The Millennial Series: Book Two

JACOB'S CAULDRON
Pam Blackwell

"Double, double, toil and trouble;
Fire burn, and cauldron bubble."
Macbeth, *Shakespeare*

To the Sangay Tulkus of the world who are
brave and honest enough to embrace
the gospel of Jesus Christ in spite of
their own religious tradition

ISBN# 0-9653327-8-0
Cover Design: Brett Peplinksi

FOREWORD

*"The most beautiful thing we can
experience is the mysterious."*
Albert Einstein

I began writing *Ephraim's Seed*, the first book in the
Millennial Series, with the goal of touching just one or two
people and giving them hope when they look to the future. The
feedback I have received from many readers tells me I have done
just that. So, as I send my next "child" out into the world, my
goal remains the same: to stimulate the reader's imagination
about the exhilarating days that lie ahead and to nurture a
longing for the Lord's return.

When I was about ten, I sat in my bedroom reading through
the Book of Revelations. Now, I didn't come from a religious
family, and it is a bit of a mystery why I was drawn to the Bible
at all. But there I sat, trying to make sense of the symbols, when
the Spirit blissfully filled me, saying "You will live to see the
events you are reading about."

I remember nearly flying down the hall to find my mother, to
share this news with her. "Mom, Mom, I'm going to see the
world come to an end!" Her response was surprising and hurtful.
"Don't be ridiculous. That book isn't literal. People believed
Hitler was the Anti-Christ and he didn't win the war, did he?" I
remember slinking back down the hall to my room thinking that
I couldn't trust my mother with my secrets any longer, for I
knew what I had experienced was true.

I share this with you, because as a young adult when I first
picked up the *Doctrine and Covenants* and opened to Joseph's
majestic visions about last days' events, I immediately knew I'd
found a resting place under his prophetic wings. That was over
thirty years now, and I look forward with a real eagerness to the
realization of the many prophecies left to be fulfilled.

Every spiritual experience ascribed to characters in this novel is real and (except for the translation process) has been related to me mostly by Latter-day Saints.

Some of my readers have asked, "Do you really believe this is the way the world will end?" And I say, "This is *a* book, not *the* Book." The challenge and the fun of being a futuristic writer is to take the bare-bone outline of prophesied events from scriptural sources and make up a real-life possibility. I'm not at all certain that events will happen as I have suggested. If someone said to me, "Pam, there's another variable you haven't considered," then I'd renew my efforts to create another scenario, another world operating with that variable added to the mix.

But whether events happen as I have written or not, I hope that *Jacob's Cauldron* will stimulate readers to study prophecy and form their own opinions. After all, we are living in the most tumultuous and exciting time in the history of the world.

My thanks go to members of the Church in different parts of the world who have shared with me their spiritual experiences, particularly Bill Chaffey and Stefinee Pinnegar; to my husband, ever brilliant and supportive; my readers: Donna Nielsen, great and longtime friend, her son, John, Robben Hixson, Beth DeBerry and Lin Bothwell–thanks to all for thoughtful and provocative feedback; to Paul Smith for his seminal suggestions; to my technical advisors–Dr. Todd Eberhard, Frank Horman, Dr. Bill Fogt and Alec Vargo; to my sister, Lyndi and nephew, David, who are not members of the LDS Church and who devoured my first draft, keeping me honest as a storyteller; and to my daughter, Dana, who has acted as cheerleader and loyal supporter in the lonely process of writing.

Footnote: The times when I use the lower case "lord" and "god", rather than upper case, are when a character is erroneously using the term to falsely denote Deity.

SYNOPSIS OF EPHRAIM'S SEED

Book One of the Millennial Series, characterized in *The Deseret News* as "a psychospiritual millennial thriller," is set early in the twenty-first century when the world is governed by the UWEN (United World Economic Network), a dictatorial organization so antagonistic to the Mormon Church that it has outlawed it. In this bleak setting, the government has also restricted travel from state to state and country to country.

Ben Taylor, a recent Jewish convert to the Church, and his wife, Peg, live in student housing at the University of Utah, where Ben is just finishing work on his doctorate. He and a number of his friends have been active in an underground economic network to benefit the people of Utah. They are exposed by the UWEN, so he and Peg flee to the southern Utah home of his long-time friend, Alex Dubik.

Alex and Moira (his Maori wife from New Zealand) have renovated Pah Tempe, an old hot springs resort where Alex has his art studio and Moira practices psychotherapy. She is pregnant with their first child at 44, so her mother, Grace, comes from New Zealand to be with her during her labor.

Also gathering to the southern Utah area are a group of LDS friends from Ukiah, California–Jed and Jody Rivers, who bring Ben's children from a former marriage–Danny and Miriam; Peter Butler, a mechanical genius who has rigged the cars to evade the UWEN travel ban; Bobby Whitmer, fresh from a mission in England; and Nate and Laurie Winder (whose marriage is in dire straits) plus their nine children.

Soon thereafter, the Chinese invade the west coast of the United States. Bobby is called up for active duty. At the same time Ben is called to work on a secret project in the closed St. George temple, translating Tibetan plates given to the Church by Sangay Tulku, an abbot (*rinpoche*) of a Tibetan monastery on Mt. Nebo.

The Chinese invasion is repulsed, but the UWEN tracks down the Taylors and friends. After a gun battle at Pah Tempe, the whole crew flees to Puerto de Luna, New Mexico. There Moira has her baby, Adam, and the group experiences rural farm life and the Hispanic culture. Then three powerful earthquakes rock the center of the former United States, creating great devastation and loss of life.

Immediately after the last quake, two apostles from the Church come to Pah Tempe to recruit priesthood holders to go to Independence, Missouri and dedicate the temple lot for the building of Zion and the return of the Lord. In this process, miraculous events occur that begin to usher in a millennial era.

MAIN CHARACTERS IN THE MILLENNIAL SERIES

Ben Taylor - Jewish convert, translator of Tibetan plates, scribe
Peg Taylor - Ben's wife, former school teacher, aspiring poet
Danny Taylor - son of Ben Taylor from former marriage
Miriam Taylor - daughter of Ben Taylor from former marriage
LaDawn Christensen - Peg Taylor's mother from Idaho

Alex Dubik - sculptor, long-time friend of Ben Taylor
Moira Dubik- Maori psychotherapist and wife of Alex
Grace Ihimaera - mother of Moira, spiritual mother to many

Nate Winder - grandson of beloved prophet, branch president
Laurie Winder - ex-wife of Nate Winder, follower of Lu Han
Ned Winder - oldest son of Nate and Laurie Winder
Mary Margaret O'Boyle - Irish mystic and Nate's love interest

Sangay Tulku - Tibetan rinpoche, meditation teacher
Joseph Dawahoya - Hopi, senior member of the Quorum of Twelve
Charles Stewart - Scottish apostle, Dawahoya's traveling mate
Lawrence Ueda - Japanese prophet of the Church
John the Beloved - apostle of the original Church
Timothy - translated Nephite apostle

Lu Han - Chinese emperor, spiritual adept
Dmitri Gornstein - head of New World Order
Hazrat Patel - general, head of armed forces for New World Order

Peter Butler - Aussie, mechanical engineer, bodyguard for apostles
Jed Rivers - outdoorsman, nurse, bodyguard for apostles
Jody Rivers - artist, married to Jed, mother of Craig and Gracie
Bobby Whitmer - returned missionary, gun *aficionado*
David Hunter - family physician
Afa Suifua - stake president in Independence, called to be apostle
Robert Olsen - Ben's former bishop and mentor

CHAPTER ONE

"The world is charged with the grandeur of God.
It will flame out, like shining from shook foil."
Gerard Manley Hopkins

The night sky was overcast but illuminated. Ben Taylor and a bewildered group of two dozen Latter-day Saints made their way silently up the hill and across the lawn of the Independence temple site. Ben blew into the humid, frigid air and instinctively pulled down the ear flaps on his woolen cap. It was, after all, February in Missouri.

Before them stood John the Beloved in white temple clothes, gesturing broadly. Although it had been dark for hours, Ben was sure he could see a golden glow around the apostle's body. John's face radiated pure delight. As had been the case in the afternoon's laying of the temple's cornerstone, Ben couldn't take his eyes off this ebullient figure. He had never seen anyone so compelling.

The group had thought they would not see John for some time. Surprisingly, they were again being summoned back into the translated apostle's presence.

"Brothers and sisters, I have called you here tonight to show you the power and majesty of the Lord. I know some of you have wondered how Zion could become a sanctuary for the pure in heart, especially in times of nuclear war, natural disasters and all the other horrors on this telestial plane."

Several of them murmured that they had.

"Well, watch closely," he said with a broad smile on his youthful face. Like a conductor leading some great stellar orchestra, John looked up at the murky sky. He raised his right arm and then commanded, in a loud voice, that the clouds part. And they did as they were bid–in slow, breath-taking movements –like dark velvet curtains being drawn back at the beginning of a ballet performance.

There, burning above them were undulating sheets of purple,

green, and red–shimmering and dancing as in an astral choreography. It was the aurora borealis. The northern lights! Everyone gasped.

After a very long silence, Peter Butler, one of the party who had witnessed the noonday ceremony, finally asked, "What's happened here? Are we seeing the northern lights? Or has the pole shifted?" He could barely ask the last question, thinking it so absurd.

"Which is it, my dear young man of science?" John asked.

Peter stared quizzically for a few seconds at the apostle, who smiled broadly. Then Peter's expression shifted from puzzlement to astonishment. "The magnetic North Pole...it's shifted? We're standing directly under the pole?"

John nodded and held up his arms toward the scintillating light show. "This beautiful solar storm was created on the sun and borne on solar winds." John projected his voice over the crowd like a Greek poet in an Athenian amphitheater. "It was drawn down by the earth's magnetic field to provide us with this bonfire of the firmament."

He lowered his voice almost to a whisper. "Just as our spirits rush towards the love of Christ, beloved brothers and sisters, and just as that love protects us from the fiery darts of the Evil One, so this energy field over Jackson County will shield the New Jerusalem from anything that man can throw against it."

The small group of Saints joyfully embraced each other and looked up in throes of admiration. Finally Peter could not wait any longer to ask, "Well, is there a southern magnetic pole?"

"There is," John replied, "but not another Zion, because that pole is in the Indian Ocean."

"I see," Peter said, his face glowing with wonder.

Suddenly the configuration of lights shifted, and the rippling sheets were replaced by a giant pale-green spiral which turned slowly in the velvet sky. In the distance came a sound like faraway thunder.

"And this will provide an endless source of energy for the people of Zion," John said turning to the assembled Saints. "We will work with Brother Peter Butler here and several other scientists, showing them how to use this tremendous source of energy for the protection and benefit of Zion."

"Is the pole star going to shift too?" another man in the party puzzled.

Mouths agape, the assembled Saints looked for the Big Dipper in the brilliant star-filled sky.

"There will be a lot of shifting in the heavens," John said quietly but with authority.

After pronouncing an apostolic blessing, John walked away across the lawn toward the wreckage of the white wooden building that had served as the headquarters for a small break-away church who called themselves the Church of Christ, Temple Lot. He disappeared into the dark. The select party stood for awhile in small groups talking quietly, trying to take in the enormity of what they had witnessed. When it became fairly certain John was not going to miraculously reappear, they slowly made their way down the hill to the LDS Visitor's Center—all except Ben.

Although he was shivering from the damp cold, Ben pushed his glasses back up on his nose and sat down on the dry bristle that served as grass. He couldn't bear to leave. The air, the hill, the sky pulsated with traces of God's presence. A line from one of his favorite poems came to his mind, "The world is charged with the grandeur of God...like shining from shook foil."

He grinned broadly and shook his head. *The establishment of Zion!* he thought. "Christ is coming!" he exulted into the dark landscape, throwing his arms into the air. "Christ is coming" echoed off the ruins of the RLDS auditorium.

This balding, 45-year-old man with intense blue eyes earlier in the day had been a witness at the dedication of the central temple lot in Zion. He had been invited to be a witness by apostles who had stopped in a small town in New Mexico on their way to Independence. He and several friends joined a motorcade of solar-powered cars which wended its way through the massive destruction of the central part of Missouri caused by the largest earthquake ever recorded–a 9.0 on the Richter scale.

Ben's reverie was cut short by the sound of Jed Rivers, one of the men with whom he had traveled to Missouri. Ben and Jed had been through a lot together. Jed and his wife, Jody, had risked their lives to bring Ben's children to him from California.

"Come lookin' for ya, man." Jed pulled Ben up with a heave. "We're gatherin' for one last meeting before we leave. Elder Dawahoya sent me out after you."

Ben flew forward off balance. "Whoa, man," he cautioned, straightening his coat. "Remember who you're dealing with here. I'm just a lowly scholar, not your wrestling partner." Jed responded with a chuckle.

For a moment the two men stood next to each other, gazing up at the aurora borealis which wove a shimmering blanket of greens, then violets, then reds. Then Ben forced himself back to the present and blushed at the thought that he might be in trouble with the President of the Quorum. Elder Joseph Dawahoya was a 72-year-old, white-haired Hopi elder and Vietnam-era colonel. A kindly man, he quietly demanded order.

The two men hurried across the acre of lawn and loped down the hill toward the heavily damaged Visitor's Center.

"Are we leaving tonight?" Ben asked.

"Dunno."

"You know, I feel torn. I want to get back to Peg and the kids and bring them back here. But I don't think I can stand wading through a bunch of snakes and bodies in the dead of night," Ben said dramatically.

"Ah, you love all this high adventure, Benjy," Jed replied, slapping him on the back.

When they reached the dishevelled building, they stepped through debris until they reached a room near the back on the first floor. It had been cleared out and served as both cafeteria and meeting room for the two dozen people who had been on the hill. Kerosene lamps on tables sent out pools of light. Ben tried not to listen to the lamps' hisses. He feared they would explode.

The group stood listening to Elder Dawahoya as the two men entered. An introvert, Ben tried to blend with the crowd, but Jed blurted out, "We're here. You can start."

Ben's face went beet red.

"Good. Thank you, Brother Rivers," the chief apostle said. Dawahoya still had a military bearing despite his years. His tanned face was smooth, except for deep lines that ran down either side of his mouth. Those, along with his square jaw, made him look a little like a boxer dog.

"Brothers and sisters, as you know, we've begun a process here that will carry us into the Millennium. But we're not there yet. I want to stress that." Joseph Dawahoya leaned forward and looked deeply into one person's eyes, then another–all around the group. "There is much that has to happen. And you must be brave and practice much restraint. Is that clear?"

The crowd murmured their assent, all but Ben who stood transfixed as he had the first time he met this extraordinary man. When he looked into the Indian apostle's eyes, he could see nothing but a mirror. It seemed like Dawahoya had been cleansed of all traces of ego. What was left was love, surprising in its intensity, disarming in its simplicity.

Then Ben became aware of the cold in the room and moved closer to the oil-burning stove. As he looked over the unfamiliar faces in the crowd, he thought, *I wonder how they were chosen to witness this incredible event. And how in the world did they survive that massive earthquake?* He felt his heart tighten to see the Polynesian couple nestle closer to each other. He ached to hold Peg.

"You'll be leaving at first light tomorrow morning," Elder Stewart told the group from New Mexico in his clipped Scottish accent. He looked like David O. McKay with the shock of white hair and tall, lanky frame. He and Dawahoya were traveling companions and close friends on the Council of the Twelve despite their different backgrounds.

After the field kitchen was cleaned, and the local people left, the six men huddled together to read scripture by kerosene light, then bedded down in the half-destroyed room that had served as a theater where proselyting films were shown. Ben struggled to get comfortable on the floor in the mummy sleeping bag he had been issued. A Russian Jew on his mother's side and an Italian Catholic on his father's, Ben told people he was a genetic worrier. Now in the dark, he could not quiet his mind, although his body had definitely moved past tired.

Images of dead bodies in the Missouri River, bumping up against his inflated raft, intermingled with the picture in the driveway of the difficult goodbyes at Puerto de Luna where he'd left his wife and children just days ago. He tried wrapping his arms around his stomach, but the sleeping bag was too snug. He pulled an arm out and straightened his beige wool cap. *Are they all right? Will we manage to get back here safely? What about the solar cars we left on the other side of the Missouri? Surely someone has taken them by now.*

And so it went for nearly an hour—one fear after another played before Ben's closed eyes. Then, as he was finally giving in to fatigue, he thought he heard soft crying. He strained to listen; yes, definitely someone crying. It was coming from an 18-year-old boy two bodies down—Neddy Winder, who'd seen everything from miraculous healings in Wichita to bloated corpses on the river. An intense 48 hours, to say the least.

Why doesn't his dad do something? Ben thought irritably, but Nate Winder lay alongside his son, snoring softly. Minutes passed and the crying continued. *Okay, okay. I'll go see what I can do,* Ben thought as he wriggled out of his sleeping bag into the frigid air.

He crawled down to Neddy, put his mouth to the boy's ear and whispered, "Neddy, what's up?" He ruffled the boy's dark, curly head, but Neddy pulled away.

"Nothing."

"Gotta be something, Buddy."

"Nope."

"I couldn't sleep either," Ben said soothingly. He drew his

shirt tightly around his chest and shivered. "I'm not sure how long I'll survive out of the womb," he warned.

No response from Neddy.

"Frankly I'm scared to death. I don't know how we're going to get back across the river, find the cars, make our way through the mobs of hungry, desperate people..."

Neddy slowly turned over on his back. "You're not kidding me, are you?" he whispered.

"No way, José. It's absolutely true. And I'm going to freeze." Ben sucked in air between his chattering teeth.

"Grab my parka over there on the chair," Neddy offered. Ben quickly reached out and slipped into the recesses of the much larger coat.

"I miss my mom," Neddy said flatly. "I never thought I would, but I do."

Ben winced. Nate Winder was divorced from his wife, Laurie, and had taken the five oldest children with him to New Mexico. Neddy had not seen his mother for over a year.

"What do you miss about her?"

"Ah...How she used to sing to me while I went to sleep." Neddy choked.

"Want me to sing? I've got great Beatles' repertoire or better yet, a smashing rendition of 'If I Were a Rich Man.'"

"No," Neddy said pointedly. "Hey, Ben, is it really true we're getting ready to build Zion? I mean *really* true. Are we really just going back to get everybody and coming here?" His words tumbled out. "And is it true this place is now perfectly safe— even from nuclear bombs?"

Ben blew into his hands, then said, "It is absolutely true. If John the Revelator says it is, that's good enough for me."

"I guess I just wasn't prepared for all this. Not too long ago, I was worrying about making the varsity basketball team in Ukiah. Now I'm on some advance scouting team with apostles who are starting Zion."

Ben chuckled and paused as Nate rolled over and muttered in his sleep. "I honestly can't take it in either," he whispered, "but I know it is absolutely true."

Neddy fell silent. Ben began to croon, "If I were a rich man, didle, didle, didle, didle, didle, didle, didle, dum...'"

Neddy laughed softly and turned on his side. "Thanks, Ben," he said in a sleepy voice. "You're almost as good as my mom."

"Hey, it's nothin', kid," Ben said in his best Bogart voice. He stood up and hung the jacket on the chair then crawled quickly back into his lukewarm bag. He lay there quiet, looking into the dark, listening to crickets. Finally he fell into an exhausted sleep without a further guilty worry.

Nate Winder was so engrossed in a realistic dream he was not aware of his son's distress. In the dream he is in the air, above a beach with two of the other men, Peter and Ben. Rather than surf the water, they are riding the air waves, literally. He felt exhilerated because he could keep up, even though he couldn't understand the technical paper that Peter was reading –something about "convection." Then he and Peter were in a town with narrow streets, English or Irish, and there was this great crush of people all crying outside what he took to be the American Embassy, waving passports. A red-haired woman in her 30's caught his eye. Her face reminded him of a medieval painting of the Madonna; beautific yet pained. Auburn curls fell over her brow highlighting her clear white skin. She was dressed in a long blue coat and had her arms around three young girls as she struggled to keep her place in the line. Nate felt so drawn to her, intense waves of energy flowed throughout his body. Suddenly he found himself in front of the gate pushing the crowd back so she could enter the embassy...when Elder Dawahoya shook his shoulder gently. Nate lay there in the dark for several minutes–his body was still throbbing from the energy of this encounter.

Ben had already been awakened by the sounds of three women moving quietly in the background and to the hissing of kerosene lamps. He watched with one open eye as an older woman poured hot water into a pan of instant oatmeal. Another carefully unwrapped a small brown bag and produced raisins. They were a rare treat in these times when the international government's issue of foodstuffs was mundane and very basic.

Elder Stewart gently shook Ben's shoulder. "It's okay, Elder Stewart. I'm awake. By the way, what time is it?" Ben asked, not really wanting to know.

"Nearly five."

"Oh, thanks." *If I haven't been run over by a Mack truck, where can I arrange for that courtesy?* Ben moaned to himself. He was a night person. Five a.m. was the end of his day, not the beginning. No shaving equipment, toothpaste, or deodorant. Rubbery oatmeal. Ben was definitely moving toward being out of sorts.

Peter Butler, a tough, muscular Aussie, grabbed Jed Rivers. "We're going for a run. Want to come, Benjy?" Jed called out. He loved to tease Ben.

Ben waved them off, slipped into his jacket and made his way to the warm stove and a cup of instant cocoa offered by a smiling, silent matron. Neddy sidled over to him. Ben looked up at him and smiled warmly. "How's it going, sport?"

"Fine." Then, a bit embarrassed, Neddy touched his puffy eyes and said, "I've decided something."

"Oh, what's that, Neddy?"

"I want to be called Ned from now on."

Nate Winder stood nearby, stretching and leaning from side to side, trying to get the kinks out of his lanky frame. "Good morning, Ben," he said with great warmth. "I hear I slept through some of my fatherly duties last night. My son tell you his big news?"

Ben winced. *Nate is taking this much too lightly,* he thought. "Yeah, he did. I remember when I wanted to change my name to Abraham—my middle name. It seemed really important to mark my shift into manhood."

Nate took the point. "You know, I can see that. Ned is a much better name for a new Melchezidek priesthood holder," he said changing his tone. Wrapping his arm around Ned's bony shoulder, Nate felt the young man let out a little sigh of relief and flashed a grateful smile in Ben's direction.

"But everyone shortened it to Abe, so I went back to Benjamin. Unless you're president, how can you get any respect with a moniker like Abe?"

The father and son chuckled. Ben felt better. "So, Nate, what are the plans?" he asked suddenly serious.

"Apostles are waiting for us to pull ourselves together," Nate replied. "I'm sure we'll hear something soon." Ben relied on Nate to know what was happening with the general authorities. A convert of seven years, he always felt at a disadvantage around life-long members of the church, especially Nate, who was the grandson of Nathan Winder, a beloved member of the First Presidency for many years.

Peter and Jed returned in fifteen minutes, ruddy and slightly winded. They wolfed down a couple of bowls of oatmeal, while Elders Dawahoya and Stewart thanked the shadowy women who ducked down to exit through the door whose frame was tilted at a 45° angle.

The seven men then gathered around the oil-burning stove. Elder Dawahoya looked lovingly at the men, then lowered his head and prayed, "Oh, Lord, Almighty God, in whose hands lies the destiny of this world, we beseech thee to hear our humble prayer. We are returning to the world–a world gone crazy with men's fears and lusts–and we ask thy divine protection as we travel on thy errands. May we, thy servants, turn our every thought to bringing about the establishment of Zion."

When the apostle paused, Peter wiped a tear from his usually stoic face.

"For thou hast promised us that your angels will be round about us, to bear us up. And thou hast promised, O Lord, to come quickly," he said with great intensity. "Hear our cries, O Savior. The earth groans in tribulation. O, come quickly." There was such pleading in his voice that Ned let out a sob. Nate put an arm around him. Never had he felt so close to his oldest son.

Ben felt like he had stumbled into Elder Dawahoya's private room in his home on the Hopi reservation and was listening to a privileged conversation between the apostle and the Lord–such was the intimate voice Joseph used.

Every man was electrified by the prayer. Gone were the aches and pains; gone were the private worries and complaints. They were on fire with devotion to the Lord's cause.

When it was over, little was said. They packed up what they had brought and bid Elder Stewart goodbye. He was staying behind to head up the massive cleanup by local members–members who had been spared death by a timely warning by the area president. They had been summoned to ward and stake houses throughout the area, and not one was killed in the devastating quake. *Not one!*

The six travelers stepped out into the brisk 20° morning just as sun streaks low on the horizon began punctuating the clouded sky. The aurora borealis shimmered in the background. There was a faint stench in the air, along with the smell of smoke that wafted off the Missouri River from burning gas lines that had erupted during the quake. In that thirty-second burst, the central part of the United States was irrevocably altered.

They walked in twos down the broken sidewalk–Elder Dawahoya with Nate, Ben and Ned, followed by Peter and Jed. From their vantage point on the hill, they were stunned to see the extent of the destruction. They had been too preoccupied on the trip to the temple dedication to really take in the scene.

"How is anyone going to rebuild this land?" Nate asked the apostle, who walked with a straight spine and the lightness of a Native American in touch with the earth beneath his feet.

"I assume that was a rhetorical question, Nate. In a month's time, you won't recognize this landscape." Joseph hopped over a large piece of concrete sidewalk jutting up at a crazy angle. "The Saints have always been builders. Look how they filled up the entire Wasatch Front in Utah. Not a square inch left from Logan to Lehi–wherever the UWEN let them build. They'll love the challenge of a new raw frontier."

"I suppose you're right, sir," Nate said somewhat morosely.

"It seems like an overwhelming job." Nate had suffered from chronic depression, partly caused by years of struggle with a difficult wife.

"Of course, I'm right. The burden of the Lord isn't heavy," the Indian apostle said lightly, taking Nate's elbow to move him along.

The inflated rafts floated at the courthouse steps, tied to the bike racks where the party had left them. The grateful men quickly pushed off and began to row against the tide of muddy flood water that moved insidiously inland over trees, buildings and lives. Back out on the Missouri in the morning light, they stared at the carnage left behind in the greater Kansas City area. Almost nothing was left standing. No one could be seen in the streets. And once again they were sickened by the sight of grey corpses bobbing downstream past their rafts and a smell of death and decay.

Ben was absolutely convinced they would not find the solar cars they had left on the opposite shore. But to his amazement, they sat like untethered horses left to graze in an open field. Elder Dawahoya raised his arms in praise to the Lord. Jed and Peter whooped for joy when they came in sight. Most people drove electric cars, but newer batteries were scarce, and older ones needed constant recharging and covered only short distances. It had been Peter's inventiveness that had pieced together these cars so that they were solar-generated and thus free to run when almost no others did.

"With a 95% conversion from solar to the electrical, you figure out how much horsepower you get on a bright day then, as long as you remain below that power requirement, you can drive 90-120 mph indefinitely, varying with the terrain," Peter explained.

After the group had finished packing the cars, they stood in a circle and offered a prayer for their safe return. Then Elder Dawahoya said sternly, "I want to reiterate what I said last night. You are to tell no one about Zion along the way. Only your families and others authorized by the church. We simply are not ready to take in the flood of refugees that will swarm to our doors."

"Yes, sir," came the chorus.

"You are going to be tempted to stop and help as we journey back. You may *not*, under any conditions," he said with great force. "The Lord needs you back in Zion as swiftly as you can get there. This may seem harsh to you, but I assure you all is in the Lord's hands."

The roads out into Kansas were still clogged with refugees, many of them women with children, walking, pushing grocery carts and pulling wagons. There were few cars. The solar cars weaved through the crowd as fast as they could lest they be swarmed by desperate people. Once, when they tried to drive past a mob in the road outside Wichita, they honked and honked. The frantic and dazed people stood their ground, so Peter and Jed got out to try to push them back. This led to a fist fight, but the two men, both martial artists, prevailed. Finally the cars were able to inch through, but the enraged crowd threw rocks after the group, smashing the back window of the last car.

The group had agreed they would drive as far as they could through Oklahoma then stop for the night, but when they approached Guymon, the apostle ordered them to keep driving. "Just trade off and sleep in shifts," he said firmly. Hardening his bulldog jaw, no man thought to argue with him.

"'I wonder why he changed his mind," Ned whispered to Ben.

"Nothing less than inspiration, I'm sure," Ben reassured the young man.

What Dawahoya knew and the rest didn't was that their families' lives depended on them arriving in New Mexico by Tuesday night. He had been told this in a dream as he lay sleeping in the back seat of the white Toyota. He saw the people of Puerto de Luna under attack–fires, pitched battles, women dragged away into the night. Waking up in a sweat, he uttered a long prayerful supplication in which he begged the Lord to let him know if what he had seen had already happened. The Holy Spirit's sweetness told him it had not.

This kind of situation where he knew something of grave importance and was not able to share it had weighed on the Native American apostle since he had been called to the quorum. He was an open man, always willing to share his knowledge and resources. It was a hard lesson to keep a closed mouth. Elder Stewart used to kid him. "I thought all Indians were taciturn, Joe, but the trick has been getting you to clam up!" It was a considerable comfort to both men to have a companion with whom they could talk about such worldly and unworldly matters.

Another person knew there was going to be trouble at Puerto de Luna–Grace Ihimaera, a Maori grandmother, who frequently demonstrated telepathic powers throughout her life, but never more convincingly than during these last tumultuous months. She sat rocking her eight-month-old grandson, Adam, in the living room of Rosa Flores.

The adobe living room was crammed with ornate, hardwood, Spanish-style furniture and memorabilia from Rosa's six grown children. She had taken in Grace and her daughter's family nine months earlier when they fled Utah on the run from the international government. Since then, the Utahns helped with chores in this small farming community and, like Israelites poised to journey to the promised land, they waited for the word that they could leave for Missouri.

Half-asleep, Adam sucked his thumb and played with Grace's braid. She rocked him back and forth until his heavy eyelids closed, then she closed her eyes and continued the rocking motion with her long, slender legs. A series of pictures began to flash behind her eyes...car lights, fire, houses with doors ajar, screams, PDL (short for Puerto de Luna) villagers running from men in dark clothes....Although Grace was accustomed to receiving precognitive messages, she definitely did not want to see this–not when everyone was so close to being safe in Zion. She stopped the rocking, stood up abruptly and walked toward the bedroom and Moira, her daughter.

Adam moaned and complained and reached for his grandmother's braid. "Iwi, come take him, please," Grace said somewhat gruffly.

Moira, a younger version of her mother, looked up from the desk and the letters she was looking through. "Why? What's the matter?" But one look at her mother's distracted face told her not to question any further.

Grace wandered into the kitchen and put on the teapot. Pulling a faded white chair from under the table, she collapsed into it and put her head in her hands. "Oh, Lord, please don't let this be true," she groaned. She reached into the pocket of her light-blue shirt and produced a silver hair pin. She deftly wound the long braid that had hung down her back into a bun and stabbed the pin into the center.

"What can be done, Father?" she pleaded and stretched her arms out across the red and white vinyl tablecloth. "Surely this doesn't have to be."

At that moment, Alex, her son-in-law, opened the old wooden screen door. Startled, she whirled around as he entered, bringing the clean smell of a brisk February day with him. He crossed the large kitchen to the sink to wash his muddy hands. "What doesn't have to be, Mom?" he asked grinning broadly.

Grace struggled for a moment, deciding whether to tell him, but she had shared much with him and Moira, so she blurted out, "I've seen something horrible, son. I've seen Puerto attacked in the way we were attacked at Pah Tempe."

Alex stood stock still, wet hands dripping on the red-tiled floor.

"When?"

"Tuesday evening. Just two nights from now."

"Does it have to happen as you saw it?"

"I think it's a warning. Last time at Pah Tempe I was sick and distracted and I wasn't in tune. At least this time we can be ready."

Alex wiped his hands on his jeans. He had been working in the herb garden next to the house. A sculptor of some note, he had left behind the art world and his home near LaVerkin, Utah to follow his wife, who was a psychotherapist, and his mother-in-law to Puerto de Luna with a small group of Latter-day Saints. It was here that he had become convinced the prophecies of Joseph Smith were true. Now he waited impatiently for the return of his long-time friend, Ben Taylor, to baptize him.

"Mom, this couldn't come at a worse time. The men have gone to Missouri. We're really depleted in manpower and we have no idea when they'll return." Alex ran his hand through his long grey hair.

"I...I do know when they'll return," Grace said. "They're on the road right now. I've been able to follow them. They're in Oklahoma."

"But will they make it back in time?"

"That I don't know."

The 55-year-old sculptor took all this in as truth. When he first married Moira, he had been very skeptical about Grace's purported powers, but they had proved accurate in several life-threatening situations over the years.

The tea kettle began to whistle. Alex grabbed it and pulled it quickly off the stove. He didn't want to wake his son. Taking a jar down from the shelf, he pinched out dry mint leaves and deftly placed them in a silver-colored tea ball. "You want honey?" he asked, ladling a teaspoon into one of the two beige ceramic cups on the counter.

Grace shook her head. Alex handed her a cup, turned a kitchen chair around and sat down next to her. He took a deep breath and asked, "Okay, who do you think is attacking us?"

"I think they're from Santa Rosa. Maybe the same gang that Peter and Jed tangled with when we first arrived. I'm sure word has spread to town that several of our men have gone."

"Revenge, then."

"No, gold plates."

"What?" Alex half-rose from his chair. "Mormons with gold

plates. But that was two centuries ago!"

"You know how people are. Someone heard about Tibetan plates, and then someone else put together the *Book of Mormon* story and who knows what else."

"That is so stupid!"

"Rosa told me she had overheard two women in the grocery store up there spreading rumors about PDL's stockpile of gold."

Moira appeared in the kitchen doorway. "Adam's asleep," she said somewhat wearily.

Alex rose and pulled out another old chair. "Tea, Iwi?" he asked solicitously.

"Thanks. What's happening, Mom? You've got *that* look on your face," Moira asked warily.

"Another attack, I'm afraid."

"Here? Oh, please, no," she said half pleading, half angry.

Grace nodded somberly.

"When?"

"Tuesday night."

Moira rose so abruptly she nearly knocked over the chair.

"Shh!" Both Alex and Grace whispered as Alex grabbed for the chair.

"We've got to warn everyone tonight," Moira said in a low, determined voice.

Within the hour, this elegant Maori woman–high cheekbones, tawny skin, dark hair half-braided down her back–had gone from door to door telling people of the possible attack. She and her deceased father had been potent political organizers for the Maori cause in New Zealand. Now everyone in Puerto de Luna knew what might happen, but very few believed her story.

Ben's stomach was in an excited knot as the caravan covered the last twenty miles over the semi-arid desert. A die-hard homebody, he couldn't wait to snuggle into Peg's spacious embrace. That and take a shower and tear into a couple of bowls of some of her split pea soup. Then hang on every word out of the mouths of his babes. Probably in that order, he decided.

Strangely the red glow on the western horizon did not die with the setting sun. Ben peered over the steering wheel. Is that coming from Puerto de Luna? Can't be. I'm just being paranoid, he thought. He tried not to look at the smudge of crimson for several miles, but it became apparent it was not going away.

"Fire!" Ben shouted and floored the gas pedal on the old Honda.

Ned, who was stretched out on the back seat, sat up so abruptly, he hit his head on the dome light. It popped on. "What! Where?" he shouted anxiously.

"There!" Ben pointed in the direction of PDL.

At that moment, the Toyota passed them going nearly ninety miles an hour. Ben just got a glance of Peter's grimacing and growling at the wheel as he and Jed raced their station wagon down the last ten miles of unpaved road.

Hay barns were set ablaze in the area that skirted the Pecos River. Nearly fifty men with black masks over their faces ran from house to house, trying to tear out the inhabitants. Shots were being fired as the apostles' bodyguards pulled up. In a few minutes the other cars screeched to a halt. All six men fresh from Zion felt a peculiar, almost superhuman, adrenalin rush as they leapt from the cars and scrambled into the chaotic scene.

Although Ben was armed and could have joined Peter and Jed, he had one thing in mind: to make it to the Martinez house to check on his family. Nate ran beside him. He had left his four younger children in Peg's care. Two burly men with torches ran ahead of them, also headed toward the adobe house. Ben shouted at them. They ran on, so he pulled his gun and fired it over their heads. They stopped and spun around.

Ben and Nate charged them. Ben, who had not been in a fist fight since grade school, ran at the larger of the two. He was a wild man, pummeling the man around the head, kicking him in the groin. His fury was too much and the invader fell to the ground, hitting his head on a rock.

Ben stood over the downed man for just one second then turned to help Nate with the other Santa Rosan. The broomstick torches the men had dropped lit the dry grass. Smoke began to smear the air. Ben jumped on the back of the black-shirted man and hit him several times in the back of the head, while Nate got in several powerful blows to the midriff. With that, the thug collapsed like a squeezed accordion.

Heart in his throat, Ben ran on and threw open the outer gate of the Martinez house, shouting for Peg.

"Ben? Is that you?" she called out in a tremulous voice.

"Yes! And Nate!" he yelled from the cobbled courtyard, as Nate caught up with him, out of breath and bleeding from his nose and lip.

"Are the kids with you?" Nate shouted anxiously.

"They are, Nate. We're fine," she answered, frantically unbarring the thick interior wooden door. As it swung open, Peg and all six kids tried to squeeze through the narrow doorway. They ran into Ben and Nate's arms, laughing and crying in relief. Nate tried to hug all four kids at the same time, while Peg and the kids nearly knocked Ben down as they struggled to reach him.

"We're not done yet, though, guys," Nate said.

"Yeah, we have to go. Lock that door again," Ben commanded. "We'll be back as soon as we can."

The concerned fathers raced back across the lawn and back into the chaos. The six men from Zion shouldn't have made such a difference in the battle, but they did. The ferocity and power with which they fought–including Elder Dawahoya–quickly turned the siege into a rout.

The apostle had taken on two men who were preparing to rape a young Hispanic woman. One crushing blow from his foot knocked one masked man to the ground. The other he pulled off the sobbing, nearly hysterical girl. The wiry attacker sprang to his feet, fists raised, ready to take down this old man, but he took one look at the powerful, almost lightening-lit countenance of the seasoned soldier and dropped his hands. Spinning around, the cowboy ran for his car and sped off down the road.

The battle continued for only a few more minutes. Then with

shouts of "Let's get out of here. The Mormons are back!" the gold-greedy invaders swarmed to their vehicles and fled. The men from PDL whooped a victory yell in unison before running to help their wives and children with the burning barns.

Ben and Nate returned to the Martinez house, shouting jubilantly, "You can come out now!" They could hear Peg struggling to pull back the bar on the door. "Ally ally outs in free," Ben hollered.

"Dad, you're okay!" Danny called out when the door was opened and he could sprint across the patio.

"Of course, I am," Ben bragged, taking stock for the first time of his bloody knuckles and torn clothes. "Come here, you guys. Let me hug you."

Peg rushed into his arms. Danny clung to his waist. The Winders formed a circle around their father, hugging and kissing him.

"Honey, I saw John the Revelator," Ben blurted out. "John, the Beloved!"

"Oh, Ben. How wonderful!"

"It's time to go to Zion!" Danny exulted.

Ben looked over Peg's shoulder at his daughter, who stood a few feet apart.

"Come here, sweetie," Ben said, stretching out a free hand.

She took a few steps forward, then stopped.

"What's wrong, Mimi?"

Miriam wrinkled her nose. "I'm sorry to tell you this, Daddy, but you stink."

CHAPTER TWO

"Take upon you the name of Christ,
by baptism–yea, by following your Lord
and your Savior down into the water,
then shall ye receive the Holy Ghost."
2 Nephi 31:13

No one was seriously injured in the attack on Puerto de Luna. Although some property was stolen and two barns were a total loss, people were spared the worst of the mob's intensity because of the timely arrival of the group of men returning from Missouri. But the members of the largely Hispanic community were shaken. Many of them talked with each other in low tones and swore under their breaths at the Mormons, "We want these people out of here. They've been nothing but trouble.... This isn't our battle."

Sensing the locals were at their breaking point, Elder Dawahoya called the populace of the small village together–214 in all, including Latter-day Saints–to the large lawn fronting Brother Hugo Martinez' house. Brother Martinez was the elderly patriarch in the area and loved by both members and non-members alike.

"Brothers and sisters–and I call you all brothers and sisters," Dawahoya said, "these are very bad times. You have suffered because of your generosity to us. This sacrifice has not gone unnoticed. The Church and the Lord are grateful to you."

The short Hopi apostle cleared his throat and said in a louder voice, "We are leaving day after tomorrow, early in the morning and we won't be back. We cannot guarantee what will become of your lovely community after our departure, for these are the very last days of the Earth's existence as we know it. So on behalf of the First Presidency of our church, we extend an invitation to you to go with us to Missouri–to a safe place–a place safe even from nuclear blasts."

"There ain't no place like that, 'specially in Missouri," an old man hooted from the back of the crowd.

"Yeah, we all know what happened to Missouri," another shouted. "Earthquake, floods, the plague. You guys are plumb crazy to head out there."

"Why should we believe you?" a woman near the front asked somewhat beseechingly .

Joseph Dawahoya looked down at his feet and then back at the crowd. "This woman," he said pointing to her, "has asked how you can believe us? This much I will say to you: The Lord Jesus Christ has prepared Zion for us in Missouri, a sanctuary for the peaceful, as prophesied in Isaiah 4:5-6. I suggest you read that scripture and pray about it." With that he turned and walked in his erect military fashion back into the courtyard of the Martinez' house, followed by the patriarch. It was as if an officer had just dismissed his squadron on the parade field.

Latter-day Saints in the crowd turned to the people next to them to try to explain what the apostle had meant, but no one was interested in listening to them. Ben was the only one who had any luck. His friend, Juan Gallegos, at least agreed to think about it.

Peg was visibly upset on their walk back into the Martinez house where she and Ben had been staying. "I give up. Honestly, I do. Now I know what Job felt like when he tried to warn the people of Sodom." Peg spread her arms expansively.

Ben tried to hold back a smile.

"What? Ben, this isn't funny. They are our friends. I don't want anything to happen to them."

"I don't either, honey. It was Jonah."

"What was Jonah?"

"I think you wanted to say, 'Jonah warned the people of Nineveh.'"

"That's what I said," she responded defensively.

Ben slipped his arm through hers and pulled her to him. "Whatever, sweetheart. I understand what you mean." He had made a vow not to pick at her quirky speech like he had done with his first wife, Linda, whose heart failure he at first had guiltily, irrationally felt responsible for.

"The saddest thing is they will be missing out on the most miraculous experiences of their lives," Peg concluded.

"I know, honey. Believe me, I know." Ben's face became tranquil as he lifted his eyes to the wispy clouds overhead and to the memory of his encounter in Zion with John the Beloved.

Puerto de Luna was a small sanctuary situated along the banks of the muddy Pecos River and dotted with small farms spaced at odd intervals. The only good land for growing alfalfa, chiles, corn and cantaloupe was along this river bank. Here in the Pecos Valley fruit trees, now bare, would blossom to produce pears, apples, plums, even peaches in a good year. Cottonwood trees, just beginning to give birth to dark buds, lined the banks of the river. At the southern end of the valley, between two tall mesas, the moon would rise dramatically during certain seasons of the year, hence the village's name—the port of the moon. It had been a timeless place, where everyone had nearly been able to forget the horrors of nuclear blasts, disease, global warming, and other natural disasters that swirled around them.

There was little preparing left to do for the Latter-day Saints. The members had spent all their time while the advance party was away in a hurried, almost ecstatic state dismantling, packing, giving away their worldly belongings. So it wasn't for them that Elder Dawahoya had delayed going to the New Jerusalem. Ben guessed that the apostle wanted to give time for the Puerto de Luna folks to make up their minds. However, he conceded the fact that he really had no idea what was happening.

One event that did occur in the subsequent 24-hour period was Alex Dubik's baptism. With his long gray pony tail pulled back by a rawhide band and dressed in a white jumpsuit, he waded into the waist-high Pecos River. He looked more serious than any of his friends or family had ever seen. Ben waited four yards out in the river. He shivered in his white shirt and white pants, but he was also beaming. He had known Alex for nearly two decades. Now he was going to give him the best gift one friend could give another.

When Alex reached Ben, he said, "I want what you've got, young whippersnapper. Let's do it."

A small crowd stood on the bank—Moira and Peg with towels, Nate Winder, the branch president, and Brother Martinez as witnesses—the rest were friends from PDL who had grown to care deeply for this 57-year-old sculptor.

In a voice loud enough to be heard clear to the road, Ben pronounced the words he had memorized from the *Book of Mormon* that were to be used at a baptism, took Alex by the wrist, and dunked him under the water. It seemed that Alex stayed under for longer than was necessary, then emerged with a serenity that one rarely saw in his taut Czech face.

He slipped his arm under Ben's and waded to shore with him. "Well, that takes care of a lifetime of sins," he said soberly.

"Yeah, and now you're too old and too lazy to amass many more," Ben teased.

The men exchanged loving glances, then, overcome with emotion of the moment, looked away.

Moira held out a large blue towel as her husband approached. Her smile was beatific. The years of waiting were over. It was just as her mother had predicted when the two first met in New Zealand at a art opening of a friend of Moira's—Alex would become a member of the Church.

Grace stood in the background with the Dubiks' son. She, too, beamed and hugged her squirming grandson close to her breast. She secretly worried that she loved Alex more than her daughter at times—particularly at times like these. He was more thoughtful, seemed more sensitive to the spirit. Not like Gordon, she thought. (Gordon Ihimaera, her deceased husband, had been a gregarious and loquacious lawyer and social activist in New Zealand, who had died at the height of his political wrangling to see that Maoris were accorded the same political status as whites. He and Moira were allies and practical realists.)

On the way to the Martinez house, Alex walked with his head down—serious and silent. Suddenly his black Doberman, Angelina, ran up from behind and shoved her muzzle into Alex's hand. "Hey, girl. How did you get out?" Alex asked affectionately as he knelt down to rub her head.

Moira motioned to Cristina, Nate Winder's daughter, to take the dog back to the house, and the processional continued into the courtyard with blue and yellow-tiled walls and cobbled floor. The group clacked across the entryway into a spacious living room filled with large pieces of mahogany furniture, black velvet paintings in ornate gold frames and at least thirty wrought-iron candelabras complete with tall white candles scattered on tables around the room.

Brother Martinez gestured to them to continue on into the large dining room dominated by a twelve-foot-long mahogany table. At the end of the table stood Elder Dawahoya beside a high-backed carved chair. Gesturing to the party to find a seat, Brother Martinez then guided Alex to the chair. Moira quickly put a clean towel down on the seat decorated with needlepoint.

"Sorry for the wet head," Alex apologized.

"Wouldn't have it any other way," Elder Dawahoya assured him.

Alex was surprised at the weight of the two men's hands as they went through the simple ceremony conferring him with the gift of the Holy Spirit. He hardly heard what was said; he was still back in the Pecos River and with the very real sensation that he had left behind in those waters the weight of years of sorrow and sin.

Amidst the shuffling of feet, he looked up to find himself surrounded by men with the tenderest expressions on their faces that he had ever seen. Now the weight of seven hands pressing on his wet head seemed to release tears which he let fall down his handsome face.

Elder Dawahoya ordained him a member of the Aaronic Priesthood, and in the process reminded everyone, "This priesthood is without beginning of days or end of years. Alex, you are now a member of the holiest order of God, without which the power of godliness cannot be manifest on the earth."

Alex sat erect and looked very sober.

"You now have priesthood power–power to teach the gospel," the apostle continued, "and to baptize others in the manner you have been baptized today. The Aaronic or Levitical priesthood also holds the keys of the ministering of angels. May you seek the Lord that you may use these powers and gifts in a way pleasing unto Him."

Moira knew something had changed when Alex rose to his feet and accepted the handshakes and pats on the back from the circle of men. Perhaps he stood a little taller or his jaw was set a little firmer. But she knew he took in what had happened with his usual, passionate intensity. So when he whispered to her that he wanted an excuse to be alone with her for a few minutes, she quickly and gracefully got them out of the crowd that now circled the mahogany table, filling their plates with the food Sister Inocencia Martinez had made.

Just inside the hall, Alex took Moira into his arms and held her close. She didn't resist in spite of his cold, soaked outfit. "Iwi, how did you ever put up with me? I have been such a stubborn jerk."

"It's been easy. You're so charming," she said, lovingly patting his arm.

"I promise I'll be the best priesthood holder you've ever married," Alex said soberly. Then he caught sight of Ben and waved to him, indicating he could use the shower first.

Returning to his first object of attention, he said, "I love you and will honor you always." Then he tenderly kissed her and held her tightly. As Alex pulled back his head from the kiss, he saw Sangay, his friend and Tibetan meditation teacher, standing a few feet away. He stared, then asked aloud in an astonished voice, "Sangay? Is that you?"

Moira turned around, not sure what she might see. The last time she had heard, Sangay was still at his meditation center on Mt. Nebo in Utah. But she too saw the small figure in the dark-red and orange robe. Sangay was a whole head shorter than Alex. A black-strapped Rolex watch on his wrist seemed a funny contrast to the strand of wooden beads he wore around his neck. There was lightness about him. He obviously liked to laugh, as the smile lines around his face showed, especially the ones near his gentle brown eyes.

Alex put his arm around her shoulder and pulled her forward to greet his mentor. Sangay flashed a huge grin. "Hello, Moira," he said, bowing slightly in deference to her.

"Hello, Sangay. I'm sorry you just missed Alex's baptism. Can I help you find a room for your things?" she asked pulling away from Alex.

"No, dear Moira, I'm not here for long." He smiled tenderly at her confusion. "And congratulations, Alex. You've taken a giant step away from the agnostic grumpy man I knew. God is now real for you."

"That He is! And thank you for coming," Alex said exuberantly, extending his hand.

Sangay didn't move to return the handshake, but again bowed politely. "As I said, I'm only here for a moment or two. I'm involved in some intrigue, but I wouldn't have missed this for the world."

"Listen, we'll not keep you," Moira said. "I'll just go back to our guests and let you two alone."

Alex flashed her a grateful smile as she disappeared through the door back into the dining room. Once the door closed, he sprang forward. "Okay! What's up?"

"God responds quickly to our heartfelt requests."

Alex looked confused.

"Your decision, Alex, to be baptized allows me to continue the teacher/pupil relationship we once had. Something I know you have been asking God for."

Alex staggered back a bit and leaned against the beige adobe wall. "How could you know that?"

"Because I was told some time ago."

"By whom?"

"By a visitor to my center–a man you know as Timothy."

"I don't know any Timothy." Alex tried furiously to think of anyone he had known in Utah that might have been involved in the meditation circles he'd moved in.

"Your mother-in-law could tell you. Hasn't she mentioned Timothy, the Nephite apostle, visiting her?"

Alex looked to his mentor with his mouth half open. "Why, yes...."

"You remember. When she was attacked by evil spirits and left her body?"

"How could I forget?"

"When she regained consciousness, she told you it was Timothy she had met on the other side."

Alex slid down the wall in his half-wet jumpsuit and landed with an unceremonious thump. He put his hands to his head. "Whoa, Sangay. Timothy comes to you and tells you I want to continue meditating with you?"

"That is the truth, my young friend." Sangay smiled an impish grin. He was enjoying this moment of disorientation with Alex. It wasn't often Alex was out of control.

"Okay. I'll have to buy that for now, but Sangay, can I ask this one question, 'Are you real? Are you still in Utah?'"

"I'm like the picture that is projected on the wall by a movie camera, and I'm not in Utah, but in Tibet. I can't stay here for much longer–just to say that you have made a choice that will accelerate your spiritual development, and if you want me to continue teaching.... "

"Sangay, I couldn't ask for more!" Alex said emphatically, as he struggled to his feet.

"Good, then it is settled. I will tell Timothy I accept his assignment." Sangay beamed and began fading. "Got to talk with Ben for a moment," he said as he brought his hands together, bent his head slightly, and completely disappeared.

Ben was drying what little hair he had and was mumbling about the cold, when he looked up into the bathroom mirror to see

Sangay standing behind him. "Good gravy," Ben nearly shouted as he whirled around. "Don't sneak up on a guy like that!" he said, putting his hand to his heart. "I'm already a candidate for a heart attack–high cholesterol, you know."

"Hello, Ben. I'm glad to see you, too."

"Sangay! I thought you might show up for this auspicious occasion. Are you really here?"

"Yes, and no."

"Say no more. We've had these astral *chats* before. I really am thrilled to see you. Other than Alex's baptism, what is the occasion?"

"For you, my friend, the occasion is the return of the plates." Sangay ceremoniously pulled from the folds of his robe a satchel about the size of a book and laid it on the bathroom sink. Then he stepped away. Before Ben's astonished eyes, the parcel seemed to vibrate in subtle variations until it looked solid. When he reached out to touch it, the rough fabric of the bag felt real.

He looked to Sangay, who nodded. "Go ahead. They are in your vibratory range now."

Ben tenderly opened the strings to the bag and pulled back the sides to reveal a stack of plates–Tibetan plates given earlier to Ben to translate, then taken away by John, the apostle. The forty plates lay in a square piece of red, yellow and blue silk. They reminded Ben of reproductions of other ancient plates he'd seen on Temple Square. The brass-colored metal leaves were about 4" x 5", the thickness of three or four sheets of paper covered with delicately chiseled characters. They were held together by three small metal rings spaced evenly apart on the left. Additional rings had fit into the top and bottom, but they had been removed altogether.

Ben knew a little of their history. In 1957 before the Chinese took over Tibet, the Dalai Lama sent older monks over the Himalayas with the Tibetan's most ancient records. These plates were among them. Ben knew that Tibet, or San-Wei as the Chinese anciently called the region, had only been a nation of Buddhists since the seventh century. Before that time, they had mostly been animists, except for at least one sect, which may have had contact with the brother of Jared on his way across Asia to the New World.

Ben had been able to translate several of the plates on which were written sacred history and latter-day prophecy. Now the thrill for Ben was nearly the same as the first time he'd seen them. "John promised I'd get these back, but I thought it would happen when we got settled in the New Jerusalem. What's the urgency, Rinpoche?" Ben asked, addressing Sangay by his high ecclesiastical title.

"I only know that they are to be returned to you. You are to keep them in your possession and continue your translating. And let's do it in order this time," Sangay said, in a mock scolding voice. Ben blushed. He'd been eager to see what was written on plates twenty and beyond, without translating the ones in between.

"I promise. I couldn't handle the guilt I felt last time."

"Good. I'll be in touch. Begin today." Sangay bowed deeply from the waist. Ben bowed back. Then the rinpoche was gone.

Ben picked up the top plate and rubbed it slowly like one would a magic lamp hoping for a genie to appear. He slipped in a meditative state that Sangay had helped him learn and stood there, towel around his midriff, rubbing and staring into the mirror, until a knock on the door pulled him back to normal consciousness.

"Hey, Benjy." It was Jed's voice. "Need to use the facilities. Sorry, guy."

"That's the second time you've interrupted me in the last few days," Ben scolded in mock anger. "Cut it out or I'll have to sic my Uncle Vito from the mob on you." Ben scurried to cover the plates with the towel he was wearing, then slip into his pants.

"Ooooo, I'm really scared." Jed joked.

"You should be," Ben said, opening the door abruptly.

After exchanging mock stares like one male gorilla passing through another male's territory, Jed disappeared into the bathroom and Ben paused in the hallway. "This has got to be one of my all-time days. Baptizing one of my best friends topped only by the return of the plates! Oh, the Lord, the Lord," he said shaking his head. He continued back to his bedroom carrying the plates like a nurse headed to the nursery with a newborn child.

CHAPTER THREE

"Some say the world will end in fire
Some say in ice
From what I've tasted of desire
I hold with those who favor fire..."
                              Robert Frost

Ben stood in the back of the dining room at the Martinez' house, which had been converted by Inocencia and her dark-haired granddaughters into a temporary chapel with rows of high-backed chairs. He glanced outside at the late afternoon sky filled with high, puffy cumulus clouds and thought, *In twelve hours we'll be leaving for Missouri!*

Tears swelled to the surface of his eyes as he watched Alex carry the sacrament tray very carefully and somberly, row by row, to the back of the room. Alex's white shirt was not designed for a tie, but now it was drawn together at the top by a dark red-striped tie lent to him by Nate. The other three sacrament trays were carried by Nate's sons, Ned, Cannon and Andrew. It didn't seem to phase Alex that he was old enough to be these boys' grandfather. This was his sacred duty to carry the bread to the mouths of waiting penitents.

Moira, who rarely showed her feelings in public, had tears dropping onto her embroidered blouse. She and her mother exchanged tender glances. Moira's baby son sat on her lap and watched his dad with a studied interest as he handed the tray to Jed Rivers who passed it to his wife, Jody and on down the line.

Testimonies were subdued. Alex simply said thank you to the room filled with emotional friends. He'd wait until he got a handle on testifying, he told Moira before the meeting.

When Peg walked to the front, Ben shifted to the end of the row, so Miriam could sit in his lap to see over the tall Winder family. Danny, who hated the public eye, slid down on his knees and drew on a yellow-lined tablet his dad had given him.

Peg was a plump forty-two. Her broad face displayed a sweet intelligence. Not a stylish dresser, she stood before the group in a slightly-wrinkled white shirt and floral skirt pinned in two places at the hem. "My friends," she began, "in the morning we will travel into tomorrow–a place the world has longed to go since Adam and Eve. I cannot thank the Lord enough for sparing me and helping me to reach this point." She paused to clear her throat and turn a pearl earring at few times in her left ear. "Alex, I have written you a short poem for the occasion of your getting the priesthood. It's a first draft, but I know you won't mind. You've been so kind to encourage my writing.

> To Alex, Freshly Knighted
> *Somewhere, perhaps just in my heart*
> *I see a curtain rise on a magnificent set.*
> *A pony-tailed man in a mail shirt strides across*
> *A tapestry-lined hall to a simple throne.*
> *There he kneels before his Master....*

Well, she's coming along, Ben thought tenderly. He couldn't help critique her work silently. The years spent studying literary criticism were too ingrained. He mentally practiced what he'd say to her–first time you read a work in public, good feeling, nice metaphor. The rest he would save. She had made it clear she didn't want an editor. But...if she asks, he thought....

The second knock on the back door got Ben's attention. He quickly sat Miriam down on the chair and in five large strides made it across the kitchen, so the noise wouldn't disturb Peg's presentation.

It was Juan Martinez. Ben's face brightened. Maybe he's come to join us, he dared to hope. He looked into Juan's shining, trusting face and opened the screen door.

"What's up, Juan," Ben asked in a low voice. "What can we do to help?"

"It's not what you can do. It's what I can do for you."

"Yes?" Ben said, glancing back at the dining room.

"Ben, because you are my friend, even though you are a *gringo*..." Juan grinned.

"Yes?"

"And because I can trust you with spiritual secrets...."

"Yes?" Ben was now slightly annoyed.

"Several people have seen the Virgin Mother next to my barn. Can you come see?"

Ben deliberately held his face in a bland pleasant expression, so as not to betray how surprised and disturbed he was at this singular message. "Just a minute, Juan." Ben motioned for him to step inside and walked quietly back to the dining room. He waited until Peg made her way through the chairs then motioned her to come out to the kitchen, its counters filled with covered dishes and plates of food.

"Juan has asked me to go to his house for a few minutes. It's important," Ben whispered. "I'll be back in time for clean-up. I'm not skipping out on my duties."

Peg smiled at Juan over Ben's shoulder. "Okay, slacker," she teased. "Hey, maybe he and his family are coming with us."

"Maybe. I'll let you know."

Ben walked alongside Juan, furiously trying to get a handle on how he felt about what he was going to see. The smell of freshly plowed fields was mixed with the odor of manure as they neared the barn. *Was it really the Virgin Mary? What if I see her?* he worried. *What if Juan can and I can't?* His reverie was cut short by the pressure of Juan's hand on his elbow.

"This way," Juan said, pointing off to the right. "We can cut through the Jimenez' side yard. We've got to hurry." A couple of tan mangey dogs crawled out from under a porch and trotted along.

Juan put his finger to his lips as they rounded the side of the house. Ben was startled to see a large group of his Hispanic neighbors assembled in the back yard. All were looking up into a large cottonwood tree. A cloud formation above the tree was situated in such a way that a brilliant shaft of light streamed down and illuminated a hole in the branches. This formed the outline of what could be a cowled woman–an outline that Ben knew to be revered by Catholics as the Holy Mother.

Looking like statues, at least twenty women stood in a half-circle repeating, "Hail, Mary, full of grace..." as they fingered their black and silver rosaries. Several men stood in silent reverence, hats in hand. An older woman with a black shawl over her head slowly fell to the ground in a faint. Two younger companions rested her head on a rolled-up sweater and fanned her with their hands but didn't attempt to move her. Each looked up and watched the phenomenon, then down at the pasty-faced woman on the beige grass stubble. The rest of the crowd, so rapt in the experience, did not even notice her figure on the ground.

"Shouldn't we help her?" Ben whispered to Juan, leaning in the old woman's direction.

Juan held out an arm to block him. "No, she does this every time the Virgin appears."

"So this has happened before?" Ben asked incredulously.

"Many times. The Holy Mother has been coming more often now because the world is so bad." Juan crossed himself.

"Can you see her?" Ben asked, then wished he hadn't.

"I can see her presence in the light."

"What does she say?"

"I don't know. But Rosa does," Juan said, nodding his head in the direction of the kneeling figure of Rosa Flores some thirty feet from the woman who had fainted. Rosa, a plain Hispanic woman in her sixties with narrow black eyes, was the midwife and unofficial healer in the area. She knelt in a black dress and white apron, her eyes shut, chin pointed skyward.

Then she began to speak in a voice loud enough to be heard by most of the crowd. "*Niños, todavia no.*" There was a long pause. No one made a sound. "*El dia del Christo es un dia de raptura.*" Pause. "*No viajen con los Mormones.*"

Juan explained, "Señora Flores speaks what the Virgin wants us to know."

"And she says you are not to come with us? That there will be a day of rapture?" Ben wanted to check if he heard correctly. His Spanish was good, but academic.

"Ai, *La Raptura.*" Juan's face lit up.

"So you hope that Christ will save you and take you up in the clouds when he comes."

"*Si.*" He nodded his head vigorously.

"But you worry that you will burn, is that right?"

Juan nodded slowly with a pained look on his face.

"Well, I think it will happen in another way, Juan," Ben said, touching Juan's sleeve slightly. "I think Jesus has provided a safe place for us to go until He comes. And then He will change the world into a paradise. Here on earth."

"Oh, that's a beautiful thought," Juan said, turning back to stare at the light streaming through the branches. "Can you see her, Ben?" he asked, pointing like a child at a Christmas tree.

"No, I don't see anything but light. But I can sense the great reverence you have for her." Ben's disappointment was betrayed by the tone of his voice.

"Well, I wanted to give you this chance before you left." Juan turned back to Ben.

Ben looked down at his black dress shoes, paused, then lifted his head and looked steadily into Juan's large brown eyes. "What I told you is true, Juan. Will you pray to the Lord about what I've said? Your life and your family's life may depend on it." Ben felt his heart nearly seize up with anxious concern.

"I don't pray that kind of prayer. He don't answer directly." Juan's eyes filled with tears. "I say my rosaries, and I hope He knows how I feel about Him." Juan looked down at his hands. "But I don't know if He listens. I can only hope the Holy Mother will intercede for me."

"He listens!" Ben grasped Juan's arm and held onto the jean jacket. "And you can know, Juan! You don't need a go-between. I promise if you'll ask Him, you'll feel a very warm feeling–right here," Ben said pointing to his chest and his yellow tie.

Juan looked back at the shaft of light which was now fading. The crowd began to murmur and stir. Rosa remained in the rigid kneeling position.

"I don't know," he said slowly. "Are you sure?"

"Look, *amigo*, I was a stranger to prayer before I met the Mormons. And if God could get through the horrible dense cloud around me, he can surely reach out and touch you," Ben said with great tenderness. He fought back pieces of memory that contained suicide notes and near-psychotic desperation.

Juan looked back at Rosa, then moved along with Ben and the crowd as they headed back to the road. Ben wrestled with whether he should tell Juan about his experiences in Zion.

The two reached an apple tree in the Jimenez' side yard. Ben stopped, faced Juan and said with great earnestness, "Juan, I have seen something so remarkable...." Then words tumbled out the trip to Missouri, the destruction, the temple dedication. "And when I walked into a room in that half-destroyed Visitor's Center, I shook hands with John the Beloved, I sat in his presence, we even laughed together."

Juan, who had been gazing out at the river, looked up abruptly and said, "No, that is blasphemy!"

"No, it isn't, Juan. John is a man, just as we are. His body has been changed in some way, so that he doesn't age, but he is real. And I'll tell you something else–Zion is real. A *real* place of safety. A place to wait for the Savior. And it's just a day's drive." Ben pointed off to the northeast. "Please come," he pleaded. "Please bring your beautiful family."

Juan wavered.

"Look, pray about it." Ben said reaching up to pull down a small, withered apple that had not been picked the year before.

"You and Maria, together. And you can always come back if it isn't true. You won't be the only Hispanics, I promise you."

The expression on Juan's face softened. "Do we have to become Mormons, if we come?"

"Absolutely not. You just have to be willing to live a decent life–and you already do." Now Ben was almost begging his friend, who had been so kind to him when the group from Utah first arrived. Juan had taken to him at once, with that beautiful and tenacious warmth so characteristic of Hispanics. He had saved Ben's dignity when he tried a hand at planting crops–always with a quick laugh and slap on the back.

While the silent crowd filed out around the two men, Juan

stood still and waited until his neighbors had reached the road before he said, "Okay, I will talk to Maria, and we'll try to pray. I like you and I like your apostle," he added. "You are honest men and I don't think you will tell me something that is not true. I will talk with Maria."

"Great!" Ben called out exuberantly as Juan reached the front of his small adobe house with children's toys cluttering the rickety front porch. "But I'll need to know by tonight, okay?"

Juan waved and disappeared quickly after opening the screen door that had several holes in it.

Rosa was spent. She walked slowly, staggered just a little as she made her way back to her house. Her black dress was dirty from the knees on down, as was the hem of the white apron. Strands of grey-black hair hung out of the bun on the nape of her neck. She had been drained by the trance she had been in. This had been a particularly difficult time–the crowd had doubts–she could feel it. How the Virgin must be upset with people thinking they are going to leave with that...that.... And Juan! What a traitor, bringing a *gringo*, and a Mormon to the Mary tree. She spit on the ground to get the bad taste out of her mouth.

And then, just as she passed by Juan's home, she heard him making a promise to Ben to contact him by nightfall with an answer. She quickly guessed what the question had been. *What sacrilege!* she cried out silently. *I know what the Virgin Mary wants for these people. For thirty-five, no, thirty-seven years, people have come to me for what they need!*

By the time she reached the courtyard to her home, she was staggering from the stab in the heart she felt. She threw open the large wooden front door, stormed by Grace and Moira in the sitting room, clacked down the dark-red tile, and slammed her bedroom door.

She paced and paced in that simple room, dominated by a large wooden cross with a small altar above the bed. She cursed the day the Mormons had come, invited by Hugo Martinez.

"What is this so-called patriarch? He has no power–nothing

like mine. Even he comes to me for herbs for his aching bones!"

And so she stewed for nearly an hour, then bolted out of her room, heading back down the dirt road toward the Gallegos' place. Juan and Maria must not go. *He must listen to me. I even delivered him into this world!* she thought fiercely.

Alex caught sight of her heading down the road and waved as he came in from the wheat fields. He was shocked at the twisted visage that she turned on him. "What's gotten into Rosa? She looks like a tornado funnel just before it touches down," he asked his wife and mother-in-law.

Ben decided to take no chances that early evening but to take Peg with him when he went back to the Gallegos'. She was the one who had been on a mission, and she was the one with the "iron-clad" testimony. "Never wavers, never doubts...she's a miracle in my life," he would brag to his friends.

Peg, known in the community as a *gringa* who led with her heart, was warmly received by Juan and Maria. Her Spanish was spotty at best, so Ben translated when needed as she explained about the plan of salvation to the six members of the family, who sat all tightly packed on the sagging couch with a red and white-striped blanket thrown over the back.

Midway through the presentation Rosa threw open first the screen door, then the front door with a resounding thump—one arm thrust into the air, the other clutching a large ivory cross around her neck.

"¡*No eschuchenles!*" the red-faced matriarch roared. "¡*Son del Diablo!*" Rosa menacingly raised her rosary in the Taylor's direction.

"Whoa, Rosa, Rosa," Ben stood to try to calm her down. "We're not some fiends...."

But Rosa waved her rosary like some battle stick. "Get out of this house. No one wants you. Go away, Mormons!" She hurled the word, 'Mormons', like a pail of slop at Ben and Peg.

They stood and moved warily toward the back door, but Juan rose and folded his arms across his chest, standing between the three. "No, Rosa, I don't want them to go," he said in a low, almost growling tone. He flung a look at his wife that she had better not contradict him.

"*Juancito*, I helped you come into this world," Rosa began. "I tell you what the Virgin wants. How can you...?"

Ben and Peg stood like statues. Neither dared to breathe. They felt as exposed as soldiers suddenly illumined by an enemy flare in no-man's land.

"I can think for myself, *Abuela*," Juan said calmly. "That Ben has taught me. I can go ask the Virgin, I can go to Jesus, I can even go to *El Padre. Myself!*" he concluded forcefully, planting his feet and setting his jaw, for he knew Rosa wasn't finished.

With each "I can" from Juan, Rosa staggered a bit. She wasn't prepared for such a thought. "Your soul will be tortured in purgatory, *hijo*," she threatened. "No one but the priest can talk to God."

Rosa scanned his defenses but found nothing to burrow into. Juan stood, and with the dignity of *el hombre de la casa* said, "Rosa, with all respect, I am going to ask you to leave. My family and I have to finish packing."

Maria gave out a little startled cry, then covered her mouth. The four young boys with big brown eyes clutched their mother's broad figure like young monkeys. They had never seen their *papacito* in such a militant pose.

"Fine. But you will never return here. Never!"

"We will come and go *como queremos*," was the retort.

That was more than Rosa could handle. She was the final authority figure in this tight-knit community. No one talked to her that way. In a black-and-white blur she was gone.

Maria spoke up timidly, "It isn't over."

"Yes, it is," Ben soothed. "We will bless this house so that it will be safe for tonight, and in the morning you will come with us."

"You don't know Rosa," Juan said quietly. "But we will be ready for you tomorrow, no matter what."

Just weeks earlier Grace had suffered at the hands of what she knew were evil spirits in her room at Rosa's house. She had literally been thrown across the room after hearing a disembodied voice say, "Now you will experience the evil of *las brujas del llano* (the witches of the plains)!" Smashing into the corner of a large dresser, she had been knocked unconscious.

For Alex, who had come to her rescue, that was his first encounter with a tangibly diabolical power. As he crossed the threshold of Grace's room, he felt as if he had stepped into a deep freezer and at the same time slowed to half speed. It took a total focus of his will to somehow move across the ten-foot span, pick up his limp mother-in-law and get out of that room. He was sure that the devil himself was going to reach out and grab him at any moment.

Although Grace had never said anything to her family, she had wondered if Rosa might have been behind the psychic attack. The two women had been quarreling rather fiercely about Grace's beliefs about the end of the world.

So when Ben came to the back door of the house later in the evening and said to Alex that he needed to talk to him about Rosa, Grace immediately interposed herself into the conversation.

"Alex, would you come with me to Juan Gallegos' house to bless him and his family?" Ben asked in nearly a whisper when the three were a few yards from the house. "Rosa's very angry with them and me." He looked furtively over Alex's shoulder into the kitchen.

"She's not here," Grace said, putting her hand on Ben's shoulder. "I think she's busy putting curses on the lot of us."

"Let's hurry then," Ben said and took large strides out to the road. He fretted but felt comforted by the warm and powerful presence of the tall Maori grandmother as he walked on one side of her, Alex on the other. Several stray dogs took up with them. Alex was inwardly thrilled to be in on a "spiritual adventure." Before, he was left to search out priesthood holders when he needed help.

"Who you gonna call?" slipped out of Ben's mouth before he could think if it was appropriate. He felt a little giddy, like he'd gone to get his mom to help with the neighborhood bully.

Alex laughed. "Ghostbusters."

"Yeah," the two friends said in unison and widened their stride.

Frowning, Grace tried to ignore their boyish banter. She knew she had to keep alert. This was no game Rosa might be playing. If she was serious about hurting the Gallegos or the Mormons, she could, and in ways the men beside her could not imagine.

As they neared the adobe house near the end of the road leading into Santa Rosa, Grace felt the hair on her arms bristle. "Ben and Alex, I want you to begin to pray as you walk," she nearly barked the order, "and when you get into the house, you let that family know you have the priesthood of God and that you are there to bless them and the house."

"Yes, ma'm," Ben said.

"What are you going to do, Grace?" Alex asked protectively.

"I'm going to stay out here for a few moments. I'll be fine," she said, patting him on the arm. "Go on."

Grace breathed a sigh of relief as she watched a light go on inside the house as the men entered–a sweet light not generated by electricity–one which burned brighter when the two men blessed the house.

"Good," she said, "now to the *brujas*."

Earlier in the summer Juan Gallegos had told her about a place at the bend on the river where the cottonwoods grew thick. He said sometimes people saw balls of bright light flashing from there. Although the phenomenon probably was caused by static electricity, locals believed it was a witches' gathering place. Grace suspected a coven or maybe a secret place where Rosa might go to evoke evil spirits.

Grace's maroon kaftan swelled around her in the stiff breeze as she walked in a determined gait east toward the river. She heard a cat's high-pitched shriek and felt a thrill ripple through her body. "Gordon, please be with me," Grace whispered.

Reaching the top of the embankment, she peered over the side into the darkness. A rank smell of fetid water wafted back up. She hesitated. *Now what am I doing?* She swallowed. *Why do I want to go down there?*

The 'there' was scarcely out of her mouth, when a blast of energy knocked her back. Although she couldn't see the source, she sensed the presence of one, two, then three female entities overflowing with hatred that topped out on an emotional scale at ten.

She leaned into the blast and shouted, "You must leave these people alone. They can do you no harm."

"Every one who leaves here tomorrow causes us great pain," a voice suddenly became audible, as the blast subsided.

Adrenalin shot through Grace's chest. "Who are you?" she asked boldly, although the tinny taste of fear had begun to slake down her throat.

"We are Legion, for there are many."

"You are women?"

"We are."

"Who have died?"

"Who have never been born!"

Grace suddenly felt a sickening feeling take over her limbs. "Gordon," she said quietly. "Please...where are you?"

She felt the pressure of a strong clasp on her left arm. She exhaled and took in a long breath. "Good. Thank you, love."

The wind picked up. The bare branches of the cottonwoods clattered together. An eerie light illuminated the trees, then it was dark. Grace shivered but decided in that moment to learn more about these entities before attempting to banish them with the Lord's name.

"You, Grace Ihimaera, must die!"

"You cannot harm me!"

Now the wind whistled and branches shook fiercely. In the distance, Grace could hear a cat fight erupt. Pulling the kaftan tightly around her, she said boldly, "I am not afraid of you. I pity you."

The voice took on a definite sneer. "You are the one to be pitied. You with the decaying body. You who cannot see your husband!"

Grace was at once terrified and exhilarated. "What do you know? You are the cowards. You can't do anything worthy of my notice." She hoped pride would trip their hand, so she could know what Rosa had set in motion.

Something which felt like a bat brushed past her. She involuntarily let out a little shriek and quickly wiped her hand in front of her face several times.

Wicked laughter erupted from the void. "Can't stand a little visit from one of our friends?"

Grace tightened her jaw then said, "Outside of childish tricks, what can you really do—not just to me, but to the people Rosa hates?" Grace was now shaking. *This is really a gamble. Will they demonstrate on me? And what powers do they have?*

Then what sounded like arguing was silenced by another female voice, this one with a lower voice, more authoritative than the last. "You want to know what we do? We draw women to their deaths."

Grace sucked in her breath. She was shocked. She'd never given thought to what female evil might specialize in. "Why do you do that?" she asked, then thought to take it back; it seemed like a stupid question, but it got the response she was hoping for.

"We cannot allow them pleasure in their bodies. We cannot permit the ultimate pleasure—bearing children."

Grace shuddered. She'd heard enough. She raised her arm in the air and said in a loud voice, "In the name of Jesus Christ, I demand that you leave me and this village alone!"

The wind picked up such velocity it blew Grace to the very edge of the river bank. Although she might not die in the tumble down the embankment, she would drown if she were knocked unconscious and fell into the water. So, in an even louder voice, she commanded the spirits to depart. And this time, the winds began to subside. Grace struggled to keep her balance and step away from the evil hole at the turn in the river.

When it was over, she stumbled back to a grassy area and fell to her knees. "Thank you, Father, for your divine protection." She let out a sob. "Help us now to leave unmolested."

CHAPTER FOUR

"This is the time of tension between dying and birth
The place of solitude where three dreams cross
Between blue rocks
But when the voices shaken from the yew-tree drift away
Let the other yew be shaken and reply."
                                        T.S. Eliot

In the early hours before everyone rose to leave for Missouri, Ben looked in on his two children, loosely curled under multi-colored quilts, and was pleased to hear them make heavy sleeping sounds. Now he assumed he was the only one awake in the house, so he tiptoed out down the hall, dressed in his dark green pajamas. He decided he would risk disappearing into the library for an hour or so with the bag of ancient Tibetan plates.

How grateful he was for the quiet library. He lit a single, simple candle and placed it in the center of a tall candelabra. He hadn't told Peg that Sangay had returned the plates–not just yet. He wanted to savor one last transcendent moment when his spirit was calmed and set in order by the breathing that Sangay had taught him–"in, hold-two-three, out, hold-two-three"–and when everything else drifted away with each steady breath. The translator would then find himself suddenly whisked away to the ancient world of Tibetan lore.

Once in his quiet state, Ben huddled over the thin metal plates. "I can't remember where I left off. I think Peg and I worked on number nine. That was the one that spoke of the earth's upheaval, transfiguring the land...." He shook his head in amazement remembering that they had translated that plate shortly before the big earthquakes hit the center of the American continent.

"I can't wait to see what other depressing news might be on number ten," he mumbled softly as he pulled the plate out and set it in front of him on the red and yellow silk cloth.

The bespectacled scholar slid the shiny candelabra with its wavering light directly in front of him and bowed his head.

"Father, forgive my many sins, for I am sinful man. Please

help your unworthy vassal in this holy task."

Then he sat up straight, eyes still closed, and placed the tips of his long, sensitive fingers on the ancient strokes and counterstrokes that filled the first line. He waited to see if he could see anything behind his eyes. Although no sight came after twenty seconds, a nearly audible voice said, "When iron birds fly, we shall be scattered as chaff in the wind."

Ben sucked in his breath in delight and groped for the small note pad he habitually carried in his shirt pocket. After he hastily wrote down those words, he ran his hand over line two. This time he both "saw" the words and heard a description of the poisonous clouds circling the skies. He also saw and heard about a hole in the sky which allowed a bad sun to scorch the earth.

"Let's see. The Chinese scattered the Tibetans in the 1960's. But the nuclear blast in Pakistan destroyed their base in Dharmsala, India, so that's probably the 'chaff in the wind' part."

He took off his glasses and placed them on the top of his balding head. "Poisonous clouds–that's got to be nuclear fallout, and the hole in the sky...." He just shook his head. Even though he tried, he couldn't help reliving the horrifying television images he had seen in Tuba City, Arizona when the first nuclear blast occurred in Alaska. He had just translated a chillingly accurate description of that event in the plates. "Now what?" he asked with slight exasperation.

He no more thought that question when the answer came back through the touch of his fingers on line four. "In that time, there will rise one, one behind another, who will rule the world like no other!" Ben jerked his hand off the surface; he saw his own startled expression mirrored in the silver surface of the candelabra. "Wow! What's this?" He quickly placed his slightly sweaty fingers back on the brass plate. "He will move like a snow leopard, yet have the feet of the bear. When he opens his mouth, he speaks like a lion, yet his name must not be known. Who can know this riddle?"

Ben sat back in the leather chair, electrified. He let out a quiet whistle and reached for a large, worn leather Bible belonging to Brother Martinez. It was written in Spanish, but Ben didn't care at this point. He read the language well enough and all he wanted now was to get to the Book of Revelations and see how closely what he had just translated matched the King James' version.

He tried to remember where it was, but this section was not one he knew well. He agreed with Martin Luther that the Book of Revelations was too bizarre to be intelligible, even though he knew Joseph Smith had said it was the easiest of the books to read.

"Ah, here it is. In chapter Thirteen. Yup, 'like unto a leopard...*los pies de oso*... mouth of a lion.' Holy Guacamole, this is creepy." Ben sat back and rubbed his hands together. "Am I going to find out something about the Anti-Christ that ancient Tibetans knew?"

Suddenly the sound of young footsteps echoed down in the hall. He quickly blew out the candle, waited, frozen, until the toilet flushing subsided. "Think I'll put this on hold for a moment," he whispered as he made his way back to his bedroom and slipped the red-cloth bundle of plates back into his backpack.

He stood for a moment looking at Peg snoring softly, then impulsively grabbed his down coat and tiptoed out the back door. It was nearly four in the morning. This was the time when he felt most alive, when his senses were fully open and vibrant. He wished the day would begin at 6:00 p.m., not a.m.

For the first time, he looked up at the night sky in Puerto de Luna and saw off to the northeast a faint illumination in the sky. "What a mindblowing experience it was, in Missouri, when we saw those northern lights with their greens and lavenders dancing between clouds overhead." Ben furrowed his brow. "I wonder what other people make of this phenomenon. Don't suppose they will put these events together with the coming of the Lord. That would be too...too spiritual."

Across the dirt driveway stood another figure, wrapped up in a parka with a fur hood. Ben squinted, moved forward a few feet, and decided it looked like Elder Dawahoya. He approached him with deference. Ben had been an admirer of the Hopi apostle since he was called into the Council of the Twelve nearly twenty years earlier.

When Ben got within twenty feet, Joseph Dawahoya turned and asked, "Ben? Is that you?"

"Yes, sir."

"I heard you were a night owl."

Ben laughed lightly. "Couldn't sleep." He came to stand alongside the short, muscular man. The two looked out at the northeastern sky for a few moments, then Ben blurted out, "Elder Dawahoya, I've been looking at the plates."

"Yes?" Joseph asked with interest. "Anything you'd like to share?"

"Yes, sir. I've begun a section that seems to give a description of the Anti-Christ and ...."

"Son, I think there are some things you should know."

And that's how Ben became aware that the Tibetan plates were part of the Lord's plan to warn the Saints in Zion of the leopard man with a lion's mouth, bear feet and a diabolical plan to rule the world.

There was a kind of hangover in the air from the night's otherworldly battles like the sickly sweet odor of napalm traces minutes after the bombers have strafed a village. People felt it as they struggled to wake at 5:30 a.m. They tasted the fear along with the delight of leaving Puerto de Luna. That mixture settled into their stomachs as they carried the last of their belongings out to the cars and stopped to notice the horizon just beginning to glow with a pencil-thin sliver of light.

Elder Joseph Dawahoya paced in the frosty morning, the collar of his sheepskin coat pulled up around his ears. Although his face did not register his excitement, his pacings and stamping did. Nate rushed up to him, clipboard in hand. "Seventeen cars–four pulling trailers, one bus. All LDS families accounted for, along with one non-member family of six–the Gallegos," he reported.

"Well done, Nate." The apostle patted him on the arm. "What about livestock?"

"Four horses, six goats, two milking cows, three dogs and six cats."

"Sounds about right," Joseph said with a sigh of relief.

"What did some hymnist write?... '...I scarce can take it in.'"

"Indeed." Elder Dawahoya looked to the north and east. "Did you see the aurora borealis last night?"

"I wasn't up that late."

"Strange to see it at this latitude," he said, his voice trailing off. "Well, okay." He roused himself. "What say we have a prayer before the wagons roll out?"

Nate, the president of this little branch, put two fingers on either side of his mouth and blew a piercing whistle. The group, except for the over-excited children, settled down and bowed their heads when they saw the chief apostle with his arms folded.

"Almighty Father, accept this first company of Saints into thy protective care and bless them on their journey that no harm will come to them, their vehicles or livestock. And may the New Jerusalem begin to bloom with these good people..."

An amen went up from the crowd, then a loud cheer. Nate went to the lead car and slipped into the driver's seat next to Patriarch Martinez. With a toot of the horn, he started up the Toyota and the Zion parade began.

Elder Dawahoya smartly returned Jed Rivers' salute to him as he drove by. Peter stood by the apostle's side. As the main mechanic of the solar-powered car, he would accompany the apostle back to Utah.

The two men watched as the line of vehicles slowly headed down the dirt road out of Puerto de Luna. A number of lights went on in houses along the way; curious faces peered out into the early dawn.

"I've heard the people of PDL say they're glad we're leaving. Then they can get back to normal," Peter said.

"Oh, there is no normal any more, Brother Butler," Joseph said somberly. "Only in Zion...only in Zion."

Once the red tail lights stopped winking in the distance, the two men gathered their belongings and climbed into the Honda. When they reached Santa Rosa, they headed away from the rays spreading light over the hills–Salt Lake City and the prophet were their destination.

It was Grace who said the world has gone into hard labor, just before the baby's crowning. If that were the case, this was a moment of panting between contractions. The UWEN, the government that until recently had ruled the international community with a heavy hand, had managed in the past to provide enough food and supplies to countries to keep them in line with only half-hearted resistance. The state of the planet was such that people were grateful for sustenance even if it came with limited freedom. The ozone was nearly stripped from the atmosphere overhead. The phenomenon known as El Niño was an annual event with each winter's warming doing more damage than the last, followed by La Niña which caused drought, fires and howling hurricanes.

Several nuclear blasts had disturbed more than the electromagnetic field. They had accelerated the warming of both poles, so that islands were being inundated as were coastlines worldwide.

One of those blasts in the Arctic was detonated by UWEN command, dropping the nuclear device on its own troops, in order to turn back a Chinese invasion of Alaska. That demoralizing act created a domino effect in which troops began to mutiny and abandon posts, allowing various regional uprisings to spread. Then, when the headquarters in Switzerland was blown up, killing many top commanders, the UWEN's power dissipated within weeks.

Epidemics, overpopulation, flagrant crime, dwindling resources, the rise of private armies, and international drug cartels–these all dragged civilization helter-skelter into the pit of anarchy and ruin–Mephistopheles plunging Faust into Hell.

In the United States, without the border checkpoints the UWEN had previously been using to keep people from migrating, aerial surveillance ceased and regional chaos ensued. In the big cities on the East Coast, ethnic gangs looted and set fire to hundreds of city blocks. Whites who hadn't fled the area were tortured, raped and murdered. The gangs also confiscated all the expensive cars left behind and wrecked them in riots of wanton destruction.

Streets were unlit; security forces often lacked the firepower to keep roaming gangs from doing whatever they wished. Vigilante justice was the rule. In some West Coast cities, gang members would ambush opposing gangs and execute them by hanging tires around their necks and setting the tires on fire. Everywhere groups of young men with crazed, roaming eyes congregated on street corners–clearly on the verge of exploding into drugged and drunken rages.

In the Midwest, where so much had been obliterated by devastating earthquakes and floods, people streamed out away from the chaotic urban centers, mostly on foot, across the plains to the north and west. As the mobs moved west, signs were placed on the eastern Colorado plains, warning people to stay away from the cities on the eastern slopes of the Rockies. Nonetheless, sick and desperate refugees overran Denver. Among them were victims of the "plague", originally carried by mice, which now had mutated into a virus transmitted by humans. The young and the elderly's demise began with a cough, then congestion that killed them within twenty-four hours.

No national government sprang back in the wake of the UWEN's dissolution in the United States–only local attempts to man the distribution centers to keep the populace from starvation. In this void, the LDS Church cautiously reemerged with its large and loyal membership still intact. Church authorities, who had been in hiding for years in the Intermountain region, began returning to their respective homes and immediately set into motion the plans laid many, many years before to care for refugees in Utah.

The Great Hall, built for general conferences but confiscated and used as UWEN headquarters, was cleaned and rededicated for church use. Volunteer security forces patrolled Temple Square. Hundreds of people who dared to come to the crime-infested downtown area cheered the relighting of Moroni on the top of the Salt Lake Temple.

Brigham Young had seen this day in a vision and described the hills filled with needy people in tents dotting the mountain sides. And so it was. Because El Niño had missed Utah for several winters, the semi-arid desert remained relatively plague-free, and refugees streamed in from the inundated West Coast as well from the Midwest. People were housed in army tents all over the Salt Lake and Utah valleys. Latter-day Saints opened their homes and businesses to feed and shelter these desperate people. Within weeks, it was the Church organization throughout the North American continent that provided order and needed supplies.

Salt Lake, with a stop in Arizona, was the overland itinerary for Elder Joseph Dawahoya and Peter Butler. Not much was said as they drove across New Mexico. There were few cars, so they pretty much had the highway to themselves. It was a time of somber contemplation. Just past Gallup, Elder Dawahoya began ruminating aloud about the task that lay ahead for him and the Church's leadership—that of organizing a mass exodus from the Wasatch Front for whomever of the two and a half million residents planned on moving to Zion.

"How many of them do you think will really pack up and leave?" Peter asked.

"Beats me." Joseph said tersely. He furrowed his brow and thought, *If half come, the logistics are horrendous. And if Isaiah's "tithe" is true, that will still leave 250,000 people to herd back to Missouri.*

The apostle slowed for a herd of deer to lope across the empty highway up ahead. "And this winter of all winters," he said aloud, "has produced the first really fierce winter in the Rockies in years, so the whole group will be forced to go south across the Colorado River and into Arizona, New Mexico and Texas–the way we went."

"Prophet probably knows," Peter said somewhat longingly.

"The prophet *definitely* knows," Joseph responded with a sigh, thankful there was one man above him in the spiritual hierarchy who carried the largest burden of all–to bring them from this point in history into the Millennium.

All of his life the Hopi elder had known he'd be called to move "men and materials" as it said in his blessing. When he was younger, he thought that part of his blessing had been fulfilled with his role in the Vietnamese War when he helped orchestrate U.S. troop movement through Southeast Asia.

The two men were very tense as they crossed the border into Arizona. Although they had a device on the car to allow them to cross, they weren't sure if any vestiges of the UWEN monitoring system were still in place. But nothing was set off. So, relieved, they headed for Hopi Land and the Third Mesa. They would stay with the apostle's nephew and family in Hotevilla before moving on to Utah.

They moved along at a fairly fast pace. The flat highway and broad curves allowed the driver and passenger the luxury of paying little attention to the car and more to the flat-topped reddish brown mesas, high country farming and occasional herd of sheep.

Two-thirds of the way across northern Arizona, Joseph announced, "We're not far now," as he turned off Highway 264 into the village of about three hundred houses which dotted the mesa.

"Good. I'm starved." Peter leaned out of the window and took in a deep breath. He was unaccustomed to being in the passenger seat and was definitely ready to stretch his long legs.

The Aussie had driven through Hopi Land on the run from UWEN troops the year before. This time he wasn't driving, so he was much more receptive to the spiritual energy the land exuded. He looked up at the deep blue sky dotted with high cumulus clouds and felt pulled up into a slightly altered awareness. *This land crackles with a sort of sacred electricity,* he thought as they drove through the streets of Hotevilla and past the only central building–the community center, which was about a football field long, a convenience store, offices, warehouses, and a post office.

Hotevilla, a town only a hundred years old, had been established by Indian Traditionalists who resisted the U.S. government's attempt to bring them into the twentieth century. It was here that Joseph's grandfather, Daniel, had been raised and where Joseph, age eight, had been left by his mother to be taught tribal ways.

After introductions to the family, the apostle left Peter in the driveway to start up an old Ford truck with the solar-generated battery from the Honda. A pungent, cleansing smell of sage, cedar and juniper hung in the windless air. Peter breathed in the crisp early evening air and the silence–a silence Peter had not experienced since his sailing days. As he loosed bolts and lifted out the air filter from the truck, he felt the back-of-the-neck shivers he knew to announce the presence of spirits just beyond the corner of his eye. Although he tried to concentrate on what he was attaching from Honda to truck, it was unnerving to sense Indian ghosts hovering nearby, checking on his every move.

When the sound of choking and sputtering from the engine of the long-unused truck reached the house, Elder Dawahoya quickly appeared around the corner of the adobe house. He had changed into a red and blue checkered shirt, Levis held up by a belt with a large silver buckle, cuffs rolled up, and heavy work boots. Over his arm he carried a maroon parka and on his head, a black knitted hat pulled down over his silver hair.

"I'm not sure when I'll be back," he said tersely. "Day or two. Have to see an old aunt and run an errand for my grandfather."

Peter knew the grandfather was dead, but didn't ask. Instead he gladly returned to the Monongye family's kitchen. There he wolfed down two portions of the dinner and sat up half the night, regaling the family with slightly exaggerated stories of his exploits as a motorcycle racer and windsurfer. He was egged on by their easy laughter. This Aussie may have been a "Bahanna," but at least he wasn't an uptight white man. They couldn't imagine their uncle keeping company with one anyway.

Elder Dawahoya drove the pickup down the jarring, washboard dirt road for five miles—a road he knew very well. He was headed for the house of his great-aunt Ruby, who had cared for his grandfather in his last years. The house had been his grandfather's before that, for as long as Joseph could remember. The foundation was mortared sandstone. On top of that were attached plywood walls and pieces of tin covered with tar paper. None of it was finished off. A propane tank that hadn't been filled for many years sat outside in the middle of the yard like a droid abandoned from some star ship. The house was warmed by a pot-bellied stove. No indoor plumbing. No electric lights. A television, once powered by a gasoline-driven generator, squatted in the corner of the living room covered with pots and plants. An upholstered couch and chair with gaping holes for arms were both covered by Indian blankets.

Two mongrel dogs began barking wildly when the Ford truck drove into the front yard. Ruby was well-attended by these servants since she was nearly deaf. The tiny figure of his aunt appeared in traditional dress with a shotgun in hand, backlit by a row of candles. Joseph waved as he approached with arms out from his sides to let her know he wasn't armed. When he got within five yards, her normally unanimated face flashed surprise, then delight.

"Oh, Joseph, how I've missed you!" she exclaimed, linking her arm in his as they entered the small house.

"And you, Auntie," he said with great feeling.

"You missed dinner."

"Couldn't be helped. I've come a long ways and I have to continue my journey back to Salt Lake. I wanted to see you and visit the mesa and Grandfather once more before I have to take on a heavy responsibility."

"I understand," she said bowing her head. "This is your home."

After Joseph washed up and took a long drink of water from a tin pitcher on the sink, he walked to a small shed next to the house where he removed a shovel and a burlap sack. He waved to Ruby as he left on foot into the high desert and onto a trail he could climb with his eyes closed. After he walked a hundred yards away from the house, he paused to watch the light go out in the house. He knew her routine. She would be in bed shortly after sundown, then up at sunrise to pray at the foot of the mesa to the Creator that He guide her through the day. This she had done all of her life, as had her people for generations into the distant past.

The apostle turned his face away from any man-made light. He stumbled at what were familiar places now washed out with the unusual rains and snows that had come and gone. The rising moon met his gaze. Its silvery light began to fill the vast, darkened area. He paused to raise his arms above his shoulders and take in a deep breath.

"My Lord..." Joseph's voice broke in supplication. "My Lord." He let his arms fall to his sides and dropped his head. "I feel overwhelmed by the task that lies ahead. We'll need a miracle...." He let out a sob. He waited for an answer, but none came.

"I need your strength," Joseph said in just a whisper. He turned to walk up the trail, squinting to see if he could find the outline of the large boulder he'd been looking for. He hiked for several minutes until he found it. He was very grateful to the Lord for that small consistency in a world where nothing seemed to remain in one place. The Hopi apostle sat down heavily. He leaned back and breathed in the clear, thin air and the sight of cumulus clouds suspended midair, illumined from within by the lunar light.

"My Lord, I know you know what it is to be alone–to be given a task so large....Wilt thou comfort your humble servant, I pray?" A light breeze blew soft sand around his boots. In the silence that ensued, he began to feel the presence of spirits gathering around him. No one he recognized.

Then came a noise from a nearby bush. Dawahoya jumped to his feet, whirled around and reached for the knife he always carried in his belt. He couldn't see anything, so he stood and waited. Scratching and shuffling. He held his breath. Then a lone desert tortoise meandered into the open area.

Elder Dawahoya let a guffaw break from his tightened throat. "What does this mean, Lord, to send me such a sign?"

"Am I to be a plodder? Will I come in last?" His mood lightened. "Or maybe I'm just to be slow and steady."

He tried to remember what day it was. "Surely the Powamu has come and gone." *And what year?* "Is this the year my grandson is initiated into the Kachina society?" He put his hand to heart. "I've been so busy on the Lord's errands, I've lost touch with..." He stopped himself before he could say, "My soul."

After the turtle disappeared into the brush, he sat back and found himself remembering when he was four at his first Powamu. This was a festival in February when people were given bean sprouts to signal the beginning of the planting season. It was also the time when people in the village dressed as Kachinas and paraded for the gathered audience. The young Joseph was especially interested in the Ogre Kachinas.

He remembered placing his small, sweaty palm into his grandfather's large rough one. And the appearance of the Kachinas who wore horrible-looking masks with bulging eyes, gigantic snouts, and mouths filled with sharp, menacing teeth. Their bodies were painted with garish colors and smelled of animal blood. The Ogres were used as a way of keeping children in line. Children were told they were going to be taken away by the Ogres and dumped in a nearby canyon where their parents couldn't get to them if they didn't obey. This kept nearly every child respectful and in tow.

The thing Joseph remembered most was the pinch on his arm from his grandfather when he began to wail as an Ogre approached. He immediately quieted down to a quivering lip and silent tears. He didn't have to be told he was to be brave in the face of such terror.

Four years later, when he was eight, he came to understand that the Ogres were there to remind the people of Masau'u, the servant of the Creator who came around 1100 A.D. He came to teach the Hopi people that the Creator wished them to live in absolute harmony with the land and each other. Their collective memory recorded 750 years of such peace with Mother Earth after the teacher's first appearance.

Masau'u also taught that the world would need the Hopi nation to teach this peace, especially at the end of the Fourth Cycle. After that, according to Hopi prophecy, Masau'u would return to rule and peace would prevail. They were to warn the world of the dire consequences of being out of touch with the Creator and Mother Earth.

The seventy-year-old's bones ached as he shifted his sitting position. He stared out to the south where the spirits of distinguished ancestors dwelt above the San Francisco Peaks near Flagstaff. "Grandfather, I have come to do what I promised– what I promised to you when I was eight."

Daniel Dawahoya had been the last remaining tribal elder whose duty it was to guard a sacred, buried object that Hopi tradition said kept the world from falling into disarray. He had shared the location and other secrets with the young man as he grew. Now Joseph was doing as he had been instructed many years ago, but he was also going against everything sacred he, as a Hopi, had been taught.

Shaking off his anxiety, he picked up the shovel and sack and walked around the boulder out into a broad and flat wash. Now Joseph was counting. "Eighty-eight, eighty-nine," as he took large strides across the open, muddy area. At "a hundred and four" the terrain began to rise. A few more large steps, and he stopped.

He pushed down hard on the shovel wedged next to a large rock and began prying it up. The apostle began sweating, and a great strain appeared across his face as he used all of his strength to extract the small boulder from its resting place. The rock made a thudding sound as it rolled to one side. Joseph didn't let up–he continued digging into the sandy clay. Four feet down he struck an object. Throwing down the shovel, he slowly and carefully scooped away the earth with his bare hands. His skin crawled. "Masau'u, I am removing this sacred object at your request (he now pulled a clay jar from its burial place), knowing it will throw all life, the earth and even the universe out of balance."

With trembling hands, he placed the jar covered with symmetrical designs into his gunny sack and laid it nearby as he shoveled dirt back into the hole and rolled the rock back into place. Joseph was not at this moment the man who had managed to bridge Indian and white worlds. He was all Hopi, his grandfather's favorite, the boy who had been initiated into the traditional elder's ways when he was twelve. It was the tribal elders who had solemnly told Joseph that he was the hope of the dying breed of Traditionalists–a group who clung to Masau'u's injunctions to live simply and in harmony with Mother Nature.

Joseph also became one of the Kiva people who performed the sacred rituals that kept the world balanced. This unearthing of the sacred jar violated everything holy, but he had been told by his grandfather that there would come a time when the sacred object must be removed and taken to the east to be given to the white brother. The brother would keep it in an important place for a time, then it would return to the land of the Hopis. This would begin the Fifth Cycle when the world would rest in great peace.

As he slowly walked back around the wash, Joseph again felt comforted by otherworldly presences who seemed almost tangible. "Welcome, Grandfather and Ancient Ones!" he sang out excitedly, recognizing the spirit of Daniel. "I do your bidding."

When the apostle reached the boulder, he lingered. He didn't want to go back to Ruby's just yet. Instead he placed the sacred bundle at his feet and leaned back to watch the clouds float slowly overhead. He wanted to feel the comfort of his grandfather a little longer.

His mind went to the first time he was aware of the truthfulness of Hopi prophecies written in pictograph on the rock wall near Orabai. It seemed to him that his life somehow coincided with these major prophecies. He was twelve, the summer of his initiation, when the long-predicted "gourd of ashes" rained down on Japan. Then, in 1969, another ancient prophecy was fulfilled which declared man would go to the moon and bring back a piece of moon rock. This event was to signal great changes for the Hopi. For Joseph, who was in Vietnam, it meant a time of spiritual awakening when a fellow soldier taught him the Gospel. And shy, faithful Susie, a childhood sweetheart, received his letters and knew for the first time that he wished to marry her in a temple.

The apostle fell asleep and spent the night warmed in his parka—strengthened and consoled by those loving, unseen presences. In the morning when he returned to Ruby's home, she was waiting. "Are you fasting?" she asked solicitously.

He nodded.

"No need to feed you then." She smiled, revealing a nearly toothless grin.

"You needn't plant this year."

Her eyes widened. "Can it be? Have I lived to the end of the Fourth Cycle?"

He again nodded soberly.

"Masau'u's instructions?" Her voice rose in disbelief.

"Yes, Auntie, it is time for the Purification. When I come back, it will be time for you to come with me."

"No," she said slowly shaking her head.

"Yes, Auntie. Or you will die."

"I will die anyway. I want to die here."

"As you wish," he said with a sigh. He knew it was pointless to argue with her. It had always been that way.

CHAPTER FIVE

"Then felt I like some watcher of the skies
When a new planet swims into his ken,
Or like stout Cortez when with eagle eyes
He stared at the Pacific–and all his men
Looked at each other with a wild surmise–
Silent, upon a peak in Darien."
John Keats

The caravan from Puerto de Luna moved along without much interference for most of the trip. The first intimations that there might be trouble came when they stopped outside Emporia, Kansas. Jed removed his CB radio from the truck and called the central communications center in Independence to get instructions about where to enter Zion.

"N7RKW, this is N8JMX," Jed called out loudly into the receiver after he pressed down the button.

"Come in, N8JMX," crackled a low male voice.

"I've got cargo, headed east. Where is point of entry?"

"When you hit Topeka, head north to Oskaloosa, then northeast forty miles 'til you reach Atchison. You can enter from there."

"I copy, N7RKW. How are road conditions?"

"Not bad until you reach the turnpike at Topeka. You'll hit a lot of debris at that point."

"Copy. ETA six hours."

"Copy that, good buddy."

Jed smiled in spite of the seriousness of the moment. He relished his time on that radio.

The party hadn't run into any UWEN troops, nor did they have any trouble crossing from New Mexico into Texas or Texas into Oklahoma. "Now we only have a six-hour drive through Kansas and we will be home...FREE!" Jed whooped. He doubled his fists and slammed them down on the hood of the truck.

This startled Jody who stuck her head out the window, "Shh! You'll wake up the Terror."

Jed crept dramatically around the back of the truck and lowered the CB unit back into the bed. Then he tiptoed up to the driver's side of the car, slowly opening the door and sliding in.

"Okay, you've made your point," Jody said in mock disgust. "*You* take care of him. *I'll* drive!"

It hadn't been easy keeping Craig occupied in the long drive. Two year-olds don't really understand the concept of "Wait for a few more miles before you ask to go to the bathroom, again," or "No, you can't drive. How many times do I have to say that?"

Jody was more short-tempered than normal. All she could think about were Saltine crackers–something that hadn't been available for nearly five years now. "If I only had crackers, I'd be able to handle this motion sickness," she said at least twenty times on the drive. Being three months pregnant was a definite drawback to this adventure. She thought about her blessing which said, 'You will help build the central Temple of Zion.' A tomboy, she had always imagined hauling rock. "Now I can't," she moaned.

"Can't what?" Jed said as he eased the truck back on the cracked highway.

"Can't help build the Temple."

"Sure you can. Pregnant women can do lots."

"Well, I can't see how," she said sourly.

"You thought about names for the baby?" Jed said cheerily, perhaps a bit too cheerily.

"It's a girl, you know."

"No, I didn't. You had another dream?"

"The last one was right, wasn't it?"

Jed had to agree that Jody had a dream when she got pregnant with Craig that was a remarkable precognitive vision of their first-born boy–particularly regarding his remarkable size and rambunctious personality.

"Grace."

"Grace, what?"

"I want to name her after Grace. And besides, she might be the first baby born in Zion and I can't call her Eve. We've already got an Adam traveling with us."

"Sure, honey. 'Grace'. I'm sure she'd be delighted." Jed said and shook his head. He loved to listen to his wife's "logical" reasoning, if he didn't have to counter it with what he considered a rational statement. That's when the fur would fly.

Peg Taylor watched as the beige flat land moved past the passenger's side window. She had never been out of the West, where the landscape was defined by mountains. This was a bit disconcerting, driving mile after mile with only an occasional rolling hill as a reference point. Barren fields, some with last year's corn husks, stood waiting to be plowed, but wouldn't be, not this year. There were no farmers to work the land.

She glanced over at Ben who seemed preoccupied, which was nothing new. The two children were playing a game of Fish with homemade cards–Miriam, lying on her stomach in the back of the station wagon, on top of the carefully packed boxes and Danny, kneeling on the middle seat facing the back of the car. The caravan passed a knot of people walking on the opposite side of the highway with sacks and suitcases in hand. They yelled and waved their arms as they passed. Peg caught a bit of what they were saying–"Go back, you're headed into no-man's land!"

Peg felt a combination of excitement tinged with sorrow. She could never ever feel really excited, because, when she did, her thoughts went to Rachel (who died at age eleven in a car accident) and how she wasn't there to enjoy the moment. And at this amazing moment, she wanted all her children with her. She tried to remember the last dream she'd had where Rachel appeared. *Oh, yes,* she thought. *She was grown and lived in Missouri. And someone said to me that she was mad at me for never visiting her. I remember feeling very confused and sad–of course I'd go to her if I knew she was alive!*

In the rear view mirror, Peg watched Miriam as she slammed down her cards and begin arguing with her brother about some call he'd made. *Rachel wasn't...isn't much like her. She is content, quiet, had those big blue eyes that seemed to take in everything. It seemed like she always had a smile on her face,* Peg remembered. "Surely she's looking down on us now," Peg said catching a sob in her throat.

"What, honey?" Ben came halfway out of his reverie.

"I was thinking about Rachel–saying she's probably looking down on us right now. When do you think I will be able to be with her, honey?"

"Gee, that's a good question, babe. Let me think," Ben said. He put his right index finger to his temple. "Probably not right away, but it can't be that much longer when we'll have the ability to see people from the other side when we want to."

"Okay," Peg said somewhat disappointed. She had hoped he would say, "As soon as we arrive," or "As soon as the temple's built."

The question bothered Ben. He wondered if people from other side really could come at will once the Millennium started. *Gees, if that's the case, I'll have to deal with my dad...and Linda!* To forestall feelings of guilt, Ben offered up one of his corny jokes to his kids, "Hey guys, you heard the one about the dyslectic devil worshipper?"

"What's dickletic?" Miriam asked.

"Somebody who can't read, because his mind turns letters around."

"Oh."

"So what about the dyslectic devil worshipper, Dad?" Danny said impatiently.

"Sold his soul to Santa."

Danny fell into peals of laughter, but Miriam had to crawl over the seat to have Peg explain the joke. Although she had heard it over and over, this one always made Peg smile when Ben told it.

It wasn't thoughts of babies and spirits that filled Moira's head as she drove behind the Taylor's car. No, it was fierce thoughts of freedom and liberation, probably brought on by her long confinement with the bearing of her son. Adam, now eight-months-old, suddenly decided he was finished with nursing. And about the same time he took his first unaided steps. He had his mother's athletic build and had scarcely crawled before he was up and scooting all over with the aid of adult's fingers or furniture. It was as if he sensed the need to grow up quickly. Although Moira said she was upset, that she wanted him to keep nursing for at least another year, she was, in fact, being stirred inwardly to return to an outer life of action that came much more naturally to her.

She, too, looked out at the open plains of Kansas, but what she saw in her mind's eye were her Native American brothers on horseback, riding freely across the plains once more. *Lamanites the dominant culture!* she wanted to shout. She thought she could see Lamanites traveling from the four points of the globe—all converging on the New Jerusalem.

No more corporate capitalist greed! Everyone sharing; no one marginalized. Everyone treating each other as brother and sister, she thought fiercely. *Heart and kinship dominating political reality. Equitable distribution of wealth!* Her heart pinched as she thought of how many years she'd longed for just such a day.

In the 1990's she had travelled from New Zealand to Canada for a world council of Third World nations four different times. Moira had been an eloquent spokeswoman for her people. It was there that she learned that many of the Indians, both North and South American, had prophecies about the end of time similar to the secret Maori oral traditions. When they met, all involved agreed that the time was not yet ripe for sweeping political changes, but it would come soon when they would take over and impress *their* values on the collective consciousness.

Moira glanced over at Alex who was dozing with Adam in his arms. She was surprised at how distant she felt from him at that moment. There was no way he knew what it was to be a member of a minority race. Even though the Maori were never conquered by the white English settlers, they had to fight politically for every right they secured from the *pakeha*.

And as if her body was responding to this "call of the wild," she pushed the accelerator to the floor and passed Ben and Peg in the brown Honda. Now there was no one in front of her but the lead car which carried the patriarch. She wouldn't pass them. She didn't know exactly where they were headed. Besides, she thought, *Brother Martinez isn't white, and he is leading the way. I can follow him at least for now.*

Grace, who had been sleeping, stirred with the wide swing of the car, as it passed the Taylors. Moira glanced back at her mother and thought, *I wonder how long Mom will be with us? I don't hear her talking about getting a house or organizing abandoned women and children, like I hope she would. If I can only get her to Zion, surely she won't get sick and die.* Moira hunched over the wheel as if to hurry the car along.

The Maori grandmother was dreaming about Gordon, leading her by the hand, gently flying over the land of Zion. She was astonished to see that there were mountains and rivers other than the Missouri River. She and he were in young bodies; she could feel the passion for him run through her body. Gordon called her his queen. As she came awake, he was saying, "Hurry and catch up with the man with sapphire eyes."

She leaned her head against the window and deliberately dozed in that half-conscious state between waking and dreaming. "Man with sapphire eyes? What could he mean? Christ? And the land of Zion. I haven't been to Missouri, but I know it doesn't have mountains. I'll just have to be patient," she said softly, knitting her long fingers together. She leaned back against the seat and savored the fading dream images of flight and passion.

Up in the lead car, Nate was all business, straining to see far enough down the road to avoid gaping holes in the concrete and fallen debris. This slowed the process considerably.

"At the rate we're traveling (forty miles an hour), we should be near Topeka near sundown," he said to the patriarch who sat next to him.

"I see. Well, I think we should finish this journey to Zion in one day. *Los angeles* have other duties to perform after they see us safely there," Brother Martinez said in his thick Spanish accent.

Sister Martinez laughed and leaned forward to pat her husband's arm. "Oscar, you never change. *Siempre lo mismo.* Push on. Don't stop. That was the way when we travelled with *la familia.* Maybe we should stop for the night and go on in the morning. It won't hurt, you know."

"No, Mama. This isn't about me. I think this is what the Lord wants."

"Oh," she said demurely and sat back. If this had been in the early years of their marriage, she would have argued with him, but now...she had had far too many experiences where her husband's connection with the Spirit proved to be both correct and vital to the situation.

Nate wasn't sure if it was the strain of being responsible for this caravan of pilgrims or the lack of sleep and endless open plains, but suddenly, before him stood the red-haired woman in his dream—this time with such an anguished look on her face that he slowed down, pulled off the road and stopped. Pretending to need to relieve himself, he walked out a few yards away from the car and stood with his back to the road. He was really unnerved to see a figure through the windshield that looked so real. "Lord, what is this? I can't make sense of what I'm seeing." He had never had an open vision before.

When no answer came, he walked over to the next car where Moira stood, who'd also gone for a walk. She stood, hands in her jeans pockets, staring out into the vast, lonely plains.

"Mind if I join you?" Nate asked.

"Don't mind at all, Nate," Moira said somewhat surprised. Nate usually kept to himself. She couldn't remember the time the two had had any substantial conversation.

"Ah...Moira...I want to ask you...ah, you see I've had this dream..."

"Go on, Nate, I'm all ears."

"Well, I've seen this red-haired woman, beautiful, obviously distressed..."

"Perhaps an anima figure."

"A what?"

"Anima figure—a feminine aspect of yourself—representing how you feel."

"Well, maybe, but I wouldn't characterize myself as greatly distressed. As far as I know, I'm stressed but greatly hopeful for what Zion will bring for us." Nate scratched his head.

"You never know what your unconscious may be needing to express." Moira tried to read his face, but she found it difficult to penetrate past his defenses.

Nate grew quiet for a moment. He felt a bit intimidated standing next to her. Tall and muscular, Moira had taken up dressing in an Indian motif--black hair braided in two braids, hanging down her back, turquoise beaded earrings, even moccasins. "I saw her again, today, on the road outside the window," he ventured.

"Someone we passed?"

"No, I don't mean that. I saw her with my eyes open this time. In a vision. She seems to be in great distress."

"Gee, Nate, I don't know. Is she someone you recognize?"

"No. Although I feel like I've known her, but never met her," Nate said, looking down. He was embarrassed at such an illogical statement—he who prided himself in being a rational man, always in control. He shivered, feeling for the first time the biting wind on his face, and pulled up his brown jacket collar around his ears.

Moira smiled at his discomfort. She was glad to see a human side to him. "Sounds like something my mother is better at handling than I am, Nate. Why not talk to her?" she said pointing to the elderly Moira woman sitting in the back seat of theJeep Wagoneer.

"Well, maybe I will. Thanks, though." Nate had no intention of telling anyone else about this embarrassing incident. As he walked back to the car, he gave himself a pep talk. I'm just tired.

I'll be fine when we get there.

"Okay, wagons ho," he shouted down the line of cars. "It's Zion or bust!"

Ned tried to stretch out his long legs across the back of the car and under Missy's legs. She was still pouting because she couldn't ride with Danny and Miriam. When he got somewhat comfortable, he leaned back and thought, *Things are going to go back to normal when we get to Zion. Maybe I'll go on a mission after all.* He watched his dad's serious face reflected in the rear view mirror for awhile. Then he shifted so he could see his siblings stretched out in the back of the station wagon–Cristina asleep, hugging a pillow, Andrew and Cannon silently fake punching each other. *We're going to be a family again,* he imagined. *Mom will come with Grandpa and Grandma from Salt Lake and they'll live down the street from us, and everybody will be happy again. Of course, Mom and Dad will have to get back together again–after all, this is Zion!*

The problem with getting to Atchison wasn't the highway being so torn up (although that contributed to it), it was the stray livestock wandering down the middle of the highway, along with groups of refugees who were using the road as a place to stop and pitch tents. Since the people from Puerto de Luna were in the only vehicles moving through the area, the closer they got to their destination, the more they saw people who were absolutely startled to see the line of cars and a bus snaking through the devastation.

As they wended their way through the chaos at ten to fifteen miles an hour, desperate people tried to jump on the cars and grab things from the truck beds. Finally looters tried to throw up a makeshift roadblock to stop the caravan completely, so men from PDL got out of the vehicles, sat on the hoods with guns and rifles drawn. When the crowd wouldn't move, the men shot into the air in order to scare off the scavengers. Then Jed pulled in front of Nate and shoved the debris off the road with his Ford truck.

"Why can't we just take them with us?" Jody pleaded over and over again.

"Apostles' orders, honey. Before we left Zion, we made a solemn oath we would take no one, no matter how bad it got."

But the situation got worse. The sound of gunfire brought more and more desperate people running to the sides of the road. Finally the Puerto de Luna party was forced to a halt. The men jumped back into the vehicles. Frightened, they rolled up the windows, locked the doors, and prayed. A crowd of nearly a hundred people swarmed over the caravan, crying out and clawing at the supplies.

It was Miriam, eight-years-old and freshly baptized, that offered the solution. "Daddy, why don't we just give them our food? They're really hungry, I can tell. And we're going to have plenty really soon."

Ben reached over the back of the seat and ruffled her hair. "Honey, I think that's a splendid idea."

"Yeah, Dad, I bet they'll let us go through if we give them what we have," Danny chimed in.

Peg instinctively reached toward the back of the station wagon. "I'm happy to share my food and supplies. But I have a lot of precious memories in here, honey, and I won't give those up. Okay?"

"Fair enough," Ben said pushing open the Honda's front door. "People," he shouted. "We are not here to harm you. We are trying to reach our families."

"You can't. There's nothing left," a man shouted back from the crowd.

"We know they're there. We've been in contact with them. And because we are so close, we are willing to share what we have with you."

The air changed from charged distress to shock. The other men from Puerto de Luna cautiously exited their cars and trucks as they saw Ben was talking to a quieted crowd gathered on the road up ahead.

"What's up, Ben?" Alex called out.

"Let's give them our supplies. In the name of the Lord."

Alex grinned. "Great!" he hollered and flashed a thumb's up sign.

With that decision, Jed walked quickly back to the rest of the vehicles and explained what they had decided to do. The crowd grew quiet with surprise as boxes of food and supplies streamed from the eighteen vehicles.

"God bless you," an elderly man called out as he carried a stack of canned goods back to a lean-to off the road. Moira pressed dried milk packages and formula cans into the arms of a woman carrying an emaciated, crying baby. A feeling of delight began to fill these Latter-day Saints as they shared what they had.

Although it didn't take long for all the goods to be distributed, the sun was setting. "It's getting dark. Now what shall we do, Patriarch?" Nate asked deferentially.

"We are to press on."

Wednesday, the day before, Elder Stewart and the five men who accompanied him reached the Far West temple site. They climbed down off the horses they were riding in order to rest. None had been on horses in years, but this was the only means of transportation available. There were few sounds, a bird or two. The normal February cold with its high humidity was absent. Instead, the weather had begun to be modified under the electric "blanket" of the aurora borealis.

"How are you doing, Elder Stewart?" asked a large Samoan man, President Suifua.

"Fabulously. Just help me down from this nag, will you, President?" Stewart asked, half in jest. He was sore and tired from the half day ride, but he hardly felt it. Exhilarated would be more like it. The Samoan grandfather quickly complied.

The apostle stood next to his horse and surveyed the scene. The white church across from the flag pole and marker had been demolished. Off in the distance to the north, they could see the house and barn Joseph Smith had used. They looked in pretty good condition.

"Horses need a rest, sir, and some water."

"Fine, and what about some lunch for us, Afa?"

"Brother Washington's serving it up any minute now."

Elder Stewart was accompanied by prominent members of the Latter-day Saint community who survived the great quake: President Suifua, Bishops Nguyen and Knox, and Elders Washington and Delgado. They were on a surveying party to explore the land from Independence to Adam-ondi-Ahman. But the land had been so twisted and contorted by the force of the 9.0 earthquake that the men, who knew the route by car, had a hard time finding landmarks.

Always erect and proper-looking, Stewart was actually a very warm, accessible man. He wore his trademark tartan beret along with a dark-brown leather coat. Tying up his horse on a huge tree root exposed from the explosive power of the quake, he walked across the pocked asphalt road to the temple site. *It is hard to imagine this place in the summer of 1838 when hundreds of homes had been built around it, along with shops, a school and hotels,* he thought.

The Saints came here to establish the New Jerusalem in Independence, but were forced to the north, he remembered. *Quickly they built up Far West, which was to be a temple city. The Quorum of the Twelve dedicated the temple lot that year.* "Then Latter-day Saints were run out, back across Missouri to Nauvoo, to the tune of Boggs' infamous extermination order," he said with disgust.

Charles Stewart was struck by the feeling that he stepped on holy ground after all these years as he walked across the cracked cement surface of the Far West temple site. "We'll build that temple the Saints wanted," he said aloud to no one. "We'll build temples wherever we want to. And soon!" He thought about all the temples the Church had been built around the world with the promise that they would survive into the Millennium. *The real test will be the St. Louis Temple,* he thought. *It's situated at the epicenter of massive quake number two.* But, as he thought about it, he had no doubt rescue parties would find it standing–and it would become a symbol of God's divine power over the elements.

It was after noon when the six finished the sandwiches that had been packed for them. They were determined to push the thirty or more miles to Adam-ondi-Ahman before dark. It wasn't easy–paved country roads that had criss-crossed the northern end of Jackson County had been obliterated. Streams coursed over sudden drops into sinkholes. The horses carefully picked their way through the chaos.

About eighteen miles from their destination they and their mounts found themselves having to climb and climb–hills that had not been there before the quake. Although not as high as the ones they could see in the distance, these unexpected hills still jutted up five hundred feet. When the party reached the summit, they cried out in surprise. Here before them lay a beautiful valley, surrounded by high mountains to the north and hills on all three of the other sides. The valley appeared to be about eighteen miles wide and about twenty miles long.

Cries came from the men, "Hosanna!" and "Surely here will the Lord come in His glory!"

As the men descended into the valley, they were filled with reverent awe. The only person not surprised was Elder Stewart. He said to himself under his breath, "This is just as I had seen it!"

They rode across the valley floor until they reached a rounded hill jutting up from the valley floor much like One-Tree Hill does in Auckland–a knoll with one tree overlooking a great open space. Elder Stewart indicated that this was Spring Hill (the place where Adam built an altar and prayed to the Lord when leaving the garden).

"This is where we will take our rest, gentlemen," Elder Stewart said in his Scottish clipped accent.

"Sir, we might be better off down near that clearing of trees.

More protection from the elements," Raul Delgado cautioned.

"Thank you, Brother. Normally that would be exactly what I would propose. But this is not an ordinary situation. We need to climb the hill and make our camp there."

The former Jesuit from Central America walked obediently back to his horse shaking his head.

After a light meal from cans heated over a small fire, the six men warmed themselves and talked of the miracles they had witnessed as Latter-day Saints were spared death by heeding the warning of home teachers and ward members.

"My family, we were going to bed," Bishop Nguyen said, "when there was a loud pounding on the door. I grabbed my gun, shoved the family into the back bedroom and headed for the door. Before I could get it open, I recognized Brother Knox's voice saying, 'Now! Get your family and get to the stake center.'"

"I never got seven people out of the house and into the car so fast. We were in our robes and pajamas. My youngest daughter had stuffed her kitten in a bag. He was meowing loudly all the way to the stake house. Cars were pulling up all over the place, people running inside." The bishop's voice choked up. "Once inside it was so peaceful. When the last car was accounted for, everyone sat down quietly in the chapel and cultural hall. The stake president at the pulpit led us in prayer. We didn't really know why we were there, just that there was danger."

The man who escaped from South Vietnam by boat paused to take a drink from his cup and looked up to see a figure just outside the fire's light. He reached for his pistol but was immediately filled with a great peace.

"So what happened, Bishop Nguyen?" the figure asked as he moved to stand behind Elder Stewart. The Scotsman turned around, smiled and rose to his full 6'3" height. "Brethren, I believe you've met the Apostle John." The group had, at the Independence temple's dedication.

The awestruck men struggled to their feet in respect. John, a small man with a slight beard and goatee stepped into the circle and bowed slightly. He was dressed in a simple white robe and sandals. His face shone with great intelligence and goodness. "Please be seated," John said with a quiet, but penetrating voice. The men quickly seated themselves. "Bishop Nguyen, would you finish your story. I'm interested."

The small Asian man stammered, having difficulty uttering the next word, so overcome by John calling him by name.

"Well," he stuttered, "then there came this enormous boom, like the biggest thunder clap you could imagine. And that was all–it was over. My wife looked at me and whispered, "I got out of bed for that?" She's got a streak of sarcasm in her. But when we stepped outside, we saw that everything had been flattened around us–I mean, everything, from the edge of the parking lot on out. And that's when my wife fainted. She's never fainted before in all the years I've known her, but she just buckled at the knees and slid right to the floor." He pointed to the ground.

There were appreciative ohs and ahs from the group. The apostle clapped his hands and said, "Thank you, Bishop. That was most interesting." As he stepped closer to the fire, the reflection from the flames on his face gave him an even more noble look than was true in daylight.

"Elder Stewart didn't mention to you that you were going to play a part in history, did he?"

The men shook their heads and looked to the Scottish apostle, who said nothing.

"Isn't this a glorious moment?" John asked rhetorically and spread his open palms skyward. "Zion–a reality! We need to build homes, plow, plant, construct roads and make ready for the largest mass immigration the world has ever known. And onto your shoulders, gentlemen, along with the 7,000 Saints left in the county, falls the task of making ready for the millions who will come here."

The men in the circle remained transfixed, eyes bound to the beatific personage before them.

"But before people begin to flow into this area, the Lord wants us to perform a sacred ordinance." John shifted his position and put his hands out toward the fire. "This is the land where Adam and Eve lived after their expulsion from the Garden of Eden. These are the plains of *Ohaha Shinehah* or the land where Adam dwelt. Those new mountains are as they were originally. And one day soon Adam, or Michael as we call him, will return once more to his telestial home."

"Yes, sir, we know. In order to transfer the authority of this world to the Savior," David Knox ventured.

"That is correct," John said enthusiastically. "All who hold keys to different dispensations will be present and report to Adam. Then the Savior will assume the reins of government by the voice of the assembled priesthood."

President Suifua said solemnly, "I understand it will be one of the most important moments in history."

"That it will, and one the world will not know about—except those who are called to be here."

"It's more than the mind can handle," Brother Washington added.

"That it is." John's eyes met those of the young African-American returned missionary, and he looked away, too filled with the apostle's loving glance to keep from tearing up.

"Our Lord has asked me to come tonight and dedicate this new land to Michael's return," John continued. "Gentlemen, would you please join me in prayer?" The men knelt as the early-church apostle raised his arms in prayer. When it was done, the rushing cadence of the Grand River could be heard in the background. The group stayed on their knees for a time in silent humility to hear such an invocation.

Later, as the fire fell into embers, John talked about the practicalities of setting the New Jerusalem into motion.

"Regarding this electronic shield which covers the state of Missouri at present, there will be twelve portals put in place through which immigrants will pass. If you can imagine a great tent with stakes, movable stakes, as the population swells. All things will prosper—the weather will become moderate for your crops. There will be no viruses to cause sickness and no poisonous snakes or insects–all will have sufficient for their needs."

He paused to let that sink in. Then he helped the men understand what would be needed to handle the influx of refugees. "We'll utilize our high priests at the portals. They will interview every adult to see if they are worthy to enter Zion. The priesthood will be, of course, backed by a security force in case of trouble."

"Trouble?"

"There will be many people who want to get into Zion but who can't abide what they perceive to be the limitations of the law."

"What about the Law of Consecration?" Bishop Knox asked. "Will everyone be asked to live it in order to be admitted?"

"No, no one will be asked to abide by it at the juncture. When it is in place, only worthy Latter-day Saints will be asked to participate."

"Then what are the basic requirements for admittance?" Bishop Knox asked.

John raised his hand and indicated he wanted the group to slow down. He looked up into the shimmering sky. The aurora borealis snaked across the sky in variegated greens. He took a long breath and said, "They must be able to live the Ten Commandments and adhere to the Word of Wisdom. There are well over two million people in the world who are quite capable of doing so–Buddhists, Hindus, Muslims, Jews, and Christians– anyone who believes in God."

"And if someone doesn't live up to their promises?"

"We'll gently escort them out the door."

That brought a small chuckle from the men.

Soon it was time for John and Elder Stewart to excuse themselves to counsel together. The two walked down the hill, heads close together, intently talking until they were thirty yards away. All that the group of men left on the hill could hear were quick, staccato exchanges. It was clear these leaders had had other conversations and that John the Beloved held Charles Stewart in high esteem.

When Elder Stewart returned alone, the men sat silent,

waiting for him to speak. He was quiet for a long while, then clapped his hands together and said, "Let's get a good night's sleep, Brethren. May we remember that we are on the Lord's errand, and the quicker we get our jobs done, the quicker He will be in our midst."

Well into the night, after the others had gone to sleep, Charles sat on his bedroll and sent silent love thoughts to his Mary, waiting for him on the other side of the veil, as he did every other night. From the new smells that came from the valley below, he was reminded of a late spring night in a small valley in the middle of Scotland when he first knew he loved her.

Instead of returning the way they had come, the men rose very early and rode out to the westward end of the unnamed valley. When they neared the banks of the Missouri, they expected to find the hordes of mice that had collected for miles around the river, but Elder Stewart explained, "The rodent population has been completely eradicated by now." No one asked how; they were just relieved.

Near Atchison, the party stopped and looked across the river; here it was very narrow and shallow, which had not been true before the earthquake. They could see a slight shimmering in the air. The apostle pointed to two small structures, five feet tall, metallic, sitting about twelve feet apart. "This is the one working entrance to Zion, Brethren. The western bank of the Missouri will serve as the western border of Zion for now. Everywhere else people will be repulsed by an electronic force field." He paused to let that sink in, then said, "I need you to stay here and guard this opening until we can send permanent replacements. Shouldn't be more than three or four days."

The five men readily agreed. They took the two pack mules with the supplies and weapons, mounted their horses and waded across to the other side. Elder Stewart waved from the near bank and called out, "Good luck and God bless." Then he mounted his horse to ride south and began to hum a song he hadn't thought about for years and years—"I'll take the high road, and you take the low road, and I'll be in Scotland afore ye..."

CHAPTER SIX

"We shall not cease from exploration
And the end of all our exploring
Will be to arrive where we started
And know the place for the first time.
Through the unknown, remembered gate
When the last of earth left to discover
Is that which was the beginning."
                                    T.S. Eliot

Once they reached the spot designated for the portal, the five men from the Kansas City area knelt in prayer. After a long and heartfelt pleading with Lord that they would have the power of discernment about who should be admitted into Zion, they began construction on a foot bridge across the shallow waters. That was done easily with logs they found nearby.

Elder Stewart had given President Suifua a hand-held device that looked like an old-fashioned VCR remote control and explained that this would signal the two collectors to alter the intensity of the electrical flow and "lift" the electronic curtain. The apostle cautioned the men to let in just one or two refugees at a time. That way they could interview each one to determine if they were suitable candidates for Zion.

"And how will we know?" they asked anxiously.

"The Spirit will be with you, that you can be certain."

Actually the space the men settled in was more like a tube than a gate. There was an outside entrance, then an area about fifteen yards by thirty yards, then another protective electronic wall. It was designed to let people in, be questioned, then let out one end or the other.

The first to come to explore the outside of the gate weren't people but a pack of hungry dogs who sniffed and snarled when they got the men's scent. The pack looked hungry enough to devour human flesh as well as anything else in their path.

Bishop Nguyen first grabbed for a shotgun. Next came Knox,

who whipped out his .357 Magnum from his coat pocket. As the pack bared their teeth, the brethren readied their trigger fingers. It was difficult for them to believe the invisible field would provide any kind of protection against these vicious animals. The lead dogs lunged forward and were struck by a high voltage shock. They fell back stunned and howling. The men lowered their guns as it became clear that the force field was in place. They also tried to calm down by breathing out several times. After all, there was nothing visible between them and the ravenous pack.

"Boy, that was spooky," President Suifua said, clearly relieved.

"Yeah, this Zion living is going to take some getting used to," Brother Delgado said.

The men relaxed and built a small fire. "How long before the Lord comes, do you reckon?" LeRoy Washington asked as he poked at a large log that hadn't caught fire.

"I hope He holds off. I'm definitely not ready." Bishop Knox laughed.

"No, I'm serious," LeRoy insisted. "As far as I can tell, we just have to get people here and a temple built."

"Nah, things have to happen in Israel that haven't happened," Knox replied.

"Like what?" Washington asked defensively. "All it's going take is a great battle and the Lord stepping in the middle of it on Mt. Tabor or wherever, and it's over."

"No, LeRoy, you're missing the three-and-half-year part about two prophets walking in their land, calling the Jews to repentance."

"That could be going on right now, for all we know."

"How about the Ten Tribes?" Emmett Nguyen interjected. "They're supposed to come here, aren't they?"

"That's my point. They could show up any day, and then the Lord will appear," LeRoy said, pushing another log toward the middle of the fire. Sparks jumped up in the air, and smoke snaked up into the night sky.

"I think you're young and real anxious to get this whole Millennium thing going," said Afa Suifua kindly. "But, son, we'll be here for a while–probably some years."

That sobered the young returned missionary. He fell silent. Finally Raul Delgado, the former Jesuit priest, asked, "President Suifua, are our bodies going to be translated before the Lord comes?"

"My reading of the Scriptures seems to suggest that some will be, so they can go out into the world and preach the gospel for one final time."

"The 144,000?"

"Right. But I don't know anything at all about the rest of us."

"Could be you, couldn't it?"

"I guess. I've never really wanted to think about that kind of thing. Any high priest is eligible," President Suifua said demurely.

"Whew! This is pretty strange stuff, living the Scriptures," LeRoy interjected. He was cut off by the sound of tires crunching on the gravel. There was no moon, but the aurora borealis' light revealed a string of cars coming up over the hill.

"Could be the party from Puerto de Luna," President Suifua stood up and grabbed his gun.

"Could be hungry hordes, too," Bishop Nguyen answered pessimistically.

"LeRoy, can you see anything?" President Suifua asked Washington, who was nearest to the gate.

"Looks like the folks we've been waiting for!" LeRoy cried out joyously, as the cars pulled into the area.

In no time Nate was out of the car. He approached the five who were poised, hands on their guns at their sides.

"Hold it right there, sir," LeRoy called out. "You don't want to get fried."

"What?" Nate asked, immediately stopping and unbuttoning his gray jacket to show he wasn't armed.

"Look, I'm President Winder of the Puerto de Luna Branch.

Isn't this the right place?"

"Yes, sir. But don't go any farther. That is a deadly force field ahead," President Suifua said as he quickly approached the entrance. "Boy, are we glad to see you; no one has heard from you since Emporia. Everyone okay?"

"Everyone's fine. We had to give up our provisions to people on the road, but we're all intact." Nate turned and waved to the tired crowd. They let loose a loud "Hurrah!" in unison.

"This is what we've been instructed to do, President Winder. We're to take in people two at a time to interview them," Afa said.

"Even the children?"

"Only those eighteen and over."

"Okay," Nate said turning back to the people. The first in line was Hugo Martinez along with his wife, Inocencia. The small elderly couple walked proudly to a point between the black electronic devices and waited.

President Suifua fumbled a moment with the switches on the control box, so overcome with emotion at the historic moment at hand. Then the seas parted, so to speak, and the couple from New Mexico walked slowly toward the men. They were taken to the far end of the "tunnel" where the stake president and the bishop from Independence interviewed them.

"...Brother Martinez, are you willing to live by the laws of the New Jerusalem—that is that you will willing to abide by the Ten Commandments?"

"Yes, I will," the patriarch said with his hand on his heart.

"And will you also live the Word of Wisdom as laid out in Doctrine and Covenants, Section 89?"

"Yes, I will."

Sister Martinez was asked the same questions with the same result, so President Suifua pressed the buttons on the "remote" and indicated that they were welcome to cross over into Zion. He pushed the key that dropped the curtain as the couple cautiously made their way over the log bridge to the other side. When they arrived, they turned and waved excitedly. "Come on, everyone.

Come to Zion!" They looked like an aged Adam and Eve.

It took two hours to get all parts of the caravan through the checkpoint and on to the other side of the river. There the group settled in for the night, but not before offering up "Come, Come, Ye Saints," putting emphasis on the "...all is well, all is well!"

After the rousing defeat of the United Arab Front in the Sinai and relocation of the Palestinians into that desert area two years ago, the Israelis settled down to a welcome respite. Supplied with top-of-line UWEN weapons from black market trading, they set up their missile defenses along with satellite surveillance along their newly expanded borders. They finally felt they had reached a degree of peace.

Then rumors of armies massing to the north reached them. So they set their security surveillance system in motion and waited with great assurance they were safe from harm. These armies, led by Dmitri Gornstein, a rabidly patriotic and paranoid Ukrainian, began by rallying forces in northwestern Afghanistan for a march across Eastern Europe and down into the Middle East. Gornstein, a small, wiry Russian Jew on his mother's side, had spent a lifetime disavowing his mother and her ways. A twisted and tortured logic led him to the bizarre conclusion that the way to be "cleansed" of his Jewishness was to destroy the Holy Land. He'd made his intentions known as a media attention grabber over the years, but the UWEN, judging Gornstein a light-weight and unwilling to dignify him and his ragtag terrorists with a response, left him alone, fully expecting his improbable group to self-destruct within a year or two.

A Russian colonel, Gornstein had stayed behind when the Russians invaded Afghanistan some twenty years earlier. And what he stayed behind to do was to form an alliance of disenfranchised Russian soldiers and so-called freedom fighters from neighboring countries. He had done his homework and lined up arms, bombs and maniacs with nothing to lose. With a rallying cry of "Down with tyranny," he and his fanatic friends set off on their bloody march. After a victory in Turkey—which caught UWEN strategists off guard–Gornstein's forces swelled like a sudden spring torrent, fed by currents of the disaffected (from Bosnian peasants to Iraqi intellectuals) and began to wash like a flash flood towards their target. And, last year, Dmitri Gornstein, who had by now fully aligned his forces with Middle Eastern terrorists, took Iran.

Drunk with this and other recent victories, Gornstein reckoned that it was now time for one of his most daring and improbable guerrilla feats. With this single stroke he would etch his name in history. Exploiting the underground expertise of his Arab cohorts and capitalizing on their suicidal fervor, Gornstein's group was able to wire an Iraqi volunteer with a very small nuclear device, send him into the UWEN compound in Zurich disguised as a Saudi Air Force colonel. There he obediently blew himself up–along with four square city blocks. Several top UWEN commanders died, and with them the illusion that the UWEN was all-powerful.

Now, while Gornstein waited for the tail end of UWEN world dominance, he established headquarters outside Tehran and turned over to his second-in-command the multi-national force that followed him. The wiley Gornstein disappeared from public view. Rumors spread throughout the Middle East that Gornstein had been assassinated by his own men (he had set this cover story in motion before he left). So the Israelis fell into an even more comfortable illusion that they were safe.

Gornstein made his way to the Tibetan Highlands to meet with Lu Han, the general in charge of the nearly successful invasion of the United States. Had the UWEN not dropped a nuclear bomb on the Chinese troops in Alaska, the U.S. might have fallen in his hands.

The two men met in a secret Sufi cell in this isolated region. This would be their first meeting in eleven years. As a young man, Dmitri had been selected to attend an elite military college near Baotau, China (on the Huang River) where both Russian and Chinese boys were trained not only in military science, but many of the ancient Taoist martial arts, as well as psychic arts.

There he shared a room with another man who now was making history on the world stage, Lu Han. The two young men had filled many nights fantasizing about how they could come to power and dominate the world. Now it seemed at least within the realm of possibility that they might transform those youthful dreams into geopolitical reality.

Not more than six hundred miles away, as the crow flies, Sangay Tulku, Ben and Alex's meditation teacher, walked across another vast plain in Tibet. A lone antelope was only a speck in the distance. Towering snow-capped mountains jutted above the terraced plain. Sangay was headed to Mt. Kangrinpoche or Kailas (as the Hindus called it), a sacred pilgrimage site. Revered by Tibet and Indian alike, it was the source of four great Asian rivers. Tradition said if some one circumambulated the mountain on a thirty-four-mile climb at least 108 times, that person would achieve Buddhahood.

The sun warmed him as it shone down directly overhead. He crossed the river Tsango and came upon *mani* stones carved with prayers and scriptures in a large pile beside the river. On the hill overhead, prayer flags on a long rope waved gently in the noon-day breeze. He remembered reading years ago about a Westerner who said about this valley, "We seem to be riding the bones of the earth, elevated above the soft body of the world...(it is easy) to feel like one is approaching the center of the universe."

Sangay had not been to the sacred mountain since he was in his twenties. As he neared the foothills, he came upon pilgrims on their knees, wearing shoes on their hands and feet, fully prostrating themselves every few feet. Among them was a dirty-faced, middle-aged man with a profoundly faraway look on his face–dark-brown shoes, yak-leather apron girded around his middle. Behind him came a middle-aged woman, beige knitted cap and red-pink shirt. A few yards behind her came a boy about ten in overly-large sheepskin coat, pink-flowered scarf picking his way over slippery shale. His mother shuffled slowly behind him, hauling a large sheepskin bedroll on her back. No one spoke; all were seeking spiritual insight, trying to achieve merit to reach a higher incarnation in the next life.

He passed this knot of pilgrims and several others in a hurry. He was not there for spiritual insight, but on an important errand that had to be carried out in a timely fashion.

Out of breath when he reached the snow line at 18,000 feet, he stopped to lean on his staff and stare at the mountain and valley below. He was reminded of the similarity and kinship he felt with central Utah when he first came there and why he chose Mt. Nebo on which to build his monastery.

"I must hurry," he chided himself. "It won't do if I'm not at the appointed narrow in the backside of the mountain by dark."

There Sangay was to rendezvous with a man who had told him in his youth he had been born to carry out a great mission to the West. The moon rose and shone off the 22,000 foot red-tinged monument to the gods–a snowy peak jutting straight up out of the bedrock. A number of falling stars or satellites streaked through the sky. Sangay hurried along the snow fields. He had seen in a vision the morning before, as he crouched over a fire in a well-used stone pit, just where the old man would meet him.

This was the very night that Joseph Dawahoya made his lonely trip to the burial place of the Hopi sacred object. Much had been made about the fact that the Hopis and Tibetans had so much in common culturally, and were, in fact, exactly on opposite sides of the world. They shared common myths of creation and the flood. One report stated that the Hopi word for love was the Tibetan word for hate and vice versa. And rumors even had the two ancient cultures trading stone tablets.

Whatever the connection, it was that very night that Sangay squeezed between the narrow walls of a hidden crevice and there encountered the now very old man, Tenzin Lhamo, who stood erect and appeared somewhat impatient.

"Your holiness," Sangay said bowing before the head rinpoche. The ancient one placed his hands on the rinpoche's head. When

Sangay arose, he was filled with a great peace. "I have come for the records, as I promised."

Without a word, the spiritual head of the Tibetans handed Sangay a box which contained plates that were similar to the ones Ben was working on. Only on these plates were the scriptures of the hidden Christian group who recorded Christ's visit to them after his crucifixion.

"Do you understand that you have only one chance to find your family before you leave?"

"I do. I have seen them in a vision. I know to what valley they are moving their herds. I am certain I will find them to bring them with me."

The men ceremoniously touched the tops of their heads together, then Sangay put his hands together and bowed very low in respect. He knew he would never see his mentor again in this life. As he walked back out onto the moonlit plain, he prayed to God, "We are moving as You would have us do. I ask your guidance and help in this migration. I cannot, as a simple man, see how my people can move through Chinese territory to the great Strait, but I know all is in your holy hands."

The grassy plain held no structures save one he could just barely see in the distance. His heart raced. He was looking for his nomadic family. They spent their time wandering throughout a vast western valley in search of good pasturage. The land and their animals gave them everything that they needed–yaks and sheep provided cheese, milk, yoghurt, along with sheepskin clothes, yak leather boots and tents. Occasionally they were honored to host the stray pilgrim who came through on his way to or from Kangrinpoche.

Now they noticed a single hiker in the distance, returning from the holy shrine. The nearer Sangay got to the nearly black yak-hair tent with its wooden stake poles tied with thick twine and the red and white prayer flag flapping in the breeze, the more he wished he could really fly, not just in meditation. He was certain the brown-clad figure in the distance was his father, although there was no reason for this belief except intuition. His parents, *Dropkas* or wanderers, had only seen their son once since they had given him to a distant monastery when he was but a boy. When he returned at age twenty, he shared some of the writing, religion, history and philosophy of Buddhism that was utterly unavailable to them. But then he was sent by the Dalai Lama to the United States. Since that time he had only heard rumors of how these elderly people with their large size yak herd had endured the brutal Chinese occupation in the 1980's where they were forced into communes to raise livestock for export to mainland China. He had heard from some visiting monks that his family had nearly starved, but were finally released to go back to their ancient ways.

Sangay's father looked up at the traveler, never guessing that his son would soon grace his tent. He was dressed in a fur cap, gray clothes covered with a dark-brown fur coat and trousers, red and gray boots and a staff in his hand. A grey goatee danced on his dirt-smudged face. The elderly man was assisting a younger one with a herd of milking goats which were looped together by a long rope. They were long-haired, white, black, grey, and brown, and had foot-long curving horns and "smiling faces".

Two young women sat nearby with a wooden loom where they worked on a pink, blue and green striped piece of cloth that they would make into a skirt. Inside the dark, smoky tent Kesang, his mother, sang as she forced a long stick up and down in a three-foot high wooden churn, working to make yak-butter tea, a staple in their diet. Her hair was bound in the traditional braid woven with cloth of bright colors and tied around her head. She was adorned with a bracelet and necklace of round ruby stones and long beaded earrings which nearly touched her breasts. Near her, on the floor, lay a baby in a sheepskin carrying pouch, quietly following her grandmother's motions. The four-month-old's face was also smudged with dirt, and she displayed two bottom teeth when she smiled.

This family was originally from Khamin from the southwest

part of Tibet where the men were noted for their size, strength and rugged features, yet they displayed an inner peace that radiated from within. This was punctuated by great, quick smiles; the women were known for their sturdiness and weaving ability as well as their gentle goodness.

"Greetings, Father," Sangay said as he raised his hands, palms together in a traditional greeting of respect.

"Greetings, pilgrim. Come in," Yeshi said kindly.

It was only after his son had removed his fur hat and the light from the hole in the top of the tent shown down on Sangay's face that the old patriarch recognized his son's grownup face and dropped his staff in such astonishment he couldn't speak for some time. His mother could only touch his face and cry.

Only after the entire extended family of fourteen had gathered around and exchanged hearty greetings did Sangay tell them what his journey was about. "I had prayed that God would put me in your path, for the time has come for the travels we spoke of so long ago. We must begin today to move across to the north, to Amdo, and beyond. The Great Lord calls to us."

An exultant shout flew out of the tent echoing into the verdant, unpopulated valley. "It is time for the Passage into peaceful times," Sangay's mother cooed to her granddaughter.

CHAPTER SEVEN

"We are stardust, we are golden,
We are caught in the Devil's bargain.
And we've got to get ourselves
Back to the Garden."
                    Joni Mitchell

As extraordinary as Joseph Dawahoya and Sangay Tulku were, and as momentous their historic acts, there was one man who was more important than any of the other players on the political or spiritual world stage–a man hidden from the world–the prophet of the Lord Jesus Christ. His name was Tatsuya "Lawrence" S. Ueda, a simple man from Sapporo, Japan.

Perhaps "simple" wasn't exactly the right word for him, for although his habits and mannerisms were simple, his mind was not. He was a brilliant historian who had graduated from Tokyo Daigaku or To-Dai, the Harvard of Japan. It was there that his interest in medieval Spain led to a study of the early medieval Arabic conquests. He became hooked on everything Arabic; he even mastered the language. He was advised to go abroad to study and chose Princeton because of its Islamic department. There he obtained the nickname Lawrence. His classmates used to kid him and say, "Be careful, Ueda. You'll end up going native like Lawrence of Arabia."

The prophet would just smile and say, "I thank you for your worry, but I have no intention of leading marauding bands. I have great respect for the Arab world. I only hope to add to the world's appreciation of these great people."

Ueda was converted to Christianity at Princeton, in spite of his interest in Islamic studies. When he returned to Japan, his parents, who were Buddhists, were very displeased. His father had been an economics professor for years at Kyoto University and his mother an *ikebana sensei* (a master of the Japanese art of flower arranging). After attending congregation after congregation looking for more about Christ, he read the work of

Kanzo Uchimura, a Japanese Christian who lived at the turn of the twentieth century and who, like Ueda, could find no church that he considered true. Uchimura founded the Myu-kyokai, or "No Church", movement which espoused the opinion that none of the Christian churches had the true gospel and that people should therefore meet together informally to teach and learn from each other about Christ.

Five years later, Ueda accepted a *Book of Mormon* from two American missionaries at a train station in Tokyo, read it from cover to cover in two nights, then tracked them down to be baptized. He met his wife, Sachiko, a life-long member of the church, when she was twenty-five and he thirty.

After obtaining his doctorate at Princeton, he worked at Brigham Young University helping translate great works of Arabic literature into English. Before being called as a general authority, his last job was working for an international think tank for whom he traveled extensively. The couple maintained a very traditional Japanese household for their two children everywhere they lived–Tokyo, London, Riyadh, Salt Lake City. They wanted their sons to have cultural roots and respect for their grandparents and ancestors.

Ueda was the first Asian apostle and a favorite one among church speakers because of his rousing passionate speeches in which he called members to live a higher law. Then the troubles came and the UWEN took over. He, being an apostle and the president of the Quorum of the Twelve, had to go into hiding. With the death of the prophet, he became the head of an outlawed church, in terribly difficult times for Latter-day Saints. And his health began to fail.

This frail man, only in his early seventies, and his wife had to move seven times in fourteen months to keep from being kidnapped by UWEN troops, tortured, put on trial for sedition, and murdered.

Recently they had managed to stay for nearly six months in a small mother-in-law apartment under a house on Murphy's Lane in Salt Lake. And it was to that apartment that Peter and

Elder Dawahoya were headed. Salt Lake City had been free of obvious UWEN presence for two of those months and was roaring back to life in the ensuing free political climate.

The two men listened to the radio as they drove into the Salt Lake Valley, surprised to hear advertisements for car sales, house lots, new furniture, bank loans. They could see sale signs draped over businesses, cars clogging malls, recreational vehicles streaming past them out into the country.

"Sounds like the good old days," Joseph commented as they listened to a local radio station whose disc jockeys interspersed their music with information for the waves of refugees—what shelters were open, what hours the food banks were operating, where residents could drop their donations of beds, bedding and clothing for both adults and children, especially warm coats and boots.

As they got closer to their destination, Elder Dawahoya, who had dreaded the thought of orchestrating a mass exodus, now found himself warming to the idea. Finally, when they were turning off 45th South onto 13th East, headed north, Joseph became agitated—squirming and leaning out the car window as each street passed by. He nearly shouted when the street sign for Murphy's Lane appeared.

"Put the pedal to the metal, Porter!"

Peter turned the car down the meandering street that ran from 13th East to Highland Drive, while the prophet tried to find the house number. Finally they stopped in front of a modest, white-shingled house midway down the lane. The car had not come to a full stop when Elder Dawahoya jumped out and sprinted up to the front porch.

"I'll stay here—guard things," Peter called after him. Dawahoya didn't look back but impatiently pressed the doorbell several times.

A pleasant-looking middle-aged woman with a broad smile answered the door, greeted the chief apostle and quickly ushered him in. She led him to a nicely appointed living room where a brisk fire crackled in the fireplace. Then she disappeared into the back of the house.

A few moments later Joseph could hear muffled voices, then the clear, slightly accented voice of the prophet. He broke into a grin even before President Ueda walked slowly in.

"Joseph!" President Ueda said with great enthusiasm and bowed. "Oh, Joseph, come sit with me," he said as he patted the nearby turquoise couch. After the Hopi elder came to sit by his right side, the prophet asked Sister Nelson, "Will you see to his companion, wherever he is?" She nodded and backed out of the room. It was clear from her expression that she was deeply moved to have the prophet in her house.

"Good woman, Sister Nelson," Ueda said after she left. "She and her husband tore out a wall in their basement so I could come up the stairs from their apartment without having to go outside."

"How is your health, Lawrence?" Joseph asked solicitously.

"It has been better. But the Lord knows what I need, so I get by. I'm so much better seeing your face, Joseph," the prophet said in a voice husky with emotion.

"And Sachiko?"

"She's fine. She's downstairs. We'll go down after our pow-wow."

Joseph wrinkled up his face with playful disapproval at the use of "pow-wow."

Sister Nelson returned with warm cocoa and the word that Peter had been attended to. When she pulled the sliding doors closed, the two men noticed two young women standing quietly in the background. They smiled in recognition. "Those are Sister Nelson's two wonderful girls."

"Looks like you are in good hands."

"Couldn't be better. The Lord always provides, doesn't He?"

The two fell silent for a moment, then the prophet continued, "Joseph, I'm sorry that it falls on your shoulders to see this exodus takes place. I wish I were in better health...."

Joseph held up his hand to stop him. "We both know this is part of the Lord's plan. Just tell me what He wants me to do."

The two sat for nearly two hours discussing the logistics of the mass exodus. Finally the prophet's voice became shaky, his face grey.

"I've got to stop. Help me up, Joseph," Lawrence said, pushing against the arm of the couch to help brace himself. "Let's go down and see the great lady."

Joseph helped the small, frail man down the steep stairs. Once inside the small two bedroom apartment, Joseph felt like he had stepped into a household in Japan. A large screen with a mountain scene hid the sink and kitchen area. Colorful floral arrangements adorned the room. The smell of new-mown hay and rich fish permeated the air. The hay smell came from fresh tatami mats that covered the carpeted floors. Since there was no Western furniture, Sachiko knelt by a low table where she was cutting a small tree branch. She struggled to her feet and bowed to the Hopi. He returned the gesture.

"How lucky you are to have the gentle graces of a good wife," Joseph said somewhat enviously.

"Surely the Lord has blessed me," Lawrence said, extending his hand in the direction of his wife, indicating she should join them.

"Now you must rest, Prophet," Sachiko said tenderly, taking the prophet's arm.

"I know what to do now," the chief apostle assured Ueda. "I will set out to see that the Lord's will is done in this manner."

Later, as the smiling apostle emerged from the house, Peter asked, "Where to, boss?"

"Downtown, to the old Church office building."

"Think that's open?"

"The prophet assured me I'd find my old office nearly the way I left it."

On their way to the car, Elder Dawahoya and Peter stopped to watch the husband, Josh, with his three sons, turning over the soil in a large backyard garden.

"I wonder if I should tell them that they won't be here to see their harvest," Joseph ruminated out loud.

As they headed downtown to the Church Office Building, Peter tried not to speed down Seventh East into the heart of the city. After all, he'd have to explain to the Lord if something happened to this modern-day Moses who was his passenger.

Joseph felt for the gunny sack that covered the jar under the passenger's front seat. It's there, he said to himself and breathed a sigh of relief. He had placed it there without looking into it. He decided he would deliver the precious object sight unseen to its designated location in Missouri. It made him less nervous not knowing what he was carrying casually under the seat of the pickup.

The pair pulled up to the grey-pillared office building that had been partially destroyed by a UWEN bomb several years earlier. Workmen were busily putting finishing touches on the restored exterior. The apostle left Peter in the lobby with the security guard and took the stairs two at a time, hurrying to his corner office on the third floor, the burlap bag hidden under his large coat.

The office was large, panelled, and very dusty. Someone had placed boxes of his memorabilia and books on the floor near the empty shelves. He stood in the doorway and thought about the good times when this office bristled with activity. Now all was in readiness for a new command headquarters–and a commander equal to the task.

Joseph pulled a handgun from his back belt-line and placed it on the large mahogany desk. "Better keep this within reach," he muttered. He scanned the room for a place to put the pottery. Finally he decided to put in a desk drawer. The irony was not lost on him. "Not for long, Great Ones, I promise, will this sacred piece remain concealed."

He picked up the telephone from the floor behind the desk and listened for a dial tone. There was one. Good, he thought. Communication systems were beginning to work again. Who should I call? I wish I could call Charles Stewart. I miss him.

Then it occurred to him that it might be possible, so he

phoned the security desk downstairs and asked how he could reach Elder Stewart in Missouri. After a long pause, a man's voice on the other end of the phone answered, "Church of Jesus Christ of Latter-day Saints. How can I help you?"

"Jed, is that you?"

"Elder D.! Where are you?" Jed asked, surprised to hear the apostle's voice.

"Salt Lake City."

"Is this phone line secured?" Jed asked abruptly.

"Don't know. But I'm not going to give you anything that anyone would be interested in. I just want to know if I can speak to Elder Stewart."

"Elder Stewart's not here in Independence. He's gone north. Not expected back until tomorrow."

"Do you know what he was doing?"

"I do not, sir. You know, these phones aren't really that secure."

"Okay, okay. I'll try back tomorrow."

Dawahoya sat back in the bright light of the afternoon sun that streamed through the western windows. He felt lonely, but excited. Then he picked up the phone again. "What about the temple?" he asked the security guard. "Are we using it again?"

"Sir, it has been in use since last Tuesday. Perhaps you'd like to go over there now?"

"I would! And I'd like Elder Butler to accompany me."

Long pause. "I'm sorry. That's not possible, sir," the clerk said, returning to the phone. "It seems Elder Butler has not been endowed. He was never able to get to a temple before they were closed."

"Well, let's get him a recommend! What's the procedure these days? Who else is around to sign it?"

And so, Peter, who in his earlier years had dreams about walking over waters to reach the Lord, found himself, in real life, walking the long tunnel between the Church Office Building and the temple with the Lord's chief apostle. He could hardly believe his luck.

Joseph was exhilarated to see people in white going about their duties at desks, speaking in whispers. The two men sensed urgency on the faces of people standing in the waiting area. People were lined up four deep at the family file desk asking for cards so they could do temple work for their deceased relatives. The area for living endowments was filled to overflowing with couples who were waiting to be interviewed for temple marriages. Word had spread that the Hopi apostle was walking through, so workers lined the route to the initiatory area, waiting to shake his hand.

"Take good care of this lad," Dawahoya said jovially to the man at the initiatory desk, patting Peter on the arm. "He's our new Porter Rockwell."

After Peter went through the endowment session, he sat with Joseph Dawahoya in the ornate celestial room on a comfortable couch. He struggled to make sense of everything that he had been through.

"You now have garments that will further protect you from harm," Dawahoya said, putting his arm around the back of the couch.

"I know you say that. It's a bit hard to understand, you can imagine."

The Hopi apostle chuckled. "I joined the Church when I was in my twenties. I remember sitting in this same room, soon to be married. And my head was reeling, as I remember it."

Peter nodded vigorously in agreement.

"And now, Brother Peter, there is one more ceremony you must strive for."

"I know, I know. Marriage," he said somewhat flippantly. "It's just that I haven't met the sheila I've wanted to settle down with."

"You can go no further on this spiritual path until you marry," Elder Dawahoya said somewhat sternly. Then the apostle took his arm away and slid a little away from the pensive Peter. Peter put his head back and looked up at the grape designs at the corners of the ceiling. A strange peace that he had never experienced before fell over him. Here he sat with a father figure, a warrior he could admire. For the first time he opened his heart to the possibility of letting a woman into his life.

"I will do as You ask," he said very quietly.

Tears began to course down his stoic face. He quickly wiped them with the shirt sleeve, but they kept on coming. He let them fall.

The first official word from Elder Dawahoya's office was of a gathering of Latter-day Saints at the Great Hall in four days. Press releases were sent to radio and television stations, as well as the burgeoning print media. Home teachers and visiting teachers went from home to home, inviting all to hear the apostle speak. It had been decided that only Elder Dawahoya would speak on behalf of the Brethren. Everyone felt it was still too risky to have a large gathering of general authorities. Peter was to act as bodyguard.

Over twenty thousand people came. Overflow crowds filled the Temple Square grounds. Elder Dawahoya was calm as he began. "My beloved brothers and sisters, the Lord is aware of your great suffering." He paused to let that soak in. "I know there has been great jubilation that you are now free to resume your normal lives, but..." Dawahoya talked in veiled terms, but ones that members who had been to the temple understood, "...you will be asked to sacrifice everything you have, including your very lives if necessary, for your commitment to the gospel...and very soon."

Several times hecklers in the crowd interrupted the apostle's speech. Peter wanted to charge into the crowd, but the apostle restrained him with a stern glance. Joseph went on to quote the prophet John Taylor, who told a woman in Cedar City in the late 1800's that he'd had a vision in which he saw Salt Lake City as a great and beautiful metropolis with cement streets extending south clear to the Point of the Mountain. Taylor had warned that the people would become indifferent to the counsel and advice of the Church authorities, growing more interested in the amassing wealth than in pursuing a spiritual life. "Please, I beg you, do not return to those old ways, before the rule of the UWEN. The recent times have been difficult, but they have allowed you to find solace in your families, and hopefully in the Lord."

The speech lasted for about thirty minutes. When it was over, Dawahoya and Butler slipped out the back of the auditorium and headed for the car parked on South Temple. As they walked through Temple Square and the milling throngs, shots rang out. They dove for cover behind a low wall just as more rounds whizzed into the swarm, hitting several people with a dull thud. Amid the screams, even more people began falling all around the two men. With no thought for their own safety, Joseph and Peter jumped up from their cover.

"You get the bodies! I'll get the shooter," Peter shouted as he weaved and dodged through the panicked crowd. Joseph began dragging the dead and wounded back behind the low wall. Peter spurted in the direction of the south wall surrounding the temple, his .357 Smith and Wesson drawn. He spotted a man wearing a black suit, white shirt, and a cloth tied around his waist, standing on the wall near the flagpole. With deadly accuracy, Peter took him out with the first shot. The man fell sideways, then rolled onto the pavement in front of the crowd. Forcefully pushing his way through the scene, the Aussie grabbed the body of the older, dark-haired man and stripped it of the bloodied temple clothing.

A group calling themselves members of the "God Returning to Earth" movement sent a rambling letter to the local television station, claiming responsibility for the shootings. In it they stated: "We warned you. Don't say we didn't. As we foretold, the Mormon Church *did* sell out to the UWEN. We warn you about the next betrayal–the Church will ask members to bring their food storage in to central warehouses, and in order to get food back, they will have everyone take on the Mark of the Beast."

Taped onto the paper was this statement: "WARNING: This attack on Temple Square is the first installment regarding the prophecy, 'Blood will run in the streets of Salt Lake City.'"

Along with segments of the letter, the station repeatedly played grizzly visual accounts of what they termed "the massacre of fifty-three innocent victims on Temple Square." They also aired an in-depth look at the assassin–a fifty-year-old West Valley City man, former member of the LDS Church, excommunicated for forming a group to reinstate polygamy and claiming he was the reincarnation of John the Baptist and rightful "heir to the prophet's throne."

Later in the week, this same group of madmen took a busload of people hostage and insisted that their demands be broadcast on a local talk show anchored by an outspoken, far-right-wing conservative host. The outrageous demands included the following: "Citizens of Utah, you should know that two of your general authorities have participated in writing the New World Constitution, which is designed to replace our God-given Constitution of the United States. They must be killed for this heresy." (The group made no mention of which two general authorities they had in mind.)

Next came a list of vague but impassioned demands that included access to the high security floors of the Joseph Smith Memorial Building and the removal of any Muslims from Fort Douglas, "because the new president of the United States will be declared a dictator for five years, and then he will have the power to introduce Islamic armies onto U.S. soil."

After the shooting, when Elder Dawahoya went back to Murphy's Lane for one final briefing with the prophet before launching the mass exodus' plans, President Ueda tried to console the apostle by saying, "You and Brother Butler managed to save several people, I understand."

"Yes, we managed to shield a number of people and get them to medical help. Martyrs for the cause," said the Hopi sadly.

"It seems Satan doesn't want people leaving here," the prophet said, his voice thick with both sadness and irony.

Dawahoya smiled weakly.

"The Lord wants us to begin implementing the evacuation plans in the same manner as we discussed before. And remember, dear friend, you can't save everybody."

Joseph looked away and tightened his jaw. In Vietnam he was known to never leave a man behind—if he could possibly avoid it. After a moment's silence, he asked, "When do you want the church records to leave?"

"Next week."

After detailed and secured conversations flew back and forth by secret transmissions from Salt Lake to Independence, stake presidents were contacted. They were told to call in everyone they knew who had remained faithful to the Church during the past difficult years. Members would be invited to leave for Missouri, but they had leave at the exact time designated, and with a 72-hour supply of food and supplies. Departure times would be staggered, so that the southerly migration wouldn't be too terribly obvious. In the interview, members were also told that if they did not leave at their designated time, the Church couldn't guarantee their safety, nor could they be guaranteed admittance to Zion when they came later. Special circumstances were discussed with individuals who needed more time to take care of matters such as illness or car repair.

The number of active members had dwindled in the Salt Lake area to 25% of the total population. And of that number only 10% elected to leave within the designated time period, so that Elder Dawahoya had only 25,000 members to help leave, not the 250,000 he had imagined. Among the reasons they gave for not going: "We don't have the money"; "We can't leave family members who are inactive—we're afraid of extreme backlash against those remaining"; "We want more time to sell the house to make a better profit on the deal"; "We heard that Missouri was devastated, not suitable for habitation"; "No, thanks. We are just beginning to recover financially now that the UWEN has withdrawn"; and even, "We're planning a family vacation."

Logistics, even for this size group, were nightmarish. The Church had to supply electrical car batteries or gasahol to members who couldn't get their cars to Missouri. They had to outfit special buses, which were driven to designated spots throughout the Valley, to pick up people who did not have transportation; the temples had to be closed and dismantled again, only months after opening; and they needed to oversee the establishment of checkpoints along the way down to Cedar City.

Besides all this, Dawahoya also had to coordinate evacuation of surrounding cities, staggering the dates so that the Jackson County facilities wouldn't be inundated.

He also had to deal with death threats, sleeping in a different place every night–Peter his constant shadow.

The following week, when the Church records were removed from the Joseph Smith Memorial Building and the vault in Big Cottonwood canyon, all who had elected to leave had done so. The route was south to St. George, down through Hopi land, and then back the way Elder Dawahoya and Peter had come–through New Mexico, Texas, Oklahoma, Kansas and finally Missouri.

John Taylor also reportedly told that same woman in Cedar City: "If you are alive at that time, be sure that you are not far behind the records, because after the Church records leave and are secure, the very powers of hell will be turned loose, and there will be such destruction that but very little life will remain."

CHAPTER EIGHT

"Through the night of doubt and sorrow
Onward goes the pilgrim band,
Singing songs of expectation
Marching to the promised land"
Sabine Baring-Gould

Within the day, the numerous anti-Mormon forces got word that this mass exodus from the Wasatch Front was underway. When the UWEN took over the state and forced the church underground, open hostility against the church was checked. Then, when that restraining force was lifted, this repressed anger came roaring back.

The alternative press began openly taunting members about their beliefs. "If you're the true church, why hasn't Jesus come to save you from nuclear blasts and the plague?" And "Just where is the prophet of the Mormon Church? Too cowardly to face the UWEN! He's been in hiding for years." Some group even hung Ueda in effigy outside Temple Square. Emboldened by the ineffectiveness of the small police force which had to be reassembled when the UWEN troops dispersed, gangs found delight in rounding up groups of clean-looking adolescents and torturing them with everything from taunts to gasahol torching.

During the UWEN years, members met in secret, in groups of ten families on other days besides Sunday, and there were no general conferences—no offerings of new revelation or counsel. In this vacuum, members, who already were on the fringe about their beliefs or adherence to standards, had a hard time staying on track with only their own spiritual resources to guide them.

In the leadership void, sub-groups of Mormons with their own twist on the faith sprang up: Many more polygamous groups; groups who mixed New Age teachings with traditional Mormon doctrine, such as ones claiming to be headed by reincarnated Joseph Smiths and Brigham Youngs; and an especially popular group who believed that the Holy Spirit had finally incarnated and was based in Winnemucca, Nevada.

With the dissolution of the UWEN command at Camp Williams, these groups now also directed threats at the main body of the church. The prophet and his wife were scarcely out of the city and passing the first Spanish Fork checkpoint when word reached them that there had been horrifying bloodbaths at light rail stations up and down the valley. The attacks were aimed at anyone who even appeared to be a Latter-day Saint. It was as though dense forces of evil, which had been kept at bay, were suddenly loosed at the very center of the Lord's Church.

Among the first groups to leave were Laurie Winder with her four children, along with her father, Elder Whitmer, his wife, Dorothy, and their nephew, Bobby Whitmer.

After divorcing Nate, Laurie had married a ski instructor who subsequently died in an avalanche. Now she appeared much subdued, not the feisty, demanding woman who had tried to seduce Peter Butler and who left her four little children with her parents to go off with the man from the Alta slopes. Since her husband's death, Laurie had let her light-brown hair grow out and wore it pulled up around to one side. Her hazel eyes now had a sunken, yet piercing look, which gave her the appearance of someone who was searching for energy from any source, no matter who or what. Analyzed by two psychologists in her teens, Laurie had been labeled histrionic by one, narcissistic by the other. But both agreed that she was short on empathy. Rarely would she role-take; and even when she did, it was a hollow performance. She neither had, nor cared to get, any sense of what another person felt.

The apostle's daughter was wearing black even a year now after the accident. She was not really in mourning, but she wore it as an outward sign that she was a devotee of a secret sect who believed that Jesus was already on the earth. She believed she was on a fast track to becoming translated, because he had incarnated as the Chinese master, Lu Han, and would take care of her if she worshipped him. The other conditions were that she forsake meat and bow to the east three times a day.

Closing her eyes, Laurie leaned her face against the car's back window and remembered the first time she had heard of the Avatar. Her friend, Kayleen Richards, had held a pearl an inch in diameter before her eyes and said dramatically, "I saw this materialize out of his palm. Straight out–no tricks. And he gave it to me so that I would remember him and have faith in his teachings." Kayleen let Laurie hold the pearl. She thought it felt miraculous to the touch. Now she fingered a pendant she always wore under her clothing–a round and stylized yin/yang symbol that all of Lu Han's devotees wore. She smiled slyly to think that she knew something her apostle father didn't as he drove south on Interstate 15 headed for Zion.

Sangay, along with his extended family, began the trek from the southwestern edge of the Himalayas across Tibet into China, across the Gobi Desert to Upper Mongolia. This involved making their way from one mountain pass to another, one valley to another until they came out on the vast windy, seemingly uninhabited plains. Dotted throughout this area from the north Arctic region to Afghanistan were secret small compounds used by Sufis from the ninth century. Sufis were an ascetic, Muslim sect, whose goal was mystical union with God achieved by fervent worship and ecstatic dance.

Less than fifty miles from where Sangay would pass, in a large building complex hidden from view by sand dunes, the occupants were nearly frenzied with activity. They had been surprised by the return of one the most adept sheikhs ever to study there–none other than Lu Han. The center contained a large chamber for Sufi whirling ceremonies, a fountain from which water was charitably distributed to the passing pilgrims, cells for the dancers (or "dervishes"), a separate quarter for the Master, a chamber of silence, and dining and bathing rooms. The honored guest, Lu Han, was secretly meeting Dmitri Gornstein for the first time in eleven years.

"This is a great meeting place, Han, if I do say so," Gornstein said as he entered and shook the sand from his great coat. He took it off and hung it on a wooden peg behind the door, then he quickly tucked in the shirt tail of his black and silver uniform.

"Thank you, friend," Han said in Cantonese. "I'm glad you found your way." He was leaning with his back against a thick, rough-hewn table set with lighted candles in wooden candle holders. The stone walls of the large room reflected the dancing light.

"I didn't know you were involved with Sufis. Last time I knew you were still training in the Taoist tradition," said Dmitri as he crossed to the table.

"Well...I have transcended traditions," Han said obliquely. "Come, sit." He patted a chair next to him as he sat down at the head of the table. "Your Chinese is quite good. Thank you for using it. It safeguards our conversations since no one here can speak it."

"It's quite easy to recall since it was taught along with Russian in my classes in primary school."

The tall, well-built Han, who looked only partially Asian with blue eyes, clapped his hands, and two men servants appeared with a plate of lamb, oil, spices and warm bread. This they gave to Gornstein. To Lu they handed a small delicately-decorated cup. The thick aroma was of Turkish coffee. The servants retreated behind a thick curtain.

"Can they be trusted?"

"With my life. They are devotees."

While Dmitri ate, Han looked him over. He seemed pleased with what he saw. "You've grown lean and hungry. I like that."

The intimate smile that Dmitri returned betrayed a moment of sexuality, then it was gone.

"You've made some name for yourself," the general said, putting his brown leather boot on an empty chair nearby. Han was dressed in a long, beige-colored robe with a multi-colored vest studded with mother-of-pearl buttons.

"I'd say the same, but I'm not sure you're in a mood to hear such a thing."

Han cleared his throat. "The invasion of ancient Chinese territory beyond the Bering Strait, as they call it, was a calculated risk, no more. I needed to know how everyone would respond."

After the UWEN dropped a nuclear bomb on the Chinese troops in Alaska, their government responded by withdrawing its troops but with a threat of nuclear retaliation. When the invaders along the West Coast of the United States were told by their leaders to redouble their efforts, the fighting intensified. More and more Chinese suicide squads were used to smash through UWEN barricades and into nominally secured areas up and down the coast.

"And did the UWEN troops react as you predicted?"

"No, they didn't. That was the fascinating thing about the whole matter. I didn't know they had among their troops fierce men from the interior of the West—a place with the inland saline lake. Within twelve days, UWEN forces, aided by this group, had ruthlessly pressed forward, north and south, in a pincer fashion, virtually destroying two of our armies of more than one hundred thousand men each. Then they took to the ridges of the inland mountain range where they succeeded in cutting down the rest of our troops trying to escape. Despite their smaller numbers, the Western troops knew the terrain and used guerrilla tactics to ambush one company after another."

"I remember hearing something to that effect," Dmitri said, then coughed. "I understand they command a considerable force that is loosely organized, but highly loyal."

"Do you know to whom?"

"A prophet!" Dmitri laughed and spit out part of his dark brown bread.

"A prophet?"

"Not Mohammed, the only true prophet. Blessed be he!"

"I see," Han mused. "I once met a woman from Salt Lake City

when I was in India. That's the name of the city where the rebels are headquartered." Han sat quietly and closed his eyes, his thoughts immediately returning to the story of the battle. "It was not so much the snowstorms that caused our war machine to sputter and stall; it was the fact that the troops were cut off from supplies. Hungry, cold, and out of ammunition, they were just a skeleton of an army by the time the fighting had reached the decisive battle high in the mountains."

"200,000 men dead!" the Russian said and whistled softly.

"Hardly a dent in our stupendous numbers, of course," Lu said with a visible glint of pride.

"And now what?" Dmitri said, wiping his front teeth with his sleeve, then picking those teeth with the little finger of his right hand.

"You were always so impatient. Take time to savor not only the victories but also the defeats. And for heaven's sake, take some time to breathe in between, being very conscious of each breath. It makes life much more ecstatic."

"Ever the philosopher."

"Ever the warmonger."

"Your wish is my command." Dmitri lowered his eyes coyly.

"I am past such activities, dear one. Mine is a twin path. I am to become emperor of China, and I am to lead souls to God."

Dmitri began to laugh, but was silenced by the look on Han's face—serious, illumined. Lu smiled at his former roommate's confusion. He had always been a bit of a mystery, not just to Gornstein, but to others who thought they knew him well.

Han was born in Vladivostok, a port in the southeastern region of Siberia, where his father, Lu Jing Guo, a highly educated man, was an executive for the Trans-Siberian Railway. Jing Guo met his wife on a trip to Moscow. She was an artistically sensitive beauty whose parents had come from Odessa on the Black Sea. Because Jing's family had been wealthy merchants in Hong Kong before the Chinese takeover, they spoke flawless English. Thus Han's father made sure his son learned English along with Cantonese and Russian.

When his mother, Irina, was approached by a member of a Taoist monastic sect who said her son had been born to be a priest, she agreed to let him go into the countryside if she could accompany him. So, from the age of five, he was trained in both healing and martial arts. Han was tall and athletic and especially sensitive to ghosts and psychic phenomena as a young boy. Because of his agility and flashing temper, he was dubbed "Snow Leopard" by his teachers.

At age sixteen, when the Taoist priests had taught him all they could, his father sent him to a military school. He was determined his son would be no introverted mystic, but a man of the world. In military matters, he also quickly excelled, so that he rapidly made his way up the ranks in an army that normally would have rejected him for his foreign blood. For there was no doubt this was an extraordinary man.

For a time, he was consumed with matters of war–but when his mother died when he was thirty-two, he turned inward with the same passion that he pursued the outer world.

"Tell me about the God part," Gornstein insisted. "I heard you took a leave of absence from the army for awhile."

"I will tell you, if you promise to listen with an open mind to this search for God. You should do it yourself, you know. "

"I...I feel like I am God's avenger, if that counts."

"Well, it will do for now." He took a sip of the coffee, then carefully entwined his long fingers and laid his hands, palm-up on his lap. "I began an urgent search for further spiritual learning after the death of my mother. I wandered into a Sufi enclave the first year of my travels and was quickly accepted as a novice. I became an ecstatic, forever whirling and dancing. Many times forgetting to eat, I wandered out in the desert in such a trance that I would be found unconscious and had to be brought back to the cell to be revived."

The sound of fierce, howling winds outside interrupted Lu's narrative.

"Dust storm. If you'll excuse me." Dmitri watched as his former roommate moved effortlessly across the room and through the heavy, woolen curtains. While the Russian waited, he could hear the sounds of animals braying and complaining, so he pulled back a shutter to see Lu with the two servants, pulling reluctant pack animals into a shed and stuffing the closed door with hay.

Gornstein sat back down and waited quietly for the Sufi master's return. He suddenly became aware of small flashes of silver light–flashes like the old RKO beacon. With each footstep that echoed down the stone hallway, the beams got more intense and came in faster bursts. As Lu rattled the door handle, Gornstein could see brilliant white light under the door. The Chinese master opened the door and, to the astonishment of Dmitri, these lightning beams were emanating from the head and body of his old friend.

Han spoke matter-of-factly, "This storm will pass in an hour."

"How...how can you be so sure?" Gornstein managed to stammer in the midst of his astonishment.

"I spoke to it. It has agreed to move on in a more easterly course than it had planned." Lu turned and hung a sheepskin coat on a peg in back of the large slatted door.

"What?" the Jewish atheist asked incredulously.

"Leave it, friend." The Asian looked at Dmitri with such a piercing look that Dmitri couldn't maintain eye contact. "Now where were we?" Han asked, sitting back in the yogic pose. "Ah, yes. Having achieved the union with God that I sought among these devotees, I moved on, past the Tibetans–whom I deem barbarian–to India. "

Overwhelmed with this display of transpersonal power, Dmitri suddenly felt exhausted. He was already tired from the six-day overland journey from Iran, but now he was thoroughly fascinated. He didn't want to disrupt the narrative.

Seeing the fatigue on the face of his old friend, Han said graciously, "Enough of this. You must be tired from your long journey." The Sufi master clapped his hands once, and the older, grey-bearded servant pulled back the curtain. "Please show my guest to his quarters."

Dmitri tried to protest, but Han insisted. After the Russian and his servant departed, Master Lu, as he was called by the people of this Sufi sect, sat back in his straight-backed chair and withdrew into a deep, meditative state–so deep that had his servant come to tell him something, he might have thought his master dead. There was no rise and fall from his chest, no breath emanated from his nose or mouth. Yet this state was not so unusual in this Sufi cell. Many of the members of this sect were able to reach such a deep state of withdrawal.

Several times during the night Dmitri woke expecting to find Han climbing into his bed as he had in their military barracks, but he didn't. Finally, about five in the morning, he awoke and left the small bedroom to walk back to the dining area. There he found Han sitting immobile–yet not sitting on the chair, but floating three feet above it.

The frightened Russian sucked in his breath in disbelief. "Han!" he called out in distress.

His floating friend opened one eye and smiled. "Yes, Dimi?"

"Are you all right?"

His eyes half-glazed, the Chinese master floated down to the waiting chair. "You look like you've just seen a ghost," he said, laughing deep from within his belly.

"I...I don't know whether I should bow or run," Dmitri said in a hushed, almost reverent voice.

"Bowing would be the proper thing. Not to me, but to the god who allows me to ascend into his presence."

The Russian sat down hard on a chair across the table from the Asian adept. "I...I don't know what to say. What in the world has happened to you?"

"I have found God. And you can too. It is far more satisfying than holding such dark sexual thoughts as I see still lurk in you."

A slight blush surfaced on the renegade commander's face spreading up to the top of his balding head.

"And if it is revenge you seek, I can promise you God has far more exquisite ways of repaying your enemies than you can imagine."

"I just never had you pegged for a..."

"A what? A god-realized avatar?"

"What is an avatar?"

"One who was born on the earth to bring salvation to God's children."

"Like Buddha, Moses, Jesus?"

Lu nodded.

Gornstein was quiet a moment, then said, "It's going to take a bit to absorb this information. I'm sorry. I didn't mean to be disrespectful." He lowered his eyes.

"And now as to why I've asked you to come." Han beamed beneficently on the subdued Russian soldier.

"Your message said we could take over the world."

"And would you have come for any other reason, my voracious friend?"

Gornstein couldn't suppress a self-derisive smile.

"The god of this world wants all his children to be happy and safe. He has told me that together we can bring everyone under a one-world umbrella, one that will supply everyone with all their needs, not like the UWEN. That was clumsy, ill-formed and poorly led."

"I like what I'm hearing," Dmitri said, running his thumb and index finger down his bushy, black moustache.

"Although the party doesn't know it yet, China is going to return to being an empire. I will accept the position of emperor but will insist on ruling only as a spiritual leader of the people. The political and military matters I will give to my friend, General Zhang."

A smirk quickly passed over Dmitri's lips. "When?"

"You doubt me," said Han with great equanimity.

"Ah, well, let's just say I'd like to wait and see," said the commander of the largest independent army in the world. He rose and began to pace—his left arm held smartly behind his back.

"That's fair, Dimi," Han said and bowed slightly. "This is all new to you. And you always were a realistic fellow. You can watch as the drama unfolds before the year is out."

"And then?"

"Ooo–so impatient! Then we will begin a series of alliances with different governments struggling to get back on their feet after the UWEN fiasco. We will be stable, generous, hopeful." Lu leaned back in the wooden chair and balanced on the back legs.

"Iran, Turkey will be included, of course?" Dmitri ventured.

"And others–among them: Japan, India, the united Korea, Russia and her satellites, France and Germany."

"And what role will I play?" The pupils of Dmitri's dark eyes were now nearly dilated.

"You, sir, are to be the benign, titular head of this united alliance."

Gornstein sucked in his breath. He had expected Lu would suggest a powerful, but subservient role.

"And you will report to no one, but me."

Dmitri's ego dragged him along with the fantasy. "And will you teach me to fly?" he heard himself ask, almost begging. He returned to the rough-hewn table and put his face close to Lu's.

"That is a promise, Dimi," Lu said, dropping his chair back to four legs. "Come, I hear the drums beginning to warm up. Let's begin with you experiencing God through dance." The Chinese master stood, slipped his arm through Gornstein's and escorted the enchanted Russian commander down the stone hallway to a large round chamber, lined with twelve foot tall pillars, each about eight feet from the outside stone wall.

Dmitri stood on the side, between two wooden pillars, watching the whirling dervishes as they turned in circles around the floor to the beat of drums and flutes, singing out an Arabic name of God.

"Go on, friend. You wanted to fly–begin now," Lu said, gently shoving Gornstein into the circle. The Russian hesitantly joined the circle of dancers, their eyes closed, all straining to see the face of God. He'll do quite nicely, thought Master Lu.

In a nomadic tent and an hour away as the crow flies, Sangay and his family sat, faces covered with cloths, trying to ride the sand storm. Sangay had entered a quiet state of meditation and concentrated on mentally quieting the family, who were upset by the intensity of the frequent desert blasts. He had been troubled all day by the feeling that there was a demon following the small group. He'd had his encounters with dark forces in the past, but this felt different–like a white light sucked into a black hole. That was how he described it to his father, as they stood and moved to the center of the tent to sup from rusted tin cups.

"I've never thought of it, Father, but you look much like an American Indian I know in the United States–Sam, a member of the Goshen tribe."

Yeshi put back his head and laughed. "That is amusing, my son! Hasn't this been a devil of a storm?"

Just as he said that, the howling wind suddenly stopped. Everyone froze, hoping against hope that the storm had subsided. Sangay stepped out of the tent and found not even a breeze as he licked his index finger and held it up in the air.

Magic, he thought darkly. This has got to be supernatural. Storms don't stop on a dime. He tapped on his black-strapped Rolex watch which he wore on his right wrist to see if it was still running. It was. The other wrist was wrapped with a strand of light-brown wooden beads which the wary rinpoche unwound and began fingering.

Why do I feel so uneasy? What could it be? he asked himself.

After noontime dinner of yak jerky and buttered tea (he would have given anything to be feasting on his favorites–*la phuk gor zoe, dho thuk, tsampa,* and, for dessert, *khapsay*), he returned to his meditation. Now, as he quieted his mind, he found himself thinking about Ben. *Why Ben?* he wondered. Rather than resist the impulse to forget him, the Tibetan abbot focussed on his student and located him sleeping in a make-shift tent in his backyard in Independence.

Entering Ben's dream, he asked, "Ben, why have you called me?" Ben was in the middle of a dream about fishing for snails when he found Sangay was suddenly standing beside him, asking him why he was using that pole when snails could be scooped up in a bucket.

"You're always a great help, Rinpoche."

"Now why did you call me?"

"I really didn't. Of course, actually returning to Zion with my family has brought me to realms of tremendous joy. Maybe I wanted to share that with you."

Ben watched in his dream as his guru picked up the box with the ancient brass plates.

"What have you been reading?" his meditation teacher asked sharply.

"The last plate I translated was about the Anti-Christ." Ben felt embarrassed that he hadn't looked at the plates for the past few days.

"That is what I've been feeling–*his* presence! So tell me what you've got," the rinpoche said eagerly.

As the dream continued, Ben struggled to remember the lines he had translated. "It goes something like...'In that time, there will rise one, one behind another, who will rule the world like no other.'"

"Go on."

"Ah...'He will move like a leopard, yet have the feet of the bear. When he opens his mouth, he speaks like a lion, yet his name must not be known. Who can know this riddle?"

Sangay disappeared from Ben's dream. Ben awoke with a tangle of images–bears, lions, Tibetans–which slowly slipped from his conscious grasp.

Sangay, on the other hand, was electrified and focused. Somewhere on this stretch of desert, and not far away, was a major source of earthly evil–a man, yet a devil, who experienced the highest visions, yet denied the source of all.

In the cool of the early evening, the Tibetans headed north, but Sangay would retain in his memory the vivid sense of evil and power darkly radiating from that secret Sufi cell. He knew he'd recognize it again if it reared its ugly head.

As they traveled across the Tibetan plateau, north and east, the rinpoche communicated telepathically with other members of the tribe of Naphtali, letting them know he was headed for a rendezvous with other heads of tribes. Their destination was a valley in the remote northeast region of Mongolia, where, it was rumored, Caucasian-looking natives lived. And, in fact, LDS missionary couples, who had been sent to the region during the early 1990's, came back home with tales of a people who wore white clothes in the fashion of temple garments and claimed an ancestry back to Noah.

CHAPTER NINE

"I do not ask for any crown
But that which all may win;
Nor try to conquer any world
Except the one within."
Louisa May Alcott

The next morning the Puerto de Luna party was greeted by a group of church officials from Independence. They ate a delicious breakfast of rations in a large tent, hastily constructed for the occasion. Along with the food cooked up by the area Relief Society, they received a warm welcome from the Presiding Bishop, Michael Levine.

"Brother and sisters, we welcome you to Zion," Levine said enthusiastically. "You are our first official immigrants. It feels a bit to us like it must have to Brigham Young and his scouting party when the first company of Saints descended into the Salt Lake Valley."

The group from Puerto de Luna beamed.

"We wish we were welcoming you into the terrestrial Zion, but unfortunately this is still the telestial plane and things are a bit messy, since we're picking up after the big quake. However, we do have a number of programs in place so that you will have food and shelter and any other of your basic needs taken care of. When you've finished eating, I would like to talk to the heads of each household, husband and wife, if that's the family structure, so that we can send you to your 'home,' and I use that word advisedly."

There were scattered guffaws from the welcoming committee.

"Because so many homes and businesses were leveled in the quake, we are in the process of rebuilding, which we will ask you to participate in."

When Ben groaned, Peg hit him in the side with her elbow. "Don't go flipping out like that, Ben. You're a guy—you can hold a hammer."

"Yeah, but it's what I do to myself and others with the tool, once I have it in my hand," Ben said smiling.

"Dad, I'm sorry to bring this up," Miriam said, pulling on Ben's checkered shirt sleeve.

"Yes, honey?"

"But where do you go to the bathroom?"

Ben laughed and said, "Just where we've been going for the last day or so. Find a bush." He pointed toward the woods.

"But you said things would be different when we got here," Miriam said with definite sarcasm in her voice. "You said we were going to a wonderful place where we would be safe and have our own house and everything would be beauti..."

Peg saved her husband by whisking her step-daughter away for a potty-stop in a pit temporarily dug for the occasion. When the two were walking back, Peg said to Miriam, "Mimi, this is just the beginning of glorious events that are going to happen to us, but you've got to be a little patient, honey. Now what is it that you've always wanted? This is a place where dreams come true."

Miriam thought for a moment. "A baby brother or sister."

That was not what Peg had in mind. Of course, she couldn't tell her that Ben had had a vasectomy. Her eyes filled with tears. She deeply wanted more children, too, but had never voiced it.

"You know I'd like that, too," Peg said merrily. "Well, let's see what the Lord can do with that request."

"And while we're on the subject, I really want a kitty. We had one when we lived with Grandpa, and I'd like a white one."

"Well, that will be a lot easier to take care of, I'll bet," Peg said, squeezing the eight-year-old's shoulders as they walked. "I'm not sure about the white, but I know there must be some kitties around here that would love a home with such a loving mistress as you."

When it was Ben and Peg's turn with the Presiding Bishop, Levine explained, "For Church members, we are going to begin with a limited Law of Consecration. This is how it will work: You will promise to give to the Zion community all your time and talents, and by that I mean that you will work at what you do best to help build the Kingdom here. And, in return, you will come to me and submit a budget for your family. This budget will be one you have prayed over—one that contains your basic needs."

He leaned back in his chair and continued, looking both Ben and Peg in the eye, "Then I will pray about it, and if I get a confirmation that it pleases the Lord, I will present you with a check for the amount you requested."

Peg and Ben squeezed each other's hand.

"This supposes that you will carefully manage this money and that you will be willing to do what is necessary, even if it is somewhat inconvenient, to help in this building phase. As the population stabilizes, we will institute an economic system that is much more sophisticated."

"Like the corporate capitalism we had before the UWEN takeover?" Ben asked, unable to conceal a slight tone of disgust in his voice.

"There will be elements of that, but, more than anything, it will be a mixed economy with communitarian and even some socialist characteristics. In short, the best of everything that we have experienced in the last century or so."

"Would it be possible to discuss this with you further, Bishop?" Ben asked, his interest piqued. "I've been a student of social change for many years, and I have been fascinated with what the practical implementation of Joseph Smith's idealistic economic ideas might look like."

"I'd enjoy that conversation, Brother Taylor," the Bishop said graciously. "Now, speaking of practicalities, let's look at your situation. Since the Church has purchased all of the land in the northern end of Missouri, we can deed you a piece of property to meet your needs. How much land do you think you can manage?"

"Just a small...," Ben looked to Peg, "house with a *very* small yard will do."

Peg pursed her lips. Levine, a former Wall Street broker, sat back and waited.

Finally Peg spoke up with a quavering voice, "Bishop, I would like ten acres. I know my husband doesn't like to even work in a garden, but I grew up on a farm and it would mean everything to me to be able to plow and plant and grow much of our own food...."

"So what about that, Brother Taylor?" the church authority interrupted. "What about your wife's desires?"

"I don't want the land. I don't know what to do with it, but if she wants and can handle that much, why not? We can always give what we can't handle back, can't we?"

Peg looked away with a hurt expression.

"Yes, you can."

"Now Sister Taylor, I'm sure you know that your husband's skills will be required at church headquarters. He will not be at home during the day."

"Then I'll get help," Peg said sharply. "I know what has to be done. My father treated me just like my brothers. I'm not afraid of hard work."

The bishop looked back at Ben. He shrugged his shoulders.

So the two signed an agreement with the Church that they could have a lease on the land *in perpetuity.* Theirs but not theirs.

"Fine, then. Let me see." Bishop Levine said, "We've tried to pick out a neighborhood where you people from New Mexico can remain neighbors." He rolled out a large blue architect's paper onto his desk. "Okay, here we have it–398 No. Orchard Road– ten acres, fruit trees, a well, pasturage, house still standing."

Peg broke into a smile and raised her fists slightly above her lap. "Yes!" she said enthusiastically under her breath.

"Who else?" Ben wanted to know.

"Well, let's see. Two blocks down, we've got the Rivers' into a two-story like yours."

The bishop shared the other designations. Then Ben realized that he hadn't heard the Gallegos mentioned. "What about them, Bishop? They aren't LDS as you know."

"Because they are non-members, we cannot offer them the same deal; however, we are leasing them a large house and have offered employment to Juan as an apprentice in the printing shop. His wages will be sufficient to pay for his home and other needs. "

"So what I understand is, if we are willing to live this limited law of consecration, we are guaranteed incomes. But if we are not LDS, the old system of salaries and rent applies," Peg said.

"It's a bit more complicated than that, Sister Taylor, but essentially that's the idea."

"But how can the church afford to give us land and money?"

"Let me give you a few figures to help you understand," the bishop said kindly. "Before the UWEN takeover which lasted only a few years, the economic situation in the world looked like this: the net worth of the world's three hundred richest people was equal to the combined income of the poorest fifty-five percent of the world's population. I said *fifty-five percent.*"

Ben whistled and said, "I had no idea it was *that* skewed."

"Actually, most of those three hundred people were part of a few wealthy families and corporations—ten to be exact."

"Those old predictions that all the wealth would fall into the hands of a few really were right on, weren't they?"

"Yes, they were. In fact, as you know, world conditions had gone from inequitable to inhuman, from unacceptable to intolerable. And that is why everyone agreed so easily to setting up a world organization that came with the promise to provide a more equitable distribution of wealth. The UWEN, of course, had no intention of doing so. We've been able to secure records that indicate they kept back fully half of the financial resources at their disposal."

"Those bast...!" Ben said and pounded on the table. He got up and pulled back the tent flap, "So how is this going to work? Surely the Church doesn't have the resources to support the twelve million..."

Suddenly a young man appeared and asked for the Presiding Bishop. While Levine stepped out, Ben remained with his back to Peg; she looked at her hands. Nothing was said until the bishop returned.

"I'm so sorry. I can't continue this conversation. Suffice to say, we can help everyone get on their feet. Life will be simple for a time, but we will certainly get by."

He quickly handed Ben several papers and an envelope which contained chits to be presented for food and basic supplies at the bishop's storehouse near their new house outside Independence.

"Bishop, have you heard the one about the two cannibals eating a clown?" Ben asked as they turned to leave.

"I don't know."

Peg interrupted, "Come on, Ben. Not now." She began to tug on his sleeve.

Ben finished up with, "Suddenly, one cannibal says to the other, 'Does this taste funny to you?'"

They could hear the bishop's laughter out into the field.

On the way to the children's play area to pick up Danny and Miriam, Ben said, "Look, Peg. I'm not a handy guy. You know that."

Peg's face turned red. "Ben, I knew that when I married you. I'm not that stupid. My brothers were farmers, my father was a farmer. I know a farmer when I meet one. I married you because you're a wonderful, sensitive guy who loves words. Just like I love words."

"But words don't put dinner on the table."

"They do here!" she retorted. "You're just as valued for your word skills as the guy who digs in the earth. Get that through your thick skull, okay?"

Ben slowly smiled. "I love it when you get angry. You're so sexy when you're upset."

She slugged him in the arm. Before he could reply, they had arrived in the makeshift play yard.

"Okay, you guys," Peg called out ebulliently to Danny and Miriam. "Let's go home!"

"Great!" both children shouted and ran for the car. Then Danny came running back, "Where's home?"

"398 North Orchard Road, Independence, Missouri!"

"All right!" he shouted as he ran back and hit the side of the car playfully. "398 North Orchard Road, *Mimi*."

"Don't call me that!" she said, trying to hit him out the window from the back seat. He laughed, put his thumbs on his ears and wagged his hands back and forth. She got out of the car and ran around the front in hot pursuit.

"Okay, okay!" Ben said, grabbing a child in each arm.

"Guess who is our very next door neighbor?" Peg asked as she escorted them back into the Honda.

"Who?" both children asked together.

"The Winders."

Danny pounded on the front seat. "Yes! Forever?"

"This time it is forever. That's a promise!"

"Yahoo! Let's get out of here," Miriam shouted. "I can't wait to see Missy!"

Early in the four-hour drive, Peg opened the pamphlet they had been given which outlined the voluntary economic program. It emphasized that the actual establishment of a Zion economy would come when there were elected officials and a government in place. At the end she began reading to herself a quote from Brigham Young: "*I have looked upon the community of Latter-day Saints in vision and beheld them organized as one great family of heaven, each person performing his several duties in his line of industry; working for the good of the whole more than for individual aggrandizement...*"She stopped and said to Ben, "Listen to this, honey. It's really great." He grunted, indicating he'd listen, so she went back and read the first part, then continued with, "...and in this I have beheld the most beautiful order that the mind of man can contemplate, and the grandest results for the upbuilding of the Kingdom of God and the spread of righteousness upon the earth. Will this people ever come to this order of things? Are they now prepared to live according to that patriarchal order that will be organized among the true and faithful before God receives his own?"

"Isn't that glorious?" she asked, having read the statement

with great feeling.

"You know, that is a really good question," responded the ever pessimistic Ben.

"What is?"

"Will they ever come to be ready for this order? I wonder."

"Oh, shush, Benjamin Abraham Taylor. You are not going to spoil this wonderful moment."

The nearer they got to Independence, the more animated Peg became. It was if something had opened up in Peg that had been quashed since she was a teenager. She was buoyant, happy, chattering, excited. The seven miles left seemed to be far too long. The prospect of having her own house and ten acres of land that couldn't be taken away, lost to early frost, insects or drought, left the beet farmer's daughter nearly breathless.

The last few miles Ben was as silent as Peg was effusive. *I just have to keep telling myself this is really Zion, and people's lives are going to really work out okay,* he thought. *Gotta trust the Lord. Trust the Lord, that's the key,* was his pep talk.

Ben had pretty much convinced himself that things were going to be okay when they began to pick their way through the potholes and broken trees and poles out on a country road. Very few houses were standing and those that were, were in pretty bad condition.

"Orchard Road!" Danny shouted and pointed.

Ben eased the car right down what had been a pleasant lane where trees were now uprooted, pavement cracked and buckling. The first house had a sign dangling from the front porch that read 388, so they kept driving for five acres, the next had no recognizable sign, then they spotted Nate's car and his kids standing out on the road, looking at a two-story farmhouse with its guts exposed. Ben's stomach sank.

Danny and Miriam hung out the windows of the Honda, shouting and waving as they approached the Winders.

"Hi, neighbors!" Peg hollered and waved.

The five were startled. Although they had seen the Honda come down the lane, they had no idea the Taylors would be living next door. "How d'ya like our icky house?" Missy called out as they drove up alongside the dejected group .

"Looks like the wrecking crew should just come in and tear it down," Danny said emphatically.

"That's what we were saying," Andrew moaned.

"Danny, get your head in here," Ben said somewhat gruffly. "They don't need your expert opinion."

The Jewish convert kept squinting to see what he could see of the acreage next door. His heart sank as he edged the car up even with the place and looked up a sloping bank to the old house, nearly a hundred years old, white stucco with dark green trim. It was standing–technically. But as he climbed out and walked around to the south of the house, it became clear that that whole side was fully exposed. The walls lay in a heap on the ground; interior stairs dangled precariously from the second floor. The kitchen was covered with debris from the collapse of the ceiling.

He continued walking through the high weeds to see the condition of the two outbuildings in back. These looked like they had been flattened between huge hands and dropped to the ground. Out in the field, dry corn stalks careened crazily right then to the left, forming a giant wave pattern. The fence on the east side of the house had been ripped out of the postholes with the force of the earthquake and lay scattered as if giant players had abandoned a colossal dominos game.

Ben's heart had plummeted to his shoe tops as he returned to the shocked family standing in the front yard. Suddenly he could see a figure running down the road. As it neared, he could make out Ned headed toward them. When the young man got within shouting distance, he shouted breathlessly, "My dad wants to know if you want to come to dinner."

The whole Taylor family burst out laughing. "At least Nate has retained his sense of humor," Ben shouted back. "Tell him we'll be there in formal garb as soon as we get washed up."

"He also said you guys can tent with us tonight if you want."

"Okay, we'll talk about that when we get there."

Peg slipped her arm around Ben's waist and said, "Really,

honey, it will be okay. You don't come from pioneer heritage."

"Oh, yes, I do. Remember Moishe Berkowitz, my great-great grandfather? He dragged that deli handcart across the plains, and wound up being Brigham Young's personal clothier and financial planner? You know the one."

Danny burst out laughing. Peg nestled her curly head next to Ben's cheek. "Honey, this is a great challenge..."

"You can say that again!" Ben nearly shouted.

"No, you don't understand. We pioneer folk love this sort of thing," Peg said in a quiet tone to calm him down. "You know, we love to look at the before and after pictures."

"Peg," Ben said seriously. "I am going to work every day in Independence. I'm not going to be here. I don't have the slightest clue what to do anyway. It's going to be up to you. Do you hear me clearly on this one?" Ben pointed a finger in Peg's face. "Don't come to me next week with a list of honey-do's. I don't know how, and I won't have the energy."

Peg pulled away and looked him straight in the eye. "Don't you think I know that, you big dummy. Bishop Levine said there will be workmen here in a couple of days to help me. Every day when you come home, things will be better."

"That's just the problem. I *should* be doing this stuff. What will they think?"

"Grrr, men!" Peg stamped her foot. "They will think you are fabulous because you're working for the church on very important projects, just like they are."

"Well, grumble, grumble," Ben said in a half-joking way.

"So enough! Let's go have filet mignon with the Winders!" Peg said, as she licked a handkerchief and tried to wipe a major dirt streak from Miriam's cheek.

Ben and Nate drove to the bishop's storehouse, while Peg and Cristina supervised the raising of four large tents. Peg sang "...come to Zion, come to Zion" so many times, the kids finally protested that they couldn't stand hearing it one more time. So she switched to "...when all the earth in glorious bloom affords the Saints a holy home like Adam-ondi-Ahman."

The group decided to camp together on the Taylors' back lawn—it being large enough and somewhat level. After a dinner of Deseret Industries' macaroni and cheese, beef jerky, dried apples and water (all of which tasted wonderful to the consumers), the kids were settled into two tents with flashlights and books.

The adults leaned on the Honda which they had driven up behind the house and partially unloaded to get to the sleeping bags, air mattresses and tents.

"I envy you your relationship," Nate said pensively to the couple.

Peg and Ben turned and looked at each other. They had never known Nate to express any intimate feelings.

"I've been unlucky in love," he said, sighing.

"Nate, you did everything you could with Laurie," Ben said adamantly. "There isn't anyone here who could have lasted half as long."

"Except my kids. They are certain it's just a matter of time now when Laurie shows up with their brothers and sisters, and we become a happy household again." The three looked over the tents where the dark green sides were lit up in random circles.

"So how do you feel about it, Nate?" Peg looked over her neighbor and wondered just who she knew that she could fix him up with. He isn't really handsome, she thought, more rugged-looking than anything. His square jaw and curly black hair offset his small eyes and large Roman nose.

"Yeah," Ben said. "I've heard rumors that Laurie changed after her husband's death on the ski slopes."

"I can't really know until I see her again. It's been more than a year, you know," Nate said wearily. "A lot of blood under the bridge." He let his shoulders slump as he exhaled.

Don't be a fool, Nate! Ben thought. A picture of Laurie arose without warning—standing in front of Ben at Pah Tempe, in a tight dress, her hand on her hip. He wanted to reach out at the image and wipe that half smile, half smirk off her face as she flirted with him. *I wouldn't trust that woman any farther than I could throw her.*

"...and I've seen her three times now, Peg." Ben furrowed his brow trying to catch the drift of the conversation.

"And last time she was bleeding from the forehead and palms of the hands?" Nate concluded with a puzzled expression.

"Who was?" Ben asked.

"Nate doesn't know," Peg said, her interest piqued.

"A red-haired woman—once in my dreams, then twice as I was awake," Nate volunteered. "I get the feeling that I'm to help her in some way, but I don't know what I can do. I don't think I've seen her before." Nate sighed and leaned back against the dirty, brown exterior of the car.

"Gee, Nate, I don't really know," Ben said. "Why not talk to Grace? She knows a lot more about psychic phenomena than the rest of us."

"I just thought you might have some ideas." His voice trailed off.

After a few moments of silence, Peg walked out away from the car and stared into the cloudy but illumined sky. "Can you really believe this? I know I've said it two hundred times today, but this seems just like a camping trip with friends, and then we'll head home."

The two men grunted in agreement.

"But you know, the air has a different feel to it," Peg said. "I can't put my finger on it, but it does—like...." Her voice trailed off. A quiet descended on the camp.

"It's strange not to hear cars or planes droning overhead," Nate said.

"I'm betting we're going to a new energy source..." Ben said.

Peg interrupted his train of thought with, "Wait. I feel a poem coming on." She whirled around and walked back to her husband and put her face up close to him. "Now, don't you moan, Benjamin," she warned, "and don't you smile either!"

"I wasn't even thinking of such a thing," Ben said, throwing his hands in the air. "Go on. Let's hear it." Ben sounded sincere.

"Promise you won't criticize."

"I don't have a critical bone left in my body after the last few days, honey."

"Well, okay...I'm going to call this simply *Mahdi*."

"*Mahdi?*"

"As I understand it, it's the Islamic Messiah soon to come." Peg half turned away from the two men, so she couldn't see the expression on their faces and began,

> "Meteors burn
> the magenta sky.
> Behind a hump-backed dune,
> tent flaps whistle."

"Honey, that's really good," Ben said with some surprise.

"Hush, I'm not through," she said with quiet fierceness.

> "Burnoose and bag
> a camel's complaint
> silent leave-taking
> (no one must follow)
> One shadow on a gauzy wall:
> the endgame chamber
> has golden curtains,
> He is red robed."

She let her voice trail off with the "red robed."

Nate put his fingers between his teeth and whistled. Several heads popped out of tents asking, "What? What, Dad?"

"Peg has just composed a really wonderful poem. You have to listen to it." So Ned, Cristina and Cannon crawled out of the tent they were in and came to stand near Peg with interest on their faces. Peg repeated the poem, this time with a bit more dramatic flair. And again, she got a round of genuine applause.

"I hope you'll write more like that, Peg," Ned said. "I'm not really sure I understand all of it, but I like the excited and intense feeling I get when I hear it."

Peg let tears trickle down her cheeks. She hadn't realized how much she missed teaching poetry; this now was doubly sweet–kids wanting to listen to *her* work. She hugged herself and grinned. "I'm not going to stop now, Ned. This feels much too good." She gave him a peck on the cheek. "This all feels much too sweet," she said to the assembled audience.

"Amen to that, Sister," Ben said in a slow Southern voice, moving to get rid of the younger, handsome Winder. Peg didn't punch Ben like she normally would. There was a definite subtle change in his voice, which she took to mean he was impressed. *That* coming from Mr. Literary Critic was sweet indeed.

CHAPTER TEN

*"Everything an Indian does is in a circle,
and that is because the power of the world
always works in circles,
and everything tries to be round."*
                                        Black Elk

Ben was grumpy as he drove back toward Independence to his new job the next morning. The night had been disastrous as far as sleep went–Peg snored, the air mattress kept leaning too far to the right dumping him out periodically onto the tent floor, and worse, the kids were up at dawn, throwing a Frisbee back and forth over the tents.

"Isn't this paradise? Aren't we supposed to be different, like living in a state of bliss or something?" he said out loud as he steered the Honda over the many cracks and bulges in the road. Besides Ben really hated new situations, and now he was headed for yet another new place of work with many people he didn't know.

The morning air was crisp and clear as he pulled the car into a slanted parking place next to the large circular lawn which was being excavated, as construction began on the central temple of the New Jerusalem. He pulled up the collar on his green windbreaker, walked across the road and into a large two-story home built in the 1920's. It stood next to a church made from local rock which had completely crumbled with the force of the quake.

He paused on the porch before opening the front door. "Lord, help me in there today. You always seem to think I can do things that I think I can't."

A warm smile greeted him from a round matron sitting behind a large desk in the entryway. "Up the stairs, Brother, then turn to your left. First door on the right."

He willed his legs up the stairs. "Moira once said I have a Jonah complex. 'God calls, but I run away.' Well, please notice. I'm here, Moira. Just want you to know."

Seated around the oblong conference table in the upper room were members of the temporary governing body of Zion. Ben had been asked to serve as the recording secretary, in addition to contributing to the committee's dialogue.

The translator's hand was cold, sweaty when Elder Stewart reached him and shook it. He had always wished he could just get into the very center of the power, not to rule, but to feel what it was like to be an insider, instead of a Jew or a new convert.

"Ben Taylor, let me introduce you around the table. This is Elder Taitano and Elder Ho of the Council of the Twelve," Elder Stewart said. The two apostles stood and reached across the table to shake Ben's hand, and he thought, *Now I know I've died and gone to heaven.* "...and you know Bishop Levine, and Nate Winder, of course," Elder Stewart finished.

Ben had been so overwhelmed he hadn't noticed Nate sitting on the right side of the room. He quickly moved toward his new neighbor and sat down, grateful for the solidity of the chair. Nate leaned over and whispered to him, "Stewart is the acting head apostle since Dawahoya is in Salt Lake. He'll chair the meeting."

"So is everybody here LDS?" Ben whispered.

"Yes, for right now. When things have settled down, we'll have something like the Quorum of Fifty in Nauvoo."

"I have no idea what that is," Ben said, slightly blushing.

"Elected officials who were both members and non-members."

"Got it." Ben looked down at the agenda in front of him, his heart pounding. He was thrilled that he could be party to such proceedings. Pulling out his favorite pen, he began to take notes.

"The prophet should be here tomorrow," Elder Stewart said with obvious excitement. "He and his lovely bride will be housed next door. I understand he is in relatively good health and in great spirits."

That news brought a round of spontaneous applause.

Charles Stewart looked around the room into the attentive faces. "I can scarcely remember what it was like to operate freely. Our main goal, gentlemen, besides bringing the Church back to the level of operations we had before the UWEN takeover, is to create a righteous society. This, of course, we have longed to have since the Church was founded in 1830. But before I get ahead of myself, President Suifua, will you give us an opening prayer?"

The large Samoan stood, face aglow, and prayed intensely for the Spirit's guidance. Then it was the presiding bishop's turn to report on the "state of the union." He noted that in the two weeks since the earthquake, the Independence area had been cleared of all corpses, major roads were opened, and three "portals" made operational. The rebuilding of houses had commenced, using stockpiled goods and furniture.

"What about the local non-member population?" Elder Stewart asked.

"Everyone who has remained here has agreed to live peacefully and follow our leadership," Bishop Levine said in a reassuring voice.

"How many non-members are there?" Elder Taitano asked.

"14,000, give or take a few."

"And the total number of residents?" Elder Ho wondered.

Bishop Levine looked down at the clipboard he was holding, then said, "As of yesterday, we had 23,677–members and non-members."

Ben whistled under his breath. Kansas City alone had been a city of 1.5 million.

Elder Stewart explained how the borders of Zion would expand by moving the electronic "stakes" farther away from the central stake as the population grew. Ben was hard pressed to keep up with all the details of a refugee-migration fund along with budget reports of the anticipated costs of housing, feeding, clothing refugees–these eventually reaching into millions of people.

It was surprising to many of the men present to hear that Jackson County was especially suited as the site of a millennial city. It was surrounded by plentiful sand and gravel pits, oil and gas fields, and fire clay for bricks. In addition, the soil and climate were especially good for raising fruits, grains and soybean crops.

President Suifua said, "We are moving rapidly toward the lifestyle mandated by Section 89 of the *Doctrine and Covenants*. Instead of meat, our principal source of protein will be soy."

"Why soy?" Ben blurted out, thinking of the white, pasty blocks Peg had occasionally made him eat.

"Besides being an excellent source of protein, Ben, we know that Asians, who consume soy daily, have lower rates of cancer and cholesterol, among other things. Don't worry though, we'll still have egg and milk production."

Ben sat back in his chair, put his hand over his stomach, sure he felt it rumbling. *I didn't count on having to change my diet, for heaven's sake, just to live in Zion.*

"...Regarding the sorghum, now that we have power over the weather, we can dry it in the field without spoilage, which, as you probably know, has been a real problem, particularly in these warm, hot years."

"Sorghum?" Ben whispered to Nate.

"For sugar and syrup."

Ben made a face; Nate couldn't help but smile.

One report that interested Ben was the decision on the part of the committee to commence work on an Internet system which would be up and running within two weeks. No one but the UWEN had had access to the Internet for many years. What a help it would be for family history work, Ben thought with some guilt. His blessing said he had "great and noble ancestors who were waiting for him to be a savior on Mt. Zion." Now it seemed he would have no more excuses for not doing their temple work.

The next items on the agenda included school construction, sanitation plants, and road maintenance. Somewhere in the middle of the discussion, Ben looked over at President Suifua and his mind wandered back to a story Peg had told him about the Samoan.

When the stake president was a young father in Samoa, his only daughter was run over and killed by a large truck–crushing her skull and internal organs. Later that day, after a brief wake with neighbors and extended family, Suifua gathered his wife and four boys in the living room next to the hastily constructed casket. "I think I can raise Malia from the dead by the power of the priesthood," he said slowly. "But I can't do it if any of you doubt me. If you think that the Lord cannot do this, please leave the house now."

After a brief discussion, all five went out into the village with great sorrow, for they thought Afa's grief had gone to his head. After they left, he pulled the cold body of his daughter out of the casket and placed it on a sleeping mat. Then he lay down next to her and began praying. All night long he cried to the Lord, begging him to return his Malia as He had the daughter of Jarius.

About five in the morning, he became hoarse and could not utter a sound without coughing, so he lay there silently imploring His Savior to grant him this one request. At six, he stopped praying and simply lay still, too exhausted to continue. As Afa looked up at the banana leaf roof, he heard the slightest whimper. He lay absolutely still to determine where the sound was coming from. Then he heard the most amazing words, "Daddy?" his daughter asked weakly. "Where am I?"

Afa scooped her up in his strong arms and rocked her until her body warmed up. Then he dashed outside, carrying her in his arms, crying for the village elders to come help him bless her.

Ben remembered asking Peg, "Was she terribly deformed or crippled?"

"No, she grew up, went on a mission, got married and had several children. That's what I heard."

As Ben tried to refocus on the meeting, he heard, "...we'll get you those numbers, Brother Taylor," Bishop Levine laughed. It had been obvious to the group that Ben was not taking notes but lost in thought. He blushed and nodded his head.

What the men were discussing was what to do with people entering Zion who had communicable diseases. "We have medical stations at each portal. With a combination of medical expertise now available to us, plus priesthood blessings, we don't have to be concerned," Elder Stewart said in a grandfatherly voice.

Ben leaned over to Nate, "What medical expertise?"

"The translated apostle has supplied us with the technology to eradicate communicable diseases, which can be a terrible problem with the influx of refugees."

"Whoa," Ben said. "Next you're going to tell me we won't need any more Jewish cardiologists. Holy cow, how will my people make a living?"

Nate quickly put a hand to his mouth to suppress a laugh.

Then the discussion turned to immigrants arriving with psychiatric disorders, and Ben thought, *Oh, well, maybe there will still be a market for Jewish psychiatrists.*

Bishop Levine told the group that this problem was one of the most pressing and problematic when the Jewish state in Israel was established in 1948.

The twelve men discussed separate housing, in-patient hospital facilities, and out-patient clinics, but nothing was settled. Uncomfortable with the problem, they put the item on the agenda for further consideration at their next meeting.

Another surprise for Ben was to hear that yurts were going be used for temporary housing. Traditionally used by Mongolian nomads, they are held up by wood poles that rise about ten feet to a peak with a round opening. A circular lattice frame creates five-foot-high vertical walls. The supporting structure is then covered with canvas and held together with a steel cable. Here, in Zion, solar panels would supply the yurts with power.

The three-hundred-square-foot yurt could house a family of five. A number of yurts would share a common bathhouse, meeting room and laundry. One drawback—outhouses. Suddenly Ben felt very grateful for the prospect of a house with indoor plumbing.

"As for Israel, they have repulsed yet another attack by the rebels in Iran. Reports are that a former UWEN officer has taken over since the death of Gornstein, but those reports are unreliable given the shaky lines of communication these days," Elder Stewart said.

Sitting in this city planning meeting, Ben felt a longing he didn't even know he still had. When he was in high school, he was elected to the student government even though he was one of a small minority of whites. Then, he had run for office because he wanted to be popular, but he also longed to have enough power to affect people's lives. When he spent the entire student body budget on parties for his Hispanic friends, he was wildly popular. However, when he tried to run again the next year, the administration understandably nixed his candidacy.

Having chosen the path of a scholar, Ben found no sense of being a mover and shaker. He never knew what effect what he wrote had on anyone. But this...*this* was exhilarating. After the first half hour, he ventured an opinion on education which the leaders listened to with respectful attention.

"I know I'm probably left of most of you politically," Ben said, his voice deferential but with a subtle touch of defiance.

"Don't count on anything here, Brother Taylor. The Lord is, after all, quite revolutionary."

Ben laughed and closed his eyes. He imagined the Lord in his red robes, tearing down ostentatious buildings, running people out on the street with a whip tied in knots. That would be very satisfying to see.

Another item on the agenda that came as a surprise to Ben was to learn that the global warming of the planet had been planned in the beginning by the Lord and others who formed the earth, as a transition back to a terrestrial climate.

As the morning wore on and the meeting drew to a close, the last item to be discussed took Ben's breath away–temple construction. He turned to Nate and pointed at the line on the page, then opened his mouth and put his hands to his cheeks. Nate nodded.

"Bishop Levine, do you have a recommendation about the limestone pits?"

"Yes, sir, we do. We've surveyed both locations and feel the limestone pit in Jasper County will serve our needs best. We've seen the samples. When the dolomite is highly polished, it can be used much like marble. It suits our needs quite well. And the location at Jasper is the least damaged."

And when we finish with the construction of this temple, Ben thought, *Jesus Christ, our Lord, will appear to his people!*

After the meeting, Ben caught up with Nate. "I didn't know you were in on this committee. Why didn't you tell me last night?"

"Why didn't you tell me?" Nate countered goodnaturedly.

"Because, ah..., never mind. Okay, Nate, tell me, what is happening with this red-headed woman you talked about last night? Fill me in. Have you had any more visions, you old mystic, you!"

Nate walked to his car and leaned against the side, folding his arms. "I've never had an experience like this, Ben. I frankly think I'm going nuts. I tell myself it's the stress of being a single parent, getting these kids here and safe. I don't know," he said, lowering his head.

Ben was frustrated. "What about her, man? Do you have any sense of where she's from?"

"The best I can get is that she may be from England or Ireland, if she exists at all. And each time I see her, she seems to be in more and more distress."

"How so?"

"Well, she seems to be pleading with me to help her escape from wherever she is. Once I saw blood on her forehead and her hands."

"Is she someone you've known?"

"Never saw her before in my life."

"Weren't you on a mission in the British Isles?"

"Yes."

"Well, maybe she's someone you knew then."

Nate started. "You know, that's a possibility. There was an Irish family, the O'Boyles. They had several young red-headed girls...."

"Good-looking?" Ben asked.

Nate let a smirk cross his face. "I taught them out in County Roscommon. But they never joined the Church to my knowledge. I think the father had a bit of a drinking problem. He wouldn't let the rest of the family join without him."

"Do you remember names?"

"Nah. I can scarcely remember faces. It's been nearly twenty years now." Then Nate broke into a grin and said, "Oh, now I remember–the feisty fifteen-year-old had a tantrum because her father wouldn't let us in the first time we tracted their home. We could hear her inside, nearly screaming, "*I want to hear them, Da!*"

"Do you think you might be connecting with her somehow?"

"You know, could be...could be....."

"Peg suggested you see Grace. Why not?"

"Too embarrassed. What do I say? This Irish woman keeps appearing to me–someone I don't even know. Grace'll probably just think I'm desperate for a love life."

"Ah, come on, Nate. You know Grace better than that. Let's go find out where the Dubiks have settled," Ben said walking back across the street to the building they had just left. Nate followed–slowly, reluctantly.

A few moments later they returned to their cars, Nate examining a piece of paper in his hand. Ben called out to him as he headed for the Honda, "Go on. Go over there. It's only three blocks down Spring Street."

"Okay, okay. I'm going," Nate said and waved to Ben. "You know you're a total pain in the rear, Taylor!" Nate called out.

Just then there was a great commotion at the temple site and around church headquarters. Word had spread to the office and construction workers that President Ueda would be arriving at any time. They quickly gathered outside, around the circular road that encompassed the temple lot. Even though it had begun to drizzle and few had umbrellas, they waited in hopes of seeing the prophet. Some had never seen him.

When the small, makeshift parade of dusty cars finally pulled onto Lexington, the crowd began to shout and wave their handkerchiefs. The figure of a small Japanese man moved to the window of the car and rolled down the window. The prophet broke into a grin. He ducked back into the car's interior, then returned to the window with a yellow scarf that was his wife's. His dazzling smile flashed to the waiting crowd as the lead car pulled into the driveway of the house next to the temporary office building. Someone in the crowd shouted, "Hooray! Now we can really get started!"

Two cars behind the prophet's was Elder Whitmer and his family. Nate, who had paused to watch the prophet's car, saw his ex-father-in-law's white Mercury van and froze. Although he couldn't see Laurie, he assumed she was inside, and that's when he involuntarily shuddered.

The front door to the house on Spring Street was ajar when Nate walked up the cracked, concrete front steps of the Dubiks' house, so he could hear what was being said in the hallway.

"...I don't know actually where she'd go, son," Grace was saying to Alex. "She's been at those intertribal councils several times. I think they've met in North Dakota and Montana, if I remember correctly," Grace said defensively. "We've been over this again and again, Al."

"You're supposed to know these things, Grace."

"I can't. I'm too upset," she said defensively.

"She said not to try and follow her, but I can't just sit here while my wife leaves the safety of this place for Indian country!" Alex sounded like he'd been stabbed in the heart.

Nate turned to walk back down the broken steps, but not soon enough. Grace caught sight of him and called out, "Nate, hello! What can we do for you?"

"Oh, hi, Grace," he said, walking back to the top step of the broad porch. "It sounds like you are busy. I can come back."

The Maori grandmother came outside on the porch. She looked slightly dishevelled like she'd been crying. "Please, Nate, come and sit," she said, sitting down on the porch swing. She was relieved to talk to someone besides a distraught son-in-law.

Nate sat down in a rusted, S-shaped metal chair and began, "Um, well..., you see, Grace, several people have suggested I see you about a series of dreams and even open visions I've had of a woman."

"Nate dear, I'm not sure I'm much good right now, but let's see. A woman. Describe her," she said, closing her eyes.

"Red-haired, lovely white skin, thirties."

"Black dress with white collar?"

"Yes!"

"I can see her. Go on!" Grace said, suddenly excited.

"It seems like she's calling out to me," Nate offered. "Once I saw her with blood on her forehead..."

"And bleeding from her palms."

"Yes!" Now Nate became animated too. "Can you tell who she is? What she wants? "

Grace's eyes rolled back and forth under her eyelids. "The name that comes to me–Marie or Mary or...."

"Mary Margaret!" Nate blurted out.

"You know her?"

"I think so. The last name was O'Boyle."

Grace was silent for a moment. "That seems right," the Maori psychic said slowly.

Then she fell silent. Nate sat quietly, looking at her lined face. He felt bad, intruding on the family when it sounded as if Moira had abruptly left.

"That looks like the stigmata she's showing," Grace suddenly continued.

"The what?"

"Christ's wounds. I've heard of people who bleed in the same places He did."

"How can I help her?"

There was a long silence. Grace shook her head. "I can't tell right now. I'm sorry, but I'm really off right now."

"Grace, please don't push yourself on my account. It isn't that important." Nate stood up and offered his hand to help her up from the swing.

"But if she exists on this plane of existence, she is a very powerful individual," Grace continued, "and I'm sure I'll be able to communicate with her, given a little time."

Alex poked his head out the door. "Hi, Nate. Sorry to be so unsociable. I'm taking care of my son."

"No problems. After nine of my own, I know the drill."

Alex disappeared, but Nate could hear the fussing of the nine-month-old in the back of the house.

"Grace, I won't bother you further today. And I wouldn't have, if this hadn't happened several times. I'm working at the church office building these days. You can leave word there if you get anything."

The Maori wise-woman hugged Nate. He looked back when he reached his car to wave to her as she retreated into the house. She looked bent and weary as she closed the door behind her.

In the back bedroom, Alex held Adam in the crook of his left arm and fingered the note Moira left: "...I have to go. This is bigger than I can explain. Please know that I love you three very much, but it's Jacob's time to vex the Gentiles. I can feel it, and I have a role to play. Forgive me, darling, but this is something I must do."

The initial shock of her leaving had worn off; now he was battling feelings that ranged from rage to quiet–all in an attempt to understand what would be so important that she would take off.

Moira, meanwhile, had taken the Jeep Wagoneer and picked her way through streets until she was able to reach Highway 29 on the outskirts of Kansas City. From there she headed north to the portal they had entered.

"I don't care what happens; I just have to go," she repeated over and over, trying to block out the responses of her family to her leaving. "This is bigger than I am; I have to go, I have to go."

When she reached the portal, the men manning the station were startled to have a car drive up containing a lone woman who wanted to leave Zion. She had practiced and practiced what she would say, "I'm on the Lord's errand. I won't be but a day."

And she hoped they wouldn't ask any other questions.

They did let her through with few questions, but as soon as she had crossed the bridge, they were on the CB radio checking with Jed, who was running the central communications center. "Did this woman leave with authorization from someone?" they asked.

Jed was startled to hear the description of the car. *Not Moira!* he thought. Maybe Grace sent her on some errand. He checked around the church headquarters but couldn't find anyone who knew anything, so he sent a young messenger to the Dubik's house. When he returned with the note, it read: "We know she's gone."

The farther from the earthquake's epicenter Moira drove toward Montana, the easier the driving got and the more she wondered at her rash decision. The dream had been so real. In it she could see the open meadow, the two hundred Lamanites in a circle, tepees in the background. She recognized the spot—north of Bozeman—where she had met with the Intertribal Council. A voice in the dream said, "Now is the time for Jacob to vex sore the Gentiles."

It was as if an electric shock had gone through her system, so strong was the feeling that she had to go. Now she was alone, driving through the dark, and she began to miss Adam—her arms ached to hold him.

"Mom will do a good job with him—so will Alex for that matter. I have to do this," she said setting her jaw.

The sun was halfway up in the sky when the Jeep bounced down the rutted road she had seen in her dream and to the dead end marked off by logs. There she saw at least fifty parked cars. "That's good." She sighed in relief. "At least I haven't been deluded about the gathering."

She bent and stretched her long legs as she stepped out of the Jeep. Then she stood to look out over the meadow. Ringed by tall pines huddled together, the meadow was muddy but tinged with the light green growth of grass. More than a hundred Indians stood in a wide circle about seventy-five yards away. Several more were riding in on horseback. Two middle-aged Indian men, dressed in buckskin, brushed past her. A young woman, also in deerskin on a pinto, walked around her. Moira smiled as she stepped to the side. Her heart was racing. She had imagined a moment like this for most of her life. "The hoop is finished," she said quietly to herself as she took long strides to join the group.

A tall, grey-haired man with Indian braids waved to her as she neared the circle. It was Running Bear, a Sioux she had become friendly with at previous meetings. "Moira, how glad I am you are here!"

"Did someone get a camping permit from the local UWEN office?" she joked. In years past, it had been very difficult to travel from place to place without UWEN approval.

But she didn't get to hear an answer, because the group suddenly grew quiet. John Gray Eagle, the spokesman for the intertribal governing body, stepped forward with a very solemn look on his face.

"In the past," he began, "we have met and said a time would come for us to take back our lands from the white man. And never was the time right." Moira admired his square jaw and long braids.

"The Great Spirit has spoken to many of us, telling us the time has come," Gray Eagle said with grave dignity.

A great whoop erupted from the crowd, and Moira felt a sob catch in her throat.

"Each of you represents a tribe from both North and South America and from the islands of the sea," Gray Eagle said looking in Moira's direction. "We will begin from this time to take back what is ours. If we can do that without killing, all the better. But, at whatever cost, this prophecy must be fulfilled."

After a spontaneous outpouring of shouting and dancing, groups formed to discuss the logistics of a sweep of the United States.

Moira was quick to point out that there were groups of her people who were on the move toward Missouri–people who should not be harmed, as they supported the cause, even though they were white. This was noted, for Moira was well-respected in the council. Although they offered no guarantees that no Mormons would be harmed, at least each group knew they should look for Latter-day Saints crossing the plains. Because, on the trek west in the 1840's and 50's, Mormons were pacificist and tried to make friends with the Indians, a traditional respect for Latter-day Saints remained.

"One of the places that we plan to raid, though, Moira, is the area around Salt Lake City. Those lands belonged to us long before the Mormons settled there."

"I realize that," Moira said. "But please give the people time to leave the area. That's all I'm asking," she pleaded. "It won't be long now."

Were it not for Moira's intervention, the same thing would have happened to the families migrating to the New Jerusalem that happened to many massacred whites throughout the West. Latter-day Saints fleeing to Zion were literally protected by the power of the priesthood as had been prophesied. More than one Indian raiding party reported that they saw a white light encircling the Mormon buses and cars as they caravaned across the midsection of the country. The sight was unnatural enough to keep the marauders at a distance.

In the days that passed, Moira felt exhilarated. *Finally these hypocritical, power-hungry Gentiles are getting what they deserve,* she thought fiercely. She did not go on raiding parties but remained in Montana at the central intelligence center, where her years in New Zealand politics now served her well as a strategician. She thought little of her family back in Missouri. Just fierce thoughts that justice was finally being served.

CHAPTER ELEVEN

*"By the roots of my hair some god got hold of me.
I sizzled in his blue volts like a desert prophet."*
Sylvia Plath

Sangay Tulku had a number of advanced students, but only two Americans. The rinpoche had two criteria: they had to be able to reach quite high states of consciousness and they had to be major players in the Lord's plan.

Both the Americans–Ben and Alex–having sensitive and artistic natures, quickly attained greater depths of inner illumination. Yet Alex was living proof of the adage that every new convert should be kept locked in a room for the first year! He began zealously scrutinizing his own thoughts and actions and those of others so obsessively, indeed so puritanically, that he grew difficult to be around. He was too quick to point out what he perceived to be other people's shortcomings, like Grace's system of paying an approximate tithing (always more generous, in any case, than she had to pay) or her tendency to overlook people's minor transgressions against the Word of Wisdom.

"Grace, you're just too lenient with people," he complained. "They're never going to be able to get a temple recommend if you pamper them."

"Son, the people who come to me for help are still struggling with much more basic issues, like if they are loved or deserve to be on earth at all. The finer points will come. They may not be ready for a temple recommend, but they sure won't be ready if I start pushing them about these little things." Alex would stalk away muttering that these were not little things, they were for "the weakest of the Saints."

The new convert changed his diet, eating meat only rarely, and then only fish because he decided that fowls of the air and beasts of the field were mentioned in the *Doctrine and Covenants*, but fish was not. Normally not an early riser, he now was out of bed at 6:00 a.m. every morning and complained if others still slept.

With Moira's departure, he intensified his self-scrutiny: *If I were only living more righteously, she would never have left. If Grace hadn't hovered so much when the baby was first born, Moira would have felt less trapped.* And so on. Thus it was that Sangay was sent to instruct Alex in a dream. Although the sculptor dreamt that his teacher sat in his bedroom and conversed with him, the rinpoche was on the other side of the earth, facing the rising sun on the vast, open plains of central Asia as he simultaneously projected himself through profound meditation into Alex's dreams.

Sangay's first words had to do with his pupil's legalistic zeal. "My, you've become an old grandfather, my friend. Almost overnight."

Alex became defensive. "I want to please the Lord. He is my whole life now."

"And do you think it pleases Him that you criticize your wife and mother-in-law?"

"No, but..."

"And do you think he is pleased with you now that you seldom laugh?"

"No, but..."

"Ah, and now surely He isn't interested in such a man who contradicts his teacher."

"But, Sangay..." Alex began, then paused and began to laugh. "Okay, okay, I get the point. A little too much of the critical function."

"Well put."

Now the dream changed, and Alex found himself with Sangay in what looked like an Indian encampment. Sangay asked, "How does that feel—to have your wife leave you?"

"I'm trying to understand what would draw her away from her family to do this," Alex said, as he searched for Moira among the crowd of American Indians who walked through the dream camp.

"Moira's like a wild animal you thought you had tamed, then

she turns on you."

"Exactly!" Alex said, then felt embarrassed to hear his less-than-politically-correct thoughts expressed aloud.

"I read minds well," Sangay said, crinkling the smile lines around his face.

"Where is she?" Alex cried. "Why bring me here to torture me?"

Sangay responded patiently, "Can you tell me what your Moira is doing right now?"

"Of course not!" Alex retorted. Then a Cherokee Indian in full regalia caught his attention. He watched as the stately man walked down to a river and scooped water up with his hands. Each drop of water that fell from his calloused, cupped hands looked like shiny silver beads.

"I am going to remind you of what you already know how to do. You remember Joseph Smith knew that Oliver Cowdery was approaching when he first came to help translate the *Book of Mormon?*"

"What I remember is that he described the inn where Oliver stayed."

"Yes, and he knew of his arrival at the farm and announced it to the family before Oliver appeared."

"And how? How was he able to do that?"

"Look at your hand," Sangay was now sitting with Alex on a hill, looking out over the valley where the Indian gathering was taking place.

"What?"

"Look at your hand."

Alex nearly woke at this point as he struggled to get his eyes to focus on his hands. Finally he fell back to sleep and held the picture of his hand.

"Good! Now, dear student, keep your hand before your face and look around to the sides—what do you see?"

"Everything going by at a really fast speed."

"Focus. Slow it down."

"I...I see a meadow...trees, people in a circle......Moira!"

The shout brought Alex straight out of sleep. "I see her!"

"Sangay?" His teacher was gone.

After his heart slowed down, he got up, wrapped himself in a blanket and sat in a rose-colored arm chair. Before long, he fell back to sleep, and he again found his hand. Behind it, he could see the Indian gathering. Slowly he lowered his hand and was able to see Moira walk away from the circle with two tall Indians toward a large tepee. He watched her until he felt a hot, burning anger rise up from his belly. Then he lost his concentration, and the vision vanished.

The next morning he was distracted, started to tell Grace about his dream experience, but thought better of it. She is so far ahead of me on this, he thought. I'll wait until I've mastered it before I say anything.

In central Asia, Sangay walked purposively, as quickly as he could, given the entourage he was escorting across the windswept plains. "Lord, I pray I will be able to reach the meeting place on time. I know other heads of tribes are on the move, for I have spoken with them in my mind. We wish only to serve you and this great cause to bring this epoch of the world to its natural conclusion." The rinpoche was interrupted in his musing by a seven-year-old niece who ran up beside him and held his hand as they walked next to the herd of goats. She was delighted when he let her use his favorite walking stick.

Alex couldn't wait for Adam to go to sleep the next evening. He was excited to drop off to sleep himself. He hoped Sangay would return, and he wasn't disappointed.

"Sangay, I can see her!" Alex nearly woke himself with the feelings of joy as the first dream of the night began and the smiling face of the Tibetan reappeared.

"You always could. You just forgot."

"Thank you for being my teacher, Rinpoche," Alex said, his low voice rich with emotion.

Sangay bowed slightly, then said, "Last night I asked you how you felt about Moira's leaving. You didn't answer me."

In the dream, Alex squirmed in a red arm chair in a large,

well-appointed house where he'd never been before. "Honestly? I hate women right now."

"Go on."

"I feel abandoned," he growled. "I just joined this church, partially for her, to be with her, and she just takes off!"

"I see. And where do you feel that abandonment in your body?"

"Right here," Alex said, placing his right hand over his navel.

"Good," Sangay said, as he slowly floated up toward the high, ornate ceiling in the dream house.

"And I'm furious with her because she's inflicting this pain on another generation. My son misses his mother."

"May I suggest that your feeling of abandonment is really the pain of being separate from God."

Alex grew quiet. "Huh, that's profound. I see. We've been dropped here on the telestial plane and abandoned by God," he said, as he too began floating toward the ceiling. "We feel like babies who are helpless to get back to our parent."

"Good. And what does that hunger, that gnawing at your intestines move you to do?"

"Ah...get drunk?"

Both men laughed. "You're regaining your sense of humor."

"Yeah, or get stoned. Anything to get away from feeling so absolutely alone." Alex now reached Sangay and bumped against the golden plaster orbs that decorated the ceiling.

"Yet, ironically, until you are willing to confront that feeling and move into an absolutely 'alone' place, does 'the dear Lord enter in.'"

Tears began to roll down the furrows of Alex's weathered yet still handsome face and slowly drop to the floor below in a string of liquid silver beads. "So it is part of my Lord's plan that I experience this loneliness? Then I can come into His presence?"

"What do you think?"

"I think so."

"Then it is a true saying, 'all things work for your good.'"

"Even if your wife leaves you?" Alex asked, sarcasm dripping from his mouth and down to the tiled floor in red, acidic dream rivulets.

"Even that. But I don't have any experience with such a thing, thank heavens," Sangay said and grinned so broadly that the smile lines around his mouth and eyes radiated out like whiskers on a Cheshire cat.

Then the dream changed again, and once again the two men were back in Alex's bedroom—Alex in bed, Sangay at the foot, standing in his traveling clothes which consisted of: a yak skin, wool-lined hat (earflaps up); dark-brown, mid-calf yak leather coat and pants; red-knitted socks pulled up over his pants' leg; a red belt tied around his waist; and, in his hand, a small object that looked like a top but was a spinning prayer wheel. This engraved silver "top" the rinpoche held by a long stick and whirled around and around, sending out prayers for every sentient being in the world.

"Tell me again how you, a Tibetan Buddhist monk, know so much about Jesus Christ," Alex nearly begged.

"Alex, I have told you, and I will tell you again, everyone who reaches a certain level of consciousness knows that Jesus is the Christ, the Master of the Universe."

Alex smiled. "Thank you for indulging me. I like hearing that said. It's like the comfort of a repetition of a favorite nursery rhyme when you are a child."

"Some day you will be able to do the same," the rinpoche said tenderly.

"I doubt it, Rinpoche. I'm such a mess. It seems like I can't do anything right."

"You are experiencing a test, an important test. If you prove yourself worthy, you will be given an important assignment for the Lord."

Alex awoke with a renewed determination to face what he had to deal with, and a softened attitude toward certain rules and requirements of the spiritual path he had chosen.

"Don't want to end up a cartoon character in a cartoon graveyard," he muttered to himself, recalling a line from an old Paul Simon song of decades ago.

But this test was hard for Alex–charming Alex–who always managed to have women around him to shield him from life's tribulations. Now, with Moira gone and Grace emotionally and spiritually unavailable, he finally was facing his own "dark night of the soul," as St. John of the Cross called it.

This Catholic mystic of the late Middle Ages wrote of the process of becoming spiritually mature. He suggested there are three phases: the halcyon days of first conversion, when the newness of the experience of God's love illumines one's soul and creates a great hope for one's ultimate salvation; then there is the eclipse of that optimism in purifying dark nights, representing the testing of one's faith, in utter and black deprivation; finally the spiritual journey culminates in the penetration of the Holy Spirit into the seeker's very soul, so that the divine and the human intertwine.

Alex, who had read St. John of the Cross many years earlier while researching a piece he was planning to sculpt, now understood why the saint had said that the ongoing work of purification of one's soul, impossible without personal effort, is nonetheless God's act, over which one has no control. One simply shows up for work–the rest is up to the dear Lord.

To make matters worse for the depressed sculptor, Sangay didn't return. And although Alex practiced watching Moira in his dreams for some time, he soon gave up, because it was so frustrating being able to see her and not having any way to communicate with her–to convince her to come back!

His only comfort was his patriarchal blessing that he had recently received from the hands of Hugo Martinez. He had already folded and unfolded the copy he carried in his wallet so many times, the creases were beginning to fray.

Alex held his sleepy, dark-haired son close on the porch swing of the bungalow as he read: "Because thou wert faithful in the premortal life, thou hast been held in reserve to be sent to earth at a time when the Lord hath need of thy time and talents," it began. Alex could recall the small hands of the patriarch as they rested on his head, and the slightly sour breath of one who had been fasting for spiritual discernment.

The new convert already knew parts of the blessing by heart: "Go forth and fear not, for the Lord loves thee, and withhold not thine hand or thy voice...Thou shalt perform miracles, even the elements will respond to thy command. Thou wilt heal the sick and stay the hand of death."

"Hey, what about that, sport?" Alex asked softly as Adam sucked his thumb and fingered his frayed "banky." The lonely sculptor pushed his boot against the weathered wood of the porch and let the swing go, back and forth, until it stopped. By that time, Adam had been transported to Slumberland.

"Lord, how am I going to become even halfway ready for these promised blessings?" he pleaded.

Lines from the blessing seemed to answer him, "Let thy mind and body be clean and pure that thou mayest become a receptacle wherein the Spirit of the Holy Ghost may continually dwell."

"I'm trying, I really am," Alex nearly sobbed.

"By doing so, thy mind will be opened to the ways of the Lord, and the time will come when the windows of heaven will be opened, and thou wilt receive visions to assist thee in thy creative labors."

Alex stood up and gently laid Adam down on the swing. He stepped out to the edge of the porch and looked up at the night sky. That night he was lucky to watch as a rare spiral of iridescent mint-green light slowly rotated in the otherwise inky sky. "Some nights, nothing happens. Some nights the sky is burning," he said, sounding like a lonesome cowboy out on the Western plains with only his horse for comfort.

Dmitri Gornstein stepped out on the floor of the *semahane* (whirling hall) feeling awkward, but exhilarated. Even as a boy he was interested in finding ways to feel "high." When he was a child playing on a swing, he'd lean back as far as he could, then quickly pull up to feel a weird rush of blood to his head. He also would hold his breath until he passed out just to feel a last-minute, exotic sensation in his head.

Three musicians sat on a riser on the north end of the round building—two flutists with long, thin, wooden flutes and one drummer. The whirling men near the center moved smoothly around and around, their arms in a square out from their bodies, hands raised to the domed ceiling. Today they were rehearsing for a *sema* ceremony, which represented a spiritual journey—the determined seeker's turning toward God and truth through dance. Gornstein would not be allowed to participate in the final production, because he was a novice. But for now, he was happily slowly turning in a clockwise circle, arms out, eyes closed, chanting, "Allah, Allah, Allah."

After a half hour of this, he was ready to stop. His face flushed, he felt excited, happy, and filled with endorphins racing through his system.

"I want to do more of this, Han," Dmitri said greedily as he returned to the sidelines behind a row of columns.

"And you shall my friend. I want to take you through what spiritual training I've been through." Lu beamed with approval. "There is no substitute for finding God."

As the two headed back down the hall to Lu's private quarters, Gornstein pointed to his Chinese friend's neck—to a large scar that ran down one side. Lu turned his head and pointed to another long scar on the other side.

"You didn't have those when we were in school. What happened?" the Russian asked as they neared the large room that usually housed the Master who headed the Sufi cell. He had moved in with the rest of the devotees when Lu arrived, so respectful was he of the Asian's powers.

"This is quite a story. Come in," Han said, gesturing broadly. "Wash up. There's a pitcher over there." The Chinese master pointed to a basin table against the stone outside wall. "Get out of those sweaty clothes. I'll have some coffee and sweets brought in."

Han caught another sexual look cross Dmitri's face.

"I have absolutely nothing in mind. You have been in the army too long, my friend. I have been celibate since I began this spiritual odyssey. It suits me well." He looked piercingly at the Russian to emphasize his point.

"As you wish," Gornstein finally agreed with a disappointed sigh.

After Dmitri cleaned up and settled into a comfortable arm chair, Han handed him a carafe of coffee. "You know, I haven't had such a captive audience in a great while. I hope I don't bore you."

"No, please," the Russian said, his interest clearly piqued in the changes his erstwhile companion had obviously gone through.

"My neck?"

"Yes."

"I was in India after I left the Sufi order. I felt there was more that I had to learn after achieving the union with God promised from the *sema*. So I went to India, to Chidambaram in southern India. At that location there is a colossal temple dedicated to Shiva as the Cosmic Dancer, Nataraja. The image stands under a roof covered by 21,600 tiles of solid gold representing the 21,600 daily respirations of the average human being."

"Whew! I had no idea such a place existed."

"There is more. Be patient." Han smiled, clearly pleased that the story had grabbed Gornstein's interest. "The temple itself covers fifty acres, including four great towers rising nearly two hundred feet. These are covered with figures of gods and goddesses carved in granite. From the porch of Chidambaram, you can see miles and miles of emerald green rice fields and palm trees."

"Amazing," Dmitri said sipping from his small coffee cup.

"A saint achieved the highest state of meditation or *samadhi* there, well over a thousand years ago. That transformative experience, along with those occurring to many,

many pilgrims a year, has supercharged the place."

"So what did you do?"

"I asked around in my best Hindi, until I found a man who would teach the basics of the yogic meditation system, and I sat there for six months."

"Six months! How did you survive?"

"On food provided by the local people there, who are very generous to spiritual seekers."

Dmitri leaned forward and placed the empty cup on the small table to his left without looking–his gaze glued to Lu's face.

"These yogic lessons," Lu continued, "which at first were elementary and boring for me, moved on to intensive postures and breathing exercises lasting up to a month at a time. It was fairly easy for me to slip into the states of consciousness that this system elicited, because of the four years of training with the Sufis."

"Four years!" Dmitri said incredulously and whistled.

Han frowned, then continued. "Within six months, however, it became apparent that I had surpassed my yoga teacher, so he sent me away."

A servant interrupted. Han left with him for a moment. Dmitri sat back and laced and unlaced his fingers. "I have to keep my wits about me here," he said fiercely under his breath. "Who knows what Lu is up to now!"

"I am sorry," Han said, resettling in the arm chair and tucking his woolen robe around his legs. "There are details of running this cell that these men can decide on without me, but I haven't been here for a long time. I think they just want to talk to me." He settled back and lit a Turkish cigarette. Then he blew a smoke circle in the air.

"How can you smoke?" Dmitri asked before he thought of what he was saying.

"And be who I am?"

"And tread such a spiritual path."

"There comes a point when it all falls away and you become a human being again."

"Oh."

"Anyway. These scars...," Lu said fingering the one on the left side. "...I wandered down to Sri Lanka–to the southern tip of the island where I was told Gautama Buddha made a pilgrimage over eight hundred years earlier. Turns out it was a sacred place for both Buddhists and Hindus. That I liked, because I really wasn't interested in joining any sect, just learning from them."

He stopped his narrative and looked deeply into Dmitri's face. *Good, he's right there with me,* he thought.

"The main temple in Katrigama was the site of many reported miracles. So I went and sat inside this temple, deep inside a forest, a forest charged with spiritual vibrations. I began to practice my *sadhana,* and, just because of the spiritually-saturated nature of the place, I found myself becoming more and more proficient."

"One day, while I was deeply withdrawn into my body, a man with a machete stepped onto the temple grounds, shouting something in an Indian dialect I scarcely understood. The only thing I could make out was that he wanted to get rid of me because I was a foreigner. Before I knew it, he had run the machete straight through my neck, severing the major artery. His screams brought several attendants to my side. I still was sitting upright in a lotus posture, and to this day I don't know how, but I slowly raised both hands to my neck and held them there. The bleeding instantly stopped, and all that was left was the scarring which you see. There is no medical reason why I am still alive. It was truly a miracle."

Dmitri's jaw hung open. His old friend was proving to be someone he would never have imagined meeting. *Power like that! How to get some? And in a hurry! No four years of whirling for me,* he thought fiercely.

The next evening Dmitri and Han headed down the stone hallway to the performance hall where a small audience waited for the *sema* to be performed. They could hear the excited crowd chattering as they approached the red-draped chamber.

Han slipped his arm through Dmitri's and said, "There are several parts to the *sema*, beginning with a singing of a eulogy to the Prophet Mohammed; then a procession in which the *semazen* or participants bow to each other acknowledging soul to soul connection."

"And where will you be?"

"In the center," Han said pointing to the red sheepskin rug positioned in the center of the hall. "As *sheikh* I provide a point of contact with the earth so that God's grace can enter into the spirits of the dancers," Han said as he headed for the changing rooms.

"And into the witnesses?" asked Dmitri as he trailed behind.

"Yes," Han said somewhat tenderly. "Into everyone present."

"Good." Dmitri sighed.

The Asian adept stopped at the curtained changing area and said, "This path, the Sufi way, is a way of devotion. The dance seeks to purify mind, emotion and spirit by turning toward Divine Unity. They are also dancing for the good of the earth and humanity as a whole.

"Very noble," Gornstein said with a hint of cynicism.

"They really *are*," Han said with great seriousness. "Now back to the ceremony: the remainder consists of four *selams* or salutes, each one symbolizing the path the devotee takes to God and back into creation." He pointed to an area between two pillars where a number of chairs had been placed. Dmitri bowed low to his friend and headed in that direction.

The twelve moustached Sufi musicians with traditional Turkish instruments–flutes, drums, tambourines–warmed up. In a circle around the outside of the dance floor stood twelve dancers each clothed in a black cloak and felt hat. Their arms crossed, they stood erect, arms folded, waiting for their cue.

The last of the forty observers settled into their seats, as did Dmitri. He watched excitedly to see how professional dancers handled the deceptively simple hand and arm movements that he had tried to perform that afternoon–focusing on his left hand, which was downturned, as the right was extended behind him. Then came the slow turning and gathering in of the arms into a circle as the dancer picked up speed.

Now the dancers moved into position. They ceremoniously discarded the black cloaks, revealing wide white skirts. These symbolized the death shroud, while the tall, felt hats they wore represented a tombstone. Dmitri sucked in his breath as the twelve began their turning, shoulder to shoulder, around each other and around Lu (the sun) who stood on the small sheepskin. Chanting low at first, the dancers' vocalization grew steadily louder, while the music simultaneously accelerated in tempo and timbre.

Mesmerized, Dmitri followed the dancers as they flew around and around until his head began to rotate on his neck. Then he found himself standing on his feet, longing to be pulled into the growing, spinning ecstasy. He licked his lips and closed his eyes, scarcely daring to take a breath.

"Allah, Allah," he called out. No one noticed him in the din. Suddenly it felt as if his breath had been sucked right out of him by a giant vacuum cleaner. His lungs stopped moving, and as it did, he felt a delicious tremor in his throat which moved up to press against a point between his eyebrows, finally ending in a cascade of molten white energy, flooding his cranium.

The dancers whirled faster; the Russian couldn't speak. The music rose to a crescendo. Then, behind his closed eyes, he saw first the figure, then the face of a brilliantly-lit figure–fire bolts bursting all around him. He strained to make out who it was. It was Lu Han.

"Aiye, god incarnate!" he called out and slumped to the floor unconscious.

Gornstein was out for a minute, no more. People on each side of him pulled him up into his chair and fanned his flushed face. "I have seen god, I have seen god," he said in a half-sob as he came to.

The ceremony over, dervishes and sheikh departed in a cacophony of joyous music. Once out in the hall, they continued to be carried in a rapturous state to the clapping of the enthusiastic audience. The performers leaned on each other laughing, trying to catch their breath. Dmitri struggled to his feet and staggered after them.

Han moved in among the Sufis, patting each on the back. "Well, well done, gentlemen. I am indeed proud of your performance." The twelve men leaned back against the stone walls, still breathing hard, but gratefully taking in the praise. Then, to the amazement of all, Lu opened his palms, and from each palm rose a gem. In the left an emerald, the right a diamond. They did not come from his pocket; they were not in his curled hand. They materialized out of the proverbial thin air.

Lu walked forward to the two men on the far left and handed each one a flawless gem worth thousands of dollars. "Thank you, my friends. You honor me by your goodness and sincere search for God."

The shocked men bowed and thanked him repeatedly. Then Lu stood in front of the next two men in line, opened his hands again and this time a pearl and a large piece of jade appeared. These he handed to the two men, who, like the first, stood slack-jawed and silent in awe until they could find words of thanks. He continued producing precious gems until all twelve men had been rewarded. Then they formed a circle around him, bowing to him and blessing him.

Only after the dervishes disappeared into their monastic cells did Lu acknowledge Gornstein, who had witnessed the miraculous manifestations as he stood at the end of the hall a couple of yards away.

"Come. Come, my friend. It is all right. You may come into my presence," Lu said and gestured for Gornstein to step forward.

The Russian walked toward him with his hands together in prayerful supplication. As he neared the adept, he dropped his gaze. "I will not doubt you again, Master Lu," he said, eyes focused on the stone-cobbled floor.

"For that I am grateful, friend," Lu said. "Come with me."

The Chinese master wheeled around and abruptly walked quickly down the hall to his quarters. Without removing his dancing garments, Lu sat down heavily on a high-backed, wooden chair with ornate embroidery on the back, arms and seat. He signalled to Gornstein to sit across from him in a straight-backed chair.

"We have much to discuss."

"Yes, please. How can I serve you?" Gornstein said with singular reverence.

"There is a threat to my plan. I discovered it when we had our little war in America. As I mentioned, I hadn't counted on the resistance from the men from the western saline lake region. They call themselves Latter-day Saints. They are now setting up an empire of their own—in the middle of the country, I am told." Lu lit up a cigarette with an impatient gesture.

"I need your help. I need to know more about them."

"How can I help?"

"Your intelligence-gathering in Israel may be of assistance. I understand these Americans believe the Jews to be one of their tribal cousins."

"Think no more about it. I will provide you with all the information that my operatives in Israel can get their hands on."

"Good. And I've located that devotee from Salt Lake City who came to India—Kayleen 'something.' She's on the move to the center of the country. I will see that she helps me."

Dmitri sat silently looking at the man whom he had once thought he knew but now could only worship.

"Anything, Master, anything," was all he could say.

CHAPTER TWELVE

"It is within my power either to serve God
or not to serve him.
Serving him, I add to my own good
and the good of the whole world.
Not serving him, I forfeit my own good
and deprive the world of that good,
which was in my power to create."
Leo Tolstoy

The morning of the third day after they arrived on Orchard Lane, Peg was visited by a dozen smiling men who arrived with two trucks loaded with building supplies. They swooped onto the property and began the renovation of her house and grounds with such efficiency–almost ferocity–she was both delighted and amazed. Within minutes, they took down the dangling staircase, swept out the debris throughout the downstairs, and divided up into teams–some framing, some plumbing, some doing drywall.

While Peg and the kids worked on cleaning up the back lawn, she began to tell them stories of her great-grandparents when they came West in the 1860's and were sent by church authorities to southwest Idaho to farm.

"I have seen my great-grandmother Lettie's diary where she described a barn-raising, done in a day. Men and women all concentrating on one goal: helping a family so they could have the necessities of life. She described how joyous the occasion was, how the food tasted extra good, how friendships were deepened. Well, kids, that's what's happening. Now that we're in Zion, we are involved in helping a lot of people create happy lives."

"I want to go to school," Miriam announced.

"And that's what pioneer girls wanted too."

"So what did they do about it?"

"They got together with some other children, and someone, who was good with children and who was smart, was designated as the teacher."

"You could do it, Mom!" Danny said exuberantly.

"I could. But I'm sure there's some master plan about who's going to teach and where you're going to learn."

"I don't care about later. Let's do school today!" Miriam enthused.

"Well, I guess we could see who at the Taylor's might like to come over. I heard the younger of Nate's kids have arrived."

"Yeah!" the two shouted as they headed out across the fields that separated the two houses.

While Peg watched Miriam and Danny sprint across the open space, she returned to her reverie about her ancestors. "Lettie," she said aloud to the clouds overhead, "are you watching? I hope so." She felt a catch in her throat. "We finally made it. I know you thought it would happen in your lifetime. But we're here!" she said exuberantly. Peg tried not to think about her widowed mother, with whom she had spoken only once— just before she and Ben fled to southern Utah. LaDawn Woodruff Christensen was an inactive member of the Church who tried to support her daughter's choices but had real difficulties believing any good would come from Peg's marriage to a Jew.

"Excuse me, Mrs. Taylor. Could you help us here for a moment?" a male voice cut through her reverie.

"Sure," Peg said heading for the house.

"We'd like to know what color you'd like us to paint the living room."

Peg couldn't believe her eyes. In an hour's time, they had patched the walls and stripped off the old wallpaper in the "parlor," which had tall bay windows that opened out onto the eastern rolling hills. She had never had a painting crew at her beck and call. "I think I'd like a mint green." *I don't know*, she thought. *Mint green? Oh, well, we can always paint over it.*

The smiling painter mixed up a color, wiped it on a stick for her perusal. She said it was fine, then she was diverted into the kitchen where the workmen wanted to know which pattern of linoleum she wanted laid. And so it went throughout the day.

About four o'clock a blue-paneled truck drove up, and the driver came to the front door asking for Margaret Taylor. He was taking orders for furniture. Peg's head was swimming. "I guess a couch, two chairs, carpet...." The man explained nothing would be new but would be in good condition. The family could use what was donated until the manufacturing of new furniture which would begin some time later that year.

"We'll be back tomorrow," the burly African-American announced with a grin on his face.

"Tomorrow? Will the house be ready?" Peg fretted.

The project coordinator replied, "Paint will be dry, plumbing will be functioning. You need a new bath tub–that one upstairs is cracked beyond repair. We'll bring one back with us tomorrow. The stairs should be finished by noon. We wanted to do a good job with them. Tried to reconstruct the railings."

In the midst of these heady decisions, Peg spent a good deal of the day being teacher as the kids "played" school. She was touched to see the sheer joy in this impromptu, natural learning process that she hadn't seen in her public school classrooms. Perhaps it's because the kids are younger, she thought. But, as the day wore on, she decided it was because they wanted to learn. They were really excited about writing poems and reciting their multiplication tables.

Peg felt warm rushes of contentment fill her. "This is my house and *my* farm and *my* kids and *my* husband's at work for the Lord." With happy tears spilling down her cheeks, she finally released the desire that she had held back since the death of her daughter and said, "And I can love this piece of land, this man, and these children. And nothing bad is going to happen." She dropped her arms to her sides and let out a sob.

Later, after the children had eaten lunch and school had lost its lustre, the Taylor kids–Elizabeth, Dana, and Holden–left. Bored, Danny and Miriam wanted to talk about animals. "Can we get that kitty cat now?" "How about sheep?" "I want two horses."

"We'll have to talk to Dad about all that," Peg said, putting off the inevitable.

When Ben drove up about six, he got out and walked to the back yard where the tents were pitched. He stayed at work longer than was necessary, because he dreaded coming home to camping, which he assumed would be their lot for months. He was scarcely out of the car before the kids were all over him. "Dad, can we get a horse?" Danny asked, hugging him around the waist.

"Dad, Danny said I'd couldn't get a sheep because my name isn't Mary," Miriam whined.

"Whoa, guys, give me a minute here," Ben said, dragging Miriam along on one arm. "Where's your mom?"

"In the house."

"What is she doing in there? It isn't safe to..." Now he was being dragged by both children in through the back door and into a kitchen painted bright yellow with brown speckled lineolum. Peg was washing out the cupboards which had been artfully reattached by the workmen. Boxes were scattered all over the floor.

"Oh, hi, honey. Sorry I didn't hear you. I'm so excited about getting this kitchen put away, so they can bring the table and chairs tomorrow."

Ben stood transfixed. "Did we have angels visit today?"

"You could call them that. It isn't perfect by any means, but everything works, and that's what we need for now."

The kids grabbed him by both arms and continued their tour through the house. "Don't touch the walls. The paint is still a little wet," Miriam called out as they mounted the stairs to the second floor. "...and down there is my bedroom. It's pink. And next door here is Danny's. The house is so big we have rooms to play in besides our bedrooms." Miriam's excited voice was high-pitched with pride. "And Daddy, Mom says we can stay in these bedrooms until we die, if we want to."

"Only she said we probably aren't going to die! Is that right?" Danny wanted to know.

"She's always right, guys. You know that," Ben said. He was overwhelmed by the work done on the house in just one day.

"Tomorrow they're going to bring my bed," Miriam asserted.

"Then we can bring the boxes out of the supply tent, and we can sleep in the house!" Miriam wasn't as interested as Danny in the possibility of immortality when compared with the prospect of Missy sleeping over.

Ben knelt down to his daughter's level and pulled her and Danny into his arms. Tears filled his eyes. He opened his mouth but couldn't think of anything to say.

Later, when the kids had fallen asleep and Ben and Peg were lying in their tent, Ben caught Peg up on news from the office.

"I got a little office of my own today. In the back of the 'office building.' It has a window that looks out over the trees."

"How great, honey!"

"And I've been given back the plates."

Peg raised up on one arm. "Ben, no!"

"I have a confession. I've had them since New Mexico."

Peg was silent.

"Sangay gave them to me."

"And why didn't you..."

"I thought you had enough on your mind..."

Peg laid back down. After a frosty silence she asked, "Will I get to work on them?"

"No."

"I see," she said and turned over away from him.

"Wait, honey," Ben protested and reached for her tense arm. "I've got permission to share with you what I find out. It's just that...Well, Grace Ihimaera wants you as a counselor. And she pulls more weight than I do around there."

Peg sat up abruptly. "Grace?"

"She's been called to be General Relief Society President."

"Oh, my gosh!" Peg's hands flew to her face.

"And she wants you–has specifically asked that you be called to be her counselor."

"Oh, my gosh!"

"You just said that."

"Oh, my gosh!" Peg fell back on her bed. "I don't believe it. I thought for sure I'd go back to teaching high school."

"Well, I understand she has a loftier position in mind for you. Education Coordinator."

"What is that?"

"Helping oversee the education of the children of Zion."

Peg began to cry. Ben pulled her into his arms and asked, "Why are you crying, cutie?"

"Oh, my heck. This is too much. It's like all my dreams are coming true. I can't handle it," Peg said nestling into his arms.

"How about more news? Give you something to *really* cry about."

"Okay," Peg said with slight trepidation.

"Laurie Winder's back with a vengeance," he said, expecting that to be news to his wife.

"I know the younger kids are back with their dad," Peg said matter-of-factly.

"Laurie's running such an obvious campaign to get back with Nate, it's a bit nauseating."

"Like what?"

"Like getting her father to talk to Nate."

"Oh, no. Poor Nate. What does he think?" Peg asked with maternal concern in her voice.

"I think he feels he needs to give the marriage another chance. Said Elder Whitmer told him they needed to bring Laurie along like Laman and Lemuel."

"Oh, boy. I tell you," Peg said vehemently, "That woman is trouble. I swear it."

"I agree. Oh, and I saw Juan Gallegos today–at the printing plant. He said to say hi."

"I wondered how he and Maria are doing."

"He appeared quite happy. Said they were renting a house in Independence, but wanted to get out of town a ways. I dared bring up the gospel. He seemed open for further discussion. I'm going to check about sending someone over to talk with the family," Ben said, pulling his arm back, which had gone numb, from under Peg's head. "Juan's such a good man. And now that he can actually see what we're about, I wouldn't be surprised if he joined the Church."

After Ben rubbed his arm to regain some blood flow, the two nestled together for awhile. Then Ben who was still feeling guilty about the plates said, "And honey, I do need some physical exercise every day. So I want you to give me some small, not-too-tough job in the yard, and I promise I'll work on it."

"Listen, mister, I'll give you some physical exercise," Peg said biting on his ear and pulling him close to her.

"Now this is the kind I don't mind being assigned to," Ben chortled.

In the Montana meadow where the tribes gathered, Moira stood around a fire with the rest of the Intertribal Council listening to Claude Lansa, a stern-looking Hopi elder, who had come to Montana at her request. Lansa was a respected tribal elder who had memorized Hopi oral traditions. Moira had persuaded him to come and share what peaceful methods the Hopis had used in the past to work things out with whites.

The tall, elegant Maori watched the hard, set faces of her friends as they scrutinized the visitor. She felt sad and pulled at one of her long black braids. She, who had been so exhilarated by the vision of Lamanites taking back what was rightfully theirs, now grew more and more uneasy at the recent turn of events. Raids upon towns and cities had become bloodier. Groups no long tried to take over just government facilities, television studios or other media to announce their cause. They abandoned these plans in favor of random violence against whites, whenever and wherever they felt like it.

Within a week after the plan had been set in motion, Indians, in lightning raids, swept into any town, robbed the banks and shops, and opened fire on people in streets and malls. They set fire to the downtown areas of major cities, inciting other non-whites to do the same. In scenes reminiscent of the destruction of Detroit or Watts in the 1960's, rabid people burnt down their own homes and businesses. What started as an attempt at non-violence didn't last long, and what happened in one city spread to another, like a virus. A buried fury, released by the Native American invaders, was more than the local residents could resist.

Hispanics, who now numbered one in four residents in the United States, also found a rage buried deep within their collective consciousness that they directed at the dominant white population. When the UWEN relaxed their hold and Mexicans poured over the U.S. borders to ransack Texas, Arizona and California towns, the local Hispanic population joined in.

It was just as Joseph Smith predicted: "...slaves shall rise up against their masters...And the remnants who are left of the land will marshal themselves...and shall vex the Gentiles with a sore vexation."

In a desperate attempt to stem the bloody tide, the ruling intertribal council recalled leaders from each tribe, for they too shared Moira's grave concern that some hideous power had been unleased. But the marauders didn't want to hear about peaceful solutions. They were interested in what Hopi prophecy had to say about the end times they found themselves in.

"Go on, Claude," Moira coaxed the silent Hopi.

Lansa cleared his throat and said, "The white man, through his insensitivity to the way of Nature, has desecrated the face of Mother Earth. It has been his desires for material possessions and power that have blinded him to the pain he has caused our Mother. All over the country, the waters have been tainted, the soil broken and defiled, and the air polluted."

Someone banged on a drum loudly. Gray Eagle put up his hand to signal silence.

"Today, almost all of the prophecies we have long waited for have come to pass: Great roads like rivers now pass along the landscape; man talks to man through the cobwebs of his telephone lines," the Hopi elder said and put out his hands toward fire to warm them. "Man travels along the roads in the sky," he continued. "Two great wars have been fought with 'gourds of ashes' raining down on the earth. Even the moon and the stars have been tampered with…"

A great whooping and thumping erupted. "And now it is our turn to rule!" shouted a Comanche elder.

"No," Grey Eagle said fiercely, waving a talking stick at the encircled audience. "Let us listen to our brother!"

"The *Bahana*, the white man, has a sweet tongue, a fork tongue, like a snake," Claude Lansa said somewhat sarcastically. "He has tried to tempt us and bring us to our knees…."

More emotional outbursts. Moira shouted at the group to be quiet. After several minutes, they settled down to murmurs.

Claude continued, "We have teachings that say, 'Blood will flow. Our hair and our clothing will be scattered over the earth. Nature will speak to us with its mighty breath of wind,'" he said dramatically, then paused to let those images soak in.

The Native Americans fell silent for several minutes. Red sparks from the fire cracked and popped into the clear night air.

"There will be corruption and confusion among the leaders of the world," Lansa continued. "All of this has been planned from the beginning of creation."

"Let's get on to the blood spilling," a Sioux shouted. Drums banged, while moccasin-clad men stomped their feet and thrust their fists in the air.

"Quiet!" a frustrated Moira shouted. "This man has come a long way to talk to us." She stared at one, then another of the hostile men. She could be ferocious—a warrior at least as wild as they were. Again silence reigned.

"The last prophecy I will tell you," Claude said with restrained anger, "says that the Red symbol will take command, putting the four great forces of nature in motion for the Sun. And when he sets those forces in motion, the whole world will shake and turn red and turn against the people who are hindering the Hopi life. That is Purification Day. People will run to the Red symbol in search of a new world and the equality that has been denied them. He will come unmercifully. His people will cover the earth like red ants. We must not go out to watch. We must stay in our houses. He will come and gather the wicked people who are hindering the red people who were here first. He is the only one who will purify us."

Moira tried to make sense of this in light of LDS prophecy. This prophecy sounded like a mixed-up version of Christ's coming, she thought. I wonder if the Red symbol is the description of the Anti-Christ. "Red" might mean the dragon.

"I'm not going to stay in my house," shouted another impatient Sioux, wearing a beaded headband. "Maybe you Hopi want to sit out there in Arizona and wait. You've got your land. But we don't. We want ours back!"

Moira felt sick. This was not what she had in mind. When she and her father had spearheaded reforms for her people in New Zealand, they never resorted to violence.

The meeting degenerated into wild shouting and howling. Over the din, Moira thanked Lansa and watched sadly as he disappeared in the shadows outside the fire's light. She stared at the dancing and whooping for a time then turned and walked through the aspens to the tepee Grey Eagle had provided for her. The Maori warrioress pulled back the rawhide flap and plopped down on a bear skin rug at the interior edge of the tent.

The despondent runaway poked at the ashes of a fire with a long stick and said to herself, "Maybe this *is* the time to wipe the white man from his towns and cities. What do I know?"

This past week had been an exhilarating time for her—swept up into leadership of a world-wide movement of Lamanites. Moira had scarcely slept, working side-by-side with friends she had cultivated over the years. In spite of the high, she couldn't shake a gut feeling that she had overstepped some fundamental boundary.

Once when she was ten, she and another girl impulsively crossed over a stream and went to play in a wooded area that her mother, Grace, had strictly declared off-limits. As the day wore on and they became thirsty, they stopped to look around and discovered they didn't recognize any of the surroundings. Lost, they spent most of the evening huddled next to each other, hungry and repentant until they were rescued by her uncle.

Now that same scared tightness gripped Moira's stomach. "But this time I'm not turning back," she said fiercely as she wrapped herself in a red and white striped blanket, lay down on the bear skin and fell into an exhausted sleep.

Grace's tunnel vision and vertigo came more frequently now. She attributed them to the pressures of her calling as Relief Society president and Moira's absence.

"Don't worry about me, son," she said to Alex the evening that Moira lay alone in that rawhide tepee in Montana. "I'm never sick, and you have your own set of problems."

The aging Maori grandmother sat on a small, overstuffed couch with a pink and green floral print. She looked out of place in this Midwestern bungalow, and she felt it. Back home in New Zealand, she would have been resting on a mat in a room above her grocery store, and she would be surrounded by kin who would have anticipated her every need. She was, after all, the village wise woman, and nearly eighty years old–venerable and capable of "seeing."

Grace gave it all up to come to the United States to be with Moira when she got pregnant. Grace had had a vision in which her grandson came to her before he was born and told her he needed her to help him come into the world. So she sold her store and left behind her entire life to do just that, knowing intuitively she'd never return.

Not that she wasn't appreciated by this culture. She was made General Relief Society President, after all. She felt it was a great honor, but it wasn't Te Kao, her hometown, and there wasn't a seashore nearby where she could walk to replenish her vital essence.

The Ihimaeras (which means "smiler" in Maori) had three children–two boys besides Moira. Albert, the oldest, became a drug addict after he migrated to Auckland and died of a heroin overdose at twenty-five. Henry, the second, stayed near home, but never quite found himself in the shadow of his powerful and prominent father. He drifted from one relationship to another, living off women and gambling his days away.

Moira was Grace's one hope for a child to whom she could pass on Maori spiritual secrets and the Latter-day Saint way of life. Although her daughter was an active member of the church, she wasn't initially interested in her mother's spiritual matters so much as her father's political activities. It was only after he died quite unexpectedly, that Grace and Moira "found" each other. So, when Adam made his urgent request, Grace hurried to her daughter's side, hoping now that Moira was going to be a mother, she would settle down to learn traditional women's ways.

And, now that her beloved daughter had left the family for political exigencies, Grace felt the life force ebbing out through a hole in her heart.

"I'm not going to be dismissed that easily, Mom," Alex insisted, pressing his concern for her health. "At least talk to me about the Relief Society–what is going on?" Alex leaned forward in a wing-backed chair he brought up to the couch and plumped a yellow-striped pillow behind her back. Grace noted the worried look on the handsome man's face. *He is so dear*, she thought.

"Son, I've been alone for so long without a man to share my innermost thoughts, I'm just not used to such masculine attention," she said smiling tenderly. "It's been well over twenty years since Gordon passed. I usually talk to him after I've gone to bed."

"Look, Mom. I need somebody to talk to. Adam's babbling is getting to me."

He looked so disconsolate, Grace began talking with a forced enthusiasm. "Oh, my, what isn't going on! With all twelve portals open and functioning, we are admitting about 3,500 immigrants a day. Most have nothing but the clothes on their back. Many of them are sick. It's like nothing I've ever orchestrated before."

It's good to talk intimately with her again, Alex thought. *I've been feeling so strangely disconnected in recent days. I had written it off as missing Moira's body as I fall asleep. But thinking about it, I* haven't reached out to anybody, not even Grace. Depression is an insidious thing, he thought. It doesn't help that I can't have my eight cups of coffee a day, either.

"Well, let's see," Grace continued. "Yesterday morning I met with the Welfare Committee about the tent city we had to put up overnight. A large influx of Hispanic families–nearly 700 people–were fleeing the Dallas/Fort Worth area. It seems there is a great deal of fighting between whites and Indians and Hispanics. These refugees did not want to fight. However many were sick with PDS. They lost twenty-six members of the party just between here and Texas."

"Does anyone have any idea about how to stop this 'plague' from spreading?" Alex asked just to keep Grace talking.

"We have hospital admitting stations right at the gateway to Zion. Doctors examine people, give them a priesthood blessing and some kind of injection that superspeeds the healing process in a way I don't understand."

"I thought I heard rumors of handkerchiefs blessed by the prophet being passed out among the portal workers. Do you know anything about that?"

"You know there are so many miracles happening these days I wouldn't be surprised."

Both laughed, then suddenly Grace put the palm of her hand to her right temple and winced. Alex was immediately on his feet, but she waved him off. "Just open a window for a bit of air, dear."

He quickly did as he was told, then asked solicitously, "You okay, Mom? I haven't liked the way you've looked recently."

"Nothing I can't handle."

A moment of silence passed, then Alex asked, "Any people coming in from Utah, Idaho in the past few days?" Alex pulled up the chair closer to her knees and put his hand on her arm. She had been holding her breath to wait for the vertigo to subside. With his touch, she breathed a little easier.

"A few," she struggled to say. "They've been having a terrible time with late spring snowstorms, so most of the stragglers have been trapped on the other side of the Rockies."

"Don't you think that's strange–the weather–after they had been warned if they didn't leave, they wouldn't have the chance to."

"I've certainly thought about that. Are you hoping for someone to come that you haven't seen?"

The sculptor hung his head for a moment, then said, "I've been thinking about Renoir, my old Golden Retriever. I don't know that she survived that bullet wound she got in the shootout at Pah Tempe. But I've hoped against hope that she might have come with Dr. Hunter. You remember David, don't you, Mom?"

"David Hunter? Of course! He healed Moira."

"Any way you could check and see if he's arrived?" Alex didn't even have the company of his black Doberman, Angelina. Because of the bungalow's postage-stamp-sized back yard, the dog was boarding with Jed and Jody Rivers.

"Help me up. I'll do it right now," Grace said as she pushed against the couch to stand up. She wobbled a bit, but she felt stronger having something on which to focus her attention. "We've just begun to compile a central listing of the immigrants." Telephones were scarce in Zion; Grace had one because of her position. Otherwise, people seeking family members or friends had to inquire personally at the Relief Society office in Independence.

The Maori grandmother stood in the kitchen for a moment, leaning against the faded white wall and thinking she might throw up. The feeling subsided; she dialed the wall phone and asked to speak to her secretary.

The afternoon sun streaming through the cottage curtains made rectangles on the old linoleum floor. The song of a robin caught her attention while she waited for the information. *I'll miss this,* she thought. *I've wanted to go home to Gordon for so long. But now that it's so close, I find I'm hanging on to every sensory delight.*

"Sister Ihimaera, there is a Doctor David Hunter just listed with us. He's in Liberty. And I have a message for your counselor, Sister Taylor. Her mother is trying to reach her."

Grace felt a thrill run through her. *Oh, what fun it is to be in a position to bring joy to good people*, she thought as she returned to the living room and Alex sitting in the wingback chair with his head in his hands.

"Perk up, dear boy. Your doctor is here in Zion." She handed him David Hunter's address.

Suddenly, instead of Alex's face, Grace could only see a long tunnel, then nothing. Alex, strong and agile as he was, couldn't get to her in time to keep her from falling onto the maroon carpet. He quickly picked her up in his arms and carried her to the back bedroom.

After he had placed a wet washcloth on her forehead, she came back around and said, "Oh, Alex, I'm so sorry. You have so much on your mind as it is. "

"What I have in mind is one of those blessing handkerchiefs if they exist. Second to that, I'm going to find David Hunter to see to this fainting business."

Grace grabbed him by the hand as he turned to leave and said, "Oh, I almost forgot. You have to tell Nate Winder that I got in touch with his mysterious redhead. Tell him there really is a Mary Margaret O'Boyle. She and her three daughters are boarding a ship. I got the impression it was England. They're headed here, and they are in a great deal of danger. This hurricane season has become so deadly people really can't travel on the ocean. We must pray for her."

Alex gently patted her hand, promising her to pass on the information. But Grace forgot about the message for Peg, as she retreated into a fog of nausea.

Adam lay sleeping in his light-blue pajamas on his stomach, scrunched up against the headboard, when Alex looked in on him. Other than caring for Adam, the prolific artist had nothing to do, and he was going stir crazy. The Brethren were vague with Alex when he requested a large piece of property out in the country to farm and rebuild an art studio. Instead they gave the Dubik family this two-story house not far from the temple site with only a small plot for gardening and no room for an active dog.

After securing a babysitter, Alex called Ben at church headquarters and asked him if he'd give him a ride to the doctor's address, which he readily agreed to.

Returning to the living room, Alex stared out the window, waiting for the Honda to pull up, and thought about the house that he had put so much work into—at Pah Tempe, a former hot springs resort near Hurricane, Utah. It was an open, two-storied structure with darkened beams that crisscrossed the ceiling. On the second-story balcony, which completely circled the upstairs, he had hung Old Navaho rugs at artful intervals. In between, plants cascaded down from earthen pots. On the main floor he had hung painting after alluring painting, all originals; none were his. He stayed with sculpting, but he had a cultivated eye for what he wanted to collect. His stunning work, however, was prominently displayed on tables and stands throughout the downstairs area. A large red patterned Oriental rug dominated the living area, along with a gigantic fireplace. Copper-colored pots hung in deliberate patterns in the open kitchen area.

"All things work for your good," ran through his mind. He grabbed onto it. "I need to believe You will somehow return a measure of what I had...before I gave it all up...to follow the Mormons," he said with an acerbic emphasis on the "Mormons."

"I'm fifty-seven years old, for heaven's sake! I don't know if I can do it again," he cried out softly. "Please don't let me get bitter, Lord. I have to be ready when you come."

CHAPTER THIRTEEN

"When you have eliminated the impossible,
Whatever remains, however improbable,
Must be the truth."
Sir Arthur Conan Doyle

When the last rays of the sun dropped into the Great Salt
Lake, Joseph Dawahoya crept to the side of the waiting Toyota,
opened the back door and slid on his side across the seat. He
clutched the precious burlap bag and its contents. As soon as the
sound of the slammed door reached his ears, Peter gunned the
car down South Temple away from the now-abandoned Church
Office Building. He swerved through slower traffic as fast as he
dared without calling attention to the car or its contents, for
Elder Dawahoya was a hunted man with a bounty on his head.

The deterioration of Salt Lake City into lawlessness was
breathtakingly swift like antimatter displacing matter. Only
two weeks had passed since Elder Dawahoya returned to the city
from Arizona to begin orchestrating the mass eastern exodus.

Many of the LDS families in the area who initially refused
to leave for Zion now panicked. They did everything they could to
flee neighborhoods where barricades had been erected to prevent
Latter-day Saints from leaving; members' houses were broken
into and stripped of anything worth selling; gun battles erupted
in quiet suburbs; and snipers on the freeways took out families in
cars trying to leave. Frantic people took to hiking into the hills
with just backpacks, but a rapid-fire series of freak, early-June
snowstorms blanketed the area with more than two feet of snow.

The apostle and his bodyguard remained as long as they
dared. Joseph had masterminded the orderly leaving of Utah by
thousands and thousands of Latter-day Saints from the Idaho
border to St. George. Other apostles had similar assignments in
different parts of the country.

The two were leaving between snowstorms under the cover of
near dark. It was eight thirty, a good time, because few snipers

had yet to take up positions on the highways leading out of Salt Lake.

"How ya doin' down there, mate?" Peter asked as he headed the car down Seventh East.

"As well as can be expected for an old man," Joseph joked. "Could you take the curves a little slower?"

"Nah, it's the race car driver in me. Can't help myself."

Peter took a sip of water from a thermos on the front seat, then checked out the rear view mirror. "Can't tell, sir, but there's been a white Mercury a few cars back for a couple of miles. Do you want me to see if they're tailing us?"

"No, let's get onto 215 and see what happens there."

Joseph rolled over to the edge of the seat and carefully placed the jar on the floor. Then he pulled out the gun he had attached to his belt and asked, "Where's the ammunition, Pete?"

"Right down there on your right," Peter replied.

The apostle loaded the pistol and put another round of bullets in his shirt pocket. The two continued until they arrived at the I-215 on-ramp. Both men held their breath. The Mercury entered several cars back.

"That Merc's gotta much bigger engine, sir."

"Don't remind me. Okay, get off going south on I-15, then pull over into the far right lane. We may have to shoot our way out of here."

What the two men didn't know was that the Mercury wasn't the only car tailing the Toyota. Word was out on truckers' CB's that the man with the $50,000 bounty on his head was on the move. Cross-country truckers noted the car's description as did at least ten other drivers on the freeway.

The only thing preventing a bloody shootout was that the bounty poster read, "The $50,000 is collectible only if the apostle is captured alive." A large apostate group put up the reward. They wanted information from him, by torturing him, if necessary. Traffic was fairly heavy around 7200 South even though the freeway had been widened to six lanes. Peter kept to the far right as instructed. The Merc followed a couple of cars behind in the middle lane. "Okay, sir, what now?" Peter queried.

"Are you as good a race car driver as I've heard?"

"Won a few races in my salad days." Peter grinned.

The apostle fell silent for a moment, then said, "See what you can do about losing these guys in this traffic."

Peter was delighted to take up that challenge. He began charging into traffic, pulling right in front of cars even though it didn't appear there was any room. He hung alongside a large truck, then veered over three lanes. After a dizzying three or four minutes, the Merc was nowhere to be seen.

"How's the stomach, boss?" Peter asked, turning around to see a white-faced Dawahoya in a ball with his knees to his chest.

"It isn't the stomach, it's the heart. You remind me of a couple of my helicopter pilots in 'Nam."

The kidding ended abruptly when a semi began to move into their lane near the Draper exit. Peter quickly veered to the right, but the truck kept coming.

"I think this bugger's trying to run us over!" Peter shouted. He slammed on his brakes, swerved behind the truck, but nearly hit another car in that lane. Then another semi came roaring up from behind, bumping the Toyota and pushing it forward toward the truck ahead. It was only the lightning quick reflexes that the Aussie had developed motorcycle racing that allowed him to jerk the steering wheel to the right and floor the gas pedal, zooming them out of the squeeze play and into a field near the prison facilities at the Point of the Mountain.

Elder Dawahoya sat up and whirled around, placing the gun on the back seat, ready to fire. Tires spun in the muddy field, then they were stuck, trapped.

"Let's get out of here!" Peter shouted.

"Wait!" Joseph said grabbing Peter's dark-green jacket. "Just wait." His breathing labored, he bowed his head. Peter looked back to see what he was doing. "The only way out of this is with some celestial help," he said softly.

Peter grunted in agreement.

The semis that tried to run them off the road had pulled up, drivers running down the pavement, ready to cut into the field.

"Fall forward, son," Elder Dawahoya barked. "Look like you're hurt. Let's ambush 'em."

Three men, guns drawn, ran across the field, then slowed down as they neared the car. Peter cleverly kept the tires spinning as he lay slumped over the steering wheel so they wouldn't think the two had tried to escape but couldn't get out of the mud. It appeared that his foot had jammed against the gas pedal with the impact.

Guns drawn, the three truckers carefully approached the car. Elder Dawahoya lay on his back in the back seat, cradling his gun on his stomach.

"There he is. That's the apostle!" one shouted as he rounded the car and peered in through the back window.

Dawahoya fired just as the back car door opened, the Remington–.38–special round striking one burly trucker in the chest with a dull thud. In front, Peter kicked open the driver's side door with both feet, crashing into the skull of another man who crumpled over unconscious, his gun flying out of his hand. The third began firing at Peter, who rolled to the front of the car and aimed his gun at the man wearing a cowboy hat.

"You'll die for nothing!" Elder Dawahoya shouted at the man. "Go on! Drop your weapon. Run! We won't shoot."

But the trucker crouched behind the back of the Toyota.

"Don't kill him, Peter! Not if you can help it," the apostle shouted.

After a tense couple of minutes, the trucker threw down his weapon. Peter ran to it and scooped it up along with the other, which had landed nearby.

"Toss me your keys!" Peter shouted at the defiant trucker. The man grudgingly complied. Elder Dawahoya grabbed jumper cables from the back as the Aussie stuck his gun in the young man's face. The Hopi apostle swiftly tied him up with the cables and his blue-striped tie.

Checking on the wounded trucker, they determined his wounds weren't fatal, so Elder Dawahoya reached into the Toyota and grabbed his precious bag. Then the two raced across the muddy field to the waiting trucks. After trying and failing to get the keys to start the first rig, Peter jumped into the second and revved the engine.

The Indian apostle laughed as he got in. "So now you drive semis?"

"No, but no worries, Mate. I watched plenty of Mad Max films in my youth!" Peter chuckled.

The two fugitives slammed the dark-green doors of the cab simultaneously. Peter put the semi's transmission into gear and eased the big truck onto the highway. "It's too bad to lose that solar-powered job," he moaned. "I got a lot of time invested in that heap."

The apostle, still hugging his precious sacred bundle, said nothing until they neared the Lindon exit in Utah County, twenty miles away. "I think you're right, Pete. Turn this rig around. I want to get that car."

Peter maneuvered the six-wheeler off at Lindon and back on the highway headed north, then began playing with the CB when he heard, "Hey, what's the skinny on the guy that's got a bounty on his head, the one in Salt Lake?"

A moment later Peter replied, "Heard there was a shootout. A couple of truckers got banged up, but they got their man."

"Ah, too bad. I was hopin' for a crack at the fifty grand," said the trucker headed to Idaho. "Got any other hot tips? I'm headed north out of Salt Lake."

"Nah, that was the big prize. Sorry you missed out, good buddy," Peter replied.

The two escapees listened for more about them, but the radio was silent. The two men glanced over at each other then broke into grins. "Now let the car be there," Peter said as he shifted gears to get the big rig over the Point of the Mountain.

The Toyota rested in the muddy field where they had left it. Relieved, Peter pulled the big rig even with the car on the opposite side of the highway. "What's it going to take to get that car out of there?" he wondered aloud.

"I bet we could grab something here to provide some leverage for the back wheels," Dawahoya answered as he reached under the passenger's seat where he found a tire iron.

"Okay, let's do it!" Butler shouted, as he threw open the cab door and sprinted across the highway, carrying the tire iron and a large piece of metal he ripped from the cab's door frame. The Hopi elder was right behind, carrying his bag. It didn't take much leverage for the back wheels to push the car forward to the shoulder of the road. From there, the men jumped in and sped off south. They decided they would go up Spanish Fork Canyon this time, and out through Price.

"But that's not goin' to take us back to your people, Guv," Peter said.

"Don't worry about it, Pete. I talked to my nephew and grandaunt before we left. They indicated they wouldn't come with us. According to Hopi prophecy, when the end comes, they are to stay in their houses. Only they call it 'the Purification,' instead of the 'end.'" The apostle sighed. "So there's really nothing I can do anyway," he said, his voice trailing off.

The moon was high in the sky when they passed through Heber. Peter pulled on a lever under the dash of the Toyota.

"What's that for?" the apostle asked, curiously.

"Collectin' solar from the moon rays."

"No! really?"

"Yes, sir. We have a coating we put all over the surface of the car to collect solar energy and funnel it into the motor and battery. That way, it's even charged for night driving. We're able to use moonlight to a limited degree."

"My, my, that's brilliant, young man."

"Works best on small light cars because of the limited power capacity."

"Of course."

Peter continued, "As I told you earlier, we've got 95% conversion from the solar to the electrical, so once you figure out how much horsepower you get on a bright day, then as long as you remain below that power requirement, you can drive clear across country. You can pretty much drive 90-120 mph indefinitely, varying with the terrain."

"Well, let's see where 90-120 mph will put us by tomorrow," the weary general authority said, laying his head back on the seat. He kept his gun in his lap and his legs pressed against the vase under the seat. He closed his eyes and said wearily, "Home, Porter...home."

Laurie Winder took no time after her arrival to drop her four youngsters off at their grandparent's Victorian house in downtown Independence and head out to find her girlfriend, Kayleen Richards. It was Kayleen who had gone to India in search of a guru and found Lu Han after his neck had been miraculously healed. And, boy, was she full of stories about her adventures there. Some of them even Laurie doubted. But, if half of what her long-time girlfriend said was true, she had a corner on some of the most exciting stuff that Laurie had heard in a very long time. Laurie hadn't been interested in hearing the whole story of her girlfriend's trip to India until her own encounter with Lu Han earlier that morning.

After Kayleen drew the blinds in the living room, she told Laurie that in 1992, when she was sick with a kidney ailment, she became convinced that Western doctors weren't going to help her. After reading *Autobiography of a Yogi* (written by one of India's greatest mystics of the twentieth century), she decided to travel to the Himalayas to find the purported immortal, Babaji. Her husband, a high councilman, and her three little children tried to dissuade her, but she was certain she'd die if she didn't go. So her husband financed the trip and sent two nurses along with her. He tried to pay a doctor to go along but couldn't find one in time.

"Nothing, or almost nothing stopped me on that path. It was by divine plan that while I was crossing the Himalayan forest, on the slopes of the Kailish Mountains, I was not harmed by tigers, serpents or lions."

Laurie sat with folded arms and tried to listen with some objectivity, fighting back a smile as she thought of Dorothy's line from the Wizard of Oz, "...lions and tigers and bears–oh, my!"

"The meeting with Babaji lasted only a few days. He didn't or couldn't heal me. His attitude was so untranscendent, so down-to-earth, I really couldn't tell if he really was translated or not. Several of us were disillusioned, but then I remembered what Yogananda said about Babaji: 'Babaji can be seen or recognized by others only when he wills it.'"

"That must have been so disappointing," Laurie said with some skepticism in her voice.

"It was," Kayleen said, ignoring Laurie's discernible doubt. "We were getting ready to leave India when someone, I don't remember who now, told me he knew of an Asian master in southern India who had full mastery over matter–objects were manifested by him which previously did not exist, but came into being at that very moment–out of the palms of his hands!"

Laurie sighed with pleasure.

"Then this guy went to tell me about other miracles. For example, a necklace of pearls appeared on a wave in the Indian Ocean and floated right up to Master Lu's feet at the instant he stepped into the waters. Then there were the hundreds of lepers who had been healed by some kind of holy ash, called *vibuti*, that spilled out of the palms of his hands."

"Wow!"

"Now my dear husband had me promise I'd be back in a month. Not only was I running out of money, my health was deteriorating. But I was absolutely determined to go see this man."

"And just on the strength of that story you left New Delhi?" Laurie's hazel eyes were now wide.

"Yes. And I will tell you I worried all the way on the train. I thought, *Weren't we warned that Anti-Christs would rise up in the last days.* She stood and paced in the darkened living room. "I was afraid that when I looked into his coal-black eyes, he would hypnotize me. And then there's the orange robe he wears? What color better for the devil's outfit than deep orange?"

"Okay, okay," Laurie said impatient with this mumbo-jumbo about the devil, to whom she had never really paid much attention. "So you got there. Then what happened?"

"There were about twenty Westerners, and we were housed in a long, low building that had small bedrooms and a common bathing area. I had to wait there for two days, and by that time I was running a fever. In fact, I was nearly delirious."

"Couldn't the nurses do anything for you?" the apostle's daughter asked.

"No, I really needed to be on dialysis."

"Gees, what courage!"

"Then, on the third morning, I looked out of the little window in my cell, and he was entering the courtyard." Kayleen seemed transported back to the small Indian village near Palni. "People from the village were running ahead of him, throwing flower petals on the ground. Sick people behind him were trying to touch him. And, all the while, he had this beautiful smile on his face."

Kayleen paused in her pacing of the living room and sighed as she looked up to the ceiling.

"Yes?" came the impatient question.

"Oh, then a middle-aged woman shooed the crowd aside, and he entered a large building. Within minutes, my name was called. I was being summoned into his presence."

Kayleen grew quiet. Her voice choked. "When I came close to him, I felt like a great warm blanket had been thrown over my shoulders. I knelt down as I saw others doing. Then he took me by the hand and raised me up. He was taller than I expected."

"How tall?" Laurie asked, now hanging on every word.

"Um...probably 6 feet, maybe 6'1", I'd guess."

"Go on."

"Then he said, 'What do you wish from me, daughter?'"

"And what did you say?" Laurie demanded, unable to stand the suspense.

"I started to cry. I thought, as I looked into his face, I can ask anything and I will get it."

"And...?"

"I finally said I wanted to be well enough to raise my children. And then he..." Kayleen held back a sob. "...he opened the palms of his hands, and before my very eyes, this white-grey ash appeared. I mean, it literally started pouring right out of his hands!"

"A miracle!" Laurie nearly shouted.

"I know! He placed the ash on my back near my kidneys, although I never said what was wrong."

"So, that's when you were healed? Right there?" Laurie, now on the very edge of the couch, almost gasped.

"On that very spot. The minute he laid his hands on me, the pain and fever disappeared."

"And that's when he gave you the pearl?" Laurie was now eager to get to what she thought was the really miraculous part, the part Kayleen had shared with her in the past.

"Yes. He opened his palm again, and this big, slightly pink pearl just came out of it. You know, you've seen it."

"I know. I just love hearing about it."

"Well, he handed me the pearl and said, 'Don't forget to thank God and his Avatar for your blessings.'"

"Whew! That is just amazing. Where is it? Where's the pearl?" Laurie asked in a low conspiratorial voice.

"Come on," Kayleen said, motioning for Laurie to follow her down the hall to a back bedroom. "George doesn't know I still have it. When I came back to the States so much better and told him what had happened, he demanded I throw the *vibuti* and the pearl away. He didn't believe it was a real gem."

"Men!" Laurie shook her head.

Kayleen opened a closet door and reached for a shoe box high on a closet shelf. "Of course, I threw out some of the *vibuti*, but never the pearl." A sweet smell, similar to baby powder, wafted into the air as she opened the box.

Carefully unwrapping a newspaper, then red tissue paper,

she finally opened to several small, light-green folded pieces of paper and a little, multi-colored purse with golden-colored strings. Pointing to the green papers, she whispered, "*Vibuti.*"

Then she pulled open the bag and reached in for the large pearl, which she proudly displayed in the palm of her carefully-manicured hand. "I had it appraised. I was told it was flawless and worth about $2000, and that was in 1982."

Both women stood staring at the object, then Laurie said, "Kayleen, I want you to cross your heart and hope to die that this is true. After all, it happened years ago, and you were delirious with a fever."

The petite woman stood to her full 5'3" height and said forcefully, "I swear to you that this is true. And the Christ is still alive. I have friends who have seen him since." She carefully rewrapped the objects and returned the shoe box to the top of the closet.

When Kayleen turned around, Laurie said dramatically, "Well...have I got something to tell you then!"

Flopping down on a nearby bed, Laurie patted the covers and indicated she wanted her friend to sit down.

"What?" Kayleen asked as she sat down close to the apostle's daughter. "I can't stand it. Tell me."

"It, and I say 'it' advisedly, happened early this morning."

"Yes, okay, hurry!" said Lu's devotee.

Laurie rubbed her hands together, then launched into the story. "I wasn't asleep because I could see my two daughters in the living room. They got up early, playing in their pajamas. Anyway, I was resting on my bed, when...(she made sure Kayleen was totally focussed on her face)...a man about this high (indicating ten inches) suddenly appeared at the end of my bed."

"Oh, my gosh, no!" Kayleen threw her hands over her mouth.

"Yes?" Laurie asked somewhat irritated.

"Laurie, I'm sorry to interrupt, but do you know who that was?" Kayleen's voice registered in the soprano range.

"Well, I found out. It was the lord, Master Lu," Laurie said proudly. "He came to find me and give me a message."

"Oh, my gosh, you are so lucky. That's happened to two other people I know. He's always that tall. I don't know why."

Laurie was now miffed with the information that this remarkable vision had been given to someone else. "*Anyway*," she continued, "the lord of the universe said that he knew who I was. He said he wanted me to know that, as he sat meditating in an attempt to find the most advanced souls worldwide, my face appeared before him."

Kayleen was now up, standing on the bed, her hands on her cheeks. "I can't stand this. This is too exciting! Did he mention me?"

"Yes, the lord said you were a lovely soul who had been a faithful disciple for many years. And that was how he could find me–through your exquisite devotion."

At that moment, Kayleen's husband, George, came through the front door. "Oh, no," she moaned. "Wait here. Don't move. I'll get rid of him," Kayleen whispered, jumping off the bed.

While Kayleen and George talked in the kitchen of the large, older home, Laurie sat on the bed flushed with excitement. "It wasn't some early morning dream. It was real!" Laurie reassured herself. "Kayleen said others have had this same kind of visitation."

Kayleen returned a few minutes later and shut the door. "I told him you weren't feeling well, and I was tending to you." She sat down at the foot of the twin bed and looked at Laurie with wondering eyes. "What did he say? What are you supposed to do?"

"I'm to be the conduit for his teachings here in Zion, until he can come." Laurie tried to act humble by lowering her eyes. "He told me I'm to speak only to small groups, people whom I know and can trust. He also warned me there may be some opposition to the idea that 'he' has already come."

"Well, it makes sense that he would choose an apostle's daughter. He came to special women when he was on earth."

"Thank you, dear," Laurie said, pretending to be touched. "But most importantly, he told me that we can be translated right *now*."

"I know that. *I* told you that." Kayleen ran her fingers through her short, dark hair.

Ignoring the interruption, Laurie continued, "In order to be worthy, we must get rid of every material desire. He says 'the original meaning of resurrection was a transcendence of the material world through which one rises up to a spiritual-divine reality.' Those are his very, exact words. He made me memorize them."

"He also said that people shouldn't expect to find eternal happiness in the other world once they have died; that world too is impermanent. Once we have exhausted our merits, we will have to return to earth."

"How depressing!" the high councilman's wife wailed. "But what about being translated? What does he mean by that?"

The sound of children filled the living room, then a door slammed. Kayleen froze. "George is out there somewhere," she whispered. "Hurry. I want to hear this before they find me."

"He has overcome the flesh, and he will teach us to do the same," Laurie whispered.

"That's a bit confusing," Kayleen said, furrowing her brow. "We do have bodies or we don't. Which is it?"

"That's the beauty of it. It's impossible to know—impossible to understand. He's just so far beyond our human intelligence. But he's promised he'll reveal all as we continue to progress."

A high pitched "Mom, where are you?" echoed down the hall.

Kayleen winced, then ignored her daughter. "So do you think he's Christ come back or a spiritual teacher preparing the way?" Laurie's confusing and contradictory message was causing Kayleen to doubt Lu Han for the first time.

"Definitely Christ. Who else could do the things he does?"

"But when I saw him, he was this...this guy. He didn't look at all like the pictures we have in Sunday School."

"Listen, Kayleen, do you remember after the Resurrection

when he appeared to those fisherman...ate with them...?"

"You're right! They didn't recognize him, did they?"

Laurie shook her head vigorously. "I have heard of people who have pictures, actual photographs of him as he *really* is. One has him walking arm and arm with Martin Luther King. So he appeared to you in a slightly different form. No big deal."

"Oh, this is so amazing!"

"And finally he told me, 'The body has no basis in fact. The mortal body is an hypnotic body, and when a woman wakes from this state of existence, she will see that it was just a kind of nightmare. He's promised to help all who follow him wake to dream no more, with his holy guidance."

"We've got to do this," Kayleen whispered as the call for "Mom" grew louder and closer.

"This?"

"Get translated!"

"We?"

"Laurie, you've got to let me help you. I found him first."

Before they could talk further, the door flew open, and there stood Kayleen's seven-year-old daughter with her hands on her hips. "I was looking for you! *Mom.*"

After Laurie left, she decided she would start presenting Master Han's teachings where she felt they would be most accepted—with her family. For Laurie had prevailed in the courtship with Nate and was moving into the house on Orchard Lane at month's end, when she and Nate would remarry in a simple ceremony conducted by her father at the older of the Independence LDS churches.

Meanwhile Nate revised the architectural plans for their house to include three more bedrooms for his four younger children. But he went about it all with a heavy heart. Although he was overjoyed to have his younger children, who had changed and grown a great deal in the year's separation, he wasn't so sure about Laurie. Rather than changing as he hoped, she still demanded and got what she wanted. She was just a little subtler about it now.

Nate felt like he was being smashed against the front railing of a large stadium in a World Cup soccer match, by a surging crowd–of one–Laurie Winder. And what was he to make of Mary Margaret, somewhere out there on the high seas, crying out for him? One night in the middle of this pressure, the weary man laid his head down on his sleeping bag and wept–something he hadn't done since he was a boy. "Thy will be done, Lord. You know best."

CHAPTER FOURTEEN

"There was a little girl who had a little curl
Right in the middle of her forehead;
And when she was good, she was very, very good
But when she was bad, she was horrid."
                    Henry Wadsworth Longfellow

Ben waited impatiently outside the meeting-room door in the upstairs of the temporary church headquarters. The seat was hard and the hallway dark. He could hear the rise and fall of the men's voices on the other side of the door, but that was all. Occasional bursts of laughter made the wait worse. *What in the world do apostles and the prophet laugh about? And are they laughing at me?* Ben fretted and pulled on his grey and red tie.

As the door opened, Ben could hear "...left the huge truck sitting along the highway and escaped! Joseph is our latter-day Moses...," then approving laughter. Ben was admitted into the presence of the presiding authorities of the Church, his armpits were dripping and his hands clammy. The contrast between the sunlit room and the dark hall made him blink.

Seven of eight members of the Quorum of the Twelve were seated around the dark, oval conference table. President Ueda sat directly opposite where Ben was standing. To the prophet's right, John the Beloved.

"Ben, how much I've looked forward to this day," President Ueda said warmly. "Sit down, young man. Please, relax. You're among friends."

"Thank you, sir." Ben said, feeling for a seat opposite the president and the translated apostle. Trying not to stare at John, he looked down at his hands.

"Let me get right to the point—why we've called you here today," the prophet said in a kind voice meant to assure Ben that he wasn't in trouble. "I've known about the Tibetan plates and your successful efforts to translate them. Congratulations."

Ben stole a peek at John to see what his expression might be.

He looked pleased.

"Thank you, sir. It certainly wasn't me; I was just a conduit." Ben looked around the room. The seven apostles he could name: Ledbetter, Ho, Mendes, Whitmer, Bashir, Arakaki, Sollars and Taitano. He had heard that Elder Dawahoya was on the plains headed for Missouri. Then his eyes met John the Beloved's. Ben had longed to see that face again. When he first encountered John at the laying of the temple's cornerstone, he thought he had never seen anyone so compelling. John's dark eyes, almost luminescent, seemed to Ben to send out rays of rapture. And, as before, Ben, who had always secretly laughed whenever anyone claimed to see auras, was sure he could see a golden glow around the apostle's body.

"Good to see you, Ben," John said with great sincerity. "I told you we would get together again." Then he nodded to the prophet to continue.

"Let me tell you what we have in mind," the prophet said, turning his soft and smiling gaze to Ben, who was struggling mightily to retain his composure. "We have need of a scribe, someone we can trust to record events for posterity. You've been recommended. How would you feel about that as a calling, Brother Taylor?"

Ben opened his mouth, then shut it. Ever since he had been baptized seven years earlier, he had wished for a way to break into what he perceived as the spiritual hierarchy. This calling, though, was more than he ever imagined.

"Do you need a little more time to think about this, Brother Taylor?" President Ueda cut into Ben's reverie.

"No, sir. I...I want to do this. It's just that...I hope I won't be a disappointment to you."

The prophet chuckled. "You can write, can't you?"

"Yes, sir, under normal circumstances. But when I have to describe the size and texture of ten foot high beasts with eight foot wing spans, my pen may fail me."

This comment brought a hearty round of laughter from the Brethren.

"You'll do nicely," President Ueda said, still laughing. "Now one more matter. Soon there will be other plates in our hands, and we'll probably want to call on your translating skills, too."

Ben nodded eagerly.

"And when you're not doing either of those two things, would you please continue your translation of the Tibetan plates?"

"No problem, sir."

"Good. Now, Ben, we'll set you apart later in the week. We'd like to have your wife with you, if you can manage that."

"She'll be delighted, I'm sure." Ben stood, wobbly and heady, as he made his way around the table shaking hands. When he came to John the Beloved, the apostle took hold of both of Ben's hands between his warm ones and said, "You underestimate yourself, Ben Taylor. The Lord never makes mistakes, and He wants you in this job."

A thrill flooded through the scribe's body, and tears welled up in his eyes. The apostle spoke just the words he needed to hear.

Ben's hands were so moist he couldn't turn the door knob on the conference room as he exited. He had to surreptitiously pull out part of his white shirt and use it to get the door open.

As the translator finally accomplished his leave-taking, he was surprised to see Alex sitting in the hall on the hard chair. "Al, what are you doing here?"

"Wish I knew. I've been a member for less than a year. Do you think they're going to excommunicate me?" he asked half-seriously.

Ben was saddened to see the dark circles around his friend's eyes. He had heard of Moira's disappearance but decided not to bring it up. "Nah, they're not going to do anything like that. They've heard what a pro you've become at changing diapers, and they want you to head the diaper detail!"

Ben gave Alex a friendly tap on the arm as he walked down the hall to his little office on the second floor. A colossal grin was plastered across his face. The words, "The Lord never makes mistakes," echoed in his ears.

The newly appointed scribe sat down at a large oak desk, removed a key from his shirt pocket, opened a lower drawer, and removed a metal box he used to store the Tibetan plates. Carefully lifting them out by the red and yellow silk cloth they lay in, Ben slid eleven plates off the top of the forty plates and held the twelfth to the light. "What do you have to tell us, little one?" He was far from becoming numb to the experience of holding four-thousand-year-old plates.

Meanwhile, Alex sat down with the spiritual leaders of the planet to what he imagined would be his "Inquisition." He sat ramrod straight, answering questions about his conversion, his faith in the Lord and his coming—answers he carefully worded to be as truthful as possible.

"Well, good," the prophet said, after a half hour's interview. He sat back and folded his hands across his midriff. "We wanted to meet you and get a feel for your spiritual mettle, Brother Dubik, because we have an assignment in mind that will require your complete devotion to the Lord and his gospel."

Alex sat quietly, all his senses alert, taking in every detail of the men's faces, even the light playing on the white robe of the ancient apostle.

"We'd like you to head a team of artists and artisans to work on the temple complex. The work will entail stained glass work, several sculptures, plus consulting on the final architectural designs." The prophet looked to Alex whose face turned totally white. "We will, of course, want your artistic contributions, not just your administrative input."

Alex's mouth fell open. *What? No excommunication? But they don't know about Moira,* he thought. *They won't want me when they find out I can't control my wife.*

John, using his telepathic ability, comforted Alex by saying, "We are, of course, all concerned about your lovely wife, Brother Dubik, but her choices have no bearing on this calling."

Blushing with embarrassment at being such an easy read, the nervous sculptor leaned forward and placed his sensitive, yet calloused hands on the table. He played with a large silver and turquoise ring on his finger that he had made.

"You may or may not know we have had the layout for this temple complex since Joseph Smith's time," the prophet said, "but there are details like elevators and cafeterias that need to be put into place. We, of course, want this project to be as aesthetically pleasing as possible."

Alex nodded vigorously, his mind already flooded with ideas for sculptures.

"You'll be given a generous budget, of course, and the latitude to decide whose work you want to include."

Alex still had not vocalized his feelings.

"I take it, then, you will agree to lend your talents to this cause?" President Ueda asked tentatively.

"Oh, yes, sir, with all my heart, I will." Alex managed to find his voice.

"Good," said the prophet who stood and offered his hand. When Alex took the small, cold hand in his large one, he thought back nearly thirty years when he was traveling through Asia, living in bleak rooms, wrestling with suicide. He remembered going to the Zen monastery, Ryoanji, and staring out at the Zen rock garden. Nothing moved there–ever. Now in this Japanese prophet's presence, he felt the same solidity.

"I was in Japan after the Vietnamese war," Alex said.

"Oh? Where were you?" Ueda asked, surprised.

"At Ryoanji."

The prophet's face brightened. "The rock garden! Can you bring some of that simplicity to your work?"

"Sir, I will try." Alex bowed slightly. "There are, however, a thousand years of meditative serenity which have produced the aesthetics at that spot."

"That's perfect, isn't it?" The church president put his hand over his heart. "We need to represent the thousand years of peace to come."

The two men smiled at each other; each finding in the other

a bright, creative intellect.

Then, just as Ben had done, Alex made his way around the room shaking hands with each apostle. The Brethren stood to take a short break, so Alex stopped to talk with John the Beloved. Although he had been introduced to John as he came in the room, the sculptor couldn't quite comprehend what a translated being really was. When the apostle John said, "We've had our eye on you for some time," Alex smiled and dismissed the comment as metaphorical.

"No, Brother Dubik, I can see you don't understand what I've just said," John said, placing his hand on Alex's arm. The apostle's touch felt warm, like a heating pad, slowly radiating out into Alex's whole arm. He was buoyed up by the sensation. In fact, he'd never felt anything quite like the energy that now surged through him—never in his long and adventurous life.

"The Lord has been aware of your creative labors and your attempts to understand him through them." John looked deeply into the sculptor's face, and Alex's breath began to fade away. He suddenly found himself suspended in a state of ecstasy.

He thought back to all the Christ-like figures he had worked on—statues whose features radiated dignity in the midst of grief. One award-winning triptych depicted a small, muscular Adonis crowned by light, flanked on one side by a male figure in rapture and, on the other side, a man sinking down in despair.

"I've tried for a long time to understand the paradoxical nature of Christ's life. And man's, for that matter," Alex said, certain John would understand exactly what he meant.

"Even after He was gone and I had been witness to all the miracles and tragedy of his death," John said in a low tone meant only for Alex, "it took me a very long time to begin to grasp how God could become incarnate and yet be loathed and despised as our Master was."

For just a moment, Alex stopped to absorb the fact that John was well over two thousand years old and was speaking not about an historical incident but an autobiographical one. It had been a while since Alex had been genuinely surprised. The last time was when Moira was miraculously healed from miscarrying.

"I try to have my work include His triumph over duality," the sculptor managed to say.

John broke into a grin, tapping lightly on Alex's arm. "I think you'll do very well in this calling, Brother Alex."

"I must admit it feels like something I've been preparing for all of my life."

"The Lord uses all the talent, known and hidden, from those who will follow Him," John said, circling the table and escorting Alex to the door.

Moira's strong and beautiful face appeared before Alex's gaze, and he sighed.

"Soon your sorrow will turn to joy," John said in a warm, fatherly tone. "I assure you, your good wife will return in a very short time."

The artist blushed and thought, *Gotta tell Grace! Gotta tell her!* And, as he shut the door, he heard John's voice lower in earnest as he addressed the Brethren who had regathered to conduct business, "The Anti-Christ is on the move..."

Indeed he was. Among other things, Lu Han now had a fanatic follower nestled in the bosom of the New Jerusalem. That afternoon, while Nate was working at the church headquarters, Laurie wasted no time in gathering her eight children around her on the grass outside the house being remodeled on Orchard Lane. Only Ned was missing—he had been called on a welfare mission with a construction crew patching up homes in the area.

Spread out on the lawn was a large red-and-white checkered tablecloth covered with paper plates, cups and napkins. She had prepared some of the children's favorites with limited food resources: tuna casserole, potato salad, three-bean salad and red Jello with canned fruit cocktail. When everyone had filled their plates and were eating contently, Laurie began talking to them in hushed conspiratorial tones. "Children, I want to tell you something very special. Only you mustn't tell anyone just yet."

Andrew, Cristina and Cannon looked at each other. Having

been away from their mother for a year, they viewed her with a bit of suspicion. Even though Nate had not said anything to them directly, they had overheard their father in discussions with his ex-in-laws and realized their mother might have some psychological problems.

Laurie looked around the circle at all the faces of her children and glowed. *How wonderful it is to know that they will be taken when he comes for me. All directly into heaven.* She sighed in delight.

"What, Mom?"

"Oh, darlings, the lord has come to the earth. He is already here."

A gasp rose up from the group. They began talking rapidly among themselves. "What does *that* mean?" Cannon asked in a slightly antagonistic voice.

She started dishing out strawberry Jello topped by miniature marshmallows and said, "It means that he will be taking us away, into heaven, much sooner than we thought. I know you're ready. You're all such spiritual children."

While the younger children clapped their hands in delight, the older ones frowned.

"He has come to me," Laurie whispered and leaned forward, looking at each child in the eye. "And he has told me that I am to be his mouthpiece until he comes to Missouri. I wanted you to be the first to know." She sat back with a proud expression on her face.

"What about Grandpa? Isn't he an apostle of Jesus," asked Holden, the youngest.

"I thought he was one of the Lord's mouthpieces," Cristina said with a snarl in her voice.

"Sweethearts," said Laurie with extra sugar in her voice, "Of course, Grandpa is His apostle. It's just that He comes to women first. Just like in the Bible." She pulled Holden to her and ruffled his hair. "It won't be long now, my darlings, and I wanted you to be the first to know."

"Oh, good, I think," Cannon said sarcastically.

Laurie let the remark go. She was letting a lot go. She reached up and touched the slightly raised red spot between her eyebrows—just to make sure "he" had visited her last night. "Go on, you guys. Finish up. It's getting dark." She wanted time to sit back and remember Lu Han's visit.

She had been sleeping in an old fold-out bed with her daughter, Missy, at her parent's house. As she started to fall asleep, a smell, somewhat like gardenia, began to waft through the room. She sat up and sniffed the air. The aroma was as intoxicating as it was beautiful. Not knowing where it came from, she first smelled the sheets, then her nightgown. *Did Mother have some new kind of fabric softener?* she wondered.

Agitated, Laurie lifted the covers on Missy's side of the bed and sniffed at her sheets and nightgown. That was not the source. So she sat back and quieted herself. Maybe this is supernatural, she thought, so she decided to try and meditate.

Leaning back against the couch with a gold fleur-de-leis pattern, she folded her legs crosslegged and placed her hands on her thighs, palms up. The minute she closed her eyes, a vision of an iridescent blue pearl appeared. She gasped aloud, then quickly put her hand over her mouth.

"What is this?" she whispered as the inner vision continued. "It's so beautiful!" Slowly she became aware of the sound of waves hitting a shoreline—occasionally crashing, sometimes hissing. "Not in Missouri." She held back a laugh. "We've got a lot going on, but not ocean waves."

"It's got to be him! Teaching me about meditation," she said as she clutched her heart. "O, divine one, come."

From over her left shoulder came the loud roar of a lion. She jumped up in spite of the fact that she knew a solid wall lay behind her. Missy struggled to wake. "Shh, honey, it's okay. Go back to sleep," Laurie said, trying to be calm.

In a moment, the quiet breathing of her daughter signaled to Laurie the coast was clear, so she called out quietly, "O lion of Judah, come to me."

And then, there in a shimmering light at the end of the bed

stood the alluring full figure of a Eurasian man, his arms outstretched–not the ten inch miniature that she had seen before.

Laurie struggled to free herself from the bedcovers and move toward the figure. "I come to thee, my lord," she half-sobbed. When she reached the end of the bed, the figure floated above her and to the right, so she fell to her knees in supplication.

What happened next was unclear to Laurie, because it happened so quickly, but there was a flash of light, an intense burning sensation filled her brow, and then he was gone.

When she reached to feel her head, there was raised bump between her eyebrows. Puzzled, Laurie searched for a meaning for the sign. "I remember now!" she said excitedly. "The red mark for Hindu women means fidelity."

"I will always be faithful, my lord," she whispered. An erotic shiver snaked through her body. "Always!"

Returning to the bed, she lay quietly in the dark next to her daughter. Her body felt lighter, almost as if she could fly.

Missy, a rambunctious eleven-year-old, couldn't wait for the evening to come, when Laurie would return to Orchard Lane and Ned would come back from his work.

She waited until Nate had gone to sleep, then she climbed out of the tent she shared with Cristina and crawled over to the boys' tent.

"Ned–you guys–you've got to hear what I heard last night," the eleven-year-old called out.

"Go to sleep, Missy," Ned complained. "I'm really tired. I've been tearing out walls all day."

"Neddy, it's important!" she insisted.

The sleepy-eyed construction worker stuck his head out of the tent. "Oh, okay. Your place or ours?"

"Yours. Cristina, come on!" Missy whispered loudly to her sister, gesturing in the direction of the boys' tent.

After all the group had squeezed in (the boys being over six feet tall), Missy began. "Neddy, did you hear what Mom told us this afternoon?"

"Yes," Ned said and hung his head a little. "Sounds pretty strange to me. I'm sure Grandpa would know if Christ were here. Besides these things are very sacred. People don't just announce them to their kids at a picnic."

"I felt sick," said Andrew emphatically, the 16-year-old who looked like his mother. "In fact, *I* couldn't eat." That brought snickers from the others. Andrew was going through a growth spurt, and they had accused him of eating tin cans along with the neighborhood goat.

"It was just the way she talked," Cannon chimed in. "Like she had some inside information that no one else had."

"What's gotten into Mom?" Cristina cried out. "I thought everything was gonna be okay once she got here."

"Will you guys stop?" Missy said frustrated. She put up a hand. "You never let me talk. And I have something important to report."

"Sorry, kid," Ned said. "You have the floor."

"Okay," she sighed. "You know I slept with the little kids back at Grandpa's house last night?"

"Yes."

"Well, I had to sleep with Mom. And I'm sleeping along, when all of sudden I wake up and she's sniffing the covers, then she's sniffing my nightgown!"

"Is she asleep?"

"No!"

"Ooo, weird," Cristina said. "That is really gross!"

"Anyway, then she starts doing some yoga and says in this icky voice (Missy now speaks in falsetto), 'Oh, lion of Judah, I come to thee,' and then..." The group broke into laughter.

"Shh, guys, don't wake Dad," Ned said. "I've got to hear what happened!"

Missy moved to the center of the tent and began punctuating her story with grand gestures. "Now she's crawling on the floor to the bottom of the bed, looks up in the air and says, 'I come to thee.'"

"Barf!" Cannon said, wrinkling his nose in disgust.

"She's really gone over the edge!" Cristina said.

Ned sat quietly. Then he pounded his fist on the ground, struggled to get up, and pulled back the tent flap.

"Ned, where are you going?" Missy asked in a worried tone.

"I'm going to tell Dad," Ned said as he stood up in the strange, aurora borealis-lit night. "She doesn't want to marry him. She's just using him!"

The kids sat frozen as they listened to Ned as he woke their father. They had knots in their stomachs, knowing they had started something that would probably end up being hard on everyone. But Missy sat there with her arms folded across her chest. The hatred she had felt for her mother in the past filled her heart again.

"She deserves it," she whispered to herself.

Nate lay resting on one elbow as his eldest relayed to him what had happened in the afternoon and Missy's version of Lu Han's visitation. The exhausted father was grateful for the dark of the tent to hide the rage that reddened his face.

"How can you marry her again?" Ned asked with anguish in his voice.

"I thought all this was too good to be true," Nate said, as he struggled to get into his pants.

"Where are you going? It's the middle of the night, Dad," Ned said, half-pleading.

"To strangle that woman!" Nate said with such malevolence in his voice, it frightened Ned. After his father had driven off at a high speed, Ned slowly walked back to the boys' tent. None of the Winders said anything as he pushed back the tent flap. Neither did he. The five sat and stared for some time before the girls wandered back to their tent.

Nate was at Laurie's window at the back of the Whitmer's house faster than he'd ever driven that route. Livid, he pounded several times on the window frame. Finally a dishevelled Laurie peeked through the curtains.

"What, Nate?" she whispered loudly.

"Get out here!" The glow from the moonlight, heightened by the northern lights, allowed Laurie to see the white rage that burned across Nate's face.

Laurie began to shake as she slipped on her pink bathrobe and slippers. She pushed back the back screen door carefully and looked for her ex-husband, but he wasn't there, so she felt her way along the sidewalk on the kitchen side of the house, brushing back the hedge's freshly-budded branches.

She stepped out onto the front lawn. There he stood near the car, looking like a black panther ready to pounce. She hesitated. He took several long strides across the lawn and grabbed her arm. "Ow! That hurts, Nate," she said in a whine.

Nate drove at the same reckless speed down the hill and out toward the town of Liberty on Highway 291. He said nothing. The air between them was frigid. Finally he pulled off the road near a large, newly-plowed field.

"Laurie, just what do you think you're doing?" Nate demanded, shoving the gear into park and pulling on the hand brake. "Just what in the..."

"I *really* don't know what you're so upset about," Laurie said, faking equanimity.

"Telling the children that Christ has come and you are his special confidante."

"They misunderstood..."

"I don't think so."

Nate jerked open the car door and walked around back. Laurie watched him nervously in the rear view mirror. She locked her door. He quickly pulled out the keys and opened it. He jerked her out, hard. He squeezed her arm so hard it left bruises.

Murder raging through his mind, Nate dragged Laurie to the side of the road and threw her down.

"I will kill you, you, you bitch, and I will be justified!"

Laurie huddled in a ball and threw one arm over her face, expecting a blow. Nate doubled up his fist and waved it in her face. "Don't you EVER say...," Nate said, sputtering, "even one more word about this to our children. NEVER! Is that clear?"

Laurie was now crying, terrified. She had never seen Nate act like this in all their eighteen years together. Her cup had always been filled with contempt for him. Laurie had been furious all their married life that Nate constantly caved in–to her, to creditors, to everyone. And so, both to punish and awaken him, she went in after him, time after time, trying to rattle his cage, to make him more aggressive. During arguments, she would mercilessly press her point again and again. By the end of their marriage, he was hollow-eyed and run down.

But this was a Nate she hadn't counted on. She had thought she could just move back into his life and create another comfortable niche, not end up murdered by the side of some anonymous road in the back woods of Missouri.

She cried out to Lu Han for help, but none came.

"And for our marriage, in case you haven't guessed, it's off!" Nate shouted right in her face. "You've haven't changed, Laurie. Your father warned me about you before we got married."

Laurie lay perfectly still.

Nate's voice choked as he asked in a softer voice, "Laurie, how could you...how could you get so far off base?"

She wept quietly.

Then he changed his tone and said bitterly, "And don't you go to your father and tell him I've beaten you or something. He's at the end of his rope with you already, even before this." He spit out the 'this.'

Whimpering.

"Get in the car! Go!"

Eyes wild, she scrambled to her feet.

"I ought to leave you out here! Let you find your own way home."

Back at her parents' house, she threw open the car door to run away. "I'm going to tell your father everything tomorrow, Laurie, everything!" he shouted at her retreating figure. "So think of your lies now."

The teenage Winder children awakened to the sound of their

dad's car returning, this time more slowly. They had lain awake, feeling guilty for their parents' second break-up–especially Ned. He loved his mother, had missed her during her year-long absence, and felt vaguely guilty for her deviance. But he had the presence of mind to pray. The Spirit filled him with the knowledge that he had done the correct thing, no matter how difficult. And he felt comforted.

As soon as the children were fed the next morning, Laurie rushed out of the house and down to Kayleen's modest home.

"What should I do about Nate? He just changed into a monster over night, for no reason." Laurie was rehearsing for her "audience" with her father. Under different circumstances, she would have made quite a good actress.

"This is a test of your loyalty to Master Lu. It always happens this way." Kayleen pulled down the living room shade as she had the day before. "Joseph Smith. Think of what he went through to have his first vision."

Laurie's eyes were nearly swollen shut from last night's crying jag. "What would the lord want me to do now?"

"Stay right here. Hold your ground. Prepare the people for his coming," said her long-time friend.

On the couch where she sat in jeans and a dirty T-shirt, Laurie held her head in her hands and let out a moan. Kayleen rushed to her side and wrapped an arm around her back. After a couple of moments of silence, Laurie lifted her head and said, "You're right. Just because Nate hates me, doesn't mean... Thanks, Kayleen! It's great to have someone who understands."

"Understand? I'm in awe," Kayleen exuded. "You must be very special for this to happen."

Laurie smiled and rose regally from the brown-stained couch.

"I know what!" Kayleen exclaimed. "Let's start an ashram."

"No," Laurie cut her off sharply. "Nothing that obvious. No buildings. I'm going to follow orders and do what the Master asked me to do. In the meantime I've got to deal with my parents."

Kayleen stood in the doorway and waved a long time at the retreating figure. She was happy, then, to close the door and return to her seemingly normal world with husband and children demanding breakfast. *It must be hard being a spiritual pioneer,* she thought.

CHAPTER FIFTEEN

*"...God hath set his hand and seal to change
the times and seasons, and to blind their minds,
that they may not understand his marvelous workings;
...that he may take them in their own craftiness."*
D&C 121:12

Master Lu spent six weeks working with Dmitri Gornstein in the Tibetan Highlands–using Sufi dance to induce ecstatic states in the Russian. When Gornstein arrived, he had been tight, withdrawn and suspicious, but the dance, plus long meditation sessions, opened him to joyous experiences he never dreamt possible. The Chinese adept's plan was to clean out the "dross," as he called it, so that he could have direct and clear telepathic communication with his disciple when he returned to Iran.

Drawing from the best of three of the major spiritual traditions (all of which he had mastered), Lu led the Russian sceptic into singular experiences, such as feeling weightless, hearing exquisite music where there was no outside source, and witnessing horrific visions of demons as he descended into the hell of his inner mind. Lu taught Gornstein that all that he experienced was illusory. And, when the Russian came through each lesson, he found the calm presence of his teacher...always many steps ahead of him.

By the time they parted, Lu could have asked Gornstein to do anything for him, even commit suicide, and he would have willingly complied, so sure was he that the Chinese emperor-to-be was god incarnate.

Between meditation sessions, the men discussed plans to put into place the underpinnings of a world government with the Russian zealot as its nominal head, but with Han as the real power behind the throne. They decided to form European and Asian alliances, reestablish UWEN connections and capitalize on the Islamic hatred for Christians and Jews. Added to all of this in their colossally Machiavellian plans was the massive power and size of the Chinese army. Genghis Khan would have gasped in admiration.

Gornstein invited surviving members of the UWEN ruling body to join "his" staff. One of them, Hazrat Patel, had been the commander of UWEN forces when they dropped the first nuclear bomb on Chinese troops, forcing them to retreat along the Bering Strait. Although it didn't make sense that Lu Han would want Patel, the Chinese master knew the Pakistani general's heart well, knew Patel had been hollowed out with ambition and could be manipulated to great advantage.

Once back in Iran, Gornstein set the plans in motion to form the New World Order. But first, Lu and Gornstein decided to deal Israel one last deadly blow before withdrawing their largely Shiite army back to Turkey.

Gornstein called General Patel into headquarters. "General, have a seat. May I offer you a cigarette?"

Hazrat graciously accepted, all the while scrutinizing Gornstein's face. The commander looked remarkably different from the last time he had seen him, Patel thought, but he couldn't figure how. Maybe the vacation was very relaxing, he decided. The sikh reached up and readjusted his red turban by tucking it in at the back of his neck. Dmitri searched through the desk drawer for a lighter.

"We're going to attack Israel," the Russian commander-in-chief announced in a matter-of-fact tone as the two took long drags off the Turkish cigarettes.

"What!?" Hazrat asked, propelling himself forward in the heavy desk chair. "Have you lost your mind, sir?" Then regaining his composure and sense of protocol, he quickly added, "No offense. I am very sorry." He put his palms together and bowed slightly. "It's just that, sir, the Israelis have the most sophisticated computer defense ever invented."

"I have not been vacationing, as has been reported. I have been conferencing with some of the best military strategists in the world, and we have put together a plan that we are certain will succeed."

"Yes, sir. Again my apologies." Patel waited to see what Gornstein, who leaned back against the beige stucco wall in a swivel chair, would say next.

"You familiar with the prophet Ezekiel in Jewish scriptures?" Gornstein asked.

"Not really," Patel admitted.

"Without going into detail, let me say that his prophesies–yes...the prophecies of a Jew," Gornstein said, raising a peremptory hand to cut off Patel's inevitable objection, "his prophecies have given us the framework of what we intend to do."

Hazrat moved his chair forward, placed his hands on the desk and began twirling the ring on his left little finger.

Gornstein closed his eyes and began quoting Ezekiel by heart, (something his master insisted on) ..."thou shalt descend and come like a storm, thou shalt be like a cloud to cover the land, thou, and all thy bands, and many people with thee."

"Like a storm? Does he mean foot soldiers?" Patel asked with some scepticism, trying to ascertain whether this man who sat across the table was barking mad or a military genius. Had he perhaps found the key to destroying his most despised enemies, the Jews–a key that had evaded the Arab grasp in the sixty or so years since Israel had recovered Palestine.

Ignoring the question, Gornstein continued, "...and thou shalt come from thy place out of the north parts, thou, and many people with thee, all of them riding upon horses, a great company and a mighty army."

Patel sighed and silently drummed his fingers on his legs.

"And do you know who has been prophesied will help us?" Dmitri asked enthusiastically

Hazrat shook his head.

"Russia, France, England, Ethiopia, Libya and Iran."

"Do *they* know that?" the Pakistani asked slight but unmistakable sarcasm in his voice.

"Indeed they do. You see, we told them, *showed* them, *cajoled* them...." Gornstein's voice trailed off into a whisper of smug self-satisfaction.

"But how can we fight against such Israeli technology? With the Palestinians out of Israel and into the Sinai, the Israelis can instantly track the movements of any stranger." Agitated, Patel rose and walked the room. "Besides all the regular tracking devices, they have video-equipped drones, even scouts with mini-cams," Patel said vehemently.

Gesturing to Hazrat to sit down, the Russian calmly continued, "The Israelis are relaxed at this point. They believe they can now live in peace. Whenever anyone relaxes and lets his guard down, there is a way to defeat him," Gornstein grandly announced as if he were addressing an assemblage of dignitaries. "And what they least expect is a full-out frontal assault by at least 50,000 foot soldiers, all willing to die for Allah..."

"... and go straight to heaven," Patel finished the sentence, a smile slowly stretching out beyond his moustache. "Very interesting, Commander. Technology always relies on the men who run it. It's true the Jews are geared for a technological war. So what is needed here is an old-fashioned 'knife fight!' Brilliant, sir!"

The next week, Gornstein arranged to plant eleven mobile missile launch pads aboard a cargo ship called the Maltese, headed for Cyprus. The ship, coming from Russia, claimed its cargo was tractors and cars for Egypt. The Turkish troops, who were actually New World Order troops, had been alerted to the sale and pledged to take military action against Cyprus for this obvious aggressive act.

Since Russia-backed Turkey and Iran had been trading partners with Cyprus, this incident gave the Russians an excuse to invade Iran. From there the Chinese jumped in on the side of the Russians. Regions of the United States, England and France, banded together to resist the eastern alliance. That was all it took to bring over 100,000 men to a staging area–right at Israel's door.

Gornstein then sent a respected former UWEN diplomat to Israel to assure the nation that no one expected them to enter into the fray, and, of course, there were no plans to invade Israel—a promise to which the Israelis turned a jaundiced but indifferent eye.

"There's nothing you can do to us anyway," the Israeli prime minister announced. "We are God's chosen people. He has decreed that we shall always defeat our enemies and live in peace in our appointed land."

When Vladimir Cosivich, Gornstein's envoy to Israel, reported these words to him and Patel, all three burst into laughter. Indeed, Patel laughed until tears came to his eyes. Then, walking the length of Gornstein's office with a swagger stick under his left arm, he spit out, "Those filthy infidels. What a surprise we have in store for them!"

"The military advisors I consult are very pleased," said Gornstein, not revealing the sacred identity of Lu Han to this Pakistani functionary whom he secretly held in contempt. "Of course, we make this situation seem real. We need to have a good-sized skirmish between Turkey and Cyprus—one that can be played out on ITN."

"Yes, sir!" Patel saluted smartly and turned to leave.

"Haz," Gornstein beamed. "Make it good."

"That's what you hired me for, isn't it?"

The two snorted.

Two hours later, Patel was riding in an open Jeep toward troop headquarters

The very next day, thousands of men died in a desert conflagration involving hand-held missile launchers, humvees and M-1 tanks. An audience of at least a billion people watched the exciting show on ITN—one of the first live coverages since world-wide television had been reinstituted some months earlier.

The fierce battle raging in the background, ITN reporters interviewed Gornstein, who assured the world that the New World Order would bring this conflict to a peaceful conclusion, as they would in any part of the world that needed their help.

Three days later, instead of coming to the peace table as was announced, Gornstein's troops swarmed across the Israeli borders in waves of tens of thousands, supported by nuclear missiles that were lobbed in such number and force that they overwhelmed the Israeli defense system. The desert's fine dust played havoc with fans and trackballs. The whole sky was so full of electronic communications that no conventional radio messages could get through. Consequently Israeli ground troops couldn't get their orders. So much information avalanched into Israeli computers, they locked up. By the time they had rebooted, Tel Aviv and Jerusalem and every other major city in the country had been overrun.

But the Israelis rallied, pulling out their own nuclear bag of tricks. When the smoke cleared, it was the New World Order that was on the run—not the first invaders to taste the fierceness of Jews.

Before Jewish refugees could return to many of the decimated cities, Israeli troops first swept the area to gather up all the nuclear hardware the invaders had left behind. They buried it, along with anything else that was nuclear "hot," in the valley of Hamon-gog. After seven months of hauling, digging and covering the lethal cache, they sealed off the area, announcing that no one would be allowed in for at least seven years.

The Israelis were responding as Lu Han expected and planned. In fact, even before the Jews had started burying the vestigial nuclear hardware, Han had the next plan well off the drawing board. He telepathically directed Gornstein to announce on world-wide television that the NWO would never allow another war. A capitol of peace would be established in Istanbul, he announced, where a new world order would guarantee prosperity and harmony for all.

Gornstein went on to announce that the capitol, Istanbul, was to be renamed Constantinople as it had been in 330 A.D., when the emperor Constantine declared it the capital of the Holy Christian Roman Empire. This was part of Han's strategy to pacify the Christian community, which, somewhat surprisingly, had great respect for the new Moslem-dominated government. The irony was, of course, that Christians were, in fact, the secret target of this predominately Islamic government.

The NWO central headquarters were to be in the Hagia Sophia, a sixth century basilica (the majority of which was still standing after many centuries) and masterpiece of Byzantine architecture. It was world-famous for its lavishly decorated interior and placement of high windows around the top of the dome in such a way that one's entrance to the basilica produced the ethereal sensation of being lifted into light, even into heaven. Now it would serve as the administrative and electronic center of the NWO's world-wide net.

Constantinople was located on the Golden Horn, the only city in the world situated on two continents–Europe and Asia–which were linked by a long suspension bridge. Turkey's chief seaport, it was famous for its rugs, bazaars, cigarettes, poppy fields–and an ethnically diverse population susceptible to the teachings of a man who could demonstrate he embraced all religions.

In fact, the first community of worshipers of the lord Lu Han opened its doors here in the capitol city to ITN coverage, scarcely a month after Israel was invaded. Within six months, every large city in the world had congregations of worshipers. Potential converts were shown exquisitely and expensively produced videos that showed Lu healing the sick, materializing precious items from thin air–even raising the dead.

Lu Han was especially interested in the symbolism of using Constantinople as the world capitol The first Christian emperor, Constantine, had had a vision there in which he claimed to see the words: *In hoc signo vinces*, "In this sign, thou shalt conquer," inscribed above the sun. Lu concluded that this place would do nicely for a new sign and miracle–*his sign*, one in which he would conquer the world.

But it was a world that was literally going to hell: more and more violent solar storms upset communications and weather patterns; earthquakes of almost unimaginable intensity rocked all parts of the world (except Zion); freak weather threatened crops with either too little or too much water; and global warming continued to play havoc with millions of years of natural evolution.

Besides the connection with Gornstein, Lu Han was able to telepathically track nearly anyone on earth, if he so desired. The only people not susceptible to his probing were those who held the Melchizedek Priesthood or those who were protected by it. The Holy Spirit's influence was so strong Han could not penetrate Latter-day Saint thought. However, someone like Laurie Winder, who attracted lower energies, was easy prey.

What the Sufi master told Laurie in her first visitation was true: He *was* scanning the Latter-day Saint frequency. He was growing more and more curious about this small group of people whose movements he could neither anticipate nor discern. Although he was a master of both Indian and Chinese astrology and could usually anticipate with great accuracy any person's decisions based on their cyclical inner conflicts, this was not true of the Mormons. It seemed to him they didn't play by the rules. Little did Han understand that his powers were limited to the telestial sphere.

His initial probe of Laurie, that ten-inch-high figure, took very little energy from him while he sat in a meditative state. It was one probe of thousands he shot off into space. In her case, the probe landed on receptive soil and began beaming back pictures to the command center. Lu was so excited to gain a foothold in this enigmatic Mormon community that he began to exert a considerable amount of energy toward Laurie. The next night he appeared to her in full-figure at his seductive best.

Han was delighted to find such a prize right in the center of the previously impenetrable camp. Once Laurie had given herself to him, he could telepathically control her, and she, like Gornstein, would obey. His short term goal was to set up a community of worshipers in Zion as in other cities. He wasn't sure what he wanted long term. He simply knew that as a group they were more powerful than he, and he wanted to discover how that was possible.

But Nate Winder was having none of it. While Laurie was away, he came unannounced to the Whitmer house. Elder Whitmer, balding with a grey fringe and weather-lined face, invited him in and sat on a maroon-and-gold-striped couch with his arms severely folded around his once-athletic frame. His wife Dorothy sat next to him, tightly wrapped in a lavender shawl. The two listened with great distress to their ex-son-in-law as he related the previous night's events. All three had long careworn looks on their faces.

Sitting backward over a kitchen chair, Nate spoke in a barely audible voice. He didn't want his little children to hear what he had to relate.

"...she's a real menace to this society. She's deluded!" he sputtered. "I'm sorry, but I have no plans to marry her now, I assure you."

"This is grave," Elder Whitmer said, reaching for his *Book of Mormon*. His wife sat silent, big tears slipping down her cheeks.

Nate continued in his baritone voice, "I'm sorry that I lost my temper with her. As you know, I've never acted that way before, no matter how she provoked me."

"Oh, we know. We know, Nate," Sister Whitmer said in a reassuring tone. "You've been the very model of restraint."

"I think I lost it because we're here now, in Zion. And I can't bear to think...."

Elder Whitmer opened the scriptures to Second Nephi and lifted his hand to interrupt, "I'm trying to remember how long Father Lehi labored with his two sons, Laman and Lemuel." He knew the answer, of course, but he felt better just resting his eyes on the passages describing how the ancient patriarch had struggled so much with his own recalcitrant sons.

"I don't know exactly how long Lehi's patience lasted, sir, but I'm finished with her!" Nate rose half out of the kitchen chair. "She can't be teaching these things to the children–or anyone for that matter!"

"No, she can't, son," Elder Whitmer said flatly. "You aren't responsible. It's mine to deal with from here."

Nate exhaled and let his shoulders fall. A few seconds passed, then he said, "The house is nearly done. I'll take all the kids off your hands when it is."

"Let's not talk about that now," said Sister Whitmer who rose and crossed the room to Nate. The wizened woman squeezed his arm and joined him as he headed for the front door.

Her husband joined her. Nate extended his hand to the apostle. "Thank you, both. Thank you for understanding."

As she watched the tall, lanky man walk down the steps, Sister Whitmer's head was swimming with the implications of this new marital breakup. *Now what will Laurie do?* she wondered wearily. It had already fallen on her 78-year-old shoulders to care for the couple's four young children for nearly two years. She was tired.

All the way back to her parents', Laurie was running over and over in her mind the story of what had happened on the road to Liberty. By the time she reached the house, she had rehearsed her version of the story so many times, she believed it. She sat in the car out front for a few more moments.

"He's a liar–he's out of control. I don't know what got into him. The children did not tell you the whole truth–they misunderstood me." She pulled over the rear view mirror, looked at her puffy eyes and daubed at them. Quite unexpectedly, a stuttering sob rose up from her solar plexus. She grabbed her stomach and cried out, "I just want someone to hold me, someone to cherish me." Then she forced herself out of the car and up the stairs to the house, all the while working herself up into a kind of victim's hysteria.

But one look at her father's face told her Nate had beaten her to the punch. She became panicky, almost disoriented.

"Hi, Daddy," she said in a high-pitched, girlish voice.

"Come see me in the dining room," he said without returning her greeting. He turned and strode very purposively down the hall. Laurie followed as far back as she dared.

Her father had already pulled up a dining room chair next to his at the end of the long, dark table when she entered the room. "Sit down, please." He was stiff, formal.

Laurie felt like she was going to throw up. She was terrified he would not believe her, not because she was afraid of being punished, but that he would then become her enemy. *Please, lord, not my own father!* she thought. *Not this as a test.*

"Nate has been here this morning," he began.

"Daddy, I..."

"Let me speak, Laurie. Do you know what heresy is?"

"Ah...it's when you're deliberately not telling the truth about a religious matter, I think," she said in almost an off-handed way, like the issue had never come up for her.

The apostle felt his stomach sink. He was silent for a moment. He looked down at his hands, carefully searching for the right words.

When he looked up, he hardly recognized his own daughter. Her eyes were hooded, almost reptilian.

Laurie stared into her father's face and saw the expression she had come to recognize as "the apostle look." He wasn't her father any more, but an apostle of the Lord Jesus Christ. "I don't know where you've come up with the idea that the Lord has come and you are his spokesperson here in Zion...." It was difficult for him even to speak those words.

She opened her mouth, but he looked so sharply at her, she shut it again.

"...but you do NOT know the truth. Is that clear?" He was now right in her face. His was dark red with repressed rage.

Laurie involuntarily put her hands to her ears. Through the muffled sounds, she could still hear him say, "You must not teach that blasphemy to your children or anyone else, or you will be excommunicated and sent away–out of Zion."

She took her hands from her ears and looked hard at her father. *He doesn't know!* Tears sprang to her eyes. *I believed him all these years, and he doesn't know what I know!*

Laurie felt herself go dead inside.

"Do you understand?"

"Yes," she said woodenly. She felt detached from her body.

The interview didn't last much longer. When he left the room, she sat staring at dust motes in a sunbeam that streamed onto the well-worn wooden floor. After a time, she rose and sat out on the steps to watch as her two youngest played on rusty swings in the back yard. The only thought that crossed her mind was, *I wonder what "he's" doing right now.*

She felt utterly alone. This must be Gethsemane, she thought bleakly. She wrapped her thin arms around her knees and put her chin down on them. Slowly an idea began to form and fill her. *I'll go to "him." That's what I'll do. Then he'll hold me and comfort me.*

Amid the high-pitched squeals of the playing children, Laurie decided that when she was contacted again by Lu Han, she'd ask to be carried to his holy side.

Another woman, desperate and alone, stared out at the frothy wake of the ship, *Ulysses*, which was sailing from Portsmouth, England to Philadelphia. She floated between this reality and an altered consciousness trying to cope with the extreme trouble in which she found herself. Mary Margaret O'Boyle was a handsome woman with striking blue eyes framed by dark eyelashes. The moonlight on her face gave it a look of arresting luminosity. Her skin was ivory; light blue veins crossed her temples. She had naturally red lips that complemented her dark red hair.

As the Irish woman turned to meander further down the deck, she murmured under her breath, "My Lord Jesus, have mercy on me." (Once she had spent two months saying, "My Lord Jesus..." a thousand times a day. When asked what she was muttering about, she said she wanted to pray without ceasing as Paul had commanded.) Now the repetition of the phrase was automatic and comforting. After weeks of waiting, she and her three girls were finally headed for Zion on terrifying seas.

This wasn't Friday or she would be "taken ill," in bed, slightly bleeding from the same places on her body as Christ's when he was crucified. Many Catholic saints in history had manifested this phenomenon, known as the stigmata. Each Friday for a number of years, Mary Margaret had also experienced it, ever since her older, alcoholic husband had been shot by UWEN troops for sedition.

Thoughts played in her disturbed mind in sweet symbols and riddles. *Can I be the Virgin Mary?...I must be if He loves me so...Maybe it's Mother, that's it...she's the Virgin...that makes me His sister... Oh, dear, how can I be His bride then?...Maybe I'm His first cousin, John's sister...No, I know!...I was born of the Virgin Mary after He was taken into heaven.*

Mary Margaret loved this state of mind. She'd wait until the girls had gone to sleep, then relax and let the bliss fill her head. The problem was to keep the negative thoughts out. If she wasn't successful, she'd be lost fighting paranoid fantasies for hours. Last Christmas Eve, she spent two exhausting days in the grip of the petrifying illusion that she was Lucifer, the fallen light.

Gripping the red rusty rail with her long white fingers, she thought back to when she first met the Ryons, her rescuers. She and the girls were on one of the last ferries to cross the North Sea before the murdering and looting that erupted as soon as the UWEN troops withdrew from Ireland. The Ryons had been waiting for a cousin at the dock in Liverpool, England. But the cousin hadn't made it. The couple anxiously searched each face, and when they saw Mary Margaret's and her three dear daughters, they insisted on taking them home.

It was there that Mary Margaret, amidst nearly incomprehensible ramblings, attempted to tell them about her first encounter with the Church. "That morning early, when I was nearing my fifteenth birthday, I ran through the briars, pulled by the face of a passer-by: someone I'd seen before–someone who *knew!* He was a person who didn't want anything; who wasn't hungry for a pitcher of milk or for a biscuit from a tin..."

(Here she paced.) " ...no broken rosary, no Guinness stains, walking down the brae with a blackthorn stick and black satchel."

She clutched her bosom and continued in a sing-song voice as the elderly couple listened, trying to piece together a coherent account.

"'There he is, Ma,' I shouted, '"the one in my dream with the crop of Bibles!' Ma shook her head in disbelief, but I had waves of gooseflesh up my legs in squames."

She paused and sighed dramatically, "I ran to the window with the knockin' on the door frame; Da drove the lads away, but I could see on the one's chest a black tag that read: Elder Winder, Church of Jesus Christ...."

She flashed them her engaging smile and said, "From then on, whenever I went to Mass, after Benediction and during the Exposition of the Blessed Sacrament, I would pray to Jesus for those waves of gooseflesh. And that's when I became aware that Christ is the ocean, forever rising and falling on the world's shore, and that on some foreign shore I'd find that lad and read his Bible, which isn't a Bible at all."

Now she laughed out loud at the memory, but her laugh didn't travel far in the heavy wind off the bow. "My name? Why Elder Winder, maybe it's Mary Magdalene or Mary, the mother...certainly not Mary Margaret O'Boyle from the town of Boyle in the County of Roscommon...laying in each palm of my hand is the grand Crucifixion...I appear to myself a stranger in the looking-glass."

Carefully putting one foot directly in front of the other, she continued her circumambulation of the ship until she found the stairs down to her cabin. "My soul is empty for the want of a periwinkle..." she sighed. The handsome Irish woman quietly opened the cabin door to look in on her three auburn-haired girls: Eilean—tall, slender, serious and sixteen; Molly—tender, maternal, fourteen, with a beautiful heart-shaped face; and Sarah—bouncy, theatrical and the definite baby of the family at age twelve.

"I want to teach them the names of flowers–the blue flowers–after the flax is taken in...." Then she lay down next to the youngest and fell into an exhausted sleep.

The Ryons, a kindly older couple from Brighton, had seen the stigmata, heard the illogical verses, and hoped the Lord would heal her, if they could just get her to Zion. There was, however, slim hope that this lone ship of Saints would reach its destination through the violent seas of a terrible hurricane season. Even if did, the passengers would find themselves caught up in the deadly chaos raging all up and down the East Coast. And, of course, there was the daunting question of just how they would make their way overland if by some miracle they did arrive alive. But they held on to a fervent belief the Lord would intervene.

CHAPTER SIXTEEN

"How else but through a broken heart
May Lord Christ enter in?"
            Oscar Wilde

Ben's eyes followed a worker dressed in blue-jean bib overalls as he filled a wheelbarrow of gray and white rock from a large pile brought in from the quarry and dumped it front of a cement mixer near the temple's outer wall. The worker then returned for another load. The scribe felt guilty that he was not out there physically building Zion but was instead translating obscure texts that didn't seem to contribute to the present good.

He had just finished with the fifteenth Tibetan plate. Although translating wasn't as difficult as it had been in the beginning, Ben still had to rely a great deal on inspiration, because the texts on the plates represented an assortment of different eras with a wide variety of orthographic systems. This plate discussed a mass migration of ten tribes. "...and the Lord and his angels opened a way—the water bridge—where our people could flee...." Try as he might to imagine a water bridge across the Atlantic or one from Israel across the Mediterranean Sea, Ben simply couldn't picture such a thing. He comforted himself with the thought that he might learn more about what was prophesied at the upcoming Sunday fireside where the prophet would speak for the first time since coming to Zion.

Hearing voices in the hall, Ben stood up, stretched, then opened his office door a crack to see Bishop Levine shaking hands with an elderly couple. After the couple descended down the stairs to the lobby, Ben sauntered to Levine's office.

"Got a minute, Bishop?"

"For you, Ben, always. Have a seat." Levine, in an expensive suit and tie, gathered up papers on his desk and placed them in a side drawer.

"You said when we first arrived that we might find time to talk about the upcoming economic structure of Zion," Ben began. "I'm really very curious about it. Is this a good time for such a discussion?"

Levine checked in his appointment book, nodded, leaned back against the fake wood wall and put his hands behind his head. He smiled at Ben, whom he enjoyed, not only because they were both Jewish converts, but because he thought the scribe was a very bright man, able to relieve the tension around the office with his slightly juvenile brand of humor.

"Where to start?" Ben asked.

"Well, how about with the model that the City of Enoch provides," Levine said. "We read in Moses that the Lord called his people Zion, because they were of one heart and one mind, and dwelt in righteousness...."

"...and there was no poor among them," Ben said, anticipating the bishop.

"Right. And one other small matter—the whole city was translated. If we are able to live this law, we will continue to live on this earth after the Millennium is ushered in. If not, we will go to the spirit world, where we work out our salvation in a different way."

"It gets right down to money, doesn't it?" Ben, ever the leftist academic, asked with a touch of sarcasm.

Levine laughed. A highly successful Wall Street broker before the UWEN came into power, he understood very well what it took to relinquish considerable wealth. In fact, before he became the Presiding Bishop, he had managed to store up a considerable fortune in gold in spite of the government crackdown. This he donated to the Church at his calling.

"Many years ago, an apostle wrote a book about what he imagined it would be like to live in the city of Enoch," Levine said. "I remember being impressed with the idea that, although the people had learned to give freely of their affection and esteem, the really hard part was to give of their goods in the same way."

"The perennial challenge!" Ben said, reciting the Socialist motto, 'From each according to his ability, to each according to his need.'"

"Well, in a *sense*," Levine said, alert to Ben's radical reference. "Right now we're working on a Church Welfare System model. But that's because we're in an emergency mode until the population stabilizes here in the next month or two. After that, we'll get on with a market-driven economy."

"With currency?" Ben asked, somewhat deflated.

"Yes, we're minting our own." Levine responded brightly. "We'll trade in gold with the outside world. They won't mind, I'm sure."

Ben put back his head and laughed. He glanced out the window where mostly Hispanic men labored on the outside temple wall. The scribe remembered the prophecy that the Lamanites would be the predominate group to help build up Zion, so he said to the Presiding Bishop, "The Church was really a Third World organization before it was outlawed. I presume that the population of the New Jerusalem will reflect that ethic mixture."

"It looks that way from the figures we're getting from intake facilities. Many more non-whites than whites–probably running two to one right now–predominately Hispanic."

"So after the Church creates a highway infrastructure, sanitation system, postal service, and so on, what will the general features of the economy be?" Ben asked.

"They will be the basic United Order principles: care for the poor through increasing employment; meaningful work; self-reliance; equality; consecration or reinvestment of excess funds; collective self-government; responsibility and morality," Levine replied.

"You practice memorizing that?" Ben joked.

"You guessed it. Quite a mouthful, huh?" Levine said.

"Yeah," Ben shot back, "like a whole bagel with cream cheese and lox."

The Jewish converts chuckled.

"Anyway," Levine continued, "the Church will endow a bank, let's call it the Bank of Zion, with sufficient funds to start up employee-owned cooperatives, governed on a one-person, one-vote basis."

"I see."

"Management will then be elected by a worker assembly and given a multi-year contract, subject to the support of the majority of workers." Levine got up and went to the window where he rested on the white sill.

"Go on," said the balding translator, who had given much thought to the establishment of the United Order.

"The bank will be the central focus of a complex of cooperatives. It will coordinate and mandate compliance with basic rules established by the majority of workers."

"Assuming it is run by righteous men and women."

"Of course, Ben," Levine said, leaning forward and looking intensely into the animated face of his listener. "Of course. But those are precisely the kind of men and women we will have in Zion! And that is what will make all the difference!" The Bishop leaned back and smiled. "In short, the bank will provide strong local autonomy on the operational level with strong central coordination."

"What about the managers who want to become billionaires?"

"In successful models we've studied, no manager may make more than six times the lowest paid worker."

"And what about a social safety net like the Scandinavian countries perfected but the U.S. never managed to master?" Ben asked pointedly—even a little aggressively. "And what about the difference between the deserving and the undeserving poor...between those who can work and don't and those who can't. Does that mean we ask an entire family to leave the protection of Zion, if, say the father doesn't pull his share of the load?"

Ben scarcely took a breath before continuing this barrage of questions. "And another thing—how to rank merit. Should we value the person who puts in the most hours? Or the best educated? Or the most talented? And what about the ill and the elderly?"

"Whoa! Ben," Michael laughed and put up his hand. "Listen,

I'll be sure you're included next time the Brethren get into some of these weighty discussions. But that's all the time I have for this session. Okay?"

Ben left the office grateful that certain members of the church hierarchy had not only asked the questions that he had wrestled with all of his life but were far ahead of him in their answering.

On the way home, Ben bumped into Nate in the church administration parking lot and said, "I hear you're leaving here to go with Elder Dawahoya on a rescue mission to the East Coast."

"You hear correctly."

"Your house finished?"

"Just about."

"And the kids?"

"We're a wee bit nosey, aren't we?"

"Peg made me ask."

"Yeah, sure. No, I've worked it out with Laurie and her parents. They'll be taking care of them in my absence."

"This wouldn't have anything to do with that sweet Irish rose that Grace is tracking for you, would it?"

"Buzz off, creep,"

"Hello! I've struck a nerve."

"Look, Elder Dawahoya asked for volunteers to go to help refugees who are pouring into eastern seaports. Mostly I just need to get out of here. Laurie is...."

"Say no more."

The ranking members of the Intertribal Council sent word they wanted to meet with Joseph Dawahoya. He immediately sent the courier back with an invitation to come to Missouri. The east coast rescue would have to wait. He was thrilled. He had been following the Indian nations' movements which had degenerated into cowboy-and-Indian shootouts reminiscent of the Wild West—only these were done from the back of pickup trucks. "So many dead brothers," he said sadly. "I hate the whole sordid mess."

Moira was one of the twelve members of the council who approached the freshly-created mountain range from the north side of Zion. Her heart hurt–a hurt that alternated with a kind of flu-like ache. She felt so torn. She had really believed she was on an errand for the good of the planet when she left her family. But now she wasn't so certain.

Moira was too proud to hope Alex would come to the valley of Adam-ondi-Ahman with the prophet. She also allowed no image of her son to enter her consciousness.

Grey Eagle, a Sioux in buckskin shirt and pants, his long, greying hair pulled back with a piece of rawhide, stood in an open meadow facing the shorter Hopi elder. "Joseph, thank you for your hospitality," he said, extending his hand.

"You know I would do anything I can," Elder Dawahoya said earnestly, taking Grey Eagle's hand.

"You are well-known for your wisdom."

The Hopi said nothing but nodded in the direction of a hastily constructed tepee village. A number of untethered painted ponies wandered among the pickup trucks. As the two Native Americans walked across the muddy meadow, Elder Dawahoya scanned the representatives from the council who were milling around. He was looking for Moira. She leaned against her Jeep Wagoneer, stoically awaiting his arrival. When the Hopi apostle reached a large white tepee covered with simple symbols, he nodded to each of the ten men and two women, indicating they should enter ahead of him and sit down on blankets spread out in a circle.

"We have come to speak to you of your prophecies," Grey Eagle said as soon as everyone was seated.

"The Church of Jesus Christ's or the Hopis'?" the apostle asked.

"We have already heard Hopi prophecy, but one of our number tells us you may be able to shed light on the times ahead, especially for our peoples."

"That may be, Grey Eagle. I have books in my truck which we

believe tell us about these times. I'll go get them."

As the apostle walked to his truck, Moira held back tears. Just to be in the presence of such a powerful priesthood holder brought her body a peace that she had not expected. Her lips trembled when he returned to the tepee with a Triple Combination under his arm.

Joseph's face shone. He felt certain this was the time spoken of in his patriarchal blessing–a time when he was promised he would be instrumental in converting thousands of his fellow Lamanites.

He began with Third Nephi 21:12. "And my people who are a remnant of Jacob shall be among the Gentiles, yes, in the midst of them as a lion among the beasts of the forest, as a young lion among the flocks of sheep, who, if he go through both treadeth down and teareth in pieces..."

And there was much nodding and grunting in approval.

"And it shall come to pass that all lyings, and deceivings, and envyings...shall be done away," the apostle read with great feeling.

"That is good," Grey Eagle interrupted. "There is much truth in these sayings."

"However, brother, it also says that 'whosoever will not repent and come unto my Beloved Son, them will I cut off from among my people...and I will execute vengeance and fury upon them, even as upon the heathen, such as they have not heard.'" Elder Dawahoya stopped and looked into each face. "This is hard teaching, but it is true."

No one stirred.

"None of the Hopi prophecies say such a thing," the apostle said somberly. "We know a red symbol will come to purify us, but we are not taught that we are saved only by Jesus Christ. But there are many promises to the man or woman who follows Him."

King Benjamin would have been proud of the sermon Joseph Dawahoya delivered to these good and noble people seated in front of him. The Spirit rested on him as he testified of the coming of the Lord, of the truth of Joseph Smith's prophetic calling and the wonderful role the tribe of Manasseh would play in the very last days.

Dawahoya continued, "It says here that 'your brethren which have been scattered shall return to the lands of their inheritances, and shall build up the waste places of Zion...no more to be thrown down.'"

His voice grew quiet, but it pierced each heart as he said, "*This* is that land. This is the place to come to begin to take back your inheritance. Not out there—not killing and looting, but here." The Holy Spirit witnessed to them that he spoke the truth in a way that was almost tangible it was so powerful.

They sat in silence. A single hawk soared overhead. Wind whistled through upper tent stakes. Then Grey Eagle stood and said firmly, "The Great Spirit has spoken. What must I do?"

Joseph beamed. "Come to Independence, learn the simple things you must do to be a disciple of the Lord Jesus Christ and help us build a city of God where all men and women are free and equal, and the earth will no more be spoiled, but be returned to her beauty!"

Every other person, save Moira, stood to accept this offer. Then all focused their attention on her. Looking down at her hands, the warrioress struggled between pride and tears. Then, unexpectedly, she thought, *What would my father have me do?*

It took just a moment for her to rise to her full 5'10." Her Maori warrior face reflected the nobility of the only indigenous people never defeated by the white man. She said in a low but intense tone, "There is no other voice under heaven that I would bow to, but I do bow to you, for I know you are a true mouthpiece for the Lord Jesus Christ. I cannot deny it." Her stoic face remained unchanged, but her heart was bursting with joy and relief.

Joseph Dawahoya rarely smiled broadly, but at that moment he couldn't help himself. *Good!* he thought. *Thank you, Lord, for returning one of your lost sheep.* The Hopi walked around the circle, heartily shaking hands. When he came to Moira, he placed her hands in his large, square ones and said, "Alex has asked that you ride with me. Could you find someone to drive your car?"

"Yes, but will he have me back?" she asked anxiously.

"I cannot speak for him," the apostle said in a grandfatherly tone. "I know that he has asked to see you. He says to tell you Adam is well."

"Well, thank you," she said, trying to keep her composure.

The former Army colonel saw to it that all had maps to the church headquarters before he stepped into his truck and led the party out of the valley of Adam-ondi-Ahman and down Highway 35.

Now I know the Lord is nearly come, he thought, as he and Moira drove along in silence. *It must be true that millions will be gathered here to help build up the waste places so they may become sanctified before the Lord. It's just hard to believe it's actually upon us.*

When Elder Dawahoya arrived in Independence, he didn't take Moira back to her house but to a building down the hill from the temple site that had been converted into a large work space for the artists laboring on the temple.

"Elder Dawahoya, you cannot know what you've done for me and our people," Moira said with great emotion as she got out of the truck. He smiled and waved her on.

Moira paused in the doorway of the studio where Alex was. She was startled to see that it conformed exactly to a dream she had had several years earlier—one in which the Lord showed her her husband working in a high-ceilinged, light-filled studio.

Her heart was in her throat. The runaway brushed her fingers through the front of her braided hair and tucked a suede blue shirt into jeans dirtied from travel. For the first time in her life she felt she was going to faint. She labored to keep her breath even.

Alex was unaware of her presence. Architectural plans, which lay unrolled on a long table near him, were held down by four rocks on each corner. He was working on a life-sized clay model of a powerful man who looked like a vibrant, triumphant

Christ figure. On other tables were sections of stained glass in various stages of completion that other artisans were crafting.

The handsome sculptor was muttering to himself. Moira could just pick out "...forgive me if this is not pleasing to You."

Slowly he became aware of her standing in the doorway. He turned around, half expecting to see an apparition, but there she stood, arms to her sides, head lowered.

"Oh...!" he exclaimed, dropping the wire tool he was using. "Iwi, is it really you?" he asked with some trepidation.

"Yes," she said demurely, afraid to see what his next expression would be after the initial shock.

He walked quickly across the studio, wiping his hands on his back pockets. "Oh, darling, darling," he almost chanted as he cleared the space between them.

Moira didn't move. When he stopped in front of her, he reached out and pulled up her chin. Then he looked deeply into her eyes. Like the first time they kissed in New Zealand, Moira felt as if a whirlwind was sweeping her into its wake.

What Alex saw was an empty Moira, stripped of pride and her usual anger. "I've missed you," he said intensely.

She pulled away and looked back down at her moccasins. "Al, I...I have been a fool or perhaps worse. I don't know if you really want me here. But I've come to at least ask for your forgiveness." Now she couldn't talk. Her shoulders began to shake and sobs arose from her solar plexus.

Alex moved in and took her in his arms. He kissed her forehead, her neck. He pulled on each braid until her ebony hair fell down her back in rivulets. Then he ran his strong hands through it, over and over, as if he needed to feel she were flesh and bones.

"My love, you waited for me for years and years before I saw the light. I have only been alone for three weeks. Where is there anything to forgive?" Alex kissed her nose.

Moira looked up into his fine, wind-worn face, her eyes brimming with tears and tenderly kissed him on the lips.

"What came over me I'll never know, but this I do know," she said. "The Lord is nearly here, and I want more than anything to be with you when that happens."

Alex put his hands in her back pockets, pulled her close to him, and pressed his lips to hers. For a long time they stood like that in the doorway, then Alex said, "There is only one thing that would draw me away from this moment, and that is that the prophet is speaking tonight. Let's not miss him."

The smell of fresh paint filled the hallways of the newly-christened Zion High School as Ben and Peg, and Nate and his three oldest children walked toward the auditorium. They waved to Jed and Jody, who walked in along with Peter. They were joining a crush of members of the Church, anxious to hear President Ueda.

Peg had been fasting and insisted on sitting very close to the front. Pulling a legal pad from her brown backpack, she noted the date at the top of the page. She hoped she would hear something of specific counsel to her and her family in what the prophet said. Leaning over to her husband, who was reading his scriptures, she whispered, "I've heard there are crematoriums near Tooele where they are rounding up Mormons and burning them alive."

"Ah, Peg, you and your rumors," Ben said flatly.

After a prayer and rousing songs from a hastily convened choir, the small figure of the prophet moved to the microphone. Everyone grew quiet. It had been years since they had been able to hear the voice of the prophet.

"My beloved brothers and sisters," President Ueda said, his voice choked. "Never did I think I would live to see this day. I thank the goodness of my Heavenly Father for preserving me to see your shining faces here in the New Jerusalem. Elder Whitmer will be our first speaker this evening."

Elder Whitmer spoke plainly, admonishing the Saints to examine themselves to see if hidden opposition to the Lord's plan lay within their hearts. He pled with members to make whatever changes were necessary, so they could enter into the temple and receive greater blessings than they had ever imagined. Only Nate knew how close to home that counsel lay and what pain the apostle felt about his only daughter.

Peg looked over at Nate and his children. She felt a tug of sadness for him—to be alone at such a momentous time. Looking around for Laurie, whom she couldn't find in the audience, her eye fell on a couple standing in the back. "Is that Alex and Moira?" she asked and poked Ben.

"Shh, honey," Ben said with some irritation. He couldn't care less who else was there; he'd never seen a prophet up close before.

When it was Joseph Dawahoya's turn to address the seven thousand Saints, he said, "Brothers and sisters, I am sad to report that there is such fighting among factions in Salt Lake City that blood is literally running in the streets and gutters." Gasps rose up from the crowd. Peg turned to Ben with a knowing look that said I told you so.

The Hopi apostle leaned forward on the lectern and continued, "And not only in Salt Lake City, but throughout the world. Christians are becoming the target of more and more violent attacks. So, as many of you know, we have begun rescue missions to bring as many good people to the shelter of Zion as possible." Then he announced the establishment of an emigration fund much like the one founded when the Mormons settled the West.

The speaker before the prophet, Relief Society President Grace Ihimaera, walked slowly to the podium. She looked very tired with dark circles under her eyes, and she spoke in a husky voice as she described the desperate shape of many refugees as they arrived at the twelve checkpoints around Zion. She described babies so malnourished they couldn't take the food that was offered but had to be fed intravenously; adults arriving with no shoes and clothes literally rags hanging off their bodies; disease victims dying in the arms of rescuers, having given every bit of their life energy just getting there.

"I don't want you to grow so content that you forget the poor.

We have whole villages of children who are orphans...."

As Grace talked about the state of those children, Peg felt herself being supercharged with the Spirit and through tears wrote down, "We must bring at least two more children into our home," only half-realizing what she was writing. Ben looked over at her but couldn't make out what she had scribbled down on the yellow legal pad. He knew, though, that Peg had received her answer by the flushed happy look on her face. How he loved her for her faith!

"Brothers and sisters, I know each of you feels like you've already been stretched to the limit in your flight here," Grace pled, "but I want to tell you the Lord needs you to stretch even more. We need volunteers to help with the needs of many good non-members."

Nate looked over at Ned and smiled at him approvingly. The soon-to-turn-19-year-old had been working long hours along with many other young people, including his cousin, Bobby Whitmer, in those refugee camps. Nate had been privy to uplifting stories of miraculous healings; families reunited with lost members whom they thought dead; the great joy the distribution of food and shelter brought to people who had walked hundreds of miles, often in miserable weather conditions, to get to the safety of Zion's spiritual and physical sanctuary.

Finally, it was the prophet's turn. Many of the audience later reported they saw a glowing light around him as he spoke. "I am here to educate you about the Lord's plans for us. We are now residing at the center place where righteous people are being gathered from the four quarters of the world as the Lord promised in *D & C* 84. This county, Jackson County, was the original center place–Eden. Brigham Young said, 'Right where the Prophet Joseph laid the foundation of the Temple was where God commenced the garden of Eden, and there he will end or consummate his work.'"

Jody looked to Jed and he back to her. Other members of the audience were equally astonished at this information.

"Likewise, the place designated as Adam-ondi-Ahman is the

land where Adam and Eve lived after they were expelled from this Garden. So, as you travel north, imagine a walk of eighty to ninety miles to Spring Hill, to a verdant wilderness, where our first parents stopped and built an altar–an altar that still stood in Joseph's time–to give thanks to their Heavenly Father for his tender mercies."

Ben squirmed in his seat. He had a hard time with the idea of two people being planted on the earth from another dimension to start the human race. Peg watched as his face clouded over, so she slipped her arm through his navy blue-jacketed one.

"And this temple lot *is* Mount Zion where we will raise a temple to our Lord. But first we must be a Zion people. The first group of Saints who tried to build Zion were expelled. In *D & C* 101, the Lord explains why."

He rustled the pages of his well-worn scriptures until he found the passage he was looking for. "'…there were jarrings, and contentions, and envyings and strifes, and lustful and covetous desires among them,' but more than anything '…they were slow to hearken unto the voice of the Lord their God.'"

The audience sat immobile.

Ueda continued in this powerful manner, "For although the Lord is merciful, he has sworn that when he comes every corruptible thing shall be consumed."

The small Japanese leader paused to let that idea sink in.

"But he will spare this place," he said, "which has been appointed for the pure in heart. Oh, Saints, how I beg you, as your friend and prophet, that you do whatever you must to do to get your affairs in order, for the day of the coming of the Lord is well nigh at hand."

After a rousing "We Thank Thee, O God, For A Prophet," the tender-hearted prophet retreated out a side door, but not before waving repeatedly to members who tearfully waved back.

Peg and Ben walked slowly out of the auditorium. Ben, who walked behind her, put his arms around her soft sweater. As the crowd thinned out and they could walk side by side, Peg said, "I'm pretty sure I *did* see Moira in the back."

"With Alex?"

"It looked like him. I'm not sure."

"That would be news, honey," Ben said, feeling a bit guilty for ignoring her earlier.

The cool misty air of the late evening felt good after being inside the high school. The sky was dark, no moon, with ghostly, green cloud formations undulating slowly overhead. The two scarcely looked up; the aurora borealis phenomenon had become old hat.

"I received an answer in there," Peg said as they walked the length of the parking lot to get to their car.

"I saw you writing furiously. What did you learn?"

"That we're to adopt at least two more children," Peg said dreamily.

Normally Ben would have joked about it or tried to dissuade her, but this time, somehow, he was surprised to find himself fully believing that she was indeed speaking the Lord's will for them. So he simply asked, "Do you know who they are?"

"No, but we'll know when it happens."

"I'm sure that's true," Ben said trying to get the keys into the passenger's side lock of the Honda. He felt a little shaky about the proposition but said nothing.

Peg slid in and closed the door. When Ben opened the other side, she was already speculating. "Grace has assigned me to Camp #3, the one on the southeast corner to help set up school programs for refugees. Perhaps they're there."

"Uh, huh," Ben rejoined, already lost in other thoughts.

"It's pretty amazing to think we have at least two more children who are ours out there somewhere."

Brought back to the subject of family, Ben surveyed, in his mind's eye, their little homestead that Peg had already transformed–the flowers beginning to bloom near the front porch, fields green with growth. She had planted corn, beans, soy, peas, tomatoes, parsley, lettuce. He could see her with the work crews, pointing out locations for the placement of fruit trees and raspberry bushes. *My little earth momma. Why not more kids?*

"You know what Danny said before we left?" Peg disturbed his reverie.

"What?"

"He'd give ten bucks for one potato chip. Just one bite of a chip."

Ben chortled.

"I told him things would get back to normal very soon," Peg said and yawned.

"Mimi seems content enough with her kitten, even though Sukey isn't all white," Ben said with some paternal concern in his voice. He maneuvered the car carefully over the cracks and bumps on Orchard Lane, a street that wouldn't be repaired for some time, considering its size.

"It took a bit for her to adjust to the fact you just don't phone someone (not that we have a phone!) and just order up a white cat."

Ben laughed and maneuvered the Honda up into their driveway. All the upstairs lights were on, so he said, "That babysitter probably got a run for her money with four Winders and two not-so-tame Taylors."

As the two walked up to the back door, Ben asked Peg, "Danny's still holding out for a horse?"

"I've told him the fencing for pasture isn't even up. But he has great faith one will materialize."

"Well, we'll see," Ben said and put out his arm to stop Peg from going in the house. Turning her around, he kissed her tenderly. The two paused outside the noisy house for a moment longer.

"Speaking of kids, when do they start to school?" Ben asked, opening the back door.

"Elementary school opens next Tuesday. I wish I were returning to teaching in some ways," Peg said longingly.

"Yeah, but you've got to get our house ready for more Taylors," Ben said, hugging her from behind as they entered the fray.

After the meeting, Alex took Moira back to the studio where he showed her what he was working on. Being in charge of the art production for the temple weighed heavily on this very talented man, like nothing else he had ever done. He showed his wife the plans for the temple. A walled complex, a huge temple with twelve towers topped by a golden dome made of material never used in any earthly construction.

She hadn't spoken of her times with Gray Eagle and the Intertribal group. Nor of the encounter with Elder Dawahoya. And he didn't ask. They made love right there. It was slow and sweet.

Then they headed back to their house and to the ailing Grace and their baby. Once Grace had told them they would live into the Millennium where their son would grow to be a great warrior for the Lord. As the couple stood over the sleeping figure of their child, Moira began to let the possibility sink in. Adam, who was a year old and large for his age, lay in yellow pajamas, arms and legs akimbo. For Elder Dawahoya, who had no knowledge of Grace's prediction, told Moira the very same thing on their drive down from Adam-ondi-Ahman.

Later, when she lay in the curve of Alex's muscular arm, Moira tried but failed to imagine how it would feel to have her body changed from the one she knew to one that would defy death or disease. Unfortunately, she relied solely on what her senses told her was real. She would be forced to rely on Alex's faith. And that wasn't easy, but it was better than losing her precious family.

CHAPTER SEVENTEEN

"And what rough beast, its hour come round at last
Slouches toward Bethlehem to be born?"
William Butler Yeats

Veteran Chinese observers were baffled by the fact Lu Han had become the emperor of China—and with such lightning rapidity! This return to an ancient form of government was considered by many diplomats and scholars to be the geopolitical enigma of the century. His ascendancy to the throne as the Son of Heaven came just after the resumption of world-wide television, playing to the global audience hungry for order and the sumptuous promise of a better life in a world careening toward chaos.

ITN gained exclusive entrance to the Forbidden City and this "momentous event in the history of the world," as Reginald Tuttle, the Beijing Bureau Chief, put it. Those parts of the palace and grounds which had been so ornate and exotic in centuries past were returned to their original glory. From the floating gardens with brilliantly decorated boats, to the golden-armored soldiers with conical hats, and the newly red-lacquered lattice walls—everything was perfect for television coverage.

The dry grass in the courtyards was sprayed green for the coronation, which was held in the Hall of Supreme Harmony. Lu, resplendent in yellow brocade, walked slowly up a long gold carpet accompanied by a retinue of servants, aides, and soldiers.

Chairman Zhu Hao, now the Lord Chamberlain of all China, bowed to Lu three times then produced a document which the emperor signed with a flourish. The Emperor pressed his jade seal on the hot wax that fell onto a sheet of wax paper. This gave Lu Han complete power over the nearly one-and-a-half billion Chinese.

At the lavish feast (which was also carried live by the television station), an official taster stood by Lu, eating the first of each of the sumptuous banquet offerings, described in great detail by the British reporter. Peacocks cried out, and yellow and black butterflies were released in great numbers to mark the auspicious occasion.

As the ceremonies progressed, Lu appeared to be blissfully grateful for each gift, each mouthful of such delicacies as turtle, serpent head soup and baked sparrow. He radiated an aura of both humility and power.

Speaking in perfect English with a slight British accent, he addressed the world-wide audience at the end of the ceremony from the Palace of Clouds in Heaven and urged the citizens of the planet to unite in the cause of peace and prosperity. When asked about the newly-formed New World Order, he exuded great confidence that it would bring political and spiritual renewal to a weary world. He smiled beatifically into the television cameras, assuring the billions of viewers that he whole-heartedly endorsed the Constantinople-based government. He also broadly hinted that the Lord Chamberlain would have news in a few days regarding a Chinese treaty with the NWO.

The effect on the television audience was galvanizing. Here was a man on earth who was wise, powerful, rich and interested in raising the standards of all people regardless of their creed, color, race or religion. And the reporter caught on tape what appeared to be a blind man being healed just by brushing the sleeve of the Sufi/Taoist master. That image was played and replayed for several weeks on stations world-wide.

Lu Han had promised certain people a private audience after the festivities were over; first in line was Dmitri Gornstein. Although the two men had been in constant telepathic contact, Dmitri had not seen the emperor since the meeting in the Gobi Desert. He had been practicing his meditation exercises and was anxious to prove to Lu that he was now adept enough for initiation into the Order of the Dragon.

"Have you heard the sound of the cricket?" Han asked from the luxurious red and gold-brocade pillow he was sitting on.

"I have. And I have seen the blue opal."

"Have you gained mastery over your breath?"

"To be completely truthful, I have not, although much of the time when I meditate, it slows of its own volition." Dmitri raised his anxious eyes to Han.

The emperor was silent, sensing where the Russian had advanced in his work. He turned to another disciple, the South African director of mines, and asked him the same questions.

Dmitri squirmed in his lotus posture, legs crossed one over the other. Sitting in this position is uncomfortable, he thought, but now to be ignored! After all I *am* the head of the New World Order.

Then the Russian remembered his evening of Sufi dance and the ensuing waves of bliss. He would give anything, *everything* to regain that sensation! So he sat and waited, calming himself by watching his in-breath.

With his eyes closed, Gornstein didn't detect the approach of the emperor until he was nearly in front of him. A light brush of a peacock feather caused him to open his eyes. As he did, he saw Lu's face, smiling with approval. Then the master reached down and rubbed his thumb on a spot between Gornstein's eyebrows. Immediately the Russian felt an electric sensation shoot down his spine. At the tail bone, it began a slower ascent, warming his torso, then his throat. He began to cry, as did several of the other handful of guests.

The energy that now filled the interior of Gornstein's head was sweet. It tasted like mango nectar. Dmitri's scalp began to itch, then his gums. Finally he thought he was being lifted right off his seat. As he struggled to keep his eyes closed, his in- and out-breath simply stopped, and a fountain of liquid light poured from the base of his spine to the top of his head–over and over–to his astonished delight.

The Chinese master moved from one disciple to another, touching each head or cheek, encouraging their surrender to the experience.

But each time the energy reached Dmitri's chest, he felt an

intense pain, as if the heart muscle were contracting. At first, he thought he was having a heart attack but didn't care. If I have to go this way, let it be, he said to himself. But after four or five passes, the tension in that part of his body began to let go. In its place came expanding waves of love that ultimately seemed to emanate out to all beings.

It was at this point that Han leaned down and gazed into Dmitri's eyes, drawing the Russian into his hypnotic gaze. Within seconds, all sense of separation vanished for Dmitri. He was Lu, Lu was he. And he was Lu's—forever.

"You must never love another," Han whispered huskily in the Russian's ear. "No man or woman."

"I will love you always."

"Prove it to me."

"Anything."

"Follow me."

Gornstein slowly gathered sufficient energy to follow the robed emperor down a long hall, past black and red screens into a small room. Two of Lu's black-robed servants stood next to a high bench. Lu indicated to Gornstein that he should climb up, lie down on his back and remove his trousers.

The older servant handed Dmitri a small rolled-up towel, gesturing that he should place it between his teeth. It was at this moment that Gornstein realized that Lu was holding a curved knife and small metal bowl and was advancing toward him.

He fainted when the knife sliced his testicles.

A eunuch for god and Master. Dmitri was now a member of the Order of the Dragons, a select group of ten men who held most of the earth's wealth and who swore undying loyalty to the Lord of 10,000 Years.

As Sangay and his family neared the appointed rendezvous at Lake Yakitiki, near the headwaters of the mighty Amguyena River on the Siberian Plateau, he felt his stomach tighten. Most of his life he had been waiting for moment. The first time the man from Israel appeared to him was when he was fourteen. He told Sangay that one day the rinpoche would meet with the heads of the other nine tribes and that would be a turning point in the history of his people. But after all the intervening years of no more visitations, the experience seemed to Sangay a myth or something he had dreamed.

There would be little nighttime this latitude, so the Tibetans took their time putting up the three yurts on the grassy slopes, even though it was after seven o'clock when they arrived. Millions of pink and purple wildflowers dotted the landscape. After watering the yaks and ponies and tying them down for the night, Sangay took a satchel from one of the yaks and left his father and cousins to take a walk toward the lake, the rolling Anadyr Mountains on his right. He turned back several times to be sure there was smoke coming from each hole in the roof. As soon as he was satisfied that the party of fourteen was settled in, he hastened his step and soon was out of sight.

A herd of white-lipped deer were startled by his presence and scattered out into the tundra. A flock of blackheaded gulls rose from the lake symmetrically and effortlessly around the water before moving north. At the water's edge two hundred yards away, Sangay observed a *sazik* (snow leopard) lapping at the lake's waters—waters that were contaminated with nuclear fallout. The large cat turned his noble face—yellow eyes, spotted white and gray face with salmon-colored nose and black lips—in the rinpoche's direction.

He didn't move, nor did Sangay. Because the rinpoche gave off no scent of fear, the beast finally turned and padded up the gravelly bank. Sangay let loose a sigh and continued his travels around the lake. He had been shown in a dream just where the meeting was going to be held. The rinpoche and his extended family camped on the southeast side of the river. Other heads of the tribes camped around the lake at other spots they had been shown. None was close enough to another that the families would be aware of each other.

Sangay touched the dark parcel he was carrying and turned

the names of the original tribes over in his mind as he walked–Dan, Reuben, Simeon, Levi, Judah, Zebulon, Issachar, Gad, Asher, Naphtali, Benjamin, and Joseph. He tried to keep his imagination from running away from him. He'd been in touch with the members of his own tribe, who included a number of Tibetans, but he wondered, *What do these other "brothers" look like? Where do they come from? What do they know that I don't?* The rinpoche broke into a grin; his straight white teeth and smile lines that descended from his oriental-shaped eyes like etched sun rays gave him a boyish radiance and made him look half his age. In fact, he felt quite young as he walked quickly around the lake.

A few hundred yards away, the rinpoche could just make out the outlines of three men in white robes standing near the lake's edge. Two were taller than the third. As he neared them, he was sure that the smaller one was the man from Israel. Never had he forgotten that man's face. John the Beloved broke into a grin as Sangay approached.

The ancient apostle hurried to meet Sangay, hands outstretched, with the two other following close behind. Sangay was nearly overcome with awe when he shook the hand of the translated apostle. John quickly introduced the others. "Master Tulku, this is the apostle Nephi and his brother, Timothy. We are so pleased you have come representing Naphtali. You are the first to arrive." The group then followed John to a campfire a little further down the lake's edge.

The four sat down on driftwood to talk. "I have brought the records as you requested." Sangay began to pull out the box he had taken from Tenzin Lhamo at Kailas, the sacred pilgrimage site of both Tibetans and Hindus.

"Please, Brother Tulku, wait for that," John said, holding up a hand.

"There will be a time for these presentations," Nephi said, as the firelight glimmering on him lent his powerful figure heroic proportions.

The men sat silent in meditation for a few moments, then

John stood and began walking to the north. Although no one could be seen, in a moment a party of three men rounded a protuberance near the lake's edge. The other apostles stood and waited for the four to return. Sangay's heart was racing.

"Gentlemen, this is Rudolf Grudzinski of the tribe of Dan, Michel Dyachenko of Issachar and Alec Hovanec of Reuben." Sangay laughed at himself for having imagined that these men would somehow not look human, but they were just ordinary men from Eastern Europe and the former Soviet Union.

It wasn't too much longer when the rest appeared—all carrying parcels or packs. And all of them *were* ordinary men but with extraordinary spiritual dispositions and destinies.

"Now that you've arrived, we will first raise a prayer to our Lord and Master, Jesus Christ, for seeing you here safely," John said cheerfully.

As the prayer was being offered by Elder Timothy, Sangay found tears flowing freely down his cheeks. His had been a lonely existence up to this point. Now he had comrades, brothers—and leaders!

The translated apostles went through the basics of gospel doctrine with these extraordinary men, although it was a refresher course for all. Then Elder Timothy led them down into the waters of Lake Yakitiki, and with the help of Elder Nephi, baptized each in the name of the Father, and the Son, and the Holy Spirit. Immediately afterward, they were given first the gift of the Holy Ghost, then the priesthood of the Most High God, by the apostle John.

The ten men warmed themselves by the fire, clearly transformed by these supernal events. Each had waited his entire life, since he was a teenager, for this very night. John counseled them to continue feasting on the word of the Lord and gave each a set of scriptures in their own language.

Nephi stood up and spoke. "These are extraordinary times in which we must do the Lord's bidding in extraordinary ways. So, gentlemen, we are going to accelerate your divine destiny as the Lord who knows your heart has directed." Then one by one they were led away from the fire by the three translated apostles, and when the first returned, Sangay half-rose in disbelief. The elderly man from the tribe of Benjamin now looked no more than twenty-five years old! And radiating the same glow around his body that the apostles displayed.

When it was Sangay's turn, he knelt on the river bank on an ocher-colored cloth and felt the six hands of the translated apostles press on his crown. The only thing after that he remembered hearing was, "In the name of Jesus Christ and by the power of the Holy Melchizadek Priesthood...."

Then a surge of ecstatic energy shot through his entire frame. When he felt his face, the lines were gone. He resisted the urge to run to the lake and look into its mirrored surface. He stood up, surprised that he felt like he could run miles. His step was light, almost giddy as he walked between Nephi and John back to the fire.

"Your bodies are now translated ones like ours," John said. "I know that several of you have been able to translocate by leaving your body behind and manifesting yourself in another location. This change in your body, now permanent, will allow you to travel at a thought and without the great expenditure of energy that you needed for the previous astral travel."

Nephi, in his baritone voice, picked up the explanation. "By the way, you'll no longer have to eat or sleep either."

Several men laughed in delight. Nephi poked at the fire, then continued, "The Lord has done this for a specific purpose. You will be needed in Zion, in Missouri, and with your tribes at important junctures, and you'll need to have the means to travel from place to place very quickly."

Timothy said, "Now, gentlemen, let's have some fun with these bodies. Sangay Tulku, see how well you do. Think that you'd like to be on the other shore and go there." The smiling rinpoche stood and closed his brown eyes. Within an eye's blink he had disappeared from the circle around the fire. Sangay, who had been accustomed to moving around at the speed of thought, had no difficulty with the exercise. He smiled as he remembered the startled look that Ben gave him when the rinpoche showed up for Alex's baptism.

"Did he make it?" Grudzinski worriedly asked Timothy.

"He certainly did. Now it's your turn," said the tall, taciturn Nephite apostle.

When the ten passed that test, John asked them to gather up their belongings and stand in a circle around a large stone up on the bank. "Can you imagine yourselves in the center of the United States? You'll find the place by the electronic force field placed over it." Then he gave exact coordinates for the plains of Olaha Shinehah.

In less than a second the thirteen men stood on Spring Hill. Where it had been Monday in Siberia, it was now Sunday, two o'clock in the morning. President Ueda walked toward them, shaking each man's outstretched hand, followed by Elders Dawahoya and Stewart. Behind them stood Ben Taylor.

"Gentlemen, welcome," the prophet said expansively, gesturing that they should all sit down around another fire—this one fueled by dried American wood gathered from the earthquake-built valley. Ben sat back behind the gathering, his note pad in his lap and his beige wool cap firmly pulled down around his ears. If someone had asked the quick-witted Jewish convert to come up with a one-liner for the occasion, he couldn't. Overcome with the moment, he just told himself, "Just keep the cameras rolling. All I ask is I don't pass out."

He'd been in bed asleep when something woke him, and he pulled back the white curtains in the upstairs master bedroom to see a car parked outside. Slipping quietly out of bed, he headed down the stairs, hanging onto the bannister for support, since he required time to get coordinated when he'd been asleep. It was only when he had the front door half open that he realized he was standing there in just his garments as an apostle of the Lord headed up the front walk.

Dressing quickly and leaving Peg a vaguely worded note, the scribe slipped out the door, slid into the back seat of the brown electric-powered Toyota, one that Peter had converted. Elder

Dawahoya drove. Ben sat in the back with Elder Stewart and behind the prophet. He hadn't asked about their destination. The situation reminded him of one when he was an undergraduate pledging a fraternity. In the middle of the night, Sigma Nu men pounced on him in his dorm room, threw a pillowcase over his head, drove him out to the Santa Monica pier, where they threatened to drop him in the chilly winter ocean if he didn't recite the entire text of "Twas The Night Before Christmas."

But this wasn't the Santa Monica pier they were approaching, this was Adam-ondi-Ahman, and Ben's choice of company had certainly improved over the years. If that weren't enough, he now stood in the company of thirteen men who had simply materialized out of thin air!

After introductions, the group settled into a discussion of world events. Sangay sat across the circle from Ben. As the fire crackled and burned brightly for a moment, his eyes met Ben's and he smiled broadly. Ben smiled back at a 25-year-old version of his meditation teacher!

Suddenly Ben remembered something Sangay had said a couple of years ago. Ben had asked Sangay what he knew of Jesus and the Tibetan teacher replied simply, "I serve Him, through my tradition." At that time Ben felt slightly superior to his meditation teacher. Poor misguided Tibetan Buddhist. He'll find out one day what I know about the gospel.

Never did Ben think he'd sit in the presence of a translated Sangay Tulku, spiritual head of the tribe of Naphtali!

He looked up from his reverie to see each of the heads of the tribes reach into their satchels, pull out scrolls or plates and place them on a large, white, silk cloth on the ground in front of them.

"Thank you, gentlemen," the prophet said soberly. "I know these records are more precious to you than anything you own."

Ben wrote furiously, describing each parcel.

"We have been guided by the knowledge given us by the Savior when He came to us after His crucifixion," Sangay said. "Now we are not limited by our ancient records but can rely on a living prophet of God!" The other heads of tribes wholeheartedly agreed.

When it was Joseph Dawahoya's turn, he proudly placed the burlap bag he had been carrying on the ground and reached into the clay pot, not sure what he would find. To the delight of the assembled group, he did not produce a scroll or plates, but a kachina. The Hopi elder knew immediately who it represented. It was Mas'sau, a forerunner of Christ. His eyes were like sunken black holes, and his mouth bristled with sharp white teeth. His head was covered with bunches of feathers and different colored blotches of paint. The doll wore a long coat made of rabbit skins. Hung around its neck was a leather pouch containing corn seeds, and hanging from a corded belt was a small gourd. One hand of the kachina doll held a planting stick and the other a stick with painted red flames on the top.

According to Hopi tradition, around the year 1100 A.D, they found Mas'sau by following a tapping on a rock out in the Black Mesa country. This Guardian of the Earth taught the Hopi people all they needed to know to live a simple life, close to creation.

"Well done, Joseph," the prophet said brightly. "You've taken the prize for the most exotic offering."

Dawahoya laughed in pleasure for his contribution and relief that the sacred object had arrived unharmed.

A delightful and spirited discussion of certain doctrinal points followed for nearly two hours. Ben wasn't sure just what to write down, so he simply recorded questions asked by each head of a tribe.

As the conversation wore down, President Ueda turned to Ben and asked him to come forward. "This man, gentleman, has been working on plates Elder Tulku gave us." The prophet's eyes twinkled as he said "Elder." Sangay returned his smile.

"Ben Taylor has proved to be an excellent worker, devoted to the Lord, and has progressed in his skills as a translator insomuch that I would like to suggest we entrust him to oversee

JACOB'S CAULDRON / 253

the translation of these plates into English, since that is the official language we will be using, until Adamic is reinstated."

Oh, boy, how did this Jewish kid end up here! Ben wondered to himself as all the participants raised their arms in assent. *So all this work on the Tibetan plates has only been preparatory. Oh, the Lord. You just never know with Him.*

"Elder Taylor, will you join us in the circle?" the prophet asked. "You can stand in for Judah, for the moment, and that way we will have all thirteen tribes represented."

"Thirteen, sir?" Ben asked.

"Joseph's inheritance went to his two grandsons, Ephraim and Manasseh. Elder Dawahoya is of Manasseh, and Elder Stewart is an Ephraimite."

"Do we know who it will be, the man of Judah?"

The prophet smiled and said, "Only his name–David."

Ben hit his head with the palm of his hand. "That was stupid," he murmured to himself.

The three translated apostles gave final instructions to the ten men who were to return to their families, swearing them to secrecy regarding their bodily transformation. They were shown how to alter their appearances so that they looked as they did before being translated.

"Gentlemen, please feel free to call on the Lord now for His help with your preparations for teaching the gospel to members of your tribes."

The group of men buzzed in pleased assent.

"Elders John, Nephi and Timothy will be present to assist with the first baptisms and priesthood ordinances. Then you'll be on your own."

The swarthy Armenian who headed the tribe of Asher assured the prophet that whole villages in his area would be baptised *en masse*, especially since he could now bear witness to the living reality of the prophet of the Lord, and the miracle that was Zion.

After an especially powerful prayer, the thirteen men simply vanished into the night air. Ben stood looking in their direction, his pen hanging loosely in his dangling hand and his mouth agape. He stood for several minutes unable to move. *Life has just taken a really interesting turn,* was his only thought.

CHAPTER EIGHTEEN

"On my American plain
I feel the struggling affection
Endur'd by roots that writhe their arms
Into the nether deep.
O what limb rending pains I feel!
Thy fire and my frost"
America: A Prophecy, William Blake

Time was running out for a rescue attempt of the passengers on the *Ulysses*. With the announcement by Zhu Hao that China would join other non-aligned nations to form the New World Order, Gornstein's government consolidated its dictatorial grip on every nation. The biggest hold-out had been the former United States, not because there was much resistance from its regional centers, but because there was essentially no government to negotiate with.

Shiite Muslims were pressed into service, making up the bulk of NWO's armed forces (although Lu Han's Chinese army could be called up at a moment's notice). Outfitted in black uniforms with a pocket monogram displaying a saber crossing a crescent moon, the two-million strong army was led by General Hazrat Patel, the former Pakistani UWEN commander. Television reporters liked to feature the colorful Patel, because he carried a swagger stick under his left arm wherever he went and wore the distinctive red turban of a Moslem sikh.

Hazrat was a severe and demanding leader who considered Mormons to be filthy infidels because they claimed that it was not Mohammed, but some Joseph Smith, who was the true prophet of God. Promising his crack army food and good wages, he dispatched them in lightning speed throughout the world. They returned to the former UWEN facilities that were still stocked with basic equipment and supplies. (The New World Order had the only operating aircraft worldwide—even most of the small airplanes had been confiscated by the UWEN.)

General Patel met with Gornstein to finalize the lightning

raids on U.S. regional centers.

"Intelligence reports tell us they are in locations formerly used by FEMA," Patel said between puffs on a Turkish cigarette. "Their emergency management centers are...here." He pointed to a number of locations on a map of the United States.

The commander of the NWO, as Gornstein liked to be called, replied, "Intelligence reports indicate there is no need to waste manpower on either coast as they have mostly been abandoned. The bulk of the population has fled inland in search of food, since it has been months since any distribution has occurred. Rumors are that many of the remaining occupants have resorted to cannibalism."

The two men smugly smiled at each other.

"Could you have imagined taking down the United States in the twentieth century," Patel asked incredulously, "...and so very easily?"

"Allah has delivered our enemy unto us as he promised."

Patel put an index finger in the air, shook it and said, "I want to caution you about a regional center in the middle of the country. Although this may be just rumor, I have been told some kind of electrical force field has been installed over much of the state of Missouri."

"How could they?" Gornstein asked, annoyed. "Wasn't that where the giant earthquake struck a year or so ago?"

Patel nodded. "And the rivers washed out all major cities along the Mississippi River. As unlikely as it sounds, there are rumors to that effect. I just wanted to warn you, that's all."

Gornstein snorted and stood up, stretching. "We'll have them, whatever it takes."

Patel smiled. He liked working for Gornstein. Since the world's arsenal of nuclear devices now rested in the NWO's hands, the "whatever it takes" was certain to mean nuclear obliteration.

Gornstein looked at the passionate, moustached Arab. He felt good to be on the side of winners rather than being a despised Jew, as he had as a boy in Russia. And, of course, the fact that he had been initiated into the Order of the Dragon—chosen as one of ten men to assist god incarnate in bringing the world from darkness into light—more than made up for his wretched upbringing. He was grateful that, with Lu Han, no one was Hindu, Buddhist, Muslim or Jew. Any spiritual aspirant could achieve a oneness with Right and Order with the help of the holy master.

The Eastern seaboard of the United States was as Patel described—city after city desolate: America's former capital was deserted and in ruins; Boston's harbor and much of the city had been inundated by a tidal wave from an off-shore earthquake, magnitude 8.6; Baltimore was in a state of ruin, just as John Taylor had seen in a vision where he stood at the 1812 square and saw "dead bodies of inhabitants piled in heaps. Even the Chesapeake Bay was befouled with dead bodies. Sickness and death were everywhere."

So this daring rescue attempt was risky, but one the prophet ordered when he heard how the five hundred Saints had managed to survive on the high seas in the worst hurricane season on record.

Peter and Jed had worked feverishly to convert three buses to solar. The rescue party consisted of Elder Dawahoya along with Nate (who had just been called a counselor in the Presiding Bishopric), the two mechanics—Jed and Peter, Ned and his cousin, Bobby Whitmer. Bobby was a small, thin and handsome young man, who, six months earlier, had survived the battle with the Chinese at Donner Pass. He was a gun *aficionado* and brought along a small arsenal of weapons.

As the small caravan pulled away from the city, Nate pointed to the temple under construction and said to Ned, "Look, son, those temple walls will be topped with a dome when we return."

"And then we'll see the Lord, right?"

"Well, we have been promised that privilege. I don't know who will be found worthy."

"I'm glad I'm old enough to have a temple recommend," Ned said, ignoring his father's pessimism "I feel sorry for the other kids. They'll have to sit outside on the grounds."

Nate's thoughts flashed to Laurie. *Would she sit with the kids outside the temple or avoid the whole scene?* he wondered. Tears came to his eyes as he remembered the sweet young woman in the lace designer gown, flushed with excitement, being escorted into the Salt Lake Temple sealing room by her father. How very sad, he thought and shook his head.

"Thinkin' about Mom?" Ned asked.

"Was I that obvious?"

"Yup. I still have hope for her, you know," Ned said somewhat defensively.

"There's always hope, son," Nate said turning his attention to stuffing a bedroll and duffel bag behind the front seat of the bus. He reached down into the recesses of his brown leather jacket and handed Ned a piece of paper.

"Here's the map Elder Dawahoya has drawn for us."

"How does he know which way we should go?"

"The prophet gave him exact instructions, son."

"How does the prophet..."

"Sit down, Ned," Nate cut in. "And close the door. No, you're not going to drive this vehicle," Nate said pushing the tall 18-year-old over to the passenger's side of the bus. "You're riding shotgun."

"Maybe literally," Ned rued.

"I pray not. We've pleaded with the Lord to protect us both in and out of that hell hole."

The buses rumbled off down the deserted early morning streets of the burgeoning city and traveled across Missouri on Highway 70, then onto the 54 past Bowling Green to the "portal" on the far banks of the low-lying Mississippi. A barge was pressed into service to ferry the three vehicles across.

Two men to a bus, the rescue team headed east, sometimes on major highways, other times on smaller two-lane roads–always faithfully following the prophet's instructions. In that way they avoided major cities and highways that had been destroyed in the three major earthquakes to hit the area. The journey which would have lasted two days, took nearly four, in spite of the fact that they drove straight through.

The scenery looked unfamiliar to several of them who had driven across the Midwest. What land they saw now was dry and drought-stricken, looking more like Sub-Sahara Africa than America's food belt. They passed gas stations with deserted cars sitting at pumps; gutted grocery stores; dead cows—frozen-looking with their stiff legs splayed in the air; and defeated, hollow-eyed people sitting on the roadside. Having become accustomed to the hordes of mice which overran the roads and were squashed under tires, the caravan faced another hazard—snakes, hundreds of them, slithering on the roads.

Near the end of the journey, Ned finally got his chance to drive, with Bobby as traveling companion.

"What I want to know is how I got short-changed," Bobby teased.

"Short-changed?"

"With the short genes."

Neddy laughed and looked over at his cousin, who was a whole foot shorter. "Well, I wouldn't hold your breath for some professional basketball scout to look you up."

"Keep your eyes on the road, Dufus."

"Do you think we'll have professional sports again?" Ned asked and sighed.

"Maybe, but not for the outrageous sums they got paid in the 1990's."

"I'm playing for a neighborhood team. Trying to keep our skills up. Don't know what for, though."

"Let it go, Louie," Bobby said and laughed.

Ned didn't laugh, didn't understand the joke.

"You're too young to remember—that was when we had commercial television. It was an advertisement about frogs and lizards."

Ned shrugged his shoulders. That was before his time. The

two lapsed into silence, listening to the repetitive sound of the tires on the rough road.

Bobby broke the silence. "I'm hoping I'll find my future wife on the ship."

Ned laughed raucously, then said in an obnoxious falsetto voice, "Ooo, Bobby's looking for a babe!"

Ignoring the outburst, Bobby stared out the windshield at the smashed moths.

"And she needs to be rescued, right?" Ned needled.

Bobby started. "What are you? A mind reader?"

"You got it, pal! And that's why you've volunteered for this dangerous mission—to rescue some damsel in distress."

Bobby punched his cousin's arm.

"Whoa, watch it, man! I've barely got control of this beast."

"I could make a crude remark, but I won't. Look, can't a guy have some kind of fantasy life? Gees, first I'm on a mission, and then I'm fighting Chinese, and then I'm in Utah babysitting your little brats, and when I get to Zion, I checked out the eligible girls and she isn't there."

"Whine, whine."

Bobby reached out to punch Ned again, but the driver reached out and grabbed his cousin's hand. "I'm serious, man. Stop it!"

The two were laughing when the red brake lights on the bus ahead of them suddenly lighted the nightscape. The two buses in front slowly pulled to the side of the road. Ned followed. When the bus rolled to a stop, Ned opened the bus door as his father's figure appeared.

"What's up, Dad?"

"Looks like a roadblock ahead. Probably saw our lights."

"I thought the map was foolpr...."

Nate cut him short. "Turn off the lights, son. Bobby, you get up front in the lead bus and get out your guns."

Bobby proudly jumped down the steps and started to the front bus, but not before giving his uncle-in-law a thumbs-up signal and saying jauntily, "Smith and Wesson makes all men equal."

The hotshot was back in a moment with two handguns and a

box of ammunition for Nate and Ned. "I'm going to ride with Peter and Jed in the first bus," he said proudly.

As the caravan moved slowly forward, they could see a crudely constructed barricade–tables, chairs, tires–in the moon's glare. A crowd of forty seedy-looking people stood behind it with sticks and bats in hand.

Peter and Bobby drew their weapons but kept them out of sight. "This ain't nothin'," Jed said sarcastically as they got closer. "Let's go for it, boys!"

He jammed the gas pedal to the floor, and the bus accelerated about fifty yards from the barricade. The other two buses followed suit. As they reached the crowd, the heavy vehicles crashed through the makeshift barrier, causing people to scatter into the fields on either side of the road. Guns raised, Peter and Bobby jumped to the back of the bus, ready to fire. But the second and third buses sailed through without a shot being fired.

"I wonder if they even had any guns," Peter asked.

"Probably some desperate, hungry mob," Bobby replied.

Philadelphia was nearly deserted. The stench of decaying bodies was overwhelming. The men covered their noses with whatever they could find and remained in the buses while waiting for the *Ulysses* to appear in the harbor. Jed was in constant contact with both the ship and Zion's communication center to coordinate the rescue effort.

"Why did they sail to Philadelphia, Dad?" Ned asked.

"They couldn't use any of the Atlantic seaports because they were destroyed in the same tsunami that swept through Boston."

"Oh, I see." The young man adjusted the handkerchief that was tied across his face. "You know, Dad, I can't eat anything. The smell is *so* bad. I never knew this is what rotting flesh was like." He paced to the rear of the bus and back. "*When* are they getting here?" he asked for the twentieth time.

"There!" Nate said pointing to a small speck in the Chesapeake Bay.

"Hey, Jed!" Nate called to the next bus and pointed out the

ship.

The rough-and-ready nurse, who in his early youth had been a Navy Seal, joined the father and son. "I hear the ship's population will be 493, not counting the crew. They lost nine at sea–two babies," Jed said sadly.

"Whew, what a tragedy," Nate said.

"The communications guy on board the *Ulysses* warned me we'd better be prepared for medical and psychiatric emergency care," Jed continued.

"Sounds like you're going to be a busy guy," Nate said admiringly. This was yet another time in the last year and a half when Jed's nursing skills had been sorely needed.

"We've got enough medical supplies in that last bus to care for a small army," Jed said proudly. "Oh, Nate, I don't want to alarm you, but Elder Dawahoya just told me he'd heard from headquarters that the NWO's sending troops our way."

"Oh, no!" Nate said. "How soon?"

"They're in Canada right now, but they could be here tomorrow at the rate they're taking over this country."

"And with all the air power in the world to support their army." Nate sounded genuinely alarmed. "Has there been any resistance from local troops?"

"Just a limited skirmish with a group of Native Americans somewhere in South Dakota. Otherwise, it's pretty much going their way."

The ship was now visible. Nate turned his full attention to the vessel. He found his hands were sweating. Grace had better be right about Mary Margaret, he thought. I've risked my life and my son's, for that matter, on a couple of dreams and the telepathic ability of some Maori grandmother.

The ship sounded its horn in welcome. The group on the shore waved their arms in the air. Well, I haven't known Grace to be wrong, Nate thought to comfort himself. "Here's goes nothing," he said through the blue bandanna he had tied over his nose.

Nate wasn't the only excited and nervous one. Bobby was, too.

He paced and jumped up and down off stacked crates. When he grew tired of playing hacky-sack with Ned, he stood at the water's edge and strained to see if he could see any young female figures on the deck.

After about half the passengers had disembarked, Mary Margaret appeared on the gang plank with her three red-headed daughters. Her eyes searched the small crowd for the young elder she had seen just once thirty years earlier. When they fell on Nate, standing near the buses, her heart quickened. "Sweet Jesus, have you answered my prayers?" she whispered. Then a breeze brought the stench to her nostrils and she gagged. "Holy Mary, Mother of God, help us in this hour of need," she said repeatedly as she made her way down the gangplank to the dock.

Dragging the three heavy suitcases into the line to get on the bus, the comely Irishwoman tried staring at the back of Nate's head to get him to turn around. She succeeded. He looked up and met Mary Margaret's eyes. Both felt a delightfully swift intake of breath and an accelerated heart rate.

She smiled demurely at him. He pressed through the crowd, his hand extended. When he reached her side, he tried to speak, but the words got caught in his throat. She laughed lightly at his awkwardness.

"May I help you, ladies?" he finally succeeded in asking—his heart now beating so wildly, he could feel the pounding in his ears.

"Would you be Elder Winder of the Dublin, Ireland Mission?" Mary Margaret asked timidly.

"I am...or I was," responded the tongue-tied suitor.

"Well, then, I'm Mary Margaret O'Boyle of County Roscommon," she said, shaking his hand.

As he took the white, delicate hand and shook it with grave formality, he said, "You look familiar. So it was in Ireland, then, that we met?" Nate said, pretending to be puzzled—half to tease her and half to keep up some measure of dignity.

She too acted coy. "Yes. You came carrying a passel of Bibles to my house. Tried to teach my family about your beliefs, but my da drove you off."

"Of course!" Nate acted surprised by the "chance" encounter.

Before more of this little drama could be played out, it was the family's turn to step onto the bus that Elder Dawahoya was driving. The apostle graciously reached for each O'Boyle and helped her aboard. He said, "Welcome to the Zion Express. We'll have you home in no time, ladies."

Mary Margaret and the girls felt immediately calmed by his presence. They found seats on the side of the bus where Nate was struggling to shove their bulky suitcases into the luggage hold. The exhausted and disoriented woman stared at Nate's dark, curly hair that was turning silver on top. Then she leaned back against the seat, took several slow, long breaths and smelled her hands. Sometimes a perfume of jasmine seemed to come from them. But not today. Today it was the smell of blood. She reached for a rosary in her sweater pocket and wound it around her wrist.

When Nate was sure he was out of sight behind the medical bus, he slapped his knee and nearly shouted, "Gracie, you're a wonder!"

It took nearly two hours to unload the passengers and baggage and reload them on the buses. They also had to take the time to stabilize the fourteen passengers who needed medical attention. During that interval, Elder Dawahoya spoke to the ship's crew, offering them safe passage to Zion with the condition that they live the gospel's basic standards. Most refused, because they didn't believe the Indian apostle that there was such a place as Zion, or they had certain Word of Wisdom problems. The majority said they'd rather take their chances on the high seas. The Hopi apostle took the seven who decided to throw their lot in with the rescue caravan to the last bus to be checked over. While there, he contacted Zion one last time to see if there had been any change of route on the return journey.

President Ueda sent word that they should return as instructed. But the radio operator added, "The prophet also told me you should get out of there as fast as possible. There's only a small window of time before the NWO troops secure the area."

As the buses rolled away in the early dawn, Mary Margaret longed to stop the caravan and insist on sitting next to Elder Winder on the second bus. She didn't even know his first name—she hadn't even seen him since she was fifteen. He had aged, of course, but not so much that his intense face still didn't stir in her an indescribable spiritual longing. It wasn't at all rational, but it seemed to her that they had known each other for many lifetimes. His voice—more than anything else—it was his voice that seemed so familiar. Mary Margaret knew her life had just taken on new dimensions, just being in his presence.

It was early on a Friday morning, a fact that hadn't slipped past her. Soon the bleeding would start. And here, in these close quarters, she wasn't sure she could hide it from her girls, or others for that matter. Her visible stigmata consisted of welts and slight bleeding on her hands, wrists and the palms of her hands—places where Christ was pierced during His crucifixion. Her feet bled from top to sole where the nails had been pounded. And a blood blister would appear on her side where the lance pierced His side.

The Irish mystic wrapped herself up as much as possible and leaned back against the seat. As she breathed in and out, she sensed the powerful presence of the Melchizedek priesthood—a comforting presence she had never felt—so she let herself go. She also could, because her tired, excited girls had fallen asleep.

Mary Margaret slipped her tongue back into her throat and thought repeatedly, *Lord Jesus, have mercy on my soul.* Soon she felt transported into the horrifying scene of His death. The swaying of the bus accentuated her own rocking, where she withdrew her senses into a prism of pure light. That was the one place no one could hurt her, and where she knew she could find the Lord.

The caravan was only a quarter of a mile from the electrical "portal" on the Mississippi River when the group headed for Zion found them pursued by NWO Advan troops in helicopters. Elder Dawahoya looked out at the machine gun turret and flashed back to Vietnam when he was frantically carrying a soldier whose right leg had just been blown off beneath the knee toward a hovering Marine chopper, its gunner firing rounds at a frantic pace to try to provide Dawahoya cover against the North Vietnamese regulars who were swarming out of the thicket. Dawahoya winced as the picture of the grenade being tossed in the chopper by a North Vietnamese soldier flashed across his mind. He remembered the explosion where the chopper burst into giant fiery fragments streaming black, yellow and red smoke as he reached for his .45 with his free hand and blew off the top of the VC lieutenant's skull.

A bull horn brought the apostle abruptly back to the present. "Stop the vehicles or we will destroy them!" shouted a voice with an Arabic accent.

The Indian apostle turned to Peter. "What do you think, Porter? Why haven't they blown us up?"

"They want the buses," Peter said.

"Probably. How much longer to the net?" Dawahoya asked in a clipped military voice.

"Eighth of a mile now."

"Let's make a run for it!" Elder Dawahoya floored the gas pedal on the lead bus, nearly knocking over Peter, who had been standing to look out the window.

"Give us a little warning, mate," Peter laughed, even at this dangerous moment.

The helicopters flew so close, they could see the man with the bull horn hollering, "One last warning! There's nowhere to run. Pull over!"

Thirty seconds–twenty seconds. The helicopter gunner pulled out a small missile launcher, rested it on his shoulder, and squinted as he began to take aim.

Five seconds.

Dawahoya's lead bus soared through the opening, then the second with Mary Margaret. Just as the missile left the launcher, the last bus with a medical team shot on through. The startled Zion guard pressed a button, and the portal instantly disappeared.

The missile hit the shield and exploded, sending the black and silver helicopter down in flames from the ricocheting debris. Before a final fireball explosion, the helicopter pilot managed to radio NWO headquarters, "Missile repulsed by unknown force!"

CHAPTER NINETEEN

*"I wanted to stop this,
this life flattened against the wall,
mute and devoid of colour,
built of pure light;
this life of vision only, split
and remote, a lucid impasse."*
Margaret Atwood

The busy refugee camp on the southeastern border of Zion was crowded with yurts, new refugees, children playing in the makeshift roadways. It opened to the South and covered parts of the former city of St. Louis. Between the vast flooding and devastating earthquakes, very little remained of the great metropolis. The one clear landmark was the St. Louis Temple, which could be seen for miles. It was a beacon of prophetic fulfillment (when it was dedicated in the 1990's, the prophet prayed that it might be spared from the ravages of the elements). Jutting up into the barren, flattened landscape, it stood white, tall, with the golden statue of Moroni still blowing his pre-Millennial horn. Most of the refugees in this camp were non-members, so one of the first questions they had when they arrived was, "What building is that, that miraculously still stands?" The answer brought a great opportunity to introduce gospel principles.

Grace walked quite slowly, stopping every few minutes to sit. When she stopped to swallow a pill, Peg ventured to ask, "Grace, are you sure you're going to make it? I can handle this Relief Society assignment on my own, really I can."

Eyes closed, Grace tried to steady herself. "Could you get me some more water, dear?"

As Peg hurried off to the kitchen in the tented area, Grace murmured to herself, "Doctor Hunter, I think you're right. This tumor *isn't* going to go away." She took another morphine pill along with a Decadron, which he had given her to try to reduce intracranial swelling.

When Peg returned, she said insistently, "Now listen, Madam President. I know you feel you must take care of all these people." The younger woman helped the matriarch bring the cup to her lips. "But you've already set so much in motion, why not let some of the rest of us get some practice in serving others?"

Grace sat back, trying to contain her vertigo, but the black tunnel that blocked out most of her vision had returned. Suddenly she grabbed for Peg but fell off the cement ledge on which she was resting.

"Go get the driver we came with!" Peg hollered at the cook who had just given her water. She pointed in the direction of a large field that served as a parking area.

An African-American woman quickly joined Peg, helping to place Grace flat on the ground, then ran to her yurt and returned with a tan blanket. Peg fussed and paced until she could hear the car bumping over the rocky border to the field. When it pulled up, the driver and the women carefully placed Grace in the back seat, and the driver drove as fast as he could back to the medical facilities a mile away.

The black woman stood with her arm around Peg. "Sister Ihimaera will be okay. She's a saint, you know."

"I know," Peg said. "I can't tell you how much time Grace's spent in all these camps. I've followed her all over, and she can't stand to let one person suffer." Peg paused to take in a long breath, then said, "She's the greatest lady I know."

"I'm Keesha Washington," the young woman offered. "Come on. You come into our humble abode until you hear about her."

Peg agreed, and they headed down a graveled walkway toward a yurt with a colorful flag waving from its top pole. Then, eyeing an outhouse, Peg excused herself and headed in its direction.

When the worried educational counselor returned and pulled open the door of the yurt, she was surprised to see six young children seated around a picnic table, quietly drawing on sheets of paper.

"This here's my little school for my daughter and kids who

are stayin' 'round here," Keesha explained. Peg moved closer and her attention was drawn to a five-year-old, light-skinned African-American girl who was lost in drawing a picture of a house. Her energy dominated the room.

"Hard to keep your eyes off her, isn't it?" Keesha asked.

"Boy, she's something else, isn't she?" Peg agreed.

"I brought her with Henry and me. Seems her folks was killed in a tornado in 'Bama–where we're from."

"What's her name?" asked Peg, craning to see what was on the beige-lined paper the little girl in the flowered dress worked on.

"Amber. Best I can understand. She hasn't remembered her last name yet. Found her wandering around a trailer park with two scraggly dogs–all three scavengin' for food."

Peg walked around the table and sat down next to Amber. "What are you drawing?"

"My Indian friends."

"Who's this?" Peg asked, pointing to a figure in the lower left.

"Diggy. He's a boy."

"And this one (in the upper right)?"

"Doa. She's five, too," Amber said firmly.

"And him?" Peg pointed to figure in the middle of the picture surrounded by a circle.

"Tanka. He's the grandfather who takes care of me."

"In Alabama?"

"Uh, huh."

"Did he come with you?"

"Yup."

"And he's your grandfather?"

"NO!" The five-year-old shook her braided hair. "He's *the* grandfather–my Indian friend. I told you!"

Peg returned to Keesha. "Does she really have a grandfather here?"

"Oh, no. She's an orphan, believe me. That's some imaginary playmates she's got there. Talks to them all the time."

"Do you think she has Indian ancestry, Keesha?" Peg asked, now interested in this child's persistence on the reality of these Native Americans.

"Wouldn't think so, from the looks of her, but you never know."

Peg looked back at Amber, and she longed to take her in her arms and comfort her. Her heart nearly burst, thinking of what the little girl must have been through. "I just want to take her home and love away all her hurts."

"Could be arranged, Miss."

"By the way, my name's Peg. Sorry I didn't introduce myself," Peg said extending her hand. "It's just that I'm so worried about Grace."

"I understand, Miss Peg. I let the folks at the food tent know where you went. Someone will come and let us know."

"Oh, thank you," Peg said, grateful for Keesha's maternal tone.

"Back to Amber, I wish someone *would* take her. She's like a little lost puppy around here."

By the time everything had been set up to transport Grace back to Independence, Peg had arranged for another rider. Just for a visit, she told herself. Just to see what Ben and the kids thought of Amber. The little girl with a turned-up nose somberly drew on a pad of paper most of the six-hour ride back to Independence. She sat between Peg and the driver, while Grace slept in the back of the car.

"You're going to get to play with my two kids, honey," Peg volunteered. "Danny, he's eleven, and Miriam, she's nearly nine. They like little kids,"

"I'm not a little kid."

"Oh, what are you?"

"An Indian."

"Oh, I see."

As this conversation was going on, back on Orchard Lane, Miriam suddenly announced, as she was setting the dinner table, that she was getting a baby sister. Puzzled, Ben questioned her carefully, thinking she might have overheard one of the couple's conversations about adoption, but she hadn't.

"I'm going to set an extra plate. She'll be hungry."

"Okay," Ben said, trying to humor her.

The three were just beginning to eat their chocolate pudding, when the sound of a car in the driveway reached them. Miriam flew out the front door before Ben could get out of his kitchen chair.

"Mimi says we're getting a baby sister. Is that true, Dad?" Danny asked.

"Beats me. Let's see who's here," Ben said rising to go to the door. But Miriam was back, flushed, excited, ahead of Peg and Amber.

"See, Daddy!" Her voice raised an octave. "See. She's here!"

Grace was rushed to the Independence medical facility where David Hunter was waiting. After examining her, he said in his best professional voice, "Grace, I'm afraid there's increasing intracranial pressure."

"I don't feel like eating."

"That's common."

"What's next?" she asked in a detached voice.

"I can keep you somewhat comfortable with morphine, as you are now. You'll need to slow way down."

"How long?"

"Months, weeks, days–hard to predict."

"I see," she said evenly. "Well, then, would you leave me to my peacemaking?" the Maori said turning her face away.

"Of course, Grace," David said in a soft voice, turning off the light as he exited the small curtained area.

Grace lay in the dark and tried to calm herself. *It isn't like I haven't wanted to go home*, she said to herself. *It's just now that we're here....*Tears coursed unchecked down her weathered cheeks.

Some time later she awakened to what she thought was the sound of the curtain being pulled back. Then a man in white (she assumed to be an orderly) stepped inside.

"Yes?" she asked groggily.

No answer.

Grace struggled to pull herself up, so her head was resting against the backboard. She peered into the half-light and, to her amazement, the figure approaching her had brilliant sapphire eyes, which shone in the half-light. She sucked in her breath and asked, "Have you come for me, as Gordon said?"

"No. Not yet, Sister Grace. You have one last task the Lord would like you to perform, then you can join your husband."

"How is he?"

"Impatient."

Grace chuckled. That was precisely the word she would use in describing her husband. "What do you want me to do? I'll do anything the Lord asks."

"There is a woman, an Irish woman..."

"Mary Margaret?"

"Yes.

"She's a very special spirit. She needs what only you can teach her."

"I do understand, sir. Just how long do I have?" she asked deferentially

"Very, very soon." Then he just wasn't in the room. A second later the light that surrounded him dissolved.

It took all of Nate's self-control to leave Mary Margaret at the Dubiks' without saying an intimate word. As the Irish mother tried to make her weary way up the front porch stairs, she stumbled. He took her elbow to steady her. He hoped she would lean into him, but she simply focused on her target—the front door.

Alex, in a maroon bathrobe, answered the door, while he held back Renoir, his Golden Retriever who had arrived in Zion with Dr. Hunter. The friendly dog kept shoving her head through the sculptor's legs, greatly curious about these newcomers.

While Alex helped the girls up the stairs, Moira introduced

herself and Adam to Mary Margaret, who fell back at Renoir's bark. "A hound from hell, to be sure," she said nervously.

Moira took the dog by the collar and dragged her into the kitchen, while Nate hung around for a few moments, hoping for some sign of encouragement. But Mary Margaret was so exhausted, she was oblivious to his attention. The only thing she longed for was clean sheets on a bed that didn't sway. Finally Nate mumbled something and excused himself.

Moira returned from the kitchen, took Mary Margaret's arm and helped her upstairs. As a therapist, Moira's antennae went up when the Irish woman slipped in and out of rational speech. As the two stood in the doorway of the bathroom and Moira was handing the tired woman a towel, the Irish woman said to her, "Moira, Mother of God, thank you."

"Excuse me?" Moira asked.

"Moira–doesn't that mean 'the Mother of God'?"

"No, it doesn't."

"You have kind eyes like she does," Mary Margaret said, her eyes wildly surveying the unfamiliar workings of an American bathroom.

"You just take your time in here. I'll check on the girls."

"The Lord bless you."

Moira shut the door and shook her head. She found the girls fighting over a dresser, settled the argument, then retreated downstairs to Alex.

"Honey, would you call David Hunter? I'm going to need him to give Mary Margaret a sedative." *And I'm going to have to put back on my therapist's hat,* she thought.

"It's nice having David back in our lives, isn't it?" Alex said.

"It sure is," Moira said softly. "We probably wouldn't have Adam if it weren't for him."

As Alex tied his frayed tennis shoes and searched for his olive-green windbreaker, she thought back to the time she first had consulted David Hunter as a doctor. She was four months pregnant with their long-awaited son, forty-four years old, and bleeding vaginally. She remembered hearing him tell Grace, "I'm going to call for an ambulance, but I want you to know that we usually don't make heroic efforts to save the fetus until it's about twenty-seven weeks along. So we'll probably have to suction her when we get to the hospital."

And as she remembered it, it was her mother who insisted that she have a blessing before leaving for the hospital. She could see Alex, his face set, pacing in and out of the open doorway of their bedroom at Pah Tempe, occasionally biting his lip. She knew he didn't believe anything would come of this blessing, and that hurt her to the core.

In her reverie, Moira recalled hearing Dr. Hunter say, "Do you have someone you'd like to act as voice?" She weakly pointed to Ben then looked over at Alex as if to say she wished she could call on him. Dr. Hunter poured a few drops of consecrated olive oil from a vial on his key chain onto her head. Then he placed his delicate hands firmly around the crown. She remembered the warm pressure from both his and Ben's hands as they silently prayed.

Hunter began, "...we, your brothers, holding the Melchizedek Priesthood..." then turned to Ben for his pronouncement. Ben stammered at first with, "We come here today as the Lord's servants...and ended with "...and you will be made whole."

Moira felt tears run down her cheeks as the memory played itself out.

When she heard Ben's deepened voice say, "I prophesy, in the name of our Savior, that your son will grow to be a great warrior in the Lord's kingdom, serving his Master faithfully and well," her spirit soared as those words began to echo within her. Suddenly she let in a tremendous rush of warmth that pulsed first through each man's hands then soared within her weakened body. She felt her temperature drop instantly.

She remembered Ben quickly reached out to grab her, thinking she was going to faint, but she didn't. "I had the most peculiar sensation just now," she said, looking into each man's worried face. "I could feel my uterus readjust itself—pull back up and in."

Alex's kiss on her cheek brought her back to the present.

"Oh, what a time," she said shaking her head. "Honey, will you ask David if he's carrying some consecrated oil? I want to ask him and you to give Mom a blessing."

Alex's eyes filled with tears. "I thought you'd never ask."

"I'm a little slow. You've known that now for while," she said patting him on the bottom as he turned to leave.

He came back for a passionate kiss.

Mary Margaret fell into a deep, dreamless sleep minutes after David administered the sedative. Then he descended the stairs to the kitchen and the waiting couple. "I'd hazard a guess the woman is suffering from post-traumatic stress. I don't think she's psychotic, but that's your department, Moira."

"I agree with your diagnosis," Moira said, sipping herbal tea at the kitchen table. "Tea, David?"

"Peppermint, thanks," David said. "I saw something I don't know to make of. Puzzling red welts on her palms and wrists. I wonder if they're self-inflicted," he said worriedly.

Alex and David looked to Moira, who shrugged. "I don't know. I'll keep it in mind."

The three sipped tea and talked briefly of the others who had arrived from the *Ulysses*.

Then Moira stood and said, "Let's go see to Mom. I'm actually more worried about her than the whole boatload of refugees."

"Of course," the tall, elegant-looking doctor said, putting his cup on the counter and indicating she should lead the way.

When they had gathered around Grace's bed, Moira stood back a bit so Alex and David could give Grace a blessing. Moira secretly hoped the men would promise her mother health and long life. Instead, Alex as voice said, "Grace Ihimaera, the Lord loves you. You have nearly completed your mission here on this earth....You will be given the strength to finish your course." No miraculous rushes of healing energy, just a quiet, peaceful scent of the Spirit permeating every part of the bedroom like distant roses.

Grace lay back, content with what had been said, but Moira couldn't let it go. "Al, let's find out what David hears," she insisted.

Alex looked hurt, but Moira didn't notice. She didn't want to lose her mother.

David looked to Alex, who shrugged. "Go ahead. I'm no spiritual giant. There may be more that I'm not tuning into," he said with a trace of bitterness in his voice.

The physician tried to center himself and listen as he placed his hands back on Grace's grey head. In the quiet, he heard, "Tell my servant, Alex, I am pleased with his spiritual progress."

"Okay," David said aloud with his eyes closed.

"Okay? What?" Moira was nearly in his face.

"Alex, the Lord would have you know that he is pleased with your spiritual progress."

Alex was bowled over. That was the last thing he thought he'd hear.

"But what about my mom?" Moira was nearly shrill.

"Your mom is in His loving hands," David said in his doctor's voice. "Be at peace."

Moira opened her mouth to insist on something else, anything but this, but finally she closed her eyes and said nothing. Doubling her fists at her sides, she tried to calm herself.

Suddenly a voice broke the tense silence. "You know, I feel a bit better. Would one of you put on some herbal tea?" Grace asked.

Two afternoons later, Grace, the Dubiks and Mary Margaret sat on the porch facing the newly landscaped temple lot. Grace rocked her grandson and held him especially close, aware there weren't going to be many more lazy afternoons on the porch. Alex and Moira swung back and forth on the old-fashioned porch swing. In the distance they could see crowds gathered to watch as four construction cranes slowly lifted a translucent dome from the earth to crown the newly constructed temple.

"I think I told you all that the dome is made of material relayed to us by John the Beloved," Alex said matter-of-factly.

"You did. And it sits on a golden solar collector of some amazing design so that when the sun shines down on the dome, it will look like it is made of gold," Moira said with some amazement in her voice.

"A symbolic precursor to the world becoming a Urim and Thummim," Alex continued.

"And the dome is smaller than the walls of the temple, allowing light to stream down into each floor," Grace said, happy she had remembered some pieces of information through the haze of pain she was enduring.

"The atrium I've spoken about—it really will be otherworldly when it's done. Already there are plants and flowers growing there—tropical plants that shouldn't grow in Missouri's climate. The place is beginning to smell like Hawaii."

"So you're satisfied with the workmanship of the temple, son?" Grace asked.

"Remarkable achievement. Exquisite architectural design. Twenty-four antechambers off the main temple complex—all topped by that." He pointed at the dome dangling midair.

"It's a unique building for a temple," Moira said.

"Why's that?" Mary Margaret ventured to ask.

"There's never been one with a dome," Alex said.

"And twelve towers instead of the usual four," Moira stated.

Alex reached for Adam, who was sleepily sucking his thumb. Grace parted with him reluctantly. The sculptor pushed the swing with his boot and said, "The word around the construction site is this is a terrestrial temple, preparing us for a celestial life.'"

"A celestial life," Grace repeated in a hushed voice.

"Really makes the circle and square motif obvious," Moira added.

Mary Margaret interjected, "The Lord is coming soon, very

soon. He's told me."

Alex said, "That's what we believe too. In a few years from now."

"Maybe not. He told me he'll come to his people first."

Grace looked to Moira with raised eyebrows. Moira mirrored her mother's facial gesture, then said, "You know, Mary Margaret, there's to be an open house of the temple very shortly. It will be open for nonmembers. Would you like to go?"

"That's very kind, but He's shown it to me."

"Ah...I see," Alex said. "And did he show you my sculpture?"

"No, just the rooms and an explanation of the function for each."

"Well, that's really interesting" Alex said, surprised at her revelation. "Maybe we can interest you in coming to see the artistic elements."

"Possibly. I'll ask."

The Irish woman stared out across the lawn and into the street where her two youngest girls, in '"new" pants and blouses from the Bishop's storehouse, were playing ball with a couple of neighbor children. They were already finding the spiritual and social climate to their liking. Mary Margaret then closed her eyes, let out a little "oh!" and stiffened into a rigid upright position.

Alex half-rose, looking to the two women. "You take Adam into the house, son," Grace said quietly. "We can take it from here."

"I'll give Adam a bath," Alex said helplessly.

"Good idea," Moira said soothingly. As Alex left the porch, he stopped to look at the beatific face of the thin woman. (Later, he would capture her translucent beauty in a famous sculpture of his.)

Moira, now the therapist, left the swing and kneeled down next to Mary Margaret who appeared to have stopped breathing.

"What do you think, Mom?" Moira asked as she looked over her new patient.

"No, you go first."

"Hysterical conversion reaction to prolonged stress, I think... maybe, with possible psychotic features." Moira stood up, tucked her saffron-colored blouse into her Jeans, and shifted back to the swing.

"What would you do with her if you had the psychiatric facilities?" Grace asked, running her fingers through her long, gray hair.

"Probably admit her and try an anti-psychotic drug."

"Uh, hum."

"You don't approve, I can tell."

"It isn't approve or disapprove," Grace said evenly. "It's just where I come from drugs aren't available."

"And you had to walk forty miles to go to school. I know," Moira said defensively.

"Iwi, don't get cheeky with me," Grace said and chuckled. "Now settle down. My sense is that Mary Margaret may be a genuine mystic, a battered one at the moment, but a mystic nonetheless."

The two women looked over at the rigid woman in the rose-print dress and scuffed white sandals.

"I don't know how those girls have managed," Moira said and sighed.

"They're darlings, that's for sure," Grace said. "I'm sure she's been a good mother in between episodes."

"What do you make of those red welts on her palms, Mom?"

"Those are my oblations, my acts of contrition," Mary Margaret said suddenly, opening her eyes.

Moira grimaced in embarrassment. "Excuse us, Mary Margaret. I'm sure you sense we mean no harm."

There was no response, so Moira rose and headed for the front door. "I'm going to leave you to it, Mom," she whispered as she passed Grace.

Then it was just the two women, both given to altered states of consciousness, who sat together in silence. Moira called the O'Boyle girls in through a side door so they wouldn't disturb the pair.

Grace closed her eyes to handle a sudden attack of vertigo, then relaxed into a meditative state. After a moment, Mary Margaret suddenly opened her eyes and stared at Grace.

"How did you get up here?" Mary Margaret asked with some incredulity.

"Get where?" Grace asked lightly.

"You know what I'm talking about. Up here. At this level of the Spirit."

Grace looked like the cat who'd just swallowed a canary. "I've been able to get into this state since I was a child. I'm a Maori, native of New Zealand. I grew up out in the country with adults who look for signs of psychic abilities in small children. When they are found, the children are encouraged to develop them, for the good of the whole community. And you, Mary Margaret, how did you learn?"

"My grandma had it; my ma, too," the Irish mystic said. "I didn't want to know about it, but I couldn't stop it. It just came on me when I was a wee girl."

"My maternal grandmother had the Sight," Grace replied. "They called her the village telegraph. She would see something happening to one of the extended family miles away and send out help. Did yours have the Sight?"

"No, ours is more of a knowin'. Knowin' what's to happen before it happens. It's a gift from the Lord Jesus."

"I agree," Grace said. "What else can you do?"

"Heal. I've been able to heal since my Tommy—my husband— died. He was murdered and so was my da. I couldn't grieve for a time. After that I felt great compassion for everyone's pain."

"How do you heal?"

"I don't!" Mary Margaret said emphatically. "It's the Lord. I'm only an instrument."

"I meant *how* do you heal—by laying on of hands or at a distance."

"Both. I've done both."

"Heal everybody?" Grace asked to see if the woman was telling the truth.

"Oh, no. I never know who, and I really don't try. It just comes to me sometimes to place my hands on a person, or to say a prayer for them. Afterwards I sometimes hear they've been made better."

Grace was definitely gaining interest in this woman. "Tell me, dear. Can you diagnose ailments?"

"Not in the usual way that a doctor does. I can sometimes see dark areas where there should be light."

"Look at me. What do you see?"

Mary Margaret asked Grace to stand up with her back to the white background of the house. She took a couple of steps back and half-closed her eyes. "I see a great light around you, Mrs. Grace, varying from white to yellow to pink—mainly a rose-pink. I think that means charity. Wait! It's everywhere except square in the middle of your head."

"What about my head?"

"It's got a dark mass. Like you had a bad headache. Do you?"

"Worse than that. A brain tumor."

"Would you like to see if the good Lord will heal it?" the Irish woman asked kindly, stopping forward with her right hand extended.

"No," Grace said, as she settled slowly back into the metal chair she'd been sitting in. "It's my time," she said matter-of-factly.

"Oh," Mary Margaret said as she too sat back down, arms tightly held around her waist.

"That makes you sad?" Grace asked. "Why, you hardly know me."

"Ah, to be sure, I'm always losin' people anyway. It would be too much to ask that I have a friend who understands me and stays with me." She began to withdraw.

Grace reached out her hand and placed it on the Irish woman's small, blue-veined one. "Wait, child. I've promised the Lord I would stay in my body until you're ready to have me go. "

But she was gone. Stiff, scarcely breathing.

Late in the middle of the night, a fireplace poker hurled itself across the living room by its own power and wrapped itself around a floor lamp fifteen feet away. The next night, dishes flew from the kitchen cabinet, crashing to the floor all the way into the dining room.

The following morning Moira sat on Grace's bed trying to get her to eat.

"I just can't. I'll sip some broth, Iwi. I can't hold anything down," Grace said firmly. "Dr. Hunter said this would happen."

"You'll starve."

"Probably go some other way, sweetheart, before I starve."

Changing the subject, Moira asked, "What are we going to do about Mary Margaret's telekinesis? We're not going to have a house left standing."

"I'm trying to get her to talk about her anger," Grace asked.

"Well, I'm going to have to sedate her soon, Mom."

"Why don't we work together. Play good cop, bad cop," Grace replied.

"Which one do you want to be?"

"I'll do good cop this time. She's come to trust me."

So, later in the day, the two brought Mary Margaret into the living room in order to speak with her. She was visibly distraught—rocking and wringing her hands. "I know it's me. I know you want me to leave. I'm so sorry...."

Grace put up a hand to stop her. "Dear, we don't want you to leave. We want you to deal with what you're feeling."

The Maori mother and daughter loomed like Amazon warrioresses next to the petite woman. She was so tiny her feet scarcely touched the rug.

Mary Margaret fingered her ever-present rosary and said after a long pause, "Well, I've got to stop runnin' sometime and somewhere."

"Good," Moira said, moving her chair up closer to the couch where Mary Margaret sat. "Tell us when this all started."

The Irish woman began to share her history of her "sorrows."

At sixteen she was married off to a much-older man, Tommy O'Boyle. The following year her house was burned down by Protestants. She endured four full-term pregnancies in six years–the first two were still births.

"When the UWEN took over the country, everybody was glad at first," Mary Margaret continued. "But then they got to be cruel. Rounded up men they suspected of carrying on the battle to rid Ireland of the Brits. My da and Tommy were caught carryin' weapons in the trunk of a car. Really stupid. The UWEN lined them up and shot them in the square. Invited the town to watch."

"How old were you then?" Moira asked.

"Twenty-two and pregnant again. The UWEN they used an Israeli tactic to keep people from continuin' their opposition to government policies–they blew up our house and left me with two wee ones, one on the way, and a mother who was very sick."

"How did you survive?" Grace asked solicitously.

"I cleaned houses until I couldn't work any more. Then I moved in with a man I met in a pub who took pity on me. That's where I had my last darlin', my Sarah. And that's where I heard my first voice from Heaven."

Both mother and daughter leaned back in their chairs. Moira squinted to try to ferret out what was reality and what was delusion in Mary Margaret's account.

"It was not a dream or delirium. I was awake," Mary Margaret continued. "Heaven was opened and a fiery light of exceedin' white inflamed my whole heart and my whole breast, not like a burnin' but like a warmin' flame, as the sun warms anythin' it touches."

Moira looked to Grace, who had all of her concentration focused on Mary Margaret.

So far everything she's said has an authentic ring to it, the Maori grandmother thought, as she mentally checked off items on her mystic's checklist.

"And I immediately knew the meaning of the Scriptures, namely the Psalter, the Gospel and other parts of the Old and

New Testaments, though I did not have the exact interpretation of the words, but I sensed in myself wonderfully the power and mystery of His message to me."

"And what was that message, dear?" Grace asked.

Mary Margaret paused. She had never shared any of this before. She grimaced before continuing on. "Ah...The voice said, 'I am living Light, who illuminates Darkness. The person I have chosen and whom I have miraculously given power, she I have laid low on the earth, that she might not set herself in arrogance of mind.'"

Taking a sip of herbal tea from a flowered tea cup set on a coffee table in front of her, she continued, "He said, 'I have closed up the cracks in her heart that her mind may not exalt itself in pride. She must love only me.'"

"And who do you think was speaking to you?" Moira asked.

"Jesus the Christ, no doubt."

"I see," Moira said and sighed.

Ignoring Moira whom Mary Margaret could sense was reluctant to believe her story, she continued, "He has taken me to secret places in the heights of Heaven where I have seen two armies of heavenly spirits arrayed against each other..."

This isn't a gray day, Mary Margaret suddenly thought. *It's a black and white day. Molly's loss is heaven's gain. Heaven smiles on those who wait...Oh, no!* she thought frantically. *If I don't stop, I'll be caught up in an endless patter of these little phrases, and I won't be able to sleep for fear I'll throw another pot across the room. Stop! I've got to stop,* she said to herself, but her thoughts seemed to have a mind of their own, flowing off into labyrinths and kaleidoscopic bursts.

Grace and Moira watched as the woman withdrew into a silent stiffness. Seeing there was nothing more to say, they rose quietly and retreated to Grace's bedroom.

After Grace lay back and settled into bed, Moira asked, "Well, Mom, what do you think? Should we confront her–get her to deal with life? Is she too fragile?"

"Leave me, Iwi," Grace said, waving her hand in the air.

"Okay, Mom."

"I've got to pray about this and see what Heavenly Father wants done."

Moira closed the curtains and tip-toed out. Grace fell asleep immediately. Near the end of the nap, she awoke to the O'Boyle girls' high-pitched kidding in the back yard. She lay thinking back to her children, Moira and her two brothers, when they were that age. Grace had learned by then not to get in the middle of the fighting and teasing. What she learned to do was enjoy the energy of their play. Suddenly the thought came into her head–"See that she has a mother"–as clear as a bell, and she knew in that moment what she needed to do about Mary Margaret.

"Iwi," she called out.

Moira immediately opened the bedroom door. "Mom, are you okay?"

"Take me upstairs to Mary Margaret. She's up there, isn't she?"

"I think so."

Leaning heavily on her daughter as they climbed the dozen stairs to the second floor, Grace wobbled her way to the Irish woman's bedroom. "Leave me, Iwi," Grace whispered. "I'll call when I want to come back down."

Grace sat on the bed next to Mary Margaret, reached out and touched her delicate, blue-veined forehead. There was no response, so Grace began to run her fingers through the distraught woman's long, thick red hair. Slowly Mary Margaret began to stir.

"What song did your mother sing to you when you were small?" Grace asked.

"'Touralouralay'–or something like that," Mary Margaret replied slowly.

"Sing it for me."

Mary Margaret began to croon an old Irish lullaby and gradually lean into Grace's body. When the song was over, she lay within the nurturing circle that Grace had formed with her arms.

Grace expected her to cry, to release her anguish, but Mary Margaret just lay there, like a wild animal that enjoys the touch but doesn't yet trust the experience.

"You have such beautiful hair," Grace said, straightening up. "Come, let's see what we can do with it."

The two moved to the vanity table. Grace stood over the lovely woman and gently brushed her long hair with a silver-backed brush. Mary Margaret closed her eyes and began to relax with each stroke.

"Did you ever love a man?" Grace asked softly.

"Why do you ask?"

"Because you remind me of nuns I knew as a child–they said they weren't for ordinary men, they were brides of Christ."

"I have had no sacred place to go. Men are boorish. They don't understand how they tread on my Holy of Holies."

Grace sat silent for a moment then said, "But if you build a retaining wall so strong that no one can get in, your Holy of Holies becomes a witch's brew, festering with anger."

Mary Margaret froze. She placed her forefingers and thumbs together to form a triangle and pressed them against her night gown a couple of inches below her navel. Even through the gown, this motion increased intense vibrations that began to flow up, although she didn't know why. A sound inside her head seemed to fill the room–boom, boom, boom.

Grace stepped back to see what she was doing.

"Oh, this is so lovely!" Mary Margaret half-cried. "Take me to Your bosom, my Beloved." Climbing onto the single bed, she lay down on her back, arms extended in the form of a cross. Grace could see welts begin to form on her forehead, then blood flowed profusely from wounds on the places where the crown of thorns had been crushed into Christ's head. Blood appeared on her palms and wrists; wounds appeared on her feet.

Grace was fascinated and horrified at the same time. *What would bring a girl to such suffering and bliss at the same time?* She wondered if she had been molested, perhaps by the man she last lived with. Once again Grace paused. *What do you want me to do here, Lord? I am your servant.*

"Alleluia!" the ecstatic woman suddenly shouted. "Light bursts from your untouched womb like a flower, Mother. Alleluia! Flower on the farther side of death. The world-tree is blossoming. Two realms are becoming one."

Grace felt constrained to stand and watch. A voice in her head said, *It will suffice to be a witness.* So, instead of getting a washcloth to clean up the bleeding woman, she sat down on the other single bed and watched for one hour, then two. Somewhere in the third, Mary Margaret called out for her.

"Mother, are you still here?" Her voice sounded more solid.

"I am."

"Will you tell me there is a boy who loves me most dear?"

"I will."

"Will you fix my hair so he'll think I'm pretty?"

"Yes, dear, I will."

Then Mary Margaret rustled in the bedcovers and sat up. Grace went for a washcloth and slowly wiped away the bloodstains on her forehead and cheeks. Ethereal, regal, the Irish woman stood and glided into the bathroom. "I'm going to get myself cleaned for his arrival," she said as she shut the door.

Grace called out downstairs for Iwi. In a moment her daughter's anxious face appeared in the hallway. "What is happening, Mom? Are you okay?"

"Call Nate Winder. I don't care what he is doing. Tell him to get here immediately!" Grace said sternly.

Moira's face disappeared immediately, and Grace sat down to wait. Nearly a half hour passed, but when Mary Margaret appeared, she was cogent and composed. She had used some of her daughter's make-up to cover most of the welts.

"Has he come?"

"I believe he's downstairs waiting."

"Grace, you've never said his name." Mary Margaret smiled wryly.

Grace grinned back. "We have both known for some time who

this suitor is. Even before he did, didn't we?"

Mary Margaret put back her head and laughed a hearty laugh. "I never thought I'd find my match, but you, Grandma Grace, are it. You're like an angel sent from God."

"And you, Mary Margaret O'Boyle, need to get on with your life. Glorious blessings await you!"

The Irish beauty walked across the bedroom and hugged Grace then began rummaging through her suitcase for a slip.

"Before you go, I want to say a couple of things," Grace said firmly.

Mary Margaret looked anxiously down the stairs.

"He'll wait."

"I'm just worried about my girls. Are they okay?"

"They're fine. They told us they were used to your 'spells'"

"I don't want them to get used to this. I want to get better. I will, won't I?" she asked Grace anxiously.

"You're on your way." Grace patted her arm. "First, there is no reaching Heavenly Father or Jesus Christ the way you've tried to do it. It won't happen, no matter how high or what phenomena you experience. That is not the path."

"But I've felt Him, seen Him."

"I have no doubt, Mary Margaret, He has comforted you and helped you to get here, but you must not run to Him like you would your father. You've got to face being a woman on this earth."

The red-haired beauty fell silent.

"It's too high, too much." Grace moved in for the kill. "You tried to escape a horrific situation by fleeing to Him. It worked, but it isn't needed any more. You're safe. You're in Zion, sweetheart."

Staring at Grace's face as if to take in every word, Mary Margaret twisted her rosary.

"You'll have all your material needs met, and you're among fellow lovers of the Lord," Grace said soothingly. "If you listen to Elder Winder, downstairs, he will help bring you your fondest dreams."

Mary Margaret jumped up and hugged Grace, clinging to her for more than a minute. "I believe you! For the first time in my life, I've found someone who knows what I know, and I believe you!"

"Good. Now let's see what you have to wear," Grace said in a motherly voice. The two looked through the five outfits hanging in the closet. They decided on a white ruffled blouse and a dark green skirt, clothes she had just picked out at the Bishop's Storehouse the day before. Mary Margaret went into the bathroom to change. When she emerged, she held out the sides of her long, flowing skirt and whirled around. She looked twenty–a real Irish rose.

CHAPTER TWENTY

*"And the rebellious shall be cut off out
of the land of Zion, and shall be sent away,
and shall not inherit the land."*
D&C 64:35

Word of the electronic shield over Missouri and the
destruction of the NWO helicopter and its missile went to
regional headquarters, then on to General Patel. By the next
morning's briefings, fighter pilots had been ordered to circle the
perimeter. At first, the flybys were quite disconcerting to the
inhabitants of Zion, but, when they could get their minds
wrapped around the idea that they were sheltered from *all*
harm, they calmed down.

"It's a negative–repeat, negative–on penetrating the force
field. Appears to be a naturally occurring thing. Related to the
magnetic North Pole shift. I know this is hard to believe, but
there's no other way to read the wacky telemetry we're showing
on all the onboard computers. Sounds nuts, I know, but...." His
voice trailed off.

"Copy that. What else?"

"There's one helluva difference between the surrounding
countryside and the area under the bubble. Outside is brown,
virtually wasted. Inside is green, a lot of agricultural activity
and considerable construction, smaller population centers, but
wide streets laid out in grids."

The New World Order finally established communications
with Zion through its Omaha military base. They demanded the
Latter-day Saint community drop its shields and cooperate with
the world government or they would suffer a horrible fate.

Elder Dawahoya took charge of communicating with the
NWO. He informed the base commander they planned on living
peacefully. They would cause no harm, but they would not
submit to the government's demands.

It was a stalemate–one that the NWO didn't press because there wasn't any large scale migration to Zion, and they had far more pressing matters for the time being than dealing with a small religious "cult" in the middle of nowhere surrounded by some freak electrical pattern. For more importantly, persecution of Christians on a worldwide basis was about to begin in earnest.

Lu Han, however, when apprised of the situation, became angry and agitated. "I knew God would pull some rabbit out of the hat to protect his people. It has been foretold," he said angrily, as he stood and wrapped himself in a yellow silk robe. He waved a hand to indicate he wanted his two male servants to leave his private quarters in the palace. Once he was certain they were out of hearing range, he said, "I may have to take a trip there soon to get this rebel band under the NWO banner." Then this thought comforted him, *I have a mole inside that place, spreading my teachings.* He smiled and patted his stomach as if he just consumed a delicacy. "Yes, that's right. Little Laurie."

Laurie walked through the backyard of her friend and co-devotee of Lu Han. She was placing hand-copied sheets of the Chinese emperor's teachings on chairs and blankets in a large circle. This was in preparation for a clandestine meeting for about twenty people she and Kayleen had recruited. They were curious to hear more about the Savior being on the planet and His desire for people to prepare to be transfigured. Many came with maladies of some kind, because Laurie had hinted that someone might be healed at the gathering.

In the previous week, Laurie's guru had manifested himself to her twice. First, in the middle of the night, while she stayed at Nate's (he was on the rescue mission in the East), she woke to the scent of *vibuti* and found on her dresser twenty-four packets of the "healing" ash. They were carefully lined up four deep.

Two nights later, Laurie was sure she was awake because she was listening for Cristina to come back to Nate's house after a date. She saw the small figure of Lu Han hovering over the end of the bed as he had in the first vision, this time in the full yellow-robed regalia of the Chinese emperor.

"Oh, Master!" she cooed.

"You have received my gift?"

"I have. I assume you want me to give them to people who need healing."

"Yes, but I want you to give them to people who come to you to hear of my teaching. You may promise them healing, and I will see to it. But gather them quietly." A sensual smile crossed his mouth.

"Oh, I will," Laurie was nearly out of her skin with delight. "Will they be able to see you too?"

"Not this time. But if you will open yourself to me, I will enter you, and you can show them my greatness." He said, *Enter you* with an enticing tongue-licking show of his teeth.

For minutes after his departure she clung to her pillow, waves of desire flooding her.

Now, as the guests trickled in, Laurie paced, trying to contain her passionate yearning. She checked the pockets of her black sweater to make sure the ash packets were still intact. *Soon we will be blessed with his presence, and I will be blessed to be his mouthpiece!* she thought. A shiver ran up her spine.

Kayleen walked out in the backyard with a tray of cups and pitchers of green Koolaid and put them on a picnic table. "What are you going to do? I can't stand not knowing."

Laurie had not told anyone of Lu Han's promise. "It's not *me*, but what *he* is going to do," Laurie taunted.

"What time is it?" Kayleen asked breathlessly.

"6:55. I wish they'd hurry," Laurie said with biting avarice in her voice. "If they don't, I'm going to have a heart attack."

By 7:15 the yard was filled with curious people. The apostle's daughter made her way through the crowd shaking hands. "...Oh, Debbe, I'm so glad you made it. Be sure you read the material on your seat." "...Hey, Betty, you brought your handsome husband," she said shaking the retired couple's hands. She waited until the group settled down and had time to read through the literature from the light from aurora borealis which was bright enough that night to illuminate the scene. Then, when there were no more people filing into the side yard, Laurie walked up to the front of the audience. She was radiant in her long black dress and silver necklace on which hung the shiny yin/yang medallion, symbol of her devotion to Lu Han. "The lord has called you here tonight to prepare you for his coming."

There were murmurs from the crowd.

"He is already here on this earth, and he seeks individuals who are ready to be translated."

After answering several probing questions from the audience, Laurie repinned her hair in a bun on the side of her head and began reading from the pamphlet of Lu Han's teachings, "...god does not descend to teach all things to man. As he has said many times, god does not come on Earth to solve all your problems. Every difficulty which you encounter and which you must face is the result of your own actions. In time, all your difficulties will automatically be resolved–by you. Why ask god?"

A man standing the back broke in, "Wait. Will you explain what you mean by God?"

"God is the principle by which we abide this life. You cannot put a definition on god. The moment you begin to define it...."

"But that makes no sense!" the short, dark man said emphatically. "How can God come to earth seeking people to translate and yet be a principle that can't be defined?"

"Exactly!" Laurie said with a self-satisfied yet dreamy smile. "It makes no sense. That's the beauty of it. And the mystery."

The crowd began to stir and talk among themselves, so Laurie decided to up the ante. "Who among you is in need of healing?" she called out.

A fifty-year-old metal worker from Detroit, seated near the front, raised his hand.

"Come up here," Laurie commanded.

As the man lumbered forward, Laurie took out a light-green satchel of the ash, dramatically held it in the air, and said to the crowd, "This is the lord's healing powder which he has given to me."

The slightly skeptical man was now standing in front of her. "Tell us what is wrong with you. What is your name?" she asked.

"George...George Blodgett. I have had chronic back pain for nearly ten years. Degenerating disc, I'm told."

"I see," Laurie said, opening the packet and pinching some gray-white *vibuti* between her thumb and forefinger. Then she raised her hand high so the crowd could see. "This holy ash, George, the lord has blessed and materialized just for your healing."

The crowd muttered among themselves then leaned forward to see what would happen. As they did, Laurie suddenly felt an electrical sensation at the top of her head, snaking its way down her spine. Her arms and hands tingled as did her feet and toes. She opened her mouth to speak, when an almost baritone voice emerged. "I heal you in my holy name," the voice proclaimed as Laurie raised her arm involuntarily and rubbed a spot of ash on the man's forehead. Then this same sensation of electricity arched through her arm and out her hand to the man's head. When it reached him, he fell back and sat down on the grass, stunned.

Kayleen rushed to his side and asked if he was okay. People quickly stood up to peer over each other. He sat there as if in a trance. Finally he indicated he wanted to stand and struggled to his feet with Laurie and Kaylene's assistance.

"How do you feel? How is your pain?" Laurie asked in the deep voice.

"It's gone! It's really not there!" the befuddled man said as he wiped off the back of his tan pants and headed across the lawn for the wooden chair which he had vacated. His blond wife held her hand to her mouth in amazement.

"Who's next? Surely there must be someone else?" Laurie peered out over the crowd, using broad masculine gestures.

A local woman, lame, who walked with a brace and a cane, raised her hand. "Come here, dear Barbara," Lu Han's voice spoke through Laurie. She struggled to get up from the low lawn chair where she was sitting. All eyes watched the greying matron hobble across the lawn to stand in front of the medium. Most knew Sister Larsen had been unable to walk without support as long as they had known her. Laurie asked, "How is your leg feeling?"

The woman mumbled that it never felt good, not since she was a teenager.

"Do you believe I can heal you?" Laurie asked breathlessly, eyes half-closed. She moved in quite close to the woman's scared face.

"I...I don't really know," Barbara stammered.

Laurie, now completely in a trance, stretched out her quite hot hands and took the thin woman's in hers.

"Barbara, don't be afraid. I won't harm you," said the emperor's silky voice, emanating from Laurie's mouth.

The frightened matron shivered. Tim, her tall, thin husband, stood up and moved protectively close to her. He asked Laurie, "Are you a faith healer?"

"I am what your Barbara wants me to be. It seems she wants me to be a healer right at this moment."

With a sob, the woman from Independence cried out, "Oh, if you could help me...these are such difficult times, and I'm such a burden to my husband."

Laurie again involuntarily raised her hand up to the woman's forehead and said in a loud voice that all could hear, "You are healed by your faith in me." As she touched Barbara's forehead with her index finger, the woman fell back with just a little "oh!" and collapsed into her husband's arms.

"Lay her down," Han's voice commanded. "I am working on her."

Then, just as Laurie raised her arms, palms out, to bless the crowd who was now quite into the scene (many believing that God was indeed working through this apostle's daughter), the back gate swung open, and her father stood in the fading light of the evening. Behind him stood a glowering Elder Stewart.

"In the name of Jesus Christ, I command you to stop!" Elder

Whitmer shouted.

Laurie slowly lowered her arms and launched a baleful, piercing stare in their direction. "What are *you* doing here?" she asked in Han's low, menacing voice.

"We are here to rid Zion of this evil," Elder Stewart said forcefully.

"How dare you interrupt this private meeting!" she demanded.

"We do our Lord's bidding," Elder Stewart responded.

A sly grin came over her face. "Then I command you in my name to leave this place, this house and allow us to continue."

Elder Whitmer strode across the yard and stood directly in front of Laurie, his eyes flashing. "Laurie, you can either walk out of this meeting under your own steam, or I will see that you are removed," he said forcefully.

Laurie reared back. "By what authority?"

"In the name of Jesus Christ!" her father said, raising his right arm in the air.

There was a kind of loud cackle, then Laurie suddenly slumped to the ground. The crowd, which had stood as the apostles entered, mulled around anxiously. Peter and Jed stepped out from the shadows of the side of the house and stood with their muscular arms folded, blocking the way out.

Elder Stewart turned to the crowd and pointed to the figure on the ground. "You have been badly fooled tonight by this woman. I suggest you forget what has happened here–it was the work of a devil."

"But I was healed!" Barbara Larsen cried out. "The pain is gone, and I can walk normally. How can that be?"

The mint-green glow of the night sky backlit the silver color of Elder Whitmer's hair, making it seem like he had a halo around his head. He said with great emotion in his voice, "Madam, Lucifer and his minions can appear in many guises and work many wonders to win souls to their side. I am happy for you–that this has happened, but you must give your thanks to

the God who made you. And never listen to this woman again."
The lightning-like countenance of the apostle caused the woman
to step back and cower in the presence of such righteous force.

Elder Whitmer pulled up his daughter to her feet and began
leading her from the yard. Peter and Jed kept others back until
she passed by. On her way, Laurie turned and cried out in her
normal voice, "Don't give up believing. He is here, I have seen
him." Then she was gone, placed in a car and driven to Church
headquarters. The crowd stood stunned for several minutes before
dispersing into the night.

John Whitmer's hand shook with anger as he grabbed the
underside of Laurie's forearm and shoved her up the stairs to the
conference room at Church headquarters.

Moira looked in on Grace, who lay propped by pillows in her
darkened, downstairs bedroom. "Are you sure you're going to be
okay, Mom? We won't be gone more than an hour, two tops."

"Go on. Don't even think about it, sweetheart. I'll be fine,"
Grace lied. The fact was she was nearly blinded by the tumor and
suffering a great deal of pain. The cortisone steroid she'd been
using was having virtually no effect. The evening before, when
David Hunter came to check on her, she asked him for something
stronger. He said she already had the best he could offer. He also
expressed his real concern that she had not eaten any solid foods
for nearly a week. "I kinda think we're coming to the end, Sister
Ihimaera."

"Don't tell the kids," Grace begged. "I want them to get
through this temple opening. Alex is so proud of his work."

"I promise," the doctor said sadly.

Alex and Moira were anxious to go through the finished
building, as they would not be attending the dedication services.
Ironically, Alex, who oversaw the artistic work, had not been a
member for a year and was not eligible for a temple recommend.
Moira insisted she would sit outside on the grounds with him.

The stunning dome with its golden illumination, which they
had seen raised into place, could be seen for miles around. The

temple exterior was of polished gray dolomite, girdered by white marble columns. Twelve spires, surrounding the dome, rose from the top of the temple walls.

Upon entering the temple grounds, the first sight was Alex's statue of Christ–this one expressing a depth of pain and pleasure in both the face and body rarely expressed in other statues of Him. On his Jewish face were smile lines as well as frown lines. His posture was not stiff but seemed to be in movement as He beckoned to His disciples to come into the holy house. Many people commented that Alex's work with dolomite was much like Michaelangelo's.

The next sensations that were aroused as one walked toward the temple's gold-embossed doors were the smell of tropical flowers and the sight of a profusion of flowers and shrubbery that gave one the feeling that she was stepping into an Eden.

A round, ruby-red stained glass design dominated the entryway, throwing crimson-colored prisms throughout the lobby. It was at the recommend desk where one experienced the first intimation of the use of light so original in this central temple. It was as if one were being surrounded and even infused with an indirect, yet pervasive light. Working with John the Beloved, Alex and the temple architects had managed to capture some of the quality of the light in the spirit world.

The pattern of polished dolomite walls with white marble columns was repeated throughout the interior. In the open waiting area past the recommend desk, one could walk through marble-like columns to go to the dressing rooms or turn right or left and walk through the outside hallways past offices designated for each of the twelve tribes. In between the walls of the interior of the temple and these antechambers was planted an atrium whose exotic ambiance and smell heightened the temple-goers' impression that they really were in a terrestrial garden.

As Alex and Moira walked down the hall past doors marked, "Dan," "Asher," "Naphtali..." they could faintly hear a choir. "Isn't that the "Hallelujah Chorus" from *The Messiah?*" Moira asked, straining to hear the voices.

"It is. They're upstairs in the assembly hall. Peg Taylor is singing in it," Alex said.

"Oh, really. Anyone else we know?"

"Don't think so," Alex said, suddenly pulling Moira close to him.

"It sounds beautiful," Moira said dreamily.

"Iwi, you are looking so beautiful these days," Alex said, scanning her tan features.

"I've felt a lot more at peace since I've come home. I believe Christ really means it when He says, 'Come unto me, and I will give you peace.'"

The two stood looking deeply into each other's eyes for a few moments, then Alex said, "See that vase over there?" He pointed to a fine, long-necked vase sitting on a simple stand with an ornate, tortoise-shell top. "Jody Rivers did that. She really got into the pottery part of this project."

Moira chuckled. "That's funny, because she kept saying, 'My patriarchal blessing says I'll help build the Temple, but I'm pregnant. How can that be?'"

"You never know how Heavenly Father is going to work out those prophetic statements. Jody came to me as an assistant. She'd never thrown a pot, but she really blossomed as we went along," Alex said with perceptible pride in his voice.

As they reached the end of the hall and turned toward the chapel, they spotted Nate and Mary Margaret passing through, so they waved.

"You know what some of the women are saying?" Moira asked.

"Who cares? I thought we were leaving gossip behind when we came to Zion."

"Well, we're winding down. It's a hard habit to break."

Now the Dubiks walked into the gorgeously-appointed chapel. Moira gasped and grabbed at Alex's arm when she looked up at the eighteen-foot-tall stained glass window depicting a triumphant Christ in a red robe. He looked so real that Moira froze for a moment. "That's uncanny–it looks like He's standing right there," she whispered and pointed in the direction of the window.

"This project was overseen by John the apostle. He kept subtly changing our work until we produced *that*...." Alex's voice trailed off in wonder.

"Whew! I can't even begin to imagine what miracles this dedication will bring."

"Me, neither." Alex tried to push away the angry thought that he couldn't be there, so he said, "Okay, what is the gossip?" mad at himself for wanting to know.

Moira smiled. "Some women are wondering if Nate isn't going from the frying pan into the fire. I know that Mary Margaret isn't mentally stable, and she's a non-member. They think he may be on the rebound—you know, apostle's daughter to Irish beauty."

"Enough already," Alex said irritated. "Why is it that women are such busy-bodies about other people's love lives?"

"Honey," Moira said, patting his arm, "we get to fall in love all over again."

"Once is enough for me," Alex grumbled.

"But you'll fall for a story of a guy who comes up against great odds and struggles to survive! It's the same with us. One of our greatest triumphs is to find a wonderful man and have him fall in love with us. Yours is to defeat a ferocious dragon."

"Okay, okay," Alex said, laughing as he raised his large, calloused hands in the air. "But, promise me you'll leave Nate alone. He looks happy for the first time since I met him."

From the chapel, they walked down the interior hall, laid with light-blue carpet, past exquisitely-decorated sealing rooms similar to ones Moira had been in in New Zealand and Hawaii. But when they reached the celestial room, something happened to the Maori which she hadn't expected. Here the effect of the light streaming in through the twelve feet high windows left Moira with the impression that the room had disappeared, and she had been lifted up into a higher, lighter realm. Even her body felt lighter. She was speechless.

After a few moments in this transported state, she returned to focus on who else was in the elegantly-appointed room. Her eye fell on Juan Gallegos and his family. She grabbed Alex's arm, and they quickly walked over to the couple who were clearly amazed at the beauty of the holy place. After warm hugs all around, Moira asked how they were.

"We are fine," Juan said, his face shining with delight. "We are listening to the missionaries and have set a baptism date."

"What great news, Juan!" Alex exuded. "When? Can we come?"

"We were just getting ready to tell you. If you don't come, we will be very sad. If it weren't for you and the Taylor's, we wouldn't have come to Missouri. And what we would have missed!"

"How are people back in Puerto de Luna?" Moira asked.

"It's really bad there. I got a letter that said the plague has killed many people."

"That's horrible! And Rosa? How is she?" Alex asked.

"Okay, I think. She's too mean to have a virus kill her. But I did hear that people aren't happy with her. The Virgin doesn't come any more."

Alex flashed a quick smile at Moira over the Gallegos' head. "Got to tell Mom about that," he mouthed.

With the mention of Grace's name, Moira suddenly stepped back and frowned.

"Honey, what is it?" Alex asked solicitously.

"I don't know. I feel really funny. I think it's Mom," Moira said. "Yes, that's it! We have to get back to her!" She looked around frantically. "Something bad has happened, honey. I can feel it." She grabbed Alex, murmured apologies and bounded down the hall, pushing her way past the entering crowd.

At that moment, Grace, lying in the darkened back bedroom, was experiencing such a searing pain in her forehead that she thought she couldn't possibly endure any more. Then suddenly it was gone. Her vision, though blurred, seemed to clear enough for her to make out a figure across the room. As it came closer, she could see it was the man with the brilliant blue eyes.

"Just who are you?" she struggled to ask.

"I am your guardian angel, and it's time, Grace. Your request has finally been granted," he said soothingly.

He stepped aside to reveal Gordon, dark and handsome, his arms outstretched. "Come, my love. It's time."

Grace struggled for a moment. "But Iwi, sweetheart. I have to say goodbye–and Alex and Adam," she pined.

"You'll see them very soon," Gordon promised.

"But they won't be able to see me," she protested.

"That's where you're wrong. Now stop arguing with your husband and come on."

With a slight tickle to the top of her head, she let out a quiet sigh and glided out. Although she'd had out-of-body experiences when she slept, this was the first in waking daytime.

Gordon, a tall, athletic man with curly black hair, led her slowly into a bright light which dissolved into a vast, green area. She immediately recognized it as one she had once visited. At the onset of that visit, she'd been knocked unconscious by being slammed into the side of the dresser and was taken to see the place where souls were entering the spirit world. Now it was her time, and she felt so free, almost frisky. Young again, and so much in love with her eternal soul mate.

Moira and Alex rushed into the house, but had to stand helplessly over a warm corpse until Dr. Hunter arrived. Moira couldn't contain herself and sobbed so hard her shoulders shook. Alex held her and rocked her until the medical examiner and Hunter arrived. To the couple David explained, "It was a brain herniation through a small opening in the back of the brain case. Couldn't have taken more than an hour." To the medical examiner he wrote down, "Supratentorial herniation," and wiped away tears that fell on the paper.

The hastily-called meeting at church headquarters to consider excommunication was attended by Laurie's bishop and stake president, two high councilmen and Elder Stewart. Elder Whitmer vacated the building, although he didn't go home to his grieving wife. It was she who had told her husband about Laurie's secret meeting. She learned about it from a friend who had been approached by Laurie and Kayleen. The matron politely declined to go but was shocked enough at the suggestion that these two women knew more than the prophet about the Lord's second coming to report it to Sister Whitmer.

A defiant, mocking Laurie sat opposite her accusers, who sat in somber contemplation.

"Do you understand that if you do not submit your will to the will of our Father and His priesthood, you will be asked to leave Zion?" her stake president asked with concern.

"What is Zion?" she spat out. "The lord isn't here. I will happily go to him." A reptilian look possessed her face. "I do not recognize your authority. Yours is a false priesthood."

Ned insisted on accompanying his mother and grandfather to the portal on the northeast end of Zion. Arrangements had been made with the Omaha headquarters of the New World Order to escort Laurie to an ashram of Lu Han's followers in Boulder, Colorado. The price was hefty–$75,000 in gold bullion that Elder Whitmer had brought with him to Zion.

Laurie stood stone-faced while the three waited for the soldiers to arrive. She carried only one suitcase and slung a large black purse over her shoulder. Ned stood with his head down, arms hanging uselessly. Elder Whitmer tried to cover his dismay by pacing back and forth, periodically stopping to talk with sentinels who administered the electronic gate.

When the black van appeared over a distant hill, Ned stepped up to his mother and said in a choked voice, "You can always change your mind, Mom."

She stiffened and stared straight ahead until the soldiers were admitted into one side of the gate. Elder Whitmer led the way, Laurie behind. He handed over the money and tried to get their assurances that they would really take her to Boulder, but he couldn't read their faces. For all he knew, they'd drive over the hill, bludgeon Laurie, leave her for dead, and drive off with the money.

After Laurie walked deliberately through the portal–not looking back once–she made her way between the black-uniformed men to the van. Elder Whitmer returned to the devastated nineteen-year-old and put his arm around the boy's waist. The two stood silent as the van pulled away. When they couldn't see the red tail lights anymore, the apostle said, "Come on, Neddy. We've got a lot of work to do to keep this family going."

"What will happen to her friend, Kayleen? Will she be kicked out of Zion, too?" Ned asked morosely.

"That will depend on the Lord."

"What do you think, Grandfather?"

"I never try to second-guess the Lord, son," the apostle said.

Ned reached up and wiped a tear running off his nose. His grandfather handed him a white handkerchief. "Mom can come back, Grandfather, can't she? If she wants to, she can come back."

"That is always an option, but I think it will be awhile before that happens. She's..." Her father couldn't go on. Shoulders hunched, head hung low, he began to sob. Laurie was his only daughter, and he had held onto hope that she would change and fulfill her spiritual promise. Now all that was left was the ghastly light of the full moon behind grey-green clouds on a distant bone-dry hill.

CHAPTER TWENTY-ONE

"I am Jesus Christ, the Son of God;
wherefore, gird up your loins and
I will suddenly come to my temple."
D & C 36:8

Peg was upstairs, wetting Danny's blond hair, trying to get it to do something other than twirl out of control like two tornadoes on either side of his head, so they could leave for Grace's funeral.

"Okay, that's better," Peg said, "But, honey, how many times I gotta tell ya, just run a comb through your hair after you shower at night?"

Danny mumbled something she couldn't understand, so she pushed him lovingly out of the bathroom and grabbed Amber as she ran down the hall. It was a new experience for Peg to work with the texture of the little girl's hair—one Peg enjoyed.

"Stand still, Amber. I just have to put a couple of bows in your hair, that's all."

"Sister Peg, when am I goin' home?" she asked longingly.

"Oh, boy, that's hard to say," Peg said. "You see where you come from nobody lives there any more, and where you were staying with Keesha Washington, well...." She felt a lump come to her throat. She had tried not to think about returning the orphan to the camp but had registered her with the Orphan's Directory. That way, Amber was like their foster child until some one came to claim her.

"Never mind," the child said and raced back down the hallway to the room she shared with Miriam. Peg could hear the two arguing about missing socks. She stood with her hands on her hips for a moment, then said silently, *Lord, I almost never ask for something that I think is selfish, but I really, really want to keep this precious child...if it could be arranged.*

Her reverie was interrupted by Ben wandering toward her,

his shirt half-buttoned and without a tie. "Oh, great finder of lost objects," he said bowing low and sweeping his right arm in front of him, "Have you seen my blue tie?"

"Oh, loser of nearly everything you own, it's on the new tie rack I put up on the back of the closet door, so you wouldn't have to look for your ties."

"Oh, yeah, I forgot."

Peg laughed and shook her head then headed back downstairs, wiping grape jelly off the bannister with a wash cloth she found on the floor. Suddenly there was a loud knock on the front door.

Who could that be, she puzzled as she tucked her white blouse into a navy skirt. *We're not taking anyone with us, are we? Unless Ben has volunteered somebody I don't know about, which is a definite possibility.*

She had just put her hand on the door knob to turn it, when there came a second, even louder and more impatient pounding. She opened to the door to find her mother, LaDawn Christensen, standing there.

"Well, thank you for not responding to my message," were the first words out of the pudgy, narrow-lipped matron.

"M...Mom!" Peg exclaimed, throwing her hands to her face. "What...I didn't get...you're here! In Zion!"

"May I come in to my own daughter's house?" LaDawn asked impatiently.

"Of course...only we're just headed out to a funeral."

"At least it isn't mine," the mother said with an acidic undertone.

Peg quickly swept through the living room to gather up stray toys and gestured to her mother to sit on the couch.

"You've put on quite a bit of weight since I saw you last," LaDawn said, squinting to take in the full effect of Peg's figure.

"Gee, I don't think so, Mom. It's only been about a year and a half, and I think I'm holding pretty steady." Peg turned as tears unexpectedly stung her eyes. She took a deep breath, quickly wiped her eyes and sat down opposite her mother in an easy chair.

"You look good, Mom. How long have you been here?"

"Nearly three weeks. My visiting teachers, Sister Johnson and Sister Swensen—you know them—convinced me I'd be safer here. I left word with that half-colored woman."

"Who?" Peg tried to think whom her mother meant. "Moira Dubik?"

"No, the older woman."

"Grace?"

"Yes, nearly three weeks ago now. You'd think she'd be more efficient, being the Relief Society General President and all."

"Mom, she's just died," Peg said, her voice choking. She couldn't believe what she was hearing from her mother. She hadn't remembered LaDawn being racist, but then there were no minorities who lived in the small town in Idaho where she was raised, just seasonal migrant workers. Peg did remember her mother was adamant that she stay away from the Hispanic kids. LaDawn would never give her a reason when pressed.

"She's been ill for some time," Peg said with indignation in her voice. "I'm sure it just slipped her mind."

"Oh, I'm sorry," LaDawn said somewhat apologetically. "Well, where's the rest of your family?"

"They'll be down in a minute. Would you like to go to Grace's funeral with us?" Peg ventured, even though her mother had not gone to church for years. *Maybe she's changed,* she thought. *She's at least made it to Zion.*

"No, I'm not dressed for the occasion."

Just then Miriam and Amber thundered down the stairs. Peg called to them to come into the living room. When they raced in, Peg grabbed each and pulled them into her lap. "Girls, this is your grandmother," she said without thinking about Amber's status with the family.

"Hi!" the girls said in chorus.

"What do we call you?" Miriam asked. "Grandma?"

LaDawn gathered herself into a rigid plank, shocked that she now had to deal with a "black" girl as well as a Jewish son-in-law. *I never taught her to be this way*, she thought fiercely.

"Well," Amber said, "What should we call you?"

"Grandmother will do," LaDawn said in a short, clipped manner indicating she didn't want to continue the conversation.

After the introduction of Danny to his grandmother, Ben took the kids to the car while Peg had last words with her mother.

"Here is my address," LaDawn said, pushing a prewritten card into Peg's hand. "I hope you'll come for a visit–alone–when we can talk about these changes."

"Mom, I...I'm so glad you've made here. I promise to come by as soon as possible, so we can catch up."

As the two women walked out of the house and down the walk together, Ben was struck with how unhappy his mother-in-law looked. *Poor Peg*, he thought, *she's going to have her hands full.*

At the funeral in the older Independence chapel still standing, Grace lay in an open coffin surrounded by a plethora of flowers. Members stood to share stories about Grace–secret acts of kindness–that Moira knew nothing about. Here was Grace, scarcely in Zion a few months, and what an impact she had had on the whole society. Moira sat with Alex's arm tightly around her in the front pew. He openly wept, but she didn't let her emotions show, although she was both proud and humbled. With her heart in great pain, she vowed to try to follow in Grace's footsteps and dedicate all her energies to the building up of the Lord's kingdom.

"She was an elect lady," said President Ueda, characterizing the Relief Society President in his eulogy. The prophet took the occasion to call all who were planning to attend the temple dedication the following day to fast and prepare themselves for a great outpouring of the Spirit.

Peg tried to ignore the squirming children as emotions raged through her. She loved Grace as a surrogate mother, and she thought it strange that Grace would be the one to forget to deliver the word that LaDawn was in Zion. *Almost like she was protecting me,* Peg thought. *And when did my mom get so bitter and rigid?*

She sighed, and Ben took her hand and kissed it lightly. "Mothers can really pull at your heart strings," he said softly.

"At least yours won't come here," Peg whispered fiercely.

Early in the next day before the temple dedication, Ben dropped his three children off at the Dubiks (they would take them onto the temple grounds for the dedication) and went to his new office in the archive repository of the temple. He walked through the rows of glass cases which held the scrolls and plates that the members of the lost tribes had given the prophet. Fiddling with the light level switch, he worried that the overhead lamps weren't exactly in place.

After finishing a rough translation of the Tibetan plates that Sangay had given the church, the scribe was now worried about the new challenge he faced as head archivist. "Now this," he said, sweeping his arm across the scene, "this is ten times as daunting as the first project. I'm going to need at least eight more people, working full time." Ben rubbed a smudge off one of the cases with his shirt sleeve. "And I'm lousy at supervision."

He paused and listened to what sounded like footsteps right outside in the hall, but when no one walked past, he resumed his tour of the archive room. *Well, when you are in the service of the Lord, I guess you continually get stretched,* he thought. The indirect light slanting off his bald head as he wandered from one case to the next looked like a buoy bobbing in a dark sea.

Then he stopped and thought, *But wait! What if I never had anything to do, ever again?* He shuddered. *No...the concept of eternal progression is definitely more appealing,* he decided.

This time Sangay didn't materialize out of thin air–he walked through the door of the repository, the sixty-year-old version of Sangay, dressed in temple whites.

"What? Sangay?" Ben stammered. "I thought you had been translated!"

"Hello, Ben. I have."

"But Sangay, the last time I saw you you were twenty-five years old, tops."

"We have the ability to alter our age and appearance slightly, as needed," Sangay said as he and Ben began meandering through the exhibits. "You remember when Joseph Smith was driving along in a wagon and an older man stepped out of the woods and hailed him?"

"Yes. And when he came back, his traveling companion asked him who that was," Ben said.

"And he casually replied, 'That was Father Adam.' Well, Father Adam isn't an older man. He's a fine specimen of a man who normally looks like he's thirty, at the most."

"Wow, I never thought about that," Ben said, frantically filing away the fact that translated beings don't necessarily look the same each time they appear. "Are you here for the temple dedication?"

"I am."

"Were you just out in the hall, a couple of minutes ago?"

"No, I've just arrived."

"By satellite, as usual?" Ben quipped.

"No, normal locomotion. Okay, Ben, I've got a new joke for you. What did the Buddhist monk say to the guy at the hot dog stand?"

"I dunno. What, rinpoche?"

"Make me *one* with everything!"

Ben put back his head and laughed a hearty laugh. When the

scribe had contained himself, Sangay said with a twinkle in his eye, "So, my ambitious pupil, is this enough for you?" He swept his hand across the considerable collection of untranslated scripture.

Ben laughed again. "You know, a person always thinks, 'If I just could get this or advance up there–then it would be all better, or better yet, all over.' But it never ends, does it?"

"Thank goodness. As I have taught you, so long as we control our minds, still our hearts, and measure our breaths, we have access to the Holy Spirit. Then we can welcome eternal change and growth gracefully."

"It's funny hearing you say 'Holy Spirit'. Why didn't you let me know earlier, when we first met, that you were a closet Christian?" Ben asked.

"Because I was asked to remain silent until certain events had transpired," Sangay said.

Chuckling to himself about the incongruous appearance of the Tibetan monk dressed in a white shirt and tie, Ben asked Sangay, "How goes the missionary effort among the tribes?".

"Many, many converts." Sangay's face lit up. "So many, in fact, it has been the fulfillment of Christ's saying, 'The field is white and ready to harvest.' Whole villages are entering the waters of baptism, now that we can teach them openly."

"But I thought the New World Order had clamped down completely on proselyting–particularly anything related to Christ."

"One can never control a man or woman's spiritual longing," Sangay mused, as he walked to the case containing his Tibetan plates, then stopped to stare at the thin, metal sheets on the brilliant yellow and red silk cloth.

"When will they come here? To Zion?" Ben asked, joining his meditation teacher.

"No man knows the hour or day, but we do know the earth must first be restored to one land piece. In addition, all our people must have the opportunity to hear the gospel and be baptized."

"Then they will come for their temple blessings."

"That is correct. Won't that be a sight? Millions pouring into Zion for their blessings." Sangay held a faraway look of sheer satisfaction for a long moment, then said, "Then you can be sure it will be finished."

"And you, as a translated being, can stay for the end, can't you?"

"Yes, that is a tremendous blessing."

"Can I ask a nosey question?" Ben said, looking down at the floor.

"Do you ever ask any other kind?" Sangay teased.

"What do you with your time if you don't eat or sleep any longer?" Ben asked sheepishly.

Sangay put back his head and laughed. His smile lines resembled a child's sun drawing. "You'd be surprised how the days are filled up with the Lord's work." He pulled at the white tie which appeared to be uncomfortable to the normally tieless monk.

"Boy, these must be exciting times for you!" Ben said admiringly.

Sangay smiled. "About as exciting as finding two such apt pupils as you and Alex."

"You flatter me," Ben said, turning red.

"No." Sangay grew serious. "I would not say such a thing if it weren't true."

Embarrassed, Ben changed the subject. "I think it's really interesting the NWO has chosen the Hagia Sophia for its world headquarters."

"Why do you say that?" Sangay asked.

"Well, it's like a pale version of this marvelous temple. Thomas Merton, a Christian monk of the mid-20th century, said something like, 'The Hagia Sophia is God Himself, or the feminine aspect of divinity.' That's how I feel about this temple. It places the masculine/feminine relationship in such harmony."

"I wonder what he'd say if he could see this," Sangay said.

"It's a wonder, isn't it?"

There was a pause while the two listened to the choir on the next floor begin their final practice, then Ben said sarcastically, "The NWO–a one-world government backed by a one-world religion. It's pathetic."

"Just as it has been prophesied for millennia. You found that on the Tibetan plates I lent you, didn't you?" Sangay asked.

"I did. It was startling to read such clear prophetic lines. *Our* prophecies are couched in such symbolic language."

The two stood side by side listening, suddenly rapt in the strains of "The Spirit of God Like A Fire Is Burning." Finally Sangay said, "You ready for today?"

Ben began to say something, then shut his mouth.

"What? What do you want to say?" Sangay asked gently.

Ben fought back tears. "Thank you, rinpoche. Thank you for being so patient with me. Thank you...oh, I don't know...for a million things. I'd never be where I am without you."

Sangay put his hand on Ben's arm. His touch was light; a slight scent of incense came from his body. Then he stepped toward the open door and bowed ceremoniously. "I have to attend to my duties. See you later."

Ben bowed back, and when he looked up the rinpoche was nowhere in sight. He walked around the room once more for good measure until deciding he'd go upstairs to the large meeting hall where Peg was practicing. *No use worrying about these beauties any longer,* he thought, as he patted an hermetically-sealed case that contained Elder Dawahoya's kachina.

It was only when he walked out the door that he realized who it was that had made the earlier sounds in the hall–two burly guards, looking all the world like Nephite warriors in white jumpsuits. He nodded to them as he shut and locked the door. *Wonder where they found those guys...in central casting?* Ben laughed to himself. *You never know with the Lord.*

Lu Han sat on an large, ornate brocade pillow in his inner chamber in the Palace of Clouds, fuming that there was now no one in Zion whom he could manipulate. He thought back to when he found Laurie in his ashram in Boulder. "What are you doing *here!*" his 10-inch figure demanded.

"I've been thrown out of Zion...by my own father," she whined. "May I now come to you, great lord?" she asked, stretching her arms beseechingly in his direction.

"Never! I have no use for people who fail me." His eyes flashed a menacing hatred in her direction. Before she could say a word more, he disappeared and commenced to send out a probe to Kayleen, but he found her energy field was shut down to him. Terrified of what had happened to Laurie, she quickly submitted herself to disfellowshipment proceedings.

"I'll waste no more energy on a woman!" He spat toward a copper spittoon. "They are useless and weak!" He uncrossed his legs and stood. "I'll have to do something myself," said the self-appointed Lord of 10,000 Years.

Ben sat near the back of the assembly hall to take in the full effect of the rehearsal's music. *These acoustics are incredible,* he thought, as he rested his head back against the wooden bench and looked up at the golden reflector and the dome beyond. The sounds of the "Hallelujah Chorus" began to swell. The light from the tall windows made the dome seem to float. Ben felt he was floating, too, surrounded by a chorus of angels. He opened his eyes several times to see if he could discern divine presences in the room.

At the break, Peg came rushing up to him, breathless. "Ben, Ben, I've got to tell you what happened this morning as I was walking down the hall to come here."

"Whoa, slow down. Sit down, honey." Ben found that when she was excited Peg always talked way too fast for him to assimilate what she had to say. She would shower him with rapid-fire sound bytes without filling in the details.

"Okay," Peg said taking a long breath. "As I was walking toward the elevator, I looked back and there stood two huge men on either side of your door. They had on feathered head dresses and massive breast plates with spears taller than they were. Like they were standing guard outside the archives!"

"No kidding!" he said half-seriously. "Well, I saw them too, but they were in white jumpsuits."

"Couldn't have been the same ones," she puzzled and went on, "And then, when I walked past the sealing office, two more of these huge guys were standing on either side of that door."

To humor her, Ben said, "You know, I've heard somewhere that people have seen Nephite warriors guarding the MTC and the Salt Lake Temple, I believe."

Peg nestled into his arms. She was slightly shaking. Ben felt big and protective. He said, "This is just the beginning, my sweet. I think we're going to have to get used to people coming and going from the fourth dimension."

The stake choir director, a large Polynesian woman, signaled the return to rehearsing, so Peg slipped out of his arms and made her way back through the seats to the riser. Ben's heart followed her. "I am so in love. I am the luckiest man alive," he said aloud.

She heard him, turned and blew him a kiss.

Ben checked his coat pocket for a white handkerchief and waited for the crowd to arrive. Soon the room began to fill with friends, neighbors–an excited Nate with Neddy and Bobby Whitmer, Jed and the very-pregnant Jody with Peter–in addition to people Ben didn't know, and a few he hadn't seen since he had fled from Utah.

One of those men, Bishop Olsen, caught Ben's eye as the saintly, arthritic man slowly made his way to the front of the hall. Jumping up and rushing through the oncoming crowd, Ben reached the bishop just as he was sitting down.

"Bishop Olsen!" Ben said, somewhat out of breath.

"Oh, Ben. How good it is to see you!" Olsen struggled to his feet and embraced his protegé. The bishop had taken Ben under his wing in Salt Lake right after Ben's baptism. It was he who had suggested Ben for the Tibetan translation project and told Ben that the Brethren were aware of him and wanted to encourage him in his spiritual progression. Ben couldn't believe that anyone at those high levels would be aware of him, yet now here he was, privy to many of the inner-most decisions of the Brethren.

Ben clearly remembered the bishop saying to him, "If you are able to withstand what testing the Lord provides for all His servants who wish to be called saints of God, you will find that you will be bound up for eternal life and have fulfilled the dearest desires of your heart."

Then Ben confessed that his one great desire in life, along with having his family happy and safe, was to be with his Savior. And the bishop had said, "I don't know a more zealous lover of Christ, Ben. You are an exceptional man, and one day soon you will have the opportunity to have that wish fulfilled."

Now here they were, in the Lord's Zion temple, with the possibility of that promise being realized that very day. But at this moment, Ben clung to this father figure, for Pete Taylor had died when Ben was seventeen.

"How is your wife?" Ben asked solicitously.

"Elizabeth bore the trip admirably. Her health is still not good, but we have every hope that the miraculous may occur here in God's kingdom. Come, sit, Ben," the bishop said, patting the bench next to him on the second row.

"Isn't this reserved for special guests?"

"Yes, but you are my guest for now." The bishop beamed. From there Ben could clearly see Peg file into the alto section. She winked at him to let him know she noticed where he was and who he was with.

Patriarch Hugo and Inocencia Martinez walked slowly down to the reserved seating area, and Ben flashed them a big smile. In that moment, he was filled with a soft contentment, as if he were a young boy nestled among loving, competent adults —something he had never actually experienced as a child.

After the two-hundred member choir in their white temple clothes were seated, the dais began to fill with the joyous general authorities. Newly-called apostles joined their colleagues on the top row. One was President Suifua who had been the head of the Independence Stake. Below them came members of the Quorum of the Seventy, most new to their positions. Sangay sat below President Suifua in his "older, pre-translated version" along with other men, heads of the Lost Tribes. Ben wondered just how many people knew they were seated in the presence of translated beings.

After the choir's opening song, the prophet rose and walked in small but steady steps to the podium. Ben's face flushed with excitement, and he whispered to himself, "Here we go!"

"Brothers and sisters, we gather together to dedicate this House of the Lord, the central temple on Mount Zion. We invite all to turn their minds to the meaning of this momentous occasion."

Ben thought it was interesting that this dedication was on September twenty-first, the day of the autumn equinox, and the time when the fruits of the harvest would soon be gathered in from the fields. Turning this and other exciting thoughts over in his mind, he scarcely heard the two speeches from members of the First Presidency, first Elder Stewart, then Elder Dawahoya. Hoping for a miraculous outpouring of the Spirit as had happened at the Kirtland Temple dedication, he looked all around, squinting his eyes in an attempt to see angels during the following song from the choir.

Then President Ueda returned to the pulpit to begin his dedicatory prayer. In it he mentioned that the holy edifice they sat in would be like no other—that the veil would be lifted, and many manifestations of the Spirit would be soon become evident.

By the time the congregation stood to sing "The Spirit of God," Ben's pulse felt like a snare drum in a marching band. It was a great relief to shout "Hosanna" and wave his handkerchief when the time came. But it was somewhere in the beginning of the "Hallelujah Chorus" that the Church's scribe felt the hair stand up on the back of his neck. When he turned his head to the left, a figure in a long, white, seamless robe began walking across the stage. With every step closer he took, it became clearer to Ben that it was the Lord, his Savior.

Ben sucked in his breath and tried not to faint. The sounds from the choir grew deeper, sweeter, more multidimensional. Ben turned in his seat, astonished to see the room filled with people in white robes, floating several inches above the floor and joining in the joyful song of adoration. Turning his attention back to the podium, the Church's scribe watched as Peg wept and tried to sing at the same time.

The Savior, His countenance powerful yet tender, came to the middle of the stage and stood quietly while the choirs continued their song of heartfelt thanksgiving for His life and sacrifice. A bright golden aura surrounded him.

Outside on the grounds, people shouted and pointed to the fiery light shooting from the top of the temple. It looked like the twelve spires were torches, burning high in the air. Mary Margaret was the first to see the white-robed translated men walking through the grounds. She called out and pointed. Amber, who was sitting at her feet, stood up and yelled, "Tanka! Over here!" Then she jumped up and ran to the side of the tall, stoop-shouldered, white-haired man who came walking down the sidewalk past the gorgeous array of planted flowers.

"This is my Indian grandfather," Amber said breathlessly as she pulled on his sleeve and brought him to the Dubiks and Mary Margaret. "He's the one who takes care of me," Amber said excitedly.

Mary Margaret stood and shook his hand, a respectful, otherworldly look on her face. "How do you do? I've heard from Amber about your care of her during the terrible tornado she passed through. What may I call you?"

"Elder Timothy. And I know that you have been a devoted servant of the Lord for some time, Mrs. O'Boyle. May you be blessed for that devotion."

Beginning to sob, Mary Margaret threw her hands over her face and looked away. So Timothy patted her arm and turned his attention to the Dubiks.

"I am deeply honored to meet you, Elder Timothy," Moira said, reaching out with a slightly trembling hand. "You knew my mother, from what she told me."

Amber hung onto Timothy's leg. "Now do you believe me?" she asked saucily. "*Now* do you believe me?"

Alex bent down and picked her up in his arms. "We do, we really do, sweetheart." He then shook the translated apostle's hand and introduced Ben's children, Danny and Miriam, to him. The two children grew shy, in the presence of Timothy's gentle intensity, as did Mary Margaret's three girls.

Then the Nephite apostle looked to Moira, who still wore on her stoic face the remnants of the loss of her mother. "Why are you so sad?" he asked.

"As you may know, my mother just passed away."

"You mean Grace?" he asked, lovingly toying with her.

Moira nodded then was distracted for a moment when Adam dropped his pacifier. When she looked up, her parents stood before her.

"You can't touch us, darling," Grace said soothingly. "But as you can see, we're here. Haven't missed a thing."

Moira began to cry and laugh at the time. "Mom, you look so beautiful–and so young. I can't believe it."

"Thank you. I certainly feel a lot better," Grace joked, leaning over to kiss Gordon on the cheek. "Nice to get back to my love."

Moira and Alex began asking them about events in the spirit world. Gordon volunteered, "Battle plans shaping up over here to take on the Anti-Christ and his armies. Everyone is so excited, so *ready* to see this drama come to an end."

Suddenly, a bright flash of lightning disrupted the discussion, then a loud boom of thunder rattled the onlookers. People began to look for cover, thinking it was going to rain. But there were no clouds in the sky. Another bolt, then another even closer...clattering claps of thunder made it impossible to talk.

Timothy excused himself and walked quickly over to another man. The two conferred briefly then made their way through the crowd to the temple's entry. Alex and Moira could see them joined by the third man. The three stood together, right arms raised, and shouted over the din, "In the name of our Lord and Savior, we command you to depart!"

In China, Lu Han staggered back against the black and red screen of his inner chamber, stunned at the power of the disciples' response. He was aware of the Savior's manifestation in Zion—an event easily detectable on the planet's psychic grid. Although he couldn't really disrupt the proceedings, he planned on using his greatly developed psychic abilities to cause all kinds of havoc with the weather, one of the more easily manipulated telestial mediums. "This is just the beginning!" Han shouted at no one in particular. "You will die at my hands, I promise you." Enraged, he grabbed a small dagger and stabbed repeatedly at his silken bed covers.

Back in the assembly hall, in the renewed quiet, the Master pronounced a blessing so beautiful on the assembled group that they were simply and utterly awash with the Spirit. Ben felt like the top of his head was ripping off. People began to spontaneously stand and prophesy about the future. Ben saw dear Sister Martinez rise out of her seat and begin talking loudly in Spanish. He even heard Jed, normally earthbound Jed, get into the celebration, speaking in what sounded like Adamic. And Peg looked to be conversing with an unseen person, tears running down her face.

Without warning, Ben watched as three white-robed men materialized on the podium near the Savior. He instantly recognized John the Beloved; he was certain the other two must be Peter and James.

Just as many translated beings were walking through crowds on the plaza outside, so they began to in the meeting hall as well. The heads of the tribes made their way through the audience, blessing people, promising them a place in the Lord's Kingdom.

It was impossible to absorb the many sublime and astonishing events occurring all around him. In fact, words deserted him. The best mental picture Ben could conjure up was when he was a kid and his mom took him to his first spectacular fireworks show.

Ben watched as Peg, face aglow, shook hands with Peter and James, as the apostles made their way through the choir stand. Then he noticed that John the Beloved was walking down off the dais, heading in his direction. Before he spoke with Ben, the translated apostle deferentially shook hands with Bishop Olsen. Then he turned to Ben and asked, "Well, translator of Sangay Tulku's plates, what do you think now?"

Ben's mind and spirit rushed to a peaceful focus on John's tender face, but he still couldn't speak. He was so filled, big tears flowed down his cheeks.

"Do you remember asking me if you could see the Lord?" John asked.

Ben nodded.

"He has sent me down here to tell you something He wants you to know," John said lovingly, glancing up to see the Lord standing at the podium.

Ben looked up. There was the Savior, smiling in affirmation of what John was saying.

Delicately putting his hand on Ben's shoulder, John said, "Our Lord would like you to know, dear Brother Benjamin Taylor, that he is very proud of you."

AFTERWORD

"A Man's life of any worth is a continual allegory
And very few eyes can see the Mystery of his life
A life like the scriptures, figurative"

                            John Keats

Joseph Smith has been called a spiritual giant by many people. The celebrated non-Mormon literary critic, Harold Bloom, wrote in his *The American Religion*, "Smith was an authentic religious genius, unique in our national history." Joseph's history is one marked by remarkable spiritual experiences, beginning in 1820, when he had an open vision of God and Jesus Christ.

In the next few years, Joseph began having a series of visits from the angel Moroni, a general who lived about 400 A.D. in southern Mexico or Central America. He told the young man where he had hidden records of his people in a hill in upstate New York. Joseph uncovered these plates and, through the help of divine inspiration, translated them into the *Book of Mormon*, which chronicles over 1000 years of history of an ancient American civilization that began when a group of messianic Jews left Jerusalem around 600 B.C. In several chapters of the book, we read prophecies about the American continent in the last days.

In the *Doctrine and Covenants*, another scriptural text of pronouncements and revelations, Joseph Smith becomes quite specific about the pattern of the last days. For instance, in Section 57 Joseph received a revelation that the city of Zion, a sanctuary for all people who seek a non-violent life, will be built on the American continent with the administrative and spiritual center in Independence, Missouri.

The litmus test for any prophet is whether something he foretold, in detail, actually came to pass. Joseph told many individuals about their future lives, and he was correct. In one of his more famous prophecies given 25 December 1832 regarding the Civil War (nearly 29 years before its occurrence!), he said, "The wars that will shortly come to pass, beginning at the rebellion of South Carolina, will eventually terminate in the death and misery of many souls....(S)laves shall rise up against their masters."

In 1844, Joseph was murdered by an angry mob in a Carthage, Illinois jail. Two days before he died, he dreamed of his death and told a companion, W.W. Phelps, of his arrival at a city, "whose gold and silver steeples and towers were more beautiful than any I had ever seen or heard of on earth." There was "the greeting of old friends, the music from a thousand towers, and the light of God himself at the return of three of his sons." (Hyrum, his brother, was also killed at the same time. His younger brother, Samuel, weakened by the stress of bringing his brothers' bodies back to Nauvoo, contracted a fever and died a month later.)

THE MILLENNIAL SERIES

Books in Print:

Ephraim's Seed, the first in a series of millennial stories which chronicles the spiritual experiences and adventures of a group of friends, who as a large extended family, gather first in southern Utah at the beginning of world war, plagues, earthquakes and societal breakdown, and follows them on to the dedication of the land Zion for the return of the Saints.

Jacob's Cauldron, book two, follows the same group of friends as they assist in the building of Zion into a social-political reality under John the Beloved's tutelage. They assist with the building of Zion as the world deteroriates physically and the Anti-Christ comes to power. Finally the temple is completed, where the Lord appears in its sanctuary to the faithful.

Books under Construction:

Michael's Fire, book three, chronicles the last three and a half years of the earth's telestial existence. We follow the same extended family in their romances and dangerous assignments. The final council at Adam-ondi-Ohman is convened; the 144,000 are sent out to teach the gospel to the world for the last time; and the lost tribes return to Zion. The story also follows two LDS prophets who preach in Jerusalem and are killed. The Battle of Armageddon explodes. The return of the Lord to the whole world occurs along with the resurrection of some Saints and the transformation of the planet into a millennial state.

Enoch's Compass, book four, covers the first one hundred years of the Millennial era. Several members of the series' extended family are among those who remain on the earth. We follow them as they struggle to build a new world, one frequented by resurrected beings. Temples scatter the land; the Lord is seen by many. Social and political struggles ensue with non-members. The first visits to other telestial planets occur.